Raven's Dawn

The Raven Crown Series
Book 1

Georgina Makalani

ISBN-10: 0-9945131-7-8

ISBN-13: 978-0-9945131-7-5

In memory of

Todd Hitchens

A kind and thoughtful friend

1

Princess Meg fidgeted with the sleeve of her dress, again, as she tried to remain as calm as possible. The longer her father remained absent, the harder it was to maintain her happy facade. She groaned inwardly and set the smile on her face as Lord Tarrant strode across the Hall toward her. She glanced around, but it was too late to hide in the crowd. She had isolated herself too well and there was no one to save her.

'Your Highness,' Lord Tarrant said loudly, bowing too low before her. 'How like your mother you look. Other than your hair, of course,' he added.

She resisted raising her hand and touching the intricately braided knots. Her hair had been snowy white since birth, yet it frustrated her that people felt the need to draw her attention to it. Her eyes were almost as pale, such a pale blue they were almost grey. Her sister Kellin was the only one who could comment without making her cringe. Kellin was so similar in looks they could have been mistaken for one another despite the twelve months between them, and the fact Kellin had red-blonde hair and bright blue eyes.

'Is there news of your father?' he asked with raised bushy eyebrows, and she wondered what kind of news Lord Tarrant hoped for.

'I'm sure he will be here shortly and you can inquire on his health yourself.'

'Are you sure he will attend?'

Meg smiled brightly. 'He is to depart for Tands in the morning. He would not travel so far if he was not well.'

'So true,' he muttered.

Grotty little man, she thought. He was only talking with her to see what he could learn, but she wouldn't be sharing any news with him, even if she had any. She had seen very little of her father herself and as far as she was aware, the trip was still planned for the morrow and the feast was to go ahead.

The Hall, usually for audiences with the king or gatherings of the court, was filled with nobles and tables. Meg enjoyed the company of the Hall but it was rare that the court would all eat together. She would at least be sitting with her sisters and not the likes of Lord Tarrant.

She waited for him to continue his questioning as he studied her silently. 'I wonder,' he said quietly, 'if your hair will turn the black of the raven one day.'

Meg opened her mouth to speak, unsure just what to say to such a comment, when the soldiers at the door stepped forward and the room dropped into silence. The carved, arched door swung open and her father appeared, filling the doorway with his tall, broad frame. And yet he appeared somewhat paler than she expected, accentuated by his raven-black hair and beard, and she wondered if this trip was as necessary as he seemed to think it was.

Meg gave a polite nod to Lord Tarrant and followed her father's path toward his throne, now sitting behind a bare table rather than in the open. As he took his seat, the servants flowed through the doorway placing platter after platter along the tables, and the throng of people moved silently toward their seats.

Meg had leaned in to squeeze her father's hand before sitting down when her eldest sister, Elalia, expertly slid between them and sat gracefully at her father's side. Meg tried not to sigh, and leaving a seat between them sat down slowly. She smoothed her dress and searched through the crowd moving between the tables.

Kellin, appearing from nowhere, sat down with a sigh between her sisters. She muttered something to Elalia, who ignored her, before she turned to Meg.

'What is it?' Meg asked quietly as more food arrived and the conversation finally lifted to a low murmur as platters were placed on the tables.

'Why do you think Father is going to Tands?'

Meg shrugged, glancing at her father as he began to stand slowly from his seat. Meg indicated that Kellin turn around, but she wondered just what her sister was so concerned about.

'Welcome, friends,' the king started by saying. 'Tomorrow I travel to our neighbours in the North. I trust you will all watch over my girls as well as they watch over you.' He sat quickly as a cheer went up from the nobles.

'Well?' Kellin hissed in her ear.

Meg looked at her seriously.

'Why is he going?'

'I don't know,' Meg said slowly. 'Why are you concerned? I am sure there have been conversations between our kingdoms previously.'

'What if he goes to discuss options for us?'

'With whom?'

'Some Tandian noble,' she said with a sigh.

'Do you have another preference?' Meg asked.

Kellin shook her head slowly.

'We will have little choice, no matter the outcome,' Meg said.

'You mean no choice. And how can you be so calm? What if he is some hideous man, like...' She nodded her head toward their sister's husband.

'We do as we must,' Meg said. She hoped that her father was sensible enough to have realised his error with Malin and that he would be more careful in his choices for them. Not that Malin had initially appeared to be of concern; it was only over the last few months that his mask had seemed to slip and his true nature come to the fore.

Kellin might be right to be concerned; at twenty and twenty-one, the two princesses were older than most to be single still. But Meg was sure her father did as he thought best. If he waited before marrying them off, it must be for a reason.

'If only he would talk with us about it,' Kellin said.

'About what? A husband?'

Kellin nodded, her eyes staring ahead. 'He doesn't talk with us about anything,' Kellin muttered, taking a gulp of wine. 'We can't get close,' she added, indicating over her shoulder as Elalia talked to the king. 'He likes Malin and Elalia by his side.'

Meg nodded slowly. They spent far more time with the king than she or Kellin were able to.

'I wonder what Father was thinking,' Kellin whispered.

'Excuse me?'

'You know well enough,' Kellin said. 'Malin and Elalia.'

Meg raised her eyebrows at her sister but gave a little nod. 'He appeared quite charming when they first wed, but there are too many rumours now.'

He was handsome enough, but there was something about him, an arrogance, superiority, perhaps. He appeared to look down on anyone that spoke to him, sometimes even Elalia, and Meg wondered if they would be truly happy together as her parents had been.

'You have to hold his interest, apparently.' When Meg stared at Kellin, she added, 'Just what I have heard around the castle.' She held up her hands in defence.

'Really?' Meg asked.

'The servants talk, and not very quietly.'

'Kellin,' Meg warned, looking about her to make sure that Elalia wasn't listening.

'He doesn't care what people say. Nor what Father might think.'

'Of course he would care,' Meg said.

Kellin squeezed Meg's arm, her gaze fixed across the room. 'He looks very handsome today,' she whispered. Lord Stand's youngest son, Marcus, the only one of the sons to attend court, pushed his dark hair from his eyes as he talked with Lord Robert. And before Meg could agree, Kellin stood and made her way around the tables to talk with him.

There had been no choice for Elalia and there would be no choice for them either. Although she was sure Kellin knew her duty, it would be hardest on her. She was too used to the freedom of talking with friends and the many young men who paid her attention. They paid Meg the same attention, but she gave them little opportunity to be any more than polite.

'Princess Megora,' Malin said, sitting beside her. 'Who is it you watch today?' he asked with a genuine smile.

'I watch no one in particular, sir,' she said. 'I simply take in the dresses and colour and movement before me.'

'Really?' he asked. 'That young man seems quite attentive to Princess Kellin,' he noted. 'Isn't he the youngest son?'

'Yet from a noble family,' she said. 'We must meet with everyone to ensure a better understanding of the world.'

'True,' he mused. 'Tell me, Meggie, has a young man taken your eye yet? I am sure you and your sister will wed soon.'

'It is up to Father to decide such things,' she said, watching the king over Malin's shoulder. 'I would rather you call me Meg,' she said, turning back to Malin. 'I'm no longer a child.'

He nodded. 'I will call you whatever you wish, Meg, and I don't think anyone here sees you as a child. Robert,' he said, addressing the man who now stood at the opposite side of the table. 'You can see our princess is no longer a child.'

The man bowed low before Meg. 'Your Highness,' he said. 'How well you look.'

'Thank you. I understand your sister has recently joined us at court.'

He nodded. 'She is quite excited, Your Highness. Although she found the travelling harder than expected.'

Meg smiled. 'I look forward to meeting Lady Sera. I remember her as a small child when I was nearly as young myself. How she has grown, I am sure.'

'Yes, quite grown up. I only hope she understands the difference between home and court.'

'I am sure she will behave perfectly.'

He bowed and moved away.

'Do you know everyone?' Malin asked.

'We all stand in this room so often, it seems everyone wants to talk with me and so I know them all,' she said. 'Only today are we afforded the luxury of eating together.'

He gave her a small nod and moved away and despite the warmth of the fires, Meg shivered. The king must have seen something in the man, some merit, but he unnerved her, more so when he appeared to be genuinely interested in her opinion. Too often he asked her about her activities as though he stood in the Temple with her or followed her around the market. She sighed; perhaps she wasn't as invisible as she thought.

'Are you well?' Kellin asked, taking her hand as she sat back down beside her.

Meg gave her hand a gentle squeeze as she gave her sister a warm smile. 'I was just thinking how nice it would be if I could stand against the walls unseen like the soldiers do.'

Kellin laughed then, and pulled her sister into a tight embrace. 'I love you,' she whispered. 'But I know you would do whatever was expected, no matter what.'

'We have a duty to the king and kingdom,' she said. 'Some days are just easier than others.'

'And I know you would never admit that to anyone but me.' She kissed Meg's cheek.

Behind Kellin, the king appeared subdued, and as he slowly stood, he faltered against the table and leaned heavily into it. Meg waited, but he took too long to stand straight and turn from the table. How old was he now? With raven-black hair and the thick beard, he usually looked such a young man. But not today. Today he looked like an old man, and Meg gulped down the strange feeling growing in her chest.

As he stumbled, Meg was on her feet and standing beside him, her hand under his elbow. 'What is it child?' the king asked softly.

'I wonder if you are well, Father?'

'Of course I am,' he said slowly, his dark eyes intense. A prickling fear covered her skin.

'I am sorry,' she mumbled, moving her hand to nestle it in the crook of his arm.

'Walk with me, Megora,' he said softly.

She nodded and walked slowly with him toward the door. As they neared it, he slowed considerably and cleared his throat. Commander Brent stepped out from the wall. Meg tilted her head to the man as he did the same to her, yet his focus was on the king. 'Are you well, Your Majesty?'

To Meg's surprise the king shook his head. 'I fear I may need more assistance than that of my daughter,' he whispered.

The commander nodded and moved quickly to assist the king from the room and then, once they were clear of the Hall, called another man forward. Meg watched as they helped him along the hallway and up the stairs. She stood frozen to the spot for a moment, and then another soldier appeared by the doorway.

'Fetch Brother Erasmus and a nurse,' she said quickly. 'But tell no one of what you do.'

The man nodded and disappeared, and Meg raced up the stairway to catch the king and his supporters.

By the time Brother Erasmus appeared in the room, the royal commander had joined them and her father had paled further. In the spacious bedchamber he appeared even smaller and frailer, dwarfed by the large bed and the heavy, crimson drapes. The Brother nodded once, his hand tight on the woven, deep-blue cord he wore around his grey wool tunic. It marked the only difference between him and the other brothers, who all wore black cords at their waists.

Meg wrung her hands and watched in silence as the nurse looked her father over. She focused on his pale face, for when she looked around the room she remembered her mother, lying across the table, her skin unnaturally grey. The simple chairs looked just the same, tucked under the table.

'Would you like a seat?' the royal commander asked, and she looked at him only briefly as she shook her head. He gave her a small smile that crinkled the skin around his eyes, deep-brown eyes that often smiled at her from his weathered, tanned face with a short-clipped beard. He had always looked older than her father. Older than most of the men she knew. Her mother had once remarked that he was a year younger than her father, but she wasn't sure if she had been jesting. 'He will be well I am sure,' he said.

'No,' Meg said too loudly. 'He won't.'

The room hushed around her and her face grew hot. 'I'm sorry, Father,' she said and made for the door.

'Stay,' he said, his voice soft and friendly, unlike anything she had heard from him in so long. She stopped and nodded.

'We will leave you to talk,' the royal commander said with a bow and indicated the commander leave with him. 'I shall return later to discuss the matter of the delegation.'

The king nodded once and Meg stepped back from the door to allow them through. The royal commander gave her arm a little squeeze without pausing in his step, and gave her the smallest wink. She sucked in a deep breath. There were times that the old royal commander was kinder and more like a father than her own was. The door clicked closed but she remained staring at it.

'Why do you worry?' he asked.

'You looked different,' Meg said gently, turning back to the man sitting on the edge of the bed. He didn't look himself. 'I cannot explain it clearly,' she whispered, 'but you looked so pale and I could only think of Mother when I found her.'

The king motioned her to him. 'It was a difficult time,' he said slowly, taking her hands in his, which were much cooler than she'd expected them to be. 'But you were so young. Do you remember her death so well?'

Meg nodded and he squeezed her hands as she knelt down before him. 'I do not want to lose you,' she said softly, resting her head on his lap, something she hadn't done since she was a child, not since her mother had died. The king appeared mortal for the first time in memory.

'I am afraid, child, that I cannot live forever. Yet I may last a little longer,' he whispered, gently running his hand over her hair. The last time he had done that, her white hair had been free, and she remembered the feeling of his fingers raking across her scalp as though it were moments ago. 'I have business in Tands that I must complete,' he continued. 'And I would like your assistance while I am away.'

She looked up into his smiling face. 'Am I to come with you?'

He shook his head, but the soft smile remained. 'I will have enough to keep me company, and the royal commander for protection.'

'Two old men together,' Erasmus muttered from the back of the room, the movement from foot to foot an indication of his agitation.

'And noblemen I trust,' the king added. 'Unless the Brothers want to come?'

Brother Erasmus shook his head and held his old body still. 'I am sure I have enough to do here, such as pray for you.'

The king laughed easily, his cheeks a little pinker. Meg longed to run her fingers over his face and feel his wiry beard, but she pulled her fingers into her fists and stood slowly.

'Now, I will not be away too long. You and your sisters will behave while I am gone.'

'Always,' Meg said quickly.

'I am sure you will,' he said. 'But Kellin and Elalia may need some direction.'

Meg laughed then. 'They will not take direction from me.'

His head tilted a little to the side. 'I'm sure you would advise them well,' he added slowly, 'if the need arose.'

Meg dropped into a low curtsy. 'Your Majesty.'

He nodded once and she was dismissed by his turning to Brother Erasmus.

⊂⊇⊆⊃

Meg stood in the courtyard as her father led the delegation through the castle gates. Several carriages and a group of soldiers on foot surrounded them, the royal commander and another commander on horseback. The cool wind pulled at her skirts. If she were sitting beside her father in his carriage, would he hold her hand as a father would, or would the distant King Oren look out the window? What could be so important in Tands that he had to travel himself? He had been as unsteady the previous evening as when he'd stepped into the carriage just moments ago. She pulled her cloak closer around her shoulders as the carriages disappeared from view.

Brother Erasmus and Brother Peras, a younger replica of the old Brother complete with the same long beard, watched her rather than the road. She tried not to sigh as she turned from the crowd waving the delegation off to face the Temple. Kellin stood chatting with Marcus, and Elalia stood silently beside Malin, both of them watching the gates. Meg didn't want to talk to any of them and continued inside.

The silence of the Temple echoed the disappointment of watching her father leave, and she tried to shake the sadness that had settled over her. In the early morning light, the rough stone walls were always golden with sunlight, and Meg's disappointment continued, for they had already faded to creamy sandstone.

The gods at least appeared to smile down on her. She moved forward quickly to complete the ritual of rubbing their feet. First Kira, then Kion, and then Kion and Kira. Her fingers lingered on Kira's feet, hoping for some comfort or confirmation that her father had done the right thing by going to Tands. Between the followers, the two pale, stone gods loomed over the expanse of the

Temple, their hands joined between them. Of the followers, Air and Earth stood to the left of the twin gods, Fire and Water to the right. Each smiled down on her as she ran her hand over their feet. She moved back to Earth and bent to kiss his feet. He would be the closest to her father as he travelled the road to Tands and she knelt before him to pray to them all.

At the sound of distant footfalls entering the Temple, Meg glanced up from her position of prayer. She enjoyed the shared space and praying with others, but there was something personal about the quiet time so early of a morning, alone with the gods, when few visited. Occasionally her father prayed early, but he rarely spoke to her if they chanced to meet.

Two young women from the kitchens walked and chatted toward the gods upon their platform. They nodded to her and dipped into a shallow curtsy as she stood slowly. Meg returned a nod before running her hand over the smooth foot of Earth, then bent to kiss his cool, salty feet. After the women had greeted the gods, Meg returned to Kira and Kion to repeat the ritual of rubbing her hands over their smooth feet before she left.

Several soldiers met her at the door, entering for their morning prayer, and she stepped back to allow them in. Only one paused for the princess and bowed, Commander Brent with his strong, square face and towering height. She barely reached the top of his breast plate.

'I thought you were to go with my father,' she said quickly. She had barely looked at any of the soldiers travelling with him and she wondered now if the right people had travelled with him. If they would ensure he returned safely to her.

He shook his head. 'No, Your Highness, the royal commander is assisted by Commander Rainger.'

She nodded and turned back to the door. As her hand pressed against the solid wood, as smooth as the feet of the Gods, he reached out a hand toward her and then stopped.

'Is there anything you need, Your Highness?' he asked quickly, looking a little unsure of himself. Not a look she had seen him wear before.

'Not at all,' she said. 'Is there something that you think I might be in need of?'

He seemed to grow more uncomfortable under her stare and he

shook his head. 'Good day to you.' He raced to catch the other men, already at the feet of the gods.

What instructions has he been left with? she wondered. She shook her head as she headed into the courtyard, where the sun tried to shine. Winter was closer than she would like. It was such a strange time for her father to choose to travel. The carriage would hardly protect him from the cold and it would be weeks before they reached Tands, although she had heard that it was warmer in the North.

'You must not worry,' Brother Erasmus offered, following her out into the courtyard. How did the man always know where she would be? Should he have travelled with them? Would the gods have allowed him to go if it were not safe?

'And yet I do,' she said. 'I'm not sure why, but I seem more worried for Father than I have ever been.'

'I am sure he knows what he does.'

'That is not what I'm worried about,' she said.

'Then what is it?' he asked, taking her arm and stopping her progress. 'Princess Megora, what could it be?' he asked again, his voice carrying across the courtyard.

'It is too far to travel and I worry what might be said while he is gone.'

He looked at her seriously, releasing her arm and tucking his hands inside his tunic. 'I doubt King Oren need worry about gossip.'

'What if he dies?' she whispered.

'All will be as it should be,' he said.

'Strangely, Brother, that does not ease my concerns.'

He gave her a little smile and a bow and she turned back for her sister's rooms. Perhaps Kellin could distract her today and Father would return before she realised he had been gone. Across the courtyard, she noticed a man leaning against the wall, and it was only as she got closer she recognised Malin. He pushed off the wall and walked quickly across the yard to join her.

'Good morning, Princess,' he said sweetly, but something about the way he said it made Meg uncomfortable.

'Sir,' she said with a nod. 'Do you not go to pray this morning?'

He gave a slight shake of his head. 'I go to the Temple when I must.'

She paused and studied him.

'The gods understand me,' he murmured, walking more slowly. 'Where do you go?'

'To see Kellin.' *As far away from you as possible*, she thought.

He nodded but said nothing.

'And where is Elalia this morning?' she asked, and he shrugged.

'How long will your father be gone, do you think?' Malin asked.

'As long as he feels he should be.'

'I am sure,' he said, pausing to bow politely and then wandering off across the yard as Meg looked after him. There must have been something there for Father to choose him. But as she walked up the stairs to Kellin's rooms, she realised that she had no idea what those features might be. He hadn't done anything to endear himself to the court or her father at all.

Meg raised her hand to the latch of Kellin's door and then stopped. It must have been something important to take the king away to Tands. She couldn't work out what that was and Kellin would be sure to have more than enough ideas for the two of them. Letting her hand drop, Meg stared at the intricately carved flowers woven across the door. Did Father think that there was a match for one of them in Tands? And if it was a good match, why had he not followed such an option for Elalia? Meg sucked in a deep breath and stood straighter, despite wanting to lean into the wood, and she moved as quickly and as quietly as she could toward her own rooms.

The room was quiet and empty as she sat before the fire. She looked over her needlework on the table and returned her gaze to the hypnotic flickering of the flames. Would she ever understand what happened around the castle? Or was she forever to simply do as she was instructed without question?

'I know my duty is to the Raven Crown and Rocfeld first,' she whispered to the flames, and they slowed in their movement as though listening to her every word. 'I'm prepared for that,' she continued, stretching her fingers toward them, and then she clenched her fingers into a fist and pulled her hands quickly into her lap. 'But I wonder if I will ever be able to decide anything of importance for myself.'

2

Elalia had spent the last month listening to noblemen whisper too loudly about what her father may be doing or negotiating in Tands. She had thought the general conversation stemmed from a frustration that they hadn't been invited to travel with the others, for she had felt some of that jealousy herself. She was the eldest, after all. And she may have been only back in Rocfeld a year, but her time with the Silent Sisters had set her up as the favoured successor.

As yet another nobleman whispered too loudly his notion of what the king might be doing in Tands, she smiled at the woman talking to her. Elalia wasn't listening and when she tried to pull her focus from the conversation behind her to the woman, she couldn't even remember her name. It wasn't important. It didn't really matter who these people were at all. She tried not to sigh as the woman paused in her ramblings. She had no idea what she was saying and Elalia was starting to think she should have stayed in her rooms.

'Why would he not simply choose to send a delegation?' someone asked, and she gave up pretending to listen to the woman before her and swung around to face the man in question.

'He did,' Elalia said smoothly, 'and he chose to travel with them.'

'What is the point of a delegation if the king travels too?'

'Perhaps he thought the matter important enough to discuss in person,' Elalia said slowly, but wondered at her own words. She had no idea at all as to why he had gone to Tands or what would be discussed.

'What could he need to negotiate? Should we be concerned?'

'I said the same thing days ago,' Lord Libry offered.

Elalia chewed her lip and then checked herself. How could she defend her father when she didn't know what he did? She didn't even know him. She longed for the safety of the Sanctuary. A desperate ache started in her chest and she closed her eyes for a moment to regroup. When she opened them, the room around her was silent and everyone had lowered themselves. Elalia was left standing above the crowd as they bowed or curtsied toward her father as he strode into the Hall.

He moved quickly to his throne and sat heavily. He looked weary and old and she moved through the crowd to stand before him.

'Father, should you not have rested before appearing here? There is nothing so important that you could not rest.'

He gave her a short nod. 'True,' he said. 'But I longed for home and familiar faces and so I came here before the solar.'

'Was your travel worthwhile?' she asked.

He looked at her closely but said nothing.

'There has been much talk,' she mumbled when his stare became too much.

He nodded then. 'It was my last chance to see Tands,' he said, his voice soft. 'A selfish move,' he added.

Kellin and Meggie appeared beside her, both curtsying low.

'Are you well, Father?' Meggie asked.

He nodded and took her hand, the movement taking Elalia by surprise, and jealousy tightened her chest. She was the eldest, after all, but little Meggie would always be favoured above the others. She might be a favourite of everyone, but was she a favourite of the gods?

'Is there any news from Tands?' Kellin asked.

Her father shook his head. 'I will share the news when I am ready,' he said. 'Now go and talk with the ladies. I will talk with the lords before I retire.'

The three of them curtsied in unison. Meggie paused for a little longer than required before turning to the crowd and following Kellin.

So much to discuss and with so many, and none of them me, Elalia thought. She searched the room for Malin and when she didn't find him she walked quickly toward the door. Would she have to talk so often with these men when she was Queen? She glanced at Meggie and Kellin talking with some other ladies as she left. Kellin laughing at something someone said, Meggie's eyes on the king.

Elalia pushed her chamber door shut and breathed in the silence. Would she ever get use to the noise? There were days when she thought she would explode from the constant chatter of the world around her, and then other times she was surprised to find at the end of the day she hadn't noticed it at all.

Leaning against the door, Elalia waited before moving into the room. There was no sign of the maid, and the fire was burning low in the fireplace. She walked quickly through to her bedchamber, her feet barely making a sound on the soft new rushes. Once inside the room she pushed the door shut and listened again before moving to a tapestry on the far wall. She reached behind it, feeling for the space in the stones, and then pushed her hand into the gap.

She sighed with the relief of the smooth wood against her fingers before she pulled the old, familiar box out. She ran her fingers over the simple, smooth lid. There was something safe about holding the box in her hands, just as she had held it when she had left the castle as a child. It had gone all the way with her to the Sanctuary of the Silent Sisters, as though it carried the memory of her mother in it. She had been allowed to keep it beneath her bed and she had carried it back again, where it had been quickly hidden away.

She sat on the floor against the wall and lifted the fragile lid. In a corner, her mother's silver ring was no longer as shiny as it had once been. She still didn't know how she had managed to keep it to herself all these years. Why had no one realised it was missing when she died or wondered where it may have been? Elalia lifted it out as though it was the most precious thing in the world and slipped it onto her finger beside her own raven-embossed ring.

It fitted as though it belonged there, yet when she was a child it had spun and slipped. She ran her fingertip over it and left it in place as she reached in to pull out the only other items in the box, two candles, one white and one black.

She held them together in both hands and blew gently over the wicks. She glanced around the room but it remained silent and the candles unlit. She mouthed a silent prayer over them, her eyes squeezed shut and then she gently placed them back into the box. 'One day soon,' she whispered, 'you will be where you belong.'

When she had left for the Sanctuary all those years ago, the box had only contained the ring and a single raven's feather, but that had crumbled long ago. She slipped the ring from her finger and gently placed it back into the box, which she closed with the same amount of care. The simplicity of its outer sheen, with no carving or adornments at all, belied the importance of what was inside. She pushed up off the floor and returned it to its hiding spot.

Again, she paused to listen at the doorway before opening it slowly. She sat quietly before the fire with a sigh. Would life be as she wanted it to be once she was Queen? So far, married life had been a disappointment. Malin didn't want to spend time with her, not like she had thought he would. How was she to grow a child when she had a husband who barely spent a night in her bed?

The Silent Sisters had mentioned sacrifice. She had expected to have to give up parts of her life, but marriage was supposed to bring with it some benefits. She sighed with the frustration again.

Was her father as disappointed with the lack of issue as she herself was? Maybe there would be more help for that as well once she was Queen. But as she stared into the flames, she had no idea what that might possibly be.

∽∾

Meg took a big breath before knocking on the king's solar door. It was Brother Erasmus that opened it to her and stood back silently, looking at the floor as she passed him. The king, reading papers at the table by the fire, didn't look up as Meg approached. Various scenarios ran through her head as she crossed the room. What news did he have for her?

'Father,' she whispered and his soft, wrinkled face turned from the papers in his hand. He seemed suddenly so much older. 'You asked to see me.'

'Sit down, child,' he said, indicating the chair.

She sat quickly and held her fingers tightly in her lap. She was desperate to ask after his health and keen to know about his trip to Tands, but she bit her lip, waiting to be told why she had been called. When she finally raised her eyes to his silence, he smiled at her.

'What is it?' she asked.

'Child, ask what you will.'

Surely it hadn't been that long since they had talked. She looked at his old face across the table and realised that perhaps it had been. Life had never been the same since her mother had died.

'I worry about you,' Meg whispered.

He nodded. 'I am feeling much older than I have for some time,' he said slowly and smiled again. 'You are a good daughter.'

She looked down at her lap then. 'I wonder at your trip to Tands.'

'You want to know what I was doing.'

She shook her head slowly as she looked up. 'I wondered what Tands was like, if it is warmer than Rocfeld and how they live.'

He looked at her seriously across the table.

'Of course I wonder at what you wanted to discuss with their king. If you search out a husband for Kellin, or myself,' she added in a barely audible whisper.

'I wanted to see an old friend,' he said, looking again at the papers, 'and to talk of matches. But I did not think of Kellin.'

Meg looked at him closely but his focus had returned to the pages before him. 'You aren't going to tell me.'

'I will when the time is right.'

Brother Erasmus coughed and they both looked at him.

'Well enough,' the king said. 'It may be that time passes too quickly. You are a good daughter,' he said, reaching out and taking her hand. 'I know you will do as you are required to do.'

She nodded. She wasn't going to be told anything else and he was again reading his papers. She wondered just what duty he was expecting of her. 'Is there anything I can do for you, Father? Was there a reason you called me to you?'

He shook his head without looking up and she stood slowly from the table. She curtsied despite his not looking and moved to the door. As she opened it, he called after her, 'Meggie, do you do your duty with the Sisters? Do you watch over the people?'

'Everyday,' she said.

He nodded and went back to his reading. Meg glanced at Brother Erasmus, who smiled and nodded. She paused in the courtyard; dark clouds threw the whole castle into a grey hue. She missed the flowers suddenly and pulled her cloak tight around her shoulders as she headed into the sharp breeze. The snow was not far away now.

Entering the Temple, Meg smiled at the people she passed on her way to the platform of the gods. He still hadn't told her anything of Tands or whether it had been warmer. It was cool inside the Temple but she felt comfortable before the gods. Perhaps some sun for her father would have been a relief for his current condition, for he had looked so pale. But she was at a loss as to why he had asked to see her at all.

Meg ran her hands over the feet of the gods and knelt to pray amongst the others that had gathered there that afternoon. Usually, with her eyes closed, it was as though she was alone with the gods, but Brother Erasmus invaded her thinking and she could not lose herself to prayer as she should. The way he had moved around the room and his subtle coughing plagued her and she found herself sighing. And then as the memory of her father's words sank in, her eyes flew open.

He didn't have long to tell her. A panic gripped her chest as she looked up into the concerned faces of the gods looking down over her. What would that mean? What would their life be when he was no longer King?

A strange uneasiness filled Meg and she stood quickly to rub her hands over the feet of the gods. Who would follow in the Raven Crown? She slowed the movement of her palms across the smooth, cool stone feet of the gods she loved. Elalia was the eldest, but she had been away so long; although her time with the Silent Sisters would be of benefit in the eyes of the gods.

Meg bent over and kissed Kira's feet, asking for forgiveness for such jealous thoughts. She couldn't be Queen. The youngest daughter would never be chosen. She didn't want to be chosen... did she? She shook her head and kissed Kion's feet, also asking for forgiveness. She did not deserve the position. And her hair had been so white since birth, it would be strange if she were marked with the raven hair.

She quickly kissed Kion's feet again, and then Kira's, and raced toward the door. As she reached it and looked back at the gods watching over the Temple, strong and tall, their faces seemed to neither smile nor frown. She hoped she had not angered them in her sudden selfishness and she raced out into the courtyard. The wind pulled at her dress and hair and she tried to hold her cloak around her as she walked toward her own rooms. She wanted to hide away for a while.

She stepped into the warmth of the rooms and stood for a moment before pulling the cloak from her shoulders. Her father intended to send her away to live with some noble's son in Tands. She would do as was required of her, no matter what it was he asked, but she hoped she could have a life she could smile at, not just battle through.

Her parents had been so happy together, always laughing and talking. She couldn't remember a time she wasn't happy before her mother died. She had lost two parents that day, her mother to the gods and her father to the crown. He was never the same, always duty bound, and he didn't have time for laughter or fun or conversation with his daughters. Would life be like that once she married, or would she have the chance to laugh with her husband as her mother had laughed with her father?

When Meg entered the Hall the next evening, everyone bowed as though she were more important than she was. She stalled in the doorway, unsure where to go or how to respond.

'Your Highness,' the royal commander said, stepping forward, and she took his offered arm and moved through the crowd. As she paused by the fire, the murmuring started and Meg's skin burned.

'What is going on?' she whispered.

'Your father has announced his intention for you.'

'What?' She turned quickly on the man and he took a step back.

'Tands,' he mumbled.

'He has announced it? When?' Meg asked as her mouth dried and her stomach dropped.

'This morning.' He looked at her seriously. 'Has he not said?'

She shook her head. *It should be Kellin*, she thought. But then he had told her that he had thought only of her on his journey. And who had he found in Tands that he thought she should marry?

'Princess?' the royal commander whispered and she looked at him seriously. 'Did you hear me?'

She shook her head.

'He has promised you to the prince of Tands.'

Meg's legs threatened to give way, but she remained standing. 'What does this mean?' she asked.

'That they have determined that you are to be joined with Tands.'

'Why not Kellin?' she asked.

'Kellin?' the royal commander asked.

Meg looked at him and shook her head. 'I think there has been a mistake, sir.'

'I was with your father,' the royal commander reminded her, but she shook off the idea.

'Why would he promise me?' she asked.

'I think you should perhaps ask him that yourself. He was very clear that you were the one he wanted to marry into Tands.'

Meg nodded, but turned away and stared into the fire. 'Does everyone know?'

He nodded. 'It is great news,' he said. 'Do you not want to marry Tands?'

Meg continued to stare into the flames. She didn't know what she wanted. She also knew she didn't really have a choice, but what if Kellin's concerns were legitimate and he was a man like Malin? Could she really be happy to do her duty with a man she couldn't respect? And so far away from home, so far away from Rocfeld.

'Princess?'

She looked up and nodded. 'I'm sorry,' she said. 'Does father wish to see me?' she asked of Commander Brent as he joined the royal commander.

'I have not seen him, I'm afraid. Would you like me to check for you?'

She shook her head and turned back to the fire.

'Are you well?' he asked her gently.

She turned quickly and both men looked quite concerned. 'I am sorry, sir,' she said again. 'I'm not quite sure what I…'

'Would you like me to walk you back to your rooms?' Commander Brent asked.

She shook her head and walked quickly toward the door. Someone asked something or said something behind her, but she didn't pause. Instead, walking straight out into the courtyard, sucking in the cool air, she was at the door to the Temple, the night closing in around her, and she realised she had forgotten her cloak. She had been bred for this, trained for this. Her life was to be the wife of whomever her father thought best. And to be the best wife she could be for the benefit of the kingdom. But the prince of Tands meant that she would one day be Queen.

She stood in the dim candlelight of the silent Temple and rubbed her hands slowly over the feet of Kira. Focused on the smoothness of the cold stone beneath her hands and not the reason she was there. She moved slowly toward Kion's feet, again slowly rubbing her hands over the stone, and she wondered at how different they looked and yet how similar they felt beneath her hands. She closed her eyes and rubbed again. If only her arms were long enough, she would have stood between the two gods and rubbed at the same time to be sure.

Could she become one with Tands? She knelt down on the cold flagstones. Her eyes still closed, she hung her head and focused on the image of their joined hands. She tried to imagine a life in which she held the hand of another. Would he want her to share his world? She couldn't imagine what he looked like. A figure with dark hair was as close as she could get. What a contrast she would make with her white hair.

Did her father think she would be marked Queen of Rocfeld?

Meg dropped down to sit on the floor of the Temple, her heart pounding too fast in her chest. She was the youngest. She struggled to get the people to see her as more than just little Meggie; even now, when she was older than most of the young women already married, she was seen as the little princess.

She stood quickly, raced forward and swept her hands quickly over the feet of the gods in the ritual required before she left. Her father must be sicker than she had realised, losing his mind as well as his health, for he had made a terrible mistake.

3

The king of Tands sighed. Reclined in his simple, wooden throne, he drummed his fingers on the armrest. Prince Brodwyn was desperate to roll his broad shoulders, but he bit his lower lip and maintained his attention-like pose. It would help neither of them if he voiced his concerns. The king waved over his adviser, and the Brother in a brown tunic standing beside Brodwyn coughed theatrically. Despite his wish to smile at the old man's behaviour, he maintained his stance and focused completely on his father.

'I do not care for such time wasting,' he boomed. 'How could it help?'

'It may be of benefit to see the girl that King Oren has suggested. He is a good man. He saw the sense in what you wanted,' the advisor, Lord Alva, said.

'The youngest. Where is the respect in that?'

'He did consider her the best of his daughters,' the advisor continued.

'Yet the youngest. Would the gods choose the girl over her elder sisters?'

'The eldest has lived with the Silent Sisters some fifteen years. To live in prayer for such a noble cause would only work in her favour with the gods,' he suggested.

'So she spent her time on her knees,' he scoffed.

Brodwyn breathed out slowly. 'They keep the goddess imprisoned in the Silence,' he said. 'How could the gods and the followers not love her for protecting us all in such a way?'

The king only glared at his interruption and turned back to the advisor.

'I have heard, Majesty,' Lord Alva continued, 'that the eldest is wed already. He is not ideal in terms of the husband of a future queen, and yet the match is done.'

'Are we sure?' the king asked, leaning forward.

'They have been wed a whole year. There is another sister, still unmarried but unmentioned by Oren.'

The king nodded and looked across at Brodwyn. 'What do you think?'

'About which aspect?' he asked.

The king narrowed his glare. 'The third daughter will not bring us together.'

'Is that what you wish for, Father? A united kingdom?'

'I do not care for the way Rocfeld becomes Tands again, but it will.'

Brodwyn nodded slowly.

'This girl may bring Rocfeld back to us, but there may be another option.'

Brodwyn waited for him to say the words, but he knew what was coming. It had been coming for some time.

'We take it by force,' he said, his voice unnaturally quiet.

'Is that necessary?' Brodwyn asked. 'What if we talked to King Oren, met the daughter? There may be another option than to break the agreement now.'

The king shrugged.

'We have lived in peace for two hundred years. Why break that?' Brodwyn pressed, and then held his breath. This was the very conversation he had wanted to avoid.

His father looked at him levelly. 'Everyone out,' he bellowed.

The room began to clear and Brodwyn stepped forward at his father's beckoning, Brother Adroth stepping forward with him. The king glared at him and he bowed low enough that his dark-green cord belt brushed the floor before he backed out of the room.

'It is the gods that choose,' he said softly and Brodwyn nodded. 'They have chosen two crowns for the last two hundred years, yet before that we were one. There was only one.'

'I am aware of the history. The king of Tands chose to give the land away,' Brodwyn said.

'To family. It was to remain in the family. She was a princess and the gift was a wedding present.'

'Yet when she died so soon after her wedding, her husband's family kept the land, the negotiations were made and the gods marked the new lord as another king,' Brodwyn continued for his father.

The king sighed. 'It can change.'

'Do you think it wise to challenge the gods?'

'There will come a time when your hair turns the black of a raven's feathers and you will be pleased at the ease with which you become King.'

'If I am worthy,' he murmured.

The king looked at him closely. 'Do you think a cousin would be better suited?'

He gave a little shrug. 'But why would you force them to return to us?'

'Because I want our legacy to be the kingdom that it was. To be one people once more.'

'Could we not negotiate such a union once I wed the princess? For the gods still mark the crown.'

'I want more for you,' he said, his face softening for the first time in his memory. 'She may be the king's favourite, but I want more than just a wife and family for you.'

'Perhaps our children will unite the kingdoms,' Brodwyn offered, wondering just what chance he had of marrying the girl.

The king slumped back in his throne and shook his head.

'You talk in circles, Father. It has been two hundred years. I ask again.'

'It is time that it came back to the fold. Perhaps if the eldest wishes to worship with the Silent Sisters, she would be willing to give it back to us.'

'You talk as though the king has no say, as though he is dead already and the gods have no influence.' Brodwyn stepped closer to the throne.

'He is a man like any other, and crowned by the gods or not he will die at some point, and what will the daughters do then?'

'What would you wish me to do if you were to die before him?' The king raised his eyebrows and Brodwyn found himself smiling. 'I do not wish to take the crown any sooner than the gods determine,' he said softly, giving his father a slow nod.

'I would want you to consider Tands before all others.'

'That I do, as I have always done,' he said. Shaking his head, he marched toward the door. He wasn't going to get anywhere with his father today. How many times in the last few weeks had he raised this same point? It was only when he came face to face with Seren at the door that he paused, turned back and bowed low to the king sitting alone in his throne room.

Once outside, he took a moment to run his fingers through his dark hair and groan loudly.

'What is your complaint?' Seren asked, giving him a shove. The man was easily his equal in height, but no matter his training, Seren was always stronger.

'The king of Rocfeld described a beautiful, intelligent young woman.'

Seren grinned at him and waved his hand for him to continue.

'I had resigned myself to marrying the girl,' he said.

'Poor you,' Seren laughed. 'Sounds hideous.'

Brodwyn pushed him back.

'Has your father changed his mind? Because if he has, there will be some ladies of Tands that will be very much relieved.'

'Seren,' he chastised. 'Hardly helpful. It isn't just that Father may have changed his mind; he seems more intent on taking Rocfeld by force.'

'Rather than by marriage? I know which way I'd rather.'

Brodwyn stalked off.

'Okay,' Seren called behind him, running across the gravel to catch him up.

They walked in silence toward the barracks. 'I haven't even met the girl,' Brodwyn muttered, stopping and watching the men around him.

'Would that help?' Seren asked.

He shook his head.

'Ho there,' Dell's deep voice boomed across the yard, and despite the heavy feeling, Brodwyn gave the man a smile. The broad, dark man towered over everyone and despite his greying hair, he was still the strongest in the yard.

'I thought your father had called for you?'

'He did, but the young prince did not like the conversation,'

Seren offered, and Brodwyn reached out and thumped his arm. Seren put his hands up and stepped back.

'What is it?' the older man asked.

'A pretty girl,' Seren continued.

Brodwyn stopped and crossed his arms, feigning offence.

'I thought the king of Rocfeld offered his daughter.'

'That is the pretty girl.'

'We don't know how pretty she is; he might have been embellishing the truth somewhat,' Brodwyn said. He knew there was little choice as to who he would marry, and if his father did see the benefits of this then the Princess Megora was as good an option as any. He chewed his lip. He would rather marry a girl he didn't know for the benefit of the kingdom than start a war for no reason other than greed. 'I fear my father wants the world as one, under one crown.'

'The whole world or just our part of it?'

'I doubt he would take on the Empire. But then I never thought he would want to claim Rocfeld back.'

'If Rocfeld returned to Tands, then there would be no threat from the Empire,' Dell said.

'If we joined with them in peace, then they would fight with us if the need arose.'

'The Empire will not take us on,' Seren offered. 'For all the sons and all the ships, Luana is still a small nation. Back from the water, they are tribes living in the desert. And they have made no threat against us or Rocfeld. Oren would have mentioned it.'

'I cannot guess at what Father will do, or why after such an offer he would still be keen to force Rocfeld to return to Tands.'

'What did you say to him, Brodwyn?'

'I said our children would unite the kingdoms.'

Dell gave him a smile. 'The wisest of young men.'

Brodwyn returned the smile and shook his head. 'You were always too lenient on me.'

'Perhaps there is an opportunity to see the girl before the marriage,' Seren said.

Brodwyn leaned against the fence as Seren stepped between the rails. He motioned to the inside of the fence, but Brodwyn shook his head.

'How do you propose I do that?'

'They visited recently on delegation to discuss trade and marriage. Perhaps your father could be convinced that such a return trip would be ideal.'

'Alva has mentioned such a venture, but if my father allows it, he won't allow me to go with them,' Brodwyn said.

'What if he didn't know that you went?' Seren suggested, swinging his sword without turning to Brodwyn.

'He would find out about it.' Brodwyn wasn't sure how his father would react if he did such a thing. He might see it as a direct threat.

'Not if you were not officially part of the party.'

'Stow away?'

'Or they take you as an apprentice of sorts. Your father need not know, and once you explain your work while gone, he can only forgive you on your return.'

'Lord Alva would never agree.'

'He might with the right words. You are always good with words, Your Highness,' he said, bowing low before him. 'Now bring your sword in here so I can remind you of your proper place.'

Brodwyn shook his head as he climbed through the fence and, with his sword raised, circled around Seren. But his mind was on what he could possibly say to Lord Alva to not only get a delegation headed for the princess, but one that would take him with them.

4

Not wanting to enter into conversation with anyone she chanced to see, Meg studied the rough cobblestones at the entrance into the Temple. As soon as she entered the main doors, she focused on the statues on the platform. Confident that they watched over her, the strain of the last few weeks lifted as it did when she entered the Temple each morning. She knew her concerns would settle heavy on her shoulders when she left, but she would appreciate the comfort while she was there.

She moved forward quickly, her soft steps echoing through the space. She greeted the gods before she knelt on the flagstones before them.

With her eyes closed, she breathed in the cool air and the smell of stone and wax filled her senses. She cleared her mind and allowed only thoughts of the gods in, trying hard to forget her father for just a little while. Even with her eyes closed, she could clearly see the faces of the gods smiling down on her from their platform. She was sure that whatever was to come, they would continue to watch over her.

A gentle hand touched her shoulder and she opened her eyes and nodded.

'I do apologise for the interruption, Your Highness,' a young Sister said, 'but your father asks for you.'

She stood slowly and moved toward the gods, wishing her time with them had been longer. She nodded to the Sister sent to fetch her before following her back to her the castle.

Kellin stood silently at the doorway to her father's rooms. Meg took her by the hand and led her slowly forward. Other than his laboured breathing, an uncomfortable silence filled the room. She gave a gentle tug on Kellin's hand, but as her sister froze she released it.

So many days she had sat beside him, listening to his breathing grow shallower. He had deteriorated so quickly in the weeks since he had returned from Tands, and she wiped hurriedly at the tears that ran hot down her cheeks. When he turned his dark eyes on her she stopped, and with some effort he raised his hand and waved her closer.

'Your Majesty,' she said in a hushed voice. 'You wanted to see us.' She knelt on the floor and sat her hands on the edge of the bed, hoping he didn't notice how much she shook.

He glanced over her shoulder only briefly. 'It is you I wished to see,' he croaked, a coughing fit taking hold of his body and causing him to sit forward awkwardly. He reached out a shaky hand and she took it, gently squeezing it, and was rewarded with a smile.

'I have been so focused on the Raven Crown. Trying to do best by Rocfeld and our people.'

'You are a great king,' she whispered.

He shook his head. 'Perhaps, yet I have not been the best of fathers. You have been raised to know your duty and you know the plans that I have put in place for you.'

She nodded.

'Your mother was determined that you should be betrothed to Tands,' he continued. 'It was her wish first and I saw the sense in her plan. You will make a fine queen.' He closed his eyes and leant back into the pillows.

'I will do my duty as required,' she said, watching him closely.

'It is more than duty,' he rasped, clearing his throat, and she leaned forward to hear him, his hand still in hers. 'You must be happy, Megora, like your mother was happy. For a happy queen is a good queen.'

'Yes, Father,' she said.

'I was not as happy without your mother.' As he coughed, spittle appeared on his chin. His voice was suddenly stronger. 'I did not want the crown.'

'Father?' She gently wiped his chin.

'I wanted to be King,' he said, his eyes still closed. 'But it was not the same without your mother. I want you to be a good queen for Tands,' he said softly, just opening his eyes enough for Meg to see the tears welling. His breathing had become ragged but his voice was still strong. 'But a happy wife and mother too. He is a good man. I have made sure he will be a good husband as well as a good king, for it would break my heart to know you were not happy.'

Meg tried and failed to stop the sob building in her chest from escaping. She had never heard her father speak of happiness before. It had always been duty and family and image first. It was a glimpse of a man she barely remembered from her childhood.

'I will try,' she said.

'He will love you,' he said. 'As I do, as Rocfeld does.'

She nodded again and squeezed his hand.

'May the gods guide you,' he whispered, his eyes closing again and his hold of her hand suddenly tight.

'And you,' she whispered. 'May Kira and Kion guide you to a better place.'

And then his grip slackened and Meg held her breath as the great king before her changed. His thick hair became fine and wiry as the black locks faded to grey. Even his beard drained of colour, and as the pale pink left his cheeks Meg found the tears flowing freely down her own. The ache in her chest was painfully sharp and she laid her head on his chest, squeezing his hand, longing for something in return, any sign that she was mistaken and he hadn't left her yet.

She sobbed for the man she had loved and yet hardly known. And then Kellin was there beside her, her warmth along her back, her cheek to Meg's and her own tears running in with Meg's. As her hand tightened on her shoulder, Meg cried all the more.

Eventually a hand gently shook her shoulder and she looked up into the kind and sad face of Brother Erasmus. Kellin's weight moved from her back and the two of them sat side by side on the edge of the bed. Meg still held her father's hand in hers and at the idea of having to let it go, more tears flowed.

Two sister-nurses curtsied before them, their faces wet with tears, and one sniffed before they offered a hand to each sister.

Meg shook her head and looked up at Brother Erasmus.

The royal commander appeared at the door, bowing low. His old face creased with sadness, and without thinking she released her father and stepped forward to take his hand in hers. He looked at her confused for a moment, as though he didn't quite recognise her, and then he gave her a gentle squeeze. Releasing her hand, he stepped to the side of the king.

'My old friend,' he whispered, his voice cracking. And one of the nurses behind Meg started to sob again.

Meg sucked in a ragged breath but the tears still flowed. 'Commander Brent,' she managed to say, as the tall man filled the doorway. 'How good of you to come.'

He nodded. 'A sad day, Your Highness, but I thought...' he stopped.

She looked at him closely. 'Commander?'

Erasmus coughed behind her as he opened and closed his mouth.

'Where is your sister?' he asked.

'I think she hides in the family chapel,' Kellin answered, pointing to the ground beneath her feet.

'Perhaps you should collect her, Commander,' Brother Erasmus said sharply. 'It is important that we ensure his spirit moves on to the gods.'

The commander nodded to Erasmus and then turned back to Meg. 'I am sorry for your loss,' he said with a low bow.

'Once you have fetched the princess, you are to return to the barracks and send the riders to tell the kingdom the news,' the royal commander directed.

Commander Brent nodded solemnly and left the room.

'Let us pray for his soul,' Erasmus said quietly.

Kellin knelt beside Meg and Brother Erasmus took his place across the bed from them. Meg took her father's hand again and pressed it to her cheek.

'Do you think he could hold the hands of the gods?' Kellin asked, taking Meg's hand.

Meg nodded slowly.

'We may not be worthy to touch more than their feet in this life, but the gods will hold us in their arms in the next,' Brother Erasmus said.

Meg pulled her father's hand closer and squeezed Kellin's hand tighter. She wasn't ready to do this without him.

Standing by the open window in the chapel, Elalia allowed the snow to float in and around her, wondering how long her father's illness would draw out. Once he finally breathed his last, one of them would be marked for the Raven Crown by the gods.

The sharp intake of breath from behind her made her sigh, but she held herself still until he coughed loudly.

'What is it?' she snapped, not turning from the window.

'I have been sent, Your Highness, to fetch you.'

'And here you are,' she turned slowly, staring him down. 'And where is it you wish to fetch me to?'

'The king is dead. Brother Erasmus has asked you to join your sisters to pray for him.'

Elalia froze for a moment before nodding once and glanced up at the ceiling and pictured her sisters sitting by her father's bedside. It wasn't possible that one of her sisters had inherited the crown, she thought, it simply wasn't possible.

Despite her slow movement and her dress taking up most of the small spiral stairwell, Commander Brent managed to squeeze past her and waited on the landing above at her father's door. She paused, unsure what it was that she would find there. Crying could be heard through the heavy wood, and she was nervous at the idea of her father laid out dead for all to see.

'Your Highness?' the commander asked from the edge of the landing. 'Are you well?' he added as she leaned heavily against the wall. The snow swirled around the castle walls, white was all that could be seen through the arrow slots.

'Where is my husband?' she asked, quieter than she had intended.

'He is still out on the hunt.'

'In this?' she muttered before she could check herself.

The commander stepped down toward her but she held up her hand. She nodded, pulled herself up and somehow glided up the last of the stairs, through the door and into the heavy sadness on the other side. The quiet murmuring ceased.

The three sisters stared at each other, all unchanged and a new kind of nervousness crept along her spine. She stared at Brother

Erasmus, who seemed perplexed, and then turned to her father, certain there was a mistake.

The king looked small and old, grey and wiry. He had always been a large man, yet there seemed to be nothing left of him now. Kellin remained stock-still and stared across the rich, red bedspread, her chin held high. Then the fight slipped from her and she laid her head down on the bed.

To ensure his spirit moved to join the gods, Elalia had to play the grieving daughter and pray for his soul. If he doubted in any way her love for him, he may stay and haunt her forever. She sat confidently on the side of the bed, pushing Kellin to the side, her large dress crunching beneath her. The smell of death was heavy on the air and if she had not just been told of her father's death, she may have believed him dead for days.

Holding her breath to prevent herself from retching, she threw herself across his still-warm body and forced out the tears of someone who had lost a father. She almost heard him whispering and cried all the louder to drive the image away.

She stayed in this position for as long as she was able, the idea of his ghost interfering with what she was sent to do spurred her on. She was sure she heard Kellin mutter, 'By the gods,' and it caused her to draw in a deep breath, which meant a lung-full of the scent of death, and she coughed and spluttered all the more.

Brother Erasmus, with his deceptively strong hands, pulled her from the bed. She felt sicker than when she had entered the room. 'His spirit is with the gods,' he muttered. 'We feel his loss.'

Elalia nodded slowly but the sick feeling stayed with her.

'We shall do all that is necessary to ensure an appropriate farewell for the king, and to guide and advise you until the crown is selected.'

Again Elalia nodded once. He would do as he thought best, whether she wanted it or not. She looked over her sisters, just as they had always been, and she chanced a moment to pull a curl forward and check that her hair had not changed.

'It is unusual,' Brother Erasmus said.

'How long will it be until we know?' Elalia asked, patting down her dress.

The old man shook his head.

'Oren's hair changed the moment your mother died,' the Royal

Commander said.

'A cousin?' Kellin asked.

Brother Erasmus coughed quietly, as though clearing his throat.

'Brother?' Elalia asked, wondering just what he knew.

'There was a time, many generations ago, when four sons were left unmarked on their father's death. It was some time before the gods made their choice clear.'

'How long?' Elalia asked, drawing out the question.

'Months or more.'

'Months?' Kellin muttered, taking Meggie's hand. 'What will happen while we wait?'

'It may not take that long,' Brother Erasmus said. 'Elalia, as the eldest, will provide leadership as we work together for the kingdom until the choice is clear.'

'I would like to rest,' Elalia said quietly. She wanted to be anywhere but discussing this with these people. 'It has been a long night.'

Brother Erasmus bowed deeply, or at least as deeply as he could with his old body.

'How long do we have with him?' Meggie asked the old man.

'You may stay as long as you like.'

Frustration threatened to boil over for Elalia that Meggie thought she could direct things, when that was her role until the mark was clear. That Meggie could influence the choice with her behaviour. Again she found herself biting her lip and trying to hold the words at bay. Why was it so hard to stay silent today?

She was sure that Erasmus gave her a knowing smile as he bowed again and left them. Then she realised that it was only the three of them alone in the room with their father.

'I do not remember being alone with him before,' Kellin said, voicing Elalia's thoughts.

'It doesn't matter now,' Elalia said, sitting heavily on the edge of the bed. 'And the world will be watching us so closely, waiting for any sign of the gods' choice.'

'Then we do the best we can until the choice is made,' Meggie whispered, kneeling down beside their father and taking his hand. 'There must be a reason why the gods have waited.'

'Or they have chosen someone outside the family,' Kellin said, standing over the basin beside the bed, peering into the water.

'I doubt it will be you,' Elalia muttered.

Kellin swung around, but despite the anger on her face she didn't charge toward Elalia as she had expected her to.

'We have not the luxury of choosing our own lives or destinies,' Meggie said calmly, releasing her father's hand and pushing herself up to stand. Elalia only then realised just how tired she looked and how much of herself she had given to their father in his last days. 'People will come from all over for Father's funeral, but they will be watching us.'

'Or attempting to influence the gods,' Elalia said.

'The gods cannot be influenced, and they will show their decision when the time is right.'

'You have such faith,' Kellin said kindly.

'How could you not?'

The two sisters embraced and despite their fair hair, Elalia could imagine them both with the raven hair that marked the crown. Would Meggie's change when she married Tands and was Queen in the North? she wondered. Or were the gods waiting for the union to show their choice?

'What do you think it will mean being Queen of Tands?' Elalia asked.

Meggie glanced at her and then back to Kellin.

'I wonder at you with raven hair,' Kellin mused, giving her a little smile.

Their mother had said Kellin had been touched by Fire, and that was the excuse Kellin still used when she was in trouble for her fiery behaviour. Elalia wondered if that would change if her hair changed to raven and she lost the red highlights.

'I have served with the Silent Sisters doing the work of Kira and Kion, protecting us from the goddess by keeping her in the Silence. There is no greater service to our gods,' Elalia said, more to herself than her sisters, but she noticed they watched her closely. A nurse reappeared in the room. She was followed by two more sisters and Elalia grimaced in their direction.

'I am retiring,' she said. 'I feel unwell in the face of Father's death.' Without waiting for any response she moved quickly from the room, her dress loud across the rushes as she walked.

Elalia pushed into her rooms with some small hope of finding her husband present, but as usual he was nowhere to be seen. The maid appeared quickly at the sound of the door and bobbed a quick curtsey before lifting her eyes. She opened her mouth and then closed it and focused on the floor.

Elalia waved her hand at the girl and sat on the chair by the table. 'Fetch a nurse, I feel unwell,' she said. Her stomach ached and the scent of her father's death was still in her throat.

'A particular nurse?' the girl asked, her feet unmoving yet her body leaning toward the door.

Elalia sighed and shook her head.

'I have run a bath, Your Highness. Perhaps that would help.'

Elalia looked up sharply at the girl and then nodded slowly. She followed the girl through to the next room. A large copper bath was set up before the fire; steam and the scent of jasmine filled the room. With the snow now thick across the grounds she wondered where they could be found, and yet, no matter the time of year, they always managed to appear in her bath. Even as a small child when her mother was the woman washing her back and laughing with her as she told her stories of Kira and Kion and their love.

She allowed the girl to unlace her dress and let it slip to the floor as she stepped out of it. Her mind was still far away as she focused on happier times, but surely her time was yet to come. If only she didn't feel so ill, and she ached. She had spent much of the night kneeling on the cold flagstones of the bare chapel beneath her father's bed, praying for her chance to show them she was Queen.

Even her breasts ached and as her under dress slipped to the floor she wondered if perhaps, finally, she was with child and life would be different. Perhaps Malin would not roam so far away. She stepped into the bath and slowly lowered herself into the hot water. The smell of death overwhelmed her senses and she allowed her head to slide down beneath the surface of the water. Her eyes squeezed closed, she held her breath as long as she was able and then slowly sat back up. As her head broke through the surface she was surrounded by the smell of jasmine once more and she leaned back against the hot surface of the bath and tried to remember the stories her mother had told her.

She had always been fascinated by the stories of Sythia and the Silence, and when her mother had died and the Silent Sisters offered her a place with them, she had been so relieved. Everyone knew the story, but only her mother had told it best.

"Long, long ago when the world was young, the gods roamed the earth in harmony. Kira and Kion were never apart, always holding hands, and the other gods loved them.

There was no jealousy and no anger, only love.

Kira and Kion watched over all the animals of the world with care. But they could not interact with the animals as they could each other, and so Kira and Kion created man and woman.

But like naughty children, they fought and argued. So Kion decided they should be ruled from amongst their own, and that one that was worthy should be crowned as ruler.

They would decide together, all the gods, who that worthy man or woman was to be, and he or she would be marked for all the world to see. Kira saw a raven flying by and decided to mark the ruler of men with the colour of the raven. And so as the first king's hair turned to the black of a raven's feathers, he was presented with a crown and the people bowed before him.

When he died an old man, the gods chose from amongst his children, and so the tradition went.

But not all the gods were happy with the choice. One amongst them wanted to rule all the heavens and earth herself. Sythia attempted to take the place of the Raven Queen. But the gods would not allow it, and despite her trickery and magic she could not change her hair to the raven colour, and the Raven Crown would never sit on her head.

Sythia made the world difficult for the Raven Queen and thus for the gods we love. She demanded power but no one would follow her.

In her hatred she killed the queen, and the gods cast Sythia out into the Silence where she could no longer hurt the people of the Raven Crown again.

The gods continued to watch over the people and mark their choice for the crown, but they did so from a distance to ensure no other god would be tempted to rule over men.

To safeguard the continued peace with the gods, the Silent Sisters watch over the Silence to ensure Sythia remains trapped there."

Elalia breathed in the scent of the jasmine and sighed across the water. She still missed her mother, but she missed the Sanctuary and the Silent Mother more. They had trained her as best they could, but her place was at the castle. She knew that she could only help them as the Raven Queen.

She looked up at the nurse standing silently beside the bath and she dipped into a curtsy. 'How may I assist you, Your Highness?'

'I need to know if I am with child.'

The woman shook her head and Elalia pushed up from the water. 'You should examine me,' she said, her voice flat despite the emotion boiling under her skin.

'I do not need to. You ask often, Highness. You are not yet with child.'

She flicked her fingers at the woman, dismissing her, and sat back down in the hot water. As the door clicked closed behind her, Elalia slapped at the water as hot tears ran down her cheeks and into the cloudy water. It was only a little thing that she wanted for herself, and yet it was the only thing she couldn't seem to get.

5

Meg tried not to fidget with her sleeve, her fingers working over the embroidery, and it was only the sideways glance from Brother Erasmus that pulled her up. She gave him a small smile and sat her hands on the table, only for her fingers to find the stem of the ornate goblet before her.

Elalia coughed loudly and she focused on her serious face. She was waiting for something but Meg had missed what that might be, and she glanced across at Brother Erasmus desperately. 'Why is Kellin not here?' she asked.

'I think the question is: why are you here?' Elalia asked unkindly and Meg was surprised by the emotionless features of her face.

'For Father,' she said, fighting the urge to stand up. She might be the eldest, but Elalia hadn't been marked yet.

'All three of you have a part in the funeral and it is only appropriate that you talk over the details,' Brother Erasmus said softly, and Meg found herself fighting back tears.

'Surely there is enough tradition to determine what is to happen,' Elalia said sharply and again Meg found herself studying her sister. Their father had only died the day before; wasn't she hurting? Or was she too caught up on being the eldest and therefore the main decision-maker until one of them was marked by the gods?

Meg remembered that moment of peace when she had first woken that morning, before the memory of his death had crashed in on her. He may have been distant, but she loved him and missed him nonetheless. Now, as she looked at her sister, she had a sinking feeling that only speculation at the choice of the gods and the delay in the choice would be foremost on the minds of those attending the funeral.

'It was only this morning you asked for assistance,' Brother Erasmus continued.

'Guidance was the word I used,' she said and again Meg sensed something else, something sharp in her voice. She shook her head and gulped at the wine before her. Elalia would feel his loss just as she did, even with the years she had lived away in the Sanctuary. She was only trying to protect herself.

'I thought it a more general request,' he said, reaching out to pat her hand, but Elalia moved it quickly into her lap.

'I have called the Silent Mother,' she said in a voice that asked no permission, and Meg sucked in a deep breath. Glancing at Brother Erasmus, she was surprised by the change in the colour of his face, his old wrinkled skin becoming a darker brown and then crimson.

'She is my friend,' Elalia continued, and Meg smiled at how her face softened. 'I am in need of a friend. And if I am to become Queen, I would appreciate her council.'

Brother Erasmus locked his fingers together and his knuckles paled with the strength of his grip. 'The Silent Mother has very important work to do. She cannot be called away at a whim.'

'It is not a whim.' Elalia's voice was level but Meg sat back from the table, sensing the danger beneath the calm. 'She will come.'

'And what of the Silence? You have spent many years praying with the Silent Sisters; you are well aware of the important work they do in keeping the goddess from this realm.'

'Do you doubt me?' she asked with a smile and the room around them seemed to crackle with the tension.

'Your Highness,' Brother Erasmus said slowly. 'The Silent Mother must remain where she is needed. You may have called, but she will not come.'

'She will. For I need her. Another can supervise at the Sanctuary. They are all as diligent to the cause as the Silent Mother. Work at the Sanctuary will continue as it has done.'

'We shall see,' he muttered, his face slowly returning to a more natural colour.

'How do the Silent Sisters keep the goddess in the Silence?' Meg asked softly, afraid to interrupt the tension at the table.

'The work of the Silent Sisters is sacred and ongoing,' Elalia said calmly as she turned her cold, green eyes on Meg, who gulped down the breath she had been holding. 'Now is not the time for lessons. We are to talk of Father and his way into the arms of the gods.'

Meg nodded mutely reaching forward for the goblet, but she found her hand shook too much, and in fear of spilling the wine over her dress she dropped her hands into her lap and her fingers found the edge of her cuff again.

'Don't fidget,' Elalia snapped.

Meg gripped one hand in the other and nodded.

'You may be right,' Brother Erasmus said softly. 'Tradition will dictate what must be done for your father.'

Elalia dipped her head to him and Meg felt the movement like a knife slicing through the air.

'Perhaps once we have passed your father to the gods, a decision will be made as to who shall wear the crown.'

She sat back and smiled then, soft and genuine, and Meg felt the air flow back into the room.

'Who will come?' Meg asked, her voice betraying the chill that seemed to have settled on her, and Brother Erasmus gave her a questioning look. 'I mean, shall our neighbours pay their respects? Will they pray with us for Father?'

'I am sure that Tands will come if they are able, Your Highness. It is far to travel. As it is from the Empire of Luana, and although we have had negotiations with them in the distant past, they do not visit with us.'

'The Empire of Luana?' Meg asked. 'I had not considered them. Surely it would be too great a distance, and we are not friends.'

'We are not enemies,' Elalia said, drumming her fingers on the table in a similar manner to the way Brother Erasmus usually did. 'If they were to come, it may be a chance to talk of trade and connection.'

'They do not follow the way of the gods,' Brother Erasmus said shortly.

'But the Luanian silk is known throughout all the lands. They may have different beliefs, but that does not make them so different we could not consider trade with them,' Elalia said.

Brother Erasmus bowed his head to her. 'Perhaps,' he muttered.

She breathed out slowly. 'Once one of us wears the crown, such communications and decisions will be so much easier.'

'Can we bury Father first?' Meg asked.

The hard, green eyes turned on her again and Meg saw a flash of something dark across them. She tried not to flinch.

'What must be done for Father?' Elalia asked Brother Erasmus.

'Pray to the gods for him. I shall meet with you in the temple once the plans are in place to confirm the prayers you are to say, along with those of your sisters.'

Meg nodded once and stood quickly from the table. She opened her mouth and then shut it again before she turned for the door.

'Wait,' Brother Erasmus said as he stood slowly from the table. 'Might you give me your arm? I fear the stairs too much for my old bones.'

Meg smiled and waited for him, tucking her hand into his elbow comfortably as he came to stand beside her, and it was only after the door had been opened and they were walking along the hallway past the tapestry-covered walls that Meg realised they hadn't said goodbye to Elalia.

'Will the Silent Mother come?' she whispered.

'I do not think so,' he said, patting her hand.

'Have you seen Malin at all since Father's death?'

He shook his head, and as they travelled easily down the stairs Meg wondered just where Malin might be and why he hadn't come forward. Perhaps their father had seen something in him that they couldn't and he was the one with the raven hair.

'Do you think the agreement with Tands will stand?' Meg asked.

'Do you want to leave us?'

She smiled into his warm face. 'That is not why I ask.'

He raised his eyebrows but then his face grew solemn. 'They may wish to wait until the gods mark the crown before they decide to continue or withdraw from such an agreement. Tell me,' he said softly, pulling her to a stop, 'why do you ask?'

She shrugged then. She had been so sure that her father meant

Kellin for the prince of Tands, and yet he had seemed so certain that it was the best match for her. 'I worry that Elalia will not let me continue to work for the people of Rocfeld as I have done, when she becomes Queen. Tands may offer a freedom I have not had.'

The Brother nodded slowly. 'But what if you are Queen?'

She shook her head slowly and allowed the old man to lead her where he would.

☙❧

The sheets were damp and twisted around his legs, and despite the fact that he didn't really want to move, Malin tried his best to untangle himself to reach the fire.

'My love?' Sera, the young woman beside him, murmured as she half woke at his movement.

'I need to stoke the fire,' he whispered, leaning over to brush her hair from her face, her exposed breast making it harder for him to move from the bed. 'We will freeze,' he finally said, pulling himself from her beauty and the twist of the sheets.

'I will warm you,' she said, sitting up, and he froze mid-step at the end of the bed as her nakedness burned through his whole body.

'But what will warm the two of you?' he asked, his eyes only on her barely swollen belly.

'Then be quick,' Sera said, running a hand over her smooth, pale skin.

He dropped the log of wood onto the fire so quickly that sparks flew about the small room. Stepping across the space and onto the bed in two strides, almost falling onto her, he was quick to nuzzle her breast. One hand moved over her belly, the other quickly between her legs.

'Slowly,' she said.

'We have not the time for slow,' he said, kissing her stomach before moving back to her breasts. 'Once we are returned to Rocfeld, I will not see you as often,' he mumbled through his full mouth.

'How can we be apart?'

'Elalia will have something to say, and her father. He may be ill, but is still a formidable man and king. We must consider this.'

She pushed him away. 'Do not jest, Malin. This is your child; it has been done before. Think of the risk I have taken for you, for us. In travelling here with you, hiding with you when I'm sure more know of what goes on than do not. Elalia may have your rooms watched and despite your love for me...'

'Oh, it is love,' he said, rolling over and pulling her with him.

'You spend too much time with your wife,' she said, her hands pushing firm against his chest.

'She is my wife,' he said. 'It is expected.'

'What shall we do?' she asked, gasping for breath as he pulled her close against him.

'Shush,' he said. 'Later.'

Malin sat bolt upright as the door crashed open.

'This had better be good, Commander,' he said, his face straight, his voice level. And yet the commander's face clearly showed his disappointment. Malin was fully aware that the man could see the woman beside him, but he knew his place in the world and he knew Malin's better. 'I had asked not to be disturbed, repeatedly.'

'Which is why I have broken down the door to deliver the message.'

Malin rolled his eyes and sighed. 'Who could need me so desperately?' he asked as sweetly as he could.

'Your wife, sir, requires you at the Temple.'

'My wife?' Malin stammered, but pulled himself in check quickly.

'The king is dead,' he said, his eyes truly sad.

'And who is our new queen?' he asked slowly.

'You mean you do not know, Your Highness?' The soldier slowly raised his eyebrows.

It was poor timing to take Sera away while the king was ill, but all he could think about was how long he would be without her. He looked at her then, wide eyed and scared. Where was the strong, cheeky woman?

'Princess Elalia sent word to you yesterday to return to the castle. I would suggest that you do not keep her waiting much longer.'

'Princess Elalia? Then who is Queen?' he asked more forcefully, pushing the woman away from him as he stepped from the bed.

'The choice is not clear,' the soldier said, turning his back on Malin and stepping out into the hallway.

'Not clear?'

'None wear the raven hair.'

'Is this usual?' Malin asked the man's back as he pulled his breeches on. The commander glanced at him over his shoulder. Malin nodded and reached for his shirt. 'I cannot remember a time when there was such a delay. When did the king die?'

'Two nights ago.'

'What does this mean?' Sera asked as he pulled the shirt over his head and pushed the door closed.

'It will be well,' he murmured, taking her into his arms. 'We will find a way for the child to be raised as he should be.'

'You are going to take him away from me,' she said fiercely, moving quickly across the bed, the sheets pulled up around her, hiding her body from him.

He shook his head, but he didn't know quite what he wanted from her or what he would be able to take. It would not be long before her body swelled to a point she could no longer continue to hide her condition. He looked at the girl, now standing by the wall, her fair hair askew, her pale-green eyes flowing over with tears. 'I have to go to Elalia,' he muttered and strode from the room. He heard the sob as the man closed the door, Commander Rainger still standing to attention in the hall.

He pushed past the commander and out into the snow. 'Come on, Commander,' he bellowed, heading for the stables. 'The princess is waiting.' He gulped down his apprehension. He would have to be firm with her, deny anything and everything and assure her he was right to be by her side. He shook his head as he lifted himself up onto his horse. With snow this thick, what had he been thinking by claiming to hunt?

Sera, he mused as they rode out onto the road back to Rocfeld. He had been thinking of Sera and her taut, pale skin.

And Elalia wasn't stupid.

6

Meg stared at her reflection in the foggy glass.

'What are you doing?' Kellin asked, stomping into the room.

'Do you think that Father's agreements will stand?' she asked, trying to smile at Kellin and failing.

'He was King; I don't see why not. Why do you ask?' The anger she had carried into the room dissipated and her blue eyes reflected the sadness Meg felt.

Meg shook her head and focused on her own face rather than her sister's in the mirror. 'Do you think Elalia will be a good queen, like Mother?' she asked.

'Why do you assume she will be Queen?' Kellin asked, moving over to the window.

'She is the eldest.'

Kellin shrugged. 'I do not know her well enough to answer. She was away so long and came back so different.'

Meg nodded slowly.

'Even her husband is not with her often,' Kellin went on. 'Could he know her?'

'I do not know enough about husbands and wives,' Meg said. 'And I wonder if I will.'

'You will be Queen and wife,' she said softly, but there was sadness in her voice. 'Do you want to be sent out as a negotiation piece?' Kellin asked quickly.

'Father knew best,' Meg said. 'I understand my place and I am happy to do my duty for Rocfeld.'

'And yet that place may be different now. No choice has been made. What if you are to be Queen of Rocfeld? What if you are Queen of both?' Kellin stared off across the room, as though contemplating what the idea would mean for her. 'If Elalia were Queen, she might marry you off to a cousin or the like.'

Meg stood up from the mirror. 'I may never be Queen of Tands.'

'I wonder if I could,' Kellin whispered and at Meg's querying look she added, 'marry a cousin.'

'Kell,' Meg said, taking her hands. 'You know you could not. If Rance were still alive it would be different.'

'If Rance were still alive I would be happy to marry a cousin.' And both girls started to laugh despite the heavy mood.

A gentle knock at the door quietened the laughter and Lora entered with a curtsy. 'Your Highnesses,' she said quietly, 'Brother Erasmus has asked for you both to attend him in the Temple, with your sister.'

Kellin groaned.

'Father must come first,' Meg said. 'Thank you,' she said, giving Lora a nod.

The maid stepped back and held the door open for them. The two sisters linked arms. Meg gave a small smile to Kellin, who pulled a face.

The Temple was cold and the twin gods stood tall and strong, the dimpled stone familiar and comforting at the far end of the space. Meg ran her hand over the smooth, worn feet in the same ritual. Despite groaning at being summoned, Kellin did the same.

Elalia and Brother Erasmus stood not far from them, discussing names of those attending the funeral and who would be directed to sit where. A young Brother standing behind Erasmus scratched down symbols on his slate. Another older Brother stood beside him and nodded or shook his head when names were mentioned to ensure the right people were grouped together, or at least the wrong people were not directed together.

Kellin coughed loudly as she came to stand beside Elalia, and the elder sister did not turn her gaze from Erasmus.

'Thank you for coming,' Brother Erasmus said. 'There is much for you to do to be a part of the ceremony to pass your father over to the gods.'

Meg found herself fighting tears and Kellin, in true form, had crossed her arms in anticipation of saying no to whatever it was they were going to be asked to do.

Elalia looked a little lost for a moment and Meg wanted to step forward and put her arms around her, but she knew Elalia would shrug her off. Meg felt the further loss of the sister she could no longer share a life with.

'Where is Malin?' Kellin asked. 'He should have a role, too, as part of the family.'

Elalia took a deep breath and looked back to Brother Erasmus. 'Do you need me for this, or could you just discuss it with them?'

Kellin opened her mouth to say something else, but Meg grabbed her arm before she had the chance. She squeezed her firmly and although Kellin rolled her eyes, she didn't say a word.

'Do you remember your mother's passing-over ceremony?' he asked Meg.

She shook her head.

'We were too young,' Kellin said. 'I remember a lot of people and father's voice booming off the walls, but not much more.' Subdued, her hand found Meg's and squeezed it tight.

'I spoke the words,' Elalia said softly and Meg again wanted to hold her sister.

'I cannot do it,' Meg said quickly, looking at Kellin as the realisation hit her as to what the Brother was asking.

'I will,' Elalia said. 'I understand the importance of his spirit moving on to join Kira and Kion.' She turned and subtly nodded to the large pair of gods dominating the Temple.

'Do you believe?' he asked.

She studied him a moment before nodding and then she eyed Meg seriously. 'I will say the words.'

'The person that says the words must believe,' Meg said slowly, unsure why she would doubt her sister's beliefs; or was it only because the Brother had stressed the importance? She had lived and worked with the Silent Sisters, after all.

'I do,' Elalia said, leaning forward. 'I believe with my whole being that father's spirit must move beyond our world to be with the gods and the followers. My time with the Silent Sisters only strengthened my beliefs.'

Brother Erasmus nodded slowly and they all turned at the noise of the doors being thrown open as Malin strode forward across the Temple. He didn't appear any different, although Meg noticed that he moved directly to Elalia rather than the gods.

He opened his mouth and then closed it, his face serious, his eyes only on his wife, and the rest of the group watched him closely. 'My dear,' he said clearly, taking her hand and pulling it to his lips. Then he surprised Meg by taking Elalia in his arms and holding her close. 'I am so sorry for your father's death,' he said. 'And that I could not be here for you.'

Meg thought Elalia looked confused before she smiled and said, 'You are here now and that is all I need.'

He released her and stepped back. 'What can I do?' he asked Brother Erasmus.

Brother Erasmus gave him a small smile but directed his words to Elalia. 'For such a king as your father, the day will be a long one. Many people will speak and there will be much prayer.'

Meg nodded. *A day just for Father seemed fitting.*

'He will be placed at the front of the Temple,' Brother Erasmus continued and he stepped towards the gods as the small group followed. 'Here,' he said, stopping between Kira and Kion. 'They will watch over him as they do us.'

'Will he be seen by everyone?' Elalia asked.

The Brother nodded and Meg found her mind wandering as they again started talking about who would be standing where. She stared up into the faces of her gods and they looked down on her, a little sad perhaps on this occasion, and she wondered what they would look like when the Temple was full for her father. Marked as King and yet no more.

She gulped down the lump that formed in her throat and tried to focus on what her sister was talking about.

'I have not received any news from the king of Tands,' she was saying, her voice harsh. 'The emperor of Luana has sent a bird that they come by boat and they will remain on their boats in the river, so we need not prepare them rooms, although they may eat with us. Have we allowed for such numbers?'

Brother Erasmus nodded. 'We have, Your Highness; the kitchens are prepared.'

'And the soldiers? For there will be so many more people moving around Rocfeld, and I am sure we would want to ensure such visitors are safe.'

'The royal commander has it in hand,' he said softly. Reaching out and taking Meg's hand, he pulled her a little closer and she found the lump in her throat slowly disappearing. But when she turned back to the gods, the idea of her father lying at their feet made her shiver.

'I am also sure,' he said, giving Meg's hand a little squeeze, 'that if the king of Tands and the emperor of Luana are to appear at such a ceremony, they would bring with them all the support and protection they would need.'

Elalia nodded and looked around the space again. 'I would still be happier if we had soldiers stationed around the castle grounds, and within the Temple for the funeral. Will you make sure the royal commander understands this?'

He gave her a single nod.

She looked at Meg for a moment, her face unreadable, and then she turned and walked to the back of the Temple. 'Tell me again, where will I be standing?' she called out across the space.

Kellin sighed and Brother Erasmus released his hold on Meg's hand. 'You can go,' he whispered. 'There is little to do that is not already set.'

Meg nodded and ran her fingers over the feet of the gods before taking Kellin's hand and heading toward the door.

CR80

Meg knelt before the gods and tried to block out the noise of those around her. The whole city was overflowing with visitors so soon after her father's death. Not just to pay their respects, but to discover who their new queen would be, she imagined.

'Your Highness,' Commander Brent whispered behind her, and she tried not to sigh as she got to her feet and moved forward to rub her hands over the feet of the gods before she turned to look at him.

'I am sorry,' he muttered, looking at her feet rather than her face. 'I do not wish to interrupt your prayer, but we are concerned that you are moving about the grounds without appropriate protection.'

She smiled then. 'Really?' she said. 'Who would be interested in me?'

'There may be all manner of men amongst the crowds, Your Highness, and I would really prefer that two soldiers were with you at all times.'

She shook her head. 'I will not have that. The men have far more important work to do than to follow me about. The same man will do.'

'Your Highness, please,' he said quickly, taking long strides to keep up with her. 'The royal commander has asked that you are watched over even more closely than usual, as with both of your sisters.'

She paused and looked at him seriously. 'You have men watching Kellin as well as Elalia?'

He nodded again. 'By her door and then two men with her as she moves around the grounds.'

'I bet she loves that,' she said quietly, walking quickly again for the door.

'She has not been entirely receptive, but she is more willing to understand the importance of it than yourself. And it may be at any moment that one of you is chosen as Queen.'

Meg sighed. 'Fine,' she conceded. 'Follow me wherever you choose.'

'Not me,' he said and she again turned to look at him.

He indicated the two men standing by the door of the Temple.

She nodded acknowledgement. Both tall, broad men, much like Commander Brent himself, and again she sighed.

'They will remain with you at all times, and they will be relieved during the night.'

She nodded and moved into the courtyard, the men falling into step behind her and the commander still striding along beside her.

'I go to see Kellin,' she said. 'Surely there will be enough protection within her rooms.'

The commander nodded and stopped to bow low to her. 'They will check your rooms before you enter.'

She nodded, trying to ignore the men behind her, their leather squeaking against their armour as they walked. The two guards on the door moved instantly to the side to allow her entry and she didn't pause to knock.

Kellin swung around as the door opened and then turned back to the fire. 'Is there anything we could be doing for Father?'

'I think Brother Erasmus has it all in hand, but he will let us know if there is anything we need to do.'

Kellin stared into the fire. 'Have our cousins arrived?'

Meg shook her head. She had tried to keep track of who had and hadn't arrived or who would come. But she had been so focused on Tands, she had forgotten her cousins. 'I'm tired of the whispers,' she said.

'Even in the Temple?'

'Everywhere I go, someone whispers something about who will be Queen and some form of speculation as to why they haven't yet been chosen,' Meg said. 'Today in the courtyard as I walked to the Temple, I heard someone say that I only went to pray to the gods to be Queen.'

'Pay no attention,' Kellin said softly, taking her hand. 'Everyone knows you have prayed every day of your life in that Temple, and more often than not, longer than everyone else.'

Meg nodded slowly. 'This will only continue until someone is marked. Why are they taking so long?'

Kellin shrugged. 'I'm sure I am third choice for the people and the gods, so I can't think on it.'

'No,' Meg said, pulling her sister into a tight embrace.

'They say the emperor of Luana is here, with several of his wives,' Kellin said, pulling away from her and sitting before the fire.

'Oh,' Meg said. 'I would like to see them. I have only heard stories.'

Kellin smiled and raised an eyebrow. 'They would be interesting stories, of a man who has more than one wife.'

'Certainly,' Meg said. 'What of Tands? Will their king come?'

Kellin shrugged. 'I know not; no one has mentioned them. I would like to walk in the market and see who is about.'

'I can't see that being allowed. We may need to wait until we are in court, or for the funeral itself.'

'And that will be soon,' Kellin muttered.

Meg nodded. *Far too soon*, she thought. She wasn't sure how she could say goodbye to such a man. The two sisters remained lost in their own thoughts staring into the fire. The flames slowly flickered and waved. Meg could almost see her father's face amongst them, dark and strong and then cold and grey. She squeezed her eyes shut to block out the memory when a soft hand touched her arm.

'I am sorry, Your Highness,' Kellin's maid, Cate, whispered. 'Would you like some supper? Cook has sent up a roast goose.'

Meg smiled at the girl and moved slowly to the table to sit beside Kellin. The two sisters ate in silence and then Kellin pushed her plate away, picked up a goblet and walked back to the fire. Standing silently before it, she stared into the flames, and Meg wondered if she saw the same image of her father. Meg quickly kissed her sister's cheek and then moved to the door to find the four soldiers standing tall. She nodded and moved through them.

If the Tandian king came, would she be allowed the chance to meet him, and perhaps his son? Her father had been so sure that he was a good man, and she would do as required no matter who he was, but she longed for a chance to see him and find out for herself if he was what her father had described.

She found herself at the solar door, unsure why she was there or what she could learn. She had put her hand on the latch when one of the soldiers said, 'There is no one there, Your Highness.'

She shook her head but opened the door anyway. It was just as it had been when her father had been there. The rooms still smelt of him and despite the time he had spent in bed before his death, it appeared as though he had just stepped out. Papers covered one table and a goblet beside the bed. The chair Meg had spent so many hours in by the fire still sat in the same position, but the fire was out and the room had a strange chill to it. She stood for a moment with her hand on the back of the chair until the soldier stepped forward.

'Would you like me to fetch someone, Your Highness?'

She looked up into his worried face and shook her head. She gave him a small smile. 'It has been a long number of weeks,' she said.

The man nodded. 'That it has.'

'I think I want to go back to my rooms now,' she said, moving toward the door. The other soldier stepped out of the way and allowed her to move through first, but she waited for the second to follow her through and close the door. 'Will you walk with me?' she asked.

He nodded and offered his arm. She slipped her hand around his elbow, grateful for the support as she moved slowly down the stairs and then back toward her own rooms. The hallways were strangely silent after the noise of the day, and she hoped she didn't lean on the man as much as she felt she was.

There were two more men by the door when they arrived. 'Is it that late?' the man at her arm asked, and they nodded in unison. They stepped aside and the soldier walked Meg into her rooms. She was grateful for the warmth of the fire and Lora standing by the table. She gave the girl a smile and released her hold. 'You will return to the barracks?' she asked him.

He nodded and bowed deeply. 'But we will be by your door when you wake.'

'Thank you,' she said, feeling comforted by the knowledge despite her reservations at such a need.

She closed the door behind him and stood silently against the warm wood as she listened to them exchange greetings and move away. When she turned back, Lora was watching her closely.

'That was not the commander,' she said.

Meg shook her head. 'No, Commander Brent had more important work to do. As they all do, I'm sure.' She moved across to the table, took a goblet already poured and gulped it down. 'I am tired,' she said. 'You can help me to bed and then you can go.'

'Yes, Your Highness,' Lora said and followed her into the room. 'I am sure that the soldiers would be only too happy to watch over you.'

Meg said nothing as Lora began to unlace her dress.

'That Raf is a very big man.'

Meg nodded. 'I am sure I am very safe with them.'

The girl smiled and curtsied. 'Good night.'

'Good night,' Meg said.

As the door closed, she sat down slowly on the floor before the fire and watched the flames flicker. It didn't appear that anything was different. The world hadn't stopped as she had thought it would, but it didn't feel the same. A father she had hardly known was gone and yet she missed him terribly.

Elalia wasn't helping Meg's state of mind either; she was distant and difficult and she wouldn't listen or talk. Her father's plans had been so clear. He had announced them to everyone, well before she had heard the news, and the agreement had been drawn up and signed by both kings.

When she had been with Brother Erasmus earlier in the day, she had noticed her name on the parchment lying across his desk. At the time, she was sure that he had left it out for her to see. Clearly it linked her name with that of the prince. Could an agreement be so easily undone by one death?

Her eyes had fallen on the papers beside it and she had found Kellin's name. She ran her finger over the words, wondering if her father had connected her to another. But the document was more of a promise to the Brotherhood than a connection to anyone else, and as Brother Erasmus had pulled it quickly from beneath her fingers together with the scroll regarding her connection, he had muttered about Brother Peras not putting things away.

'I saw nothing but my own name,' she had said, her voice carrying strangely in the Brother's study. 'Would you tell me more of Tands?'

He wasn't as forthcoming as she had hoped. Just as the royal commander had evaded her questions, Brother Erasmus was unable to give her anything useful or allay any fears she had of Tands or Prince Brodwyn.

Meg stared into the flames, wondering if she should tell Kellin what she had discovered, or if a new queen could undo such an agreement. Kellin would be heartbroken that Father would have wanted the Brotherhood for her; she would be expecting a lavish marriage, a house of her own. Meg couldn't understand why he would have thought being a Sister an ideal future for her. She would spend her life fighting against the Brotherhood's expectations. Maybe they could change the decision and allow her to marry some nice nobleman, but to whom she couldn't guess. Meg focused on the flames again.

They would do as was requested of them, although Kellin might make a fuss, whichever way it went.

She gulped at the wine. It was not her place to question, but something sat uncomfortably in Meg's throat as she imagined Elalia in her black finery and her grin as she looked over the court. She was so far removed from the quiet, uncomfortable woman that had returned to them from the Silent Sisters.

She gulped down the remainder of the goblet. She hoped it

wasn't jealousy that made her think such thoughts. That she would make a better queen. For she didn't think such thoughts, did she? She knew her place and her duty. But would Elalia make a good queen? Meg felt uneasy. She sighed. She would do what was required of her even if she didn't agree with the new queen, or even her father's wishes for that matter, because the crown knew best. Guided by the gods.

But no matter how many times she tried to convince herself, she couldn't understand where such a direction would come from. What reason her father had for Kellin to be placed with the Brotherhood. She tried to envisage her sister in the simple clothing of the sisters, but couldn't. And what would she do? She wasn't very good with small children and Meg had never seen her attend to anyone that was ill. Even when their father had lain dying she had stayed away unless he particularly called on her, and he hadn't done that until the very last.

Meg allowed the tear that was building to run down her cheek. A single moment of selfish regret. She stood slowly and climbed into her bed. She was tired and a choice surely had to be made soon. Tands may even wish her to visit before the marriage. If only they would come for the funeral... but time was running out and Tands was far away.

7

Malin stretched and rolled out of the bed in a smooth, fluid movement. Elalia missed the warmth of his body against hers instantly, but she gave no indication of it as she watched him pull his breeches on and then stand by the fire poking at the wood with savage stabbing motions.

Two consecutive nights he had called upon her and not disappeared before she woke. It was what she had wanted at some distant point, but his behaviour had her doubting him.

'What do you want?' she asked, and he stood slowly but didn't turn from the flames.

'What do you mean?'

'I don't think you need to continue the game when we are alone. You haven't done very well at it before now.' She slipped out of the bed and pulled a shawl around her shoulders. He still held the poker in his hand and she stepped up to him, ran her hands over his still bare chest. 'I enjoy your new enthusiasm,' she whispered. 'But I fear it will not continue.'

'Until you are marked as Queen, we must present as best we can.'

She laughed as she stepped back. 'It is the raven hair that you find appealing? I had heard rumours of blondes. And will your appearances slip once the choice is clear?'

He sighed as he placed the poker back in the stand and sat heavily in the chair beside the fire. 'If I don't make an effort, you shall not title me appropriately.'

'You must wait until after I am Queen for such a decision. But at least you make the effort. You may not receive a title of any kind.'

His face hardened and it took all of Elalia's strength not to shiver at the coldness that swept over him. 'I accept that. But it is your decision as to what position I hold.'

She sat slowly beside him at the fire. She had not given much thought to what he would be once she was Queen. Her only focus had been on getting the title herself. For that was what she had trained for and what she needed to be. A husband didn't fit into the plans of the Silent Sisters, and he only had one role in her plan.

'What title do you want?' she asked softly.

Malin cocked his head to the side, studying her far too intently. 'You would give me the choice?'

'I am asking the question,' she said. 'Tell me what you want and I will see what can be done.'

'I want the highest you can give me, the one with the power to do as I please, to go without question.'

'Really?' she said. 'And where would you go?'

'I will not leave you. I simply want to live as I wish.'

'You do not wish to be of service to your kingdom or your queen?'

'Maybe with the right title and position, I could be a great asset to Your Majesty.' He moved swiftly from the chair, kneeling before her and surprising her with his broad smile. He carefully took her hand in his and raised it slowly to his lips. 'What do you want in return for such a gift?' he breathed across her fingers and she shivered with the unexpected pleasure.

'Children,' she said without hesitation. 'I want a family that will carry on my legacy.'

She saw something flit across his face that she couldn't quite capture and she pulled her fingers from his hold. 'I know you spread your seed throughout the castle,' she snapped. 'Is it too much to ask, as your wife?' She pushed against him and stood quickly from the chair, marching across the room, her mind whirling with possibilities to achieve what she wanted without him when a strong grip closed around her arm.

'I can give you children,' he said. 'I will start one growing within your belly this very day if that is what you require in return for my title.'

She nodded mutely, unsure that he could do as he promised. 'You have tried before,' she whispered.

'Not as well as I could have,' he said, releasing his tight hold of her arm. 'I will,' he said reaching out and cupping her face in his hands. 'I will work hard to give you the child you desire and I get what I want.'

She nodded slowly, running her hands over his bare chest again. 'You will be the highest-ranking man in all the land, once I am Queen... with child.'

He smiled and pushed the shawl from her shoulders. 'I cannot promise that I will be the husband you wanted.'

'I don't need a husband,' she murmured as his lips worked across her neck. 'I need a child.'

'That I can deliver.' He hurriedly pulled at her slip, tearing the material a little to expose her breasts and slender body. He sighed.

'I am yours, my prince.'

'We are agreed?'

'We are.' She stepped back and held out her hand. He looked at it for what Elalia thought was too long, before shaking it firmly.

CRSO

Brother Erasmus's face paled and his breathing became laboured. Meg reached out to take his hand but he was looking beyond her, and she stopped as she noticed the Sister in white. Elalia wore a strangely unsettling smile as she walked toward them, the Sister dressed in white beside her.

'No,' Brother Erasmus wheezed, leaning against the platform on which the gods stood watch over the Temple.

'Brother,' the Sister said softy, 'it has been too long.'

'Silent Mother,' he replied, his voice strong, and if Meg had not witnessed his earlier reaction she would not have believed it had happened. 'What has happened that you would leave the Sanctuary and your duty to attend us here?'

'My friend requires my counsel,' she said, her hazel eyes cold, and Meg wondered how long it had been since a Silent Sister had left the Sanctuary.

'You have work to do,' he said.

'There are others that would maintain our hold over the Silence, Brother. Do not fear for us.'

He shook his head.

'I did say she would come.' Elalia smirked but the glance from the Silent Mother dampened her smile.

'I shall ask for a room to be prepared amongst the Sisters,' Brother Erasmus said, turning toward a Sister across the Temple and waving her over.

'There is no need,' Elalia said. 'I have a room by mine. I want her close.'

'Fear not, Erasmus,' the Silent Mother said. She stepped to the feet of the gods, touched her fingertips against the stone and almost instantly lifted them again from Kira's feet. 'So long since I have been within the Temple,' she whispered, staring up into Kira's face. 'Come child,' she said, smiling at Elalia and taking her hand. 'I will see my room now, and then we shall pray in solitude.'

They disappeared from the Temple as quickly as they had entered it.

'The Silent Sisters do the greatest work in keeping the goddess at bay,' Meg said softly, 'and yet she did not greet the gods as one who loves them.'

Brother Erasmus sighed loudly, as though he had been holding his breath. 'They do not worship in a Temple; they worship and pray to ensure the Silence holds the goddess. We cannot question a Silent Sister. But I wonder at the wisdom of the Silent Mother leaving the Sanctuary, for I have never heard it done before.'

Meg nodded mutely, for she couldn't think of an appropriate response. If the Brother had not heard of such a thing, then it had never happened, and she wondered why it would now. She watched as they disappeared through the door and out into the world, one dressed in black, the other white. The shadow and the light, she thought and then shook her head and looked up at Kira's worried face.

She turned back to Brother Erasmus to find him already across the Temple and talking with the sister he had summoned earlier. She had never seen him so nervous, and the fact that he had also not touched the gods made her worry. What would it mean if the Silent Mother was here? She didn't appear to be concerned that the goddess might be at risk of escape from the Silence.

Meg knelt down before the gods, but their faces all showed more concern than she would like to have seen. The Silent Mother had protected them from Goddess Sythia for a long time; if there was any risk, she would not have come. She would have to trust in her, and Elalia, that she would not endanger them by calling the Sister to her in some act of selfishness as Brother Erasmus seemed to think.

But as she closed her eyes to pray, Meg could only imagine a weakness forming in the Silence, the essence of the goddess finding her way out and that essence infiltrating their world. She opened her eyes as she took a deep breath and looked up at Kion, who looked more sad than concerned now, and she wondered what would happen to the world if the goddess did return.

⊗⊗⊗

The Silent Mother knelt before the candles in the royal family's private chapel and rested her forehead on her hands upon the ground. The tension she had felt in the Temple washed away in the silence of the room.

'Mother...' Elalia began to say.

'Hush,' she said, reminded of Elalia as a child when she had first come to them, so willing to learn. 'Let us pray.'

She returned to her own thoughts. Brother Erasmus might become a problem. It may have been a very long time since a Silent Sister had left the Sanctuary, but it was now time. Elalia needed her near to guide her and help her become the queen she was meant to be. She had a moment of doubt that Elalia could do this, that the right choice would be made.

She watched the woman beside her bent over in the prayer of the Silence. If Elalia needed her help then she would give it.

The two candles stood side by side, only inches apart. One glowed golden with a bright yellow flame. A black flame bobbed and weaved on the second. The two flames formed a strange flickering of light and dark, shadow and sun, within the room.

As Elalia sat up from her bent position to look at the candles, the shadows changed from the random flickering to form a shape. The woman was slender and tall, elegant with her crown. Elalia put a hand over her heart and whispered, 'Thank you.' The shadow queen curtsied and disappeared. The shadows moved across the walls and ceiling of the room with the flickering candlelight.

She turned to the Silent Mother as she nodded and threw her arms around her neck. 'I knew all would be well,' she said.

'You will be the Raven Queen,' she said slowly. 'It is as I said it would be. Do you doubt us? Do you doubt your place in the world?'

Elalia shook her head vigorously, and the Silent Mother was again reminded of the child that had come to them so many years ago. The child that had embraced their way of life so easily, so enthusiastically and without question. Any other may have destroyed what they worked for. She closed her eyes thinking of Brother Erasmus, but at least he still believed in them. The youngest princess appeared somewhat sceptical. She would wait and see how that developed. Their reputation was one of faith, strength and determination. The Brotherhood would support her against any ill thought. She would have to watch the little one to ensure she didn't get in the way.

'Silent Mother, she will come, won't she?'

'Of course she will,' she said softly, taking her hand and smiling. 'Before long the choice will be clear, and then all will be as it should be.'

Elalia smiled and seemed to relax a little.

'You must remain calm. You must continue as you are meant to be.'

Elalia nodded and stood slowly, brushing the dust from her dress and moving toward the candles.

'Leave them,' the Silent Mother said. 'I wish for a little longer.'

'Of course, Mother,' Elalia said softly. 'I shall wait for you in my rooms.'

She bowed her head to the girl and turned back to the candles, listening to the soft footfalls of the retreating princess. It would all be well, she thought. Elalia knew what was expected of her; she had been trained long enough. They would start at first light. She bent over in prayer, resting her head on the floor of the chapel.

She sat up slowly and watched the flickering shadows form into the shadow queen again, and she smiled.

8

The flow of people through the doors of the Temple didn't stop. Brothers glided around, directing people to various stations or positions. Everyone acknowledged the king, laid out at the feet of the gods. It was the only time Elalia could remember when people were not expected to greet the gods when they first entered the Temple.

The whole place murmured as one as they swapped news and views on the new world of Rocfeld. Despite the hushed voices, Elalia could pick up every word uttered. She was mentioned a lot, with quite some scepticism, she was surprised to find. One woman passing by even suggested to her friends that the Silent Mother had only appeared as a device to show the gods she was the best choice, but Princess Megora wouldn't need such tricks for the gods. Elalia tried to keep the smile on her lips as she searched the crowd for the Silent Mother.

"Malin" was another word that more and more people said as the Temple filled. She was sure that was because he had been away when the king had died. There were tales of a king and queen that had changed to the same raven hair at the death of his father. The two had ruled happily together for many years.

Elalia looked up at the gods watching over the people. How could they wait to show the next queen? she wondered. Why would they wait? She tried not to sigh. And then her mouth dried and she struggled to catch her breath.

'Calm,' the Silent Mother whispered in her ear and then slowly shook her head when she opened her mouth. 'All will be well.'

Elalia nodded slowly and allowed the woman to lead her toward her father. She would have to wait until they were free of the Temple before she voiced her thoughts. Glancing up again at their sad faces, Elalia wondered just how much the gods knew of what they did.

Another conversation from behind drew her attention. The king had only visited Tands a short time before his death, and yet the Tandian king had not come. Did they not trust that one of his daughters would be chosen, or were they waiting to see if the promised youngest one was to be Queen?

Brother Erasmus coughed politely before her and she tried to smile as she focused on him. 'I would like to present to you, Your Highness, the Tandian delegation.'

She looked over the small group of men with disappointment. No king, and now old men and a surly young man who looked about everywhere but at her. She offered a slow nod of her head.

'I am Lord Alva, Your Highness,' an older gentleman with a white-grey, short-cropped beard, offered with a very low bow. 'I am sorry for your loss, and our king offers his condolences and apologies.'

'Apologies?' she asked.

'That he was not able to attend. He fears it too far now for him to travel by horse and given the distance from Tands...' he trailed off as she waved her hand dismissively. She slowly lowered it and held it in place with the other; without glancing at Brother Erasmus, she knew the disappointment his face would wear.

'And we were already en route when we received the sad news. I am accompanied, Your Highness,' he continued slowly, 'by two of my king's favourites, Lord Caris and Brother Adroth.'

Again Elalia gave the men a short nod. 'And the young man who would rather be with the young ladies?' she asked, looking at the back of the group to the man who still looked everywhere but at her.

'Lord Danel,' he said sharply and the young man turned, looked confused for a moment and then bent into a deep bow. 'He was sent for the experience, Your Highness,' Lord Alva said with a sigh.

Elalia gave him a nod. 'I thank you for coming,' she said. *It is a disgrace. He couldn't even send the son.*

'This way,' Brother Erasmus said, directing them to the front of the Temple. 'The younger sisters stand by their father.'

Elalia looked at the Silent Mother beside her, graceful and still, as though she too were a statue. No matter what Elalia did, her younger sisters always looked like better daughters. She headed toward them, wondering if the great statues at the front of the Temple were looking over her sisters or if it was an illusion.

Malin smiled sadly as he joined her, squeezing her arm just enough for people to notice, and whispered loudly in her ear, 'Such a difficult time, my dear.'

She nodded slowly and the murmuring around them stopped; she knew they were waiting to see what would happen next. She wanted to ask where he had been, but she held herself in check.

A small group approached them almost immediately.

'Lord Robert,' she said sweetly, 'how nice to see you and your sister again.'

He bowed deeply and the young sister bobbed into a low curtsy, her face flushed. Elalia tried not to look her up and down as she straightened, for the girl appeared to have plumped up significantly since she had last seen her. 'You are settling in Rocfeld?' she asked the girl, who nodded quickly.

'Walk with me,' she said to Malin, pulling him close to her side and away from his friends. He seemed to look back at them for too long before smiling at her and despite her fluttering stomach she nodded, calmer in the knowledge that he would do what he had to for the position he wanted so badly. 'If only you were here to say your goodbyes to the king.'

'I am now,' he said, patting her hand on his arm and leaning in to kiss her cheek. 'I know how much you want to be Queen,' he whispered.

She glanced up at him then, but his gaze was on the crowd of people they moved through as he led her toward her father, laid out at the front of the Temple. Her throat seemed suddenly dry.

She gently touched her fingers to her father's feet and then took her place beside her sisters, Kellin uncharacteristically quiet and pale and Meggie already crying.

King Oren was dressed in his black cape fringed with raven feathers and the silver crown, the only indication that he was King.

The raven hair that had marked him was now as silver as the crown placed amongst the curls. Elalia was reminded of just how old he was. He had always looked so strong, and she wondered what she would look like old and grey, and no longer beautiful.

When marked as Raven Queen, she would do better than a collar of feathers. She would have the dressmaker come to her rooms later to see what could be done for her.

⊗≈⊙

The royal commander squinted through the tightly pressed bodies filling the Temple. Brother Erasmus had wanted him at the front, but he could see better from the fringes. Or so he thought, for now as he watched the crowd he was sure he could see someone he shouldn't. Or at least who hadn't been announced. He could have sworn that the young man that made up the Tandian delegation was the young prince himself. But he was at the back of the group, not placed prominently and he appeared to do as directed by Alva.

The royal commander shook his head again. Emperor Baghi of Luana paid too much attention to Princess Meg, but there was little he could do other than groan inwardly and regret that Oren was no longer here to remove the horrid little man. He stepped sideways and bumped into someone, 'Sorry,' he muttered, but he was still watching the emperor through the crowd.

'What is it?' Commander Brent asked.

'What?'

'What do you see?' he asked in a hoarse whisper and the royal commander put his finger to his lips.

'Sound travels, lad.'

Brent gave him a look of frustration.

'I don't like the way the Emperor of Luana looks at our girls,' he returned and found Brent with a wry smile and a raised eyebrow.

He heard a cough on the far side of the Temple and looked across at the two Luanian guards with their hands on the hilts of their large, curved swords. He stared across at them. Something was off, but he wasn't sure what it was.

'Do you think he means to steal them for himself?' Brent asked, but he wore a grin.

'He's watching something,' he muttered. *Or someone,* he thought. Not Meg; he was watching the young Tandian man. But he wore his collar high, and his back was to the emperor, a little lost or obscured amongst his group. 'He doesn't want to be seen,' he murmured.

'Who?'

'Shh,' the royal commander hissed and several of those around them turned. He gave a polite nod and indicated the front of the Temple.

Brother Erasmus's voice rang out; the gods smiled down on all those that had gathered for Oren, although it did appear as though Water looked a little stern compared to the others, and her eyes watched in the direction of the Luanian delegation. But he shook his head. They may have come by boat, but he was starting to read a lot more into this room than he should.

'Are the watch still on the girls?' he whispered.

Brent nodded. 'Until one is marked to wear the crown, we are watching them all as though each is Queen.'

'Good.'

'Are you worried?'

He shook his head. But it was better to be safe. There were too many hidden agendas in the Temple as it was. He wondered just how many of those the gods saw.

Brother Erasmus stood silent before the people, his eyes on the fallen king. As he looked to the three sisters, none yet marked to wear their father's crown, the room dropped to a silence that made the royal commander hold his breath.

This will be a test for all three. Elalia seemed to be the favourite for the crown, given her time with the Silent Sisters. As she took her place at the feet of the gods, the old man found himself smiling. She looked so like her mother, despite the younger sisters having more similar features to the former queen. From this distance, with the darkest hair, he could have been standing in the same spot some thirty years before. But would he ever think of her as more than the daughter of a queen?

He tried not to sigh, and despite her strong voice carrying the words of love and devotion through the Temple—her wishes for her father's spirit to be free and to live with the gods, to be held in their arms—he wasn't listening. He could have said the words by heart. He wanted to be sure that she meant them, but he couldn't look at her face to see if she did. He didn't want the truth of her acting.

A movement caught his attention and he noticed the young Tandian man searching the room rather than listening to the prayers and proceedings. As the young man stretched his head to the side, the royal commander grunted.

'What?' Brent whispered.

He shook his head. The Tandian king might not have come, but the son had. He stopped and the royal commander realised that he had found what he was looking for, Meg. This was going to be messy. Surely the boy didn't think he could sneak in and then get the chance to meet her? He had thought him brighter than that. But being promised to another might be difficult when the other hadn't been seen.

He was fairly sure by the way he continued to stare that the princess met with his expectations; and when one of the other advisors elbowed him sharply in the ribs he nearly cursed aloud. The royal commander smiled. This was a lad he could like. He turned quickly, but the emperor wasn't looking in his direction. The lad raised his collar again.

How had he got to the point that he thought it was children now running the kingdom? Girls and lads. He raised his eyes to the faces of the gods, serious and stern, looking over the people gathered before them. At the sharp nudge, he turned to a lad he knew would go far. Brent indicated the front of the Temple and the royal commander noticed the slow movement of people. He sucked in a deep breath and strode forward, running his hands over the king's feet as he lay before his people, before completing the usual ritual and heading out into the crisp winter air.

The youngest princesses were ahead of him, standing together, quiet and pale and holding hands as the snow softly whirled around them in the courtyard. He bowed low before them and Meg gave him a small smile. He rested a hand on her shoulder before he stalked toward the barracks. He wasn't going to stand around talking to people today. They would head for the Hall to continue the speculation as to who would be Queen and why the choice was not yet made, but not him.

As he passed the Tandian delegation, he paused and gave a

subtle nod to the young prince, who sighed and gave the same in return. The young man may have only come to see if his betrothed would be Queen, he thought as he stomped forward, allowing the cold day to blow around him and pull the heaviness of his loss away just a little.

9

'I have something that could help you, Highness,' a serving girl whispered in Meg's ear as she sat at the table. Before she could speak, the girl nodded toward her goblet and then she was gone.

Meg lifted it slowly to her nose and the bitter scent made her draw back quickly. She sat it down gently and looked around the room. Who would direct the girl to offer her a potion so openly? she wondered. Several people smiled at her as they met her gaze, some narrowed their eyes in suspicion, and another couple looked away.

Her heart beat faster. Someone was trying to help her win the crown with deceit or remove her from the race. Glancing over at the Tandian delegation, she wondered if it was a race she was truly invested in. She only wanted to do what was best for Rocfeld, and the gods knew who would be best to lead them. She would trust in the gods.

As Lord Tarrant appeared before her, she reached forward and tipped the goblet over, spilling the red liquid across the table and splashing him. 'I am so sorry,' she said, standing quickly.

'Do not fear. It is only wine,' he said through clenched teeth, and hurried off.

'I know it has been a difficult day,' Kellin whispered, 'But do not feel that the only way to keep annoying lords away is to pour wine over them. There won't be enough to drink.'

Meg nodded slowly. For the first time she could remember, she feared for herself. That someone would use magic to assist her to the throne. 'Do you think people fear we might cheat our way into the crown?' Meg asked her sister.

'I hadn't thought of that,' she returned. 'Do you think Elalia might cheat?'

Meg shrugged, watching her sister across the room, her hand tight on her husband's arm. That in itself didn't look right; they had been so distant and Elalia barely talked to the man, yet now they seemed to be inseparable.

'How could she cheat?' Kellin asked quickly, her hand tight on Meg's arm.

'Magic,' Meg whispered.

Kellin shook her head.

'The wine,' she continued in hushed tones, 'was not wine.'

'Magic?' Kellin asked, the colour draining from her face.

'Or poison.'

'No,' she said, sitting back, her voice clear and her face determined. 'Who would want to poison you or magic you?' she added more slowly, the certainty lost from her voice.

'Maybe someone thinks they are helping me, or helping someone else by killing me.'

'Do you suggest that someone might want me to be Queen and so kill you off?' she asked, leaning forward, her own goblet in her hand. She looked at it and then set it down. 'Who?'

Meg shook her head. They had only just said their goodbyes to her father. Were they so determined to design who should come next?

She was startled as Brother Erasmus put a gentle hand on her arm and then indicated the seat beside her. She nodded once and he sat down. 'Are you well?'

She nodded too quickly and he smiled reassuringly.

'It has been a long day,' he said softly.

'Meggie worries that someone may be using magic to mark one of us as Queen,' Kellin whispered across her.

Brother Erasmus looked at her seriously and then back to Meg.

'The serving girl put something in the wine,' she whispered, pointing to the fallen goblet.

He lifted it carefully to his nose and sniffed. 'Magic,' he muttered.

'Better than poison,' Kellin said.

'Commander Brent,' the Brother called out, motioning the commander closer.

'Brother. Princesses,' he said with a slight bow of his head. 'How might I be of assistance?'

'You do watch over the princesses?'

'Yes,' he said, looking at Meg with a serious face. 'I know the princess is not happy with the arrangement, but I think it best.'

'I think the princess agrees,' Brother Erasmus said as Meg looked down at her lap.

She hadn't taken any idea of risk seriously, but he was right and she was scared.

'I think we both do,' Kellin said quickly.

'Perhaps a sister should accompany you back to your rooms,' Brother Erasmus said. 'I think you need someone closer. Someone inside the room with you.'

'I'm sure the soldiers can keep them safe from harm.'

'There may be more than a physical threat.'

The commander's face hardened as he stared down the Brother and Meg felt a further uneasiness. How could her life have changed so dramatically in so few days?

'I would not expect you, Brother, to talk of magic in such a way.'

'We all know there is magic out there, some good, some bad, but it is all frowned upon by the gods. There is also much speculation as to why the next to wear the Raven Crown has not been marked. Some may be trying to assist that decision.'

'Surely a queen marked by magic rather than the gods would be clear.'

'To some,' he said, 'but not all. When the gods are ready, the choice will be clear.'

Meg nodded quickly.

'How long?' Kellin asked.

Brother Erasmus smiled and took her hand, but he shook his head slowly.

Cʒ℘

Days after her father's funeral, Meg blinked into the unexpected winter sunshine as she left the Temple. The world was covered in bright white snow, and then part of it moved. The Silent Mother, her white tunic all but lost to her surroundings, was crossing the courtyard ahead of her. Brother Erasmus's concern came back to her and she wondered just how the Silent Sisters kept the goddess at bay. Meg skipped carefully across the icy stones to catch her up.

'Excuse me, Silent Mother,' Meg said as she reached the woman just as she entered the castle. 'I wonder if you have a moment to tell me about the Sanctuary?'

The woman that turned on her was not what she expected, the comfortable smile replaced by a thin-lipped grimace and cold, hazel eyes. 'What would you want to know?' she asked, her voice level and low, and Meg tried to shake off the growing unease.

Perhaps she was unused to conversing with so many, Meg thought. 'I only know of the Silence and your work from stories. I would love to know the truth of it.'

'The truth is not always easy,' she said as she headed deeper into the castle, and Meg found herself skipping again to keep up with her quick pace.

When they reached the private chapel, Meg paused at the doorway. Had it been so long since she had been here? she wondered, for there was nothing familiar about the space at all. The small wooden altar seemed out of place, and the lack of gods unnerved her. 'Surely they were here before,' she muttered.

'You question the lack of gods?' the woman asked unkindly. 'We are to focus only on our task, and they are simply a distraction.'

'But you do what you do for the gods,' Meg said, frustrated that a Sister of the gods could see them in such a way. Stepping into the room, despite the hair prickling on the back of her neck, Meg continued, 'Candles?'

The Silent Mother stared at the black-and-white candle on the small alter for a moment before answering. 'Silence lives in the shadows,' she said, stepping forward and giving a small bow to the altar.

'Are you to keep the shadows at bay, keep the Silence away?' Meg asked quickly.

'We must embrace the Silence to achieve our goal,' she said, kneeling down.

'To keep the goddess in the Silence,' Meg whispered.

'We do what we do for all the world,' she said, and the smile was the first Meg had seen, but it made her more uneasy than the earlier unfriendly look.

'Have you seen the goddess in the Silence?' Meg asked, stepping forward.

'Would you want to see her?' she asked softly, her focus back on the candles.

Meg shook her head. 'I only seek to understand. To ensure Kira and Kion are safe.'

'You do not care for the people of Rocfeld in the same way?'

'Of course, as long as the gods are secure then so can the people be.'

'Do you really think it is that simple, child?' she asked, looking over Meg as though she were but a small child with limited understanding of the world.

'I trust the gods.' Meg squared her shoulders and stared the woman down.

'Is that enough?' she asked, unflinching under Meg's stare. 'For the gods are yet to make a choice for the crown.'

'You have dedicated your life to their work; do you not feel the same?' Meg asked. 'The decision as to who wears the crown will be made at the right time.'

'You do not fully understand what I have devoted myself to,' she said slowly, standing, and Meg found herself backing up. 'It is important, more important than anything you could ever put yourself to. More important than even the Brotherhood understands. It cannot be explained.'

Meg nodded quickly. 'May I pray with you?' she asked.

The Silent Mother looked at Meg seriously. 'You would not know how to pray for Silence.' Meg opened her mouth to speak but the Silent Mother continued. 'It is not something that can be explained or taught. If you were to serve with us, you would know. You would understand.'

'Does Elalia understand?' Meg asked, surprised by the hurt in her own voice.

The same strange smile returned. 'Yes, she has always understood what it is we do.'

Meg nodded once and turned for the door.

'Go and pray in your Temple and leave us to the Silence,' the

Silent Mother said behind her.

Meg was tempted to run back to the Temple, to kneel at the feet of the gods she loved and ask them for understanding. But she headed back to her rooms instead. The Silent Mother had not been what she expected, a quiet woman like other Sisters of the Brotherhood, devoted and yet open to discuss points of faith or duty. But the Silent Mother didn't appear to want to share anything of her life or how the Sisters protected them. She was defensive, as though Meg had an alternate reason for asking the questions she did.

She pushed open the door of her rooms to only the sounds of the crackling fire. She could live in silence if that was what the gods required of her, if that would keep the kingdom and her people safe.

Meg stopped, her hand on the back of the chair, and she blinked in the strangely foggy room. The air smelt strange, an acrid, burnt smell, as though someone had dropped something into the fire that they shouldn't have. Stepping forward, she noticed the fire burnt green, the flames the strangest colour, as though some magic had taken them and changed them into something else.

It became harder to breathe in the strange firelight, the room unnatural and her chest tight. Could it be that the Silence had been breached with the Silent Mother away from the Sanctuary? she wondered, just as Brother Erasmus had feared. She should be warned. But as Meg swung around she came face to face with the woman standing in her doorway. The Silent Mother stepped forward slowly and closed the door.

Meg coughed as the bitter smoke filled the room, her eyes burning.

'What do you think you can do?' she asked as Meg reached for the window.

Her fingers slipped against the latch as she started to cough again and her vision blurred from the tears trying to wash the stinging smoke from them. Finally she grabbed the latch tight, but it would not budge. When she looked toward the door, the Sister stood unaffected by the smoke, her eyes closed, and Meg dropped to her knees as the bitterness filled her lungs.

The door was her only chance, but the Silent Mother was in the way. She tried to crawl forward but she couldn't breathe at all, and as she lay down on the rushes, she could just make out the white tunic of the Silent Mother as the world faded to black.

Meg gulped in a large lungful of air and sat up to find herself in her bed.

'Slowly now,' Brother Erasmus said from the end of the bed. 'Do you know what happened?'

Meg blinked and rubbed at her eyes, no longer burning, and her breathing came easily. She put her hand on her chest, expecting some of the same burning she had felt within the smoke-filled room. 'Was there any damage?' she asked.

'From what?' he asked, stepping forward, his old face creasing in concern.

'The fire,' she whispered. 'The smoke.'

'The fire was out when I found you, Your Highness,' Lora said, appearing from behind the Brother. 'You were lying on the floor.'

'Perhaps you fainted,' Brother Erasmus offered.

She glared at him. 'I don't faint,' she said. 'There was someone in the room, causing the fire to burn green and smoke to fill the room. I couldn't breathe, I couldn't see.'

'Who? How could someone make the fire burn green?'

Meg opened her mouth and then closed it again. They wouldn't believe her.

'Go for a nurse,' he said softly to Lora, and when it was only the two of them left in the room he sat carefully on the side of the bed. 'Tell me,' he whispered.

'The Silent Mother.'

He shook his head. 'You must have been mistaken. When she is not with your sister, she is in prayer.'

'I met with her in the private chapel. I wanted to know about the Sanctuary, but she didn't want me knowing, didn't like me asking questions. And then when I returned to my room, the fire burned green and I couldn't open the window.'

Brother Erasmus stood slowly. 'The guard on the door saw no one arrive or leave other than yourself. You are mistaken,' he said firmly. 'We have talked of magic; it is someone trying to frighten you.'

'They have succeeded,' she said, wrapping her arms around herself. 'But it was the Silent Mother.'

'You are mistaken,' he said again. 'Or you suggest that the Silent Sisters work against the gods, work with magic that is not their own. That they do not guard the Silence as we hope.'

'What if they guard the Silence in a way we cannot understand?' she asked slowly, as the brevity of the Brother's words sank in. If the Silent Sisters were not what they were thought to be, if they weren't protecting them as they thought, what could that mean?

'The goddess is lost in the Silence and they keep her there. Generations of Silent Sisters have protected us and the gods. I fear you hit your head.'

Meg nodded slowly, lay back and closed her eyes. Perhaps the Brother was right and it was another evil, tricking her into seeing the Silent Mother when she was not there. Meg shuddered and sat back up. Who would do such a thing?

Brother Erasmus slowly shook his head and as the nurse entered the room he left it. She lay back and allowed the nurse to probe her for injuries or signs of illness, but she couldn't close her eyes with such images in her mind, studying the pattern painted on the canopy of her bed instead.

10

Elalia stood still and straight and tried to focus on those moving through the gates and not think on who hadn't yet arrived. It was the distance, she reassured herself, that was why some families had not made it to the castle in time for the funeral. But they would be there when her hair turned the raven black that marked her as Queen. She was certain the mark would come and she tried to hide her frustration at the delay of the gods.

She had attempted to meet with everyone as they arrived, but it wasn't always possible. There seemed to be a constant flow of people. Her mother would have met with everyone and she was keen to be seen in the same light, to be compared to such a great queen. Although as more people arrived, the more certain she became that they were only coming to see if they were right as to who would be the next queen, or if the crown would move outside the family.

A rider had been sent ahead to say that her cousins were close and she was genuinely pleased at the idea of familiar faces tied to happy memories. Although he had only mentioned cousins, she wondered why her aunt would not attend, and was a little relieved that her uncle wouldn't be there with his cold eyes. She shivered at the idea of him. She had always been scared of him as a child.

Creena's round, smiling face was the first to appear at the carriage door and Elalia smiled easily back. She realised, as she stepped forward to take her cousin's hands in hers, that it had been a long time since she had smiled naturally.

'You are beautiful,' Elalia said, squeezing her hands and looking her over, her hair perfectly in place, her dress not even wrinkled from the days inside the carriage. Her perfect, pale skin highlighted the brilliant blue of her eyes and Elalia felt the familiar stab of jealousy at her cousin's effortless beauty.

Creena curtsied before her, her hands still tight in Elalia's, and then she threw her arms around her. 'Oh, Elalia, how long it has been.' But before Elalia could find comfort in the embrace, she released her and stepped back as her older brother, Morley, stepped from the carriage. He was such a contrast to his sister, with his dark hair and a short, square frame. His large, bushy eyebrows reminded Elalia how much older than her he was.

Only a step behind him, a beautiful blond woman took his hand and emerged into the light. Elalia had forgotten he had married recently. The girl would have been no more than eighteen summers, and her tanned skin appeared as though she had spent every one of those in the sun. She smiled at Morley and looked around her in awe. They made a strange couple, Elalia's short, broad cousin nearly twice the age of the beautiful, slender woman standing next to him.

'I am sorry, Your Highness,' said Morley with a deep bow, 'for your loss and that we missed your father's funeral.'

'I understand it is a long way to travel,' she said, holding out her hand and allowing him to take it. The delegation from Tands lived much further away and yet they had managed, but it wasn't worth questioning her uncle's behaviour now, or his motives.

When another man stepped from the carriage, Elalia's smile faltered.

It was Rance, their middle brother.

No. Rance had died years ago.

She forced the smile back into place and focused on Morley.

'Have we missed who was marked as Queen?' he asked, far too casually.

She shook her head, knowing full well they all knew, but she was distracted by the other man. 'Not at all, your timing is perfect.'

'Elalia,' Creena said, drawing her attention back. 'This is Morley's new wife, Annar.' She indicated the tall woman with a graceful sweep of her hand. Elalia gave her a nod as she dipped into a shallow curtsy, but her eyes moved quickly to the man standing at the back of the group and grinning widely. 'This is our cousin, Tyne,' Creena added.

He stepped forward and bowed low before her, his smiling eyes and broad grin unnerving, as well as looking like her dead cousin. 'Cousin,' he said, in a voice that could have belonged to Rance as well.

She gave him a questioning look.

'I am cousin to your cousins and so I feel we are as closely related.'

She nodded that she understood his meaning, but wondered just how close a relation this cousin was.

'You must be tired from your journey,' Elalia said. 'A week by carriage is not as much fun as when we were children.'

'So true,' said Creena, 'And in this snow it appeared to take so much longer. I fear I am still cold.'

Elalia nodded. 'I shall have you shown to your rooms.' She waved a footman who had been waiting silently behind her to come forward.

'The rooms are together,' Morley said, more statement than question.

'They are close to each other.' Elalia looked at the footman and he nodded.

'We wish to be together,' Morley said, 'in the same rooms.'

Elalia studied him for a moment and despite his smile she knew he was serious. 'There are many visiting with us at the moment,' she said.

'Yet we are in a strange place and we would appreciate being together,' Annar said simply.

'You are with family,' Elalia said, clutching her hands before her and trying to keep the frustration from her voice.

The girl gave her a shy smile.

'I shall see what can be done.' Elalia sighed.

'You are too sweet, Cousin,' Annar said, leaning forward, but Elalia stepped just out of reach. She did not want this woman's kisses upon her cheek.

A quiet cough emanated from the carriage, and Elalia wondered if her aunt had come after all and had been forgotten by her children as an old hand gripped the door frame. It was Annar that moved forward to help the old woman out, but as she emerged shrivelled and bent into the light, Elalia could only stare.

'Father thought it best that we bring the soothsayer with us,' Annar said, supporting the woman by the elbow. 'It has been too long without an heir marked.'

'I'm sure the gods will make the right decision in the right time,' Elalia said, unable to take her eyes from the unblinking stare of the soothsayer. She shivered involuntarily and cursed her body for betraying her as the young Annar grinned.

'You must come to the Hall,' she said, turning and walking quickly ahead, 'for warmth and sustenance.'

Once they reached the Hall, Elalia extended her arm to guide them in ahead of her, but she remained in the doorway. 'You do not join us, cousin?' Tyne asked.

'I am afraid I have many others to meet. A man will show you to your rooms once they are ready.'

He nodded and looked around. 'When may I meet my other cousins?'

'They are occupied at present, but I am sure you will meet with them this evening.' She nodded and raced down the hallway away from the room before he could ask anything else. It was only as she entered the cool air of the courtyard that she wondered what the Silent Mother would make of the soothsayer. Did they think that the crown may fall to one of them? Perhaps she should have pressed for the reason her aunt and uncle had not thought it worth the time to travel. Especially her aunt, for she had just lost her brother.

CR80

'Creena,' Meg called as she entered the Hall, 'I am so pleased to see you.' She threw her arms around her cousin and pulled her close.

'I am sorry that we were not able to make it for the passing-over ceremony,' Creena said to her and then, lowering her voice, added, 'There was too much discussion as to who should attend, and then the journey was so slow through the snow. Winter seems so harsh this year.'

'It is a test,' Kellin said, joining them and pulling Creena close to kiss her cheek. 'For we must wait for the coming season for life to settle again, and it seems so unsettled. So much waiting.'

'Kellin,' Creena said. 'You were impatient as a child and I see you still are.'

Kellin gave her a friendly smile and turned to look at Morley and the woman with him across the room. 'Annar is beautiful,' she said, studying the woman's slender figure. All three women looked her over and then Kellin and Meg turned back to Creena as she said, 'Perhaps.'

'You possess your mother's skin,' Meg said.

'You do not need to flatter,' Creena said. 'She is beautiful, yet beside my brother it is enhanced, I think.'

Again the women studied the small party talking with Elalia by the fire, and Morley's dark hair, thick eyebrows and short, stocky frame did indeed seem enhanced by his young wife's beauty.

'And how do you fare, Meg?' Creena asked suddenly, taking her hand and pressing it tightly between her own. 'I heard whispers that you fainted. That seems so unlike you.'

Meg tried not to grimace. 'I am well,' she said. 'And I have never fainted.'

Creena smiled, but seemed to study Meg for far too long. 'So I told Morley.'

'And who is the man with Morley?' Kellin asked, drawing their cousin's gaze across the room. Meg, realising she had been holding her breath, tried to release it slowly.

'My cousin Tyne, on Father's side,' Creena said.

'I could be distracted by his eyes,' Kellin said and the other two laughed.

'He looks like Rance,' Meg said. 'I am sorry,' she added quickly.

'No need for apologies. He looks very much like Rance and I think it may be why Morley keeps him close. He has the way of Rance about him. I sometimes think it would have been very different if he had not died as he did.'

Meg nodded slowly. 'How are your parents? Such a shame they could not come.'

'Mother said it was too far for her and Father had more pressing business, although I am unsure what it could be. He may join us later.'

'When we were children, we seemed to move between the two

homes so often. Perhaps the memory of childhood is unreliable,' Kellin said, her eyes still on Tyne. 'Yet for a brother, I would have thought your mother would travel.'

'She knew he would be gone by the time she arrived and so not worth the journey,' Creena said quickly. And then at Kellin's look of surprise she added with a smile, 'He would have been with the gods and Mother felt her grief would be the same at home as here. There are so many people here,' she said, looking around the room.

Meg's gaze followed hers; there were more people in the Hall, in the castle even, than she had ever remembered. So many had come for her father's funeral, even more for the marking of the new queen. 'I hear rumours that you arrived with a soothsayer,' she said to her cousin.

'Father suggested that she may assist in telling who might wear the Raven Crown.'

'I hope the gods choose soon. The soothsayer can say what she pleases, but if the gods do not mark the queen it will make no difference,' Kellin said.

'Or king,' Creena said.

'Do you think that the crown might leave the family?' Meg asked.

Creena shrugged and smiled sweetly. 'I cannot guess at what the gods might do, but it is strange that no one is marked yet.'

Meg had heard this same sentiment too many times since her father's death. She was looking for a distraction when Kellin squeezed her arm.

'Where do you suppose he has been?' Kellin asked, subtly pointing at Malin as he entered the room with Robert.

'Where is the Sister?' Meg found herself asking.

'A Silent Sister?' Creena asked.

She shook her head. 'Robert has a younger sister, fair and beautiful; she is usually only a pace or two behind him.'

'Perhaps she is unwell,' Kellin said lightly. 'She has not looked quite herself for some time.'

'In what way?' Creena asked.

'She seems to be putting on weight,' Kellin said with a wink and Meg scowled at her.

'And she spends much time with Elalia's husband?'

Kellin's eyes dropped to the floor. Gossip about Malin was not somewhere she should go, even with her cousin. They watched Malin cross the room, talking and laughing with people as he went, and arrive at his wife's side where he put a gentle hand to her elbow.

'Come,' Meg said, pulling Creena by the hand and away from the conversation she knew would come. 'Let us introduce you to some ladies and we shall see what other interesting people we can find.'

'Are you saying I am not interesting?'

Meg stopped and then relaxed at the sight of her cousin's smile. 'Hardly,' she said. 'For we have royalty from across the seas and delegates from the North.'

'Tands is here?' she asked.

'A delegation. Not the king, nor the prince,' she added quietly. 'And I have had very little chance to talk to any of them. Come, we shall try for a better introduction and it will be a great excuse to find out who some of these people are.'

'And then you can introduce us to Annar,' Kellin said. 'Such skin, I want to know all of her secrets.'

'I'm not sure she will share many of them with you,' Creena said, looking away from her brother and his wife, 'but I'm sure she would gladly share her opinion of all sorts of other things.'

Sitting before the fire, Meg only glanced up as Kellin sat beside her and took her hand in hers. 'Are you sure you are well?' she asked.

'I do wish you would stop asking. I'm fine. Creena looks well,' she said softly, watching the flames flicker in the hearth. 'Although I didn't quite believe her reasons for our aunt staying away or for bringing a soothsayer. What will Brother Erasmus say?'

'I don't like Annar,' Kellin said quickly.

When she didn't continue, Meg asked, 'Is there a reason for your dislike?'

Kellin shrugged. 'She seemed too sure of herself.'

Meg laughed. 'That is a strange thing to say.'

'What did you think of her then? And the strange cousin that looks more like Rance than even Rance did himself. Why would he come?'

Meg opened her mouth to answer but closed it again without

speaking. Of all the visitors in the Hall this evening, she seemed to know her cousins least of all. Morley was too much like her uncle, and she too couldn't understand the attendance of Tyne at such an event. Particularly when they had never met before.

'Annar,' Kellin said.

'What?' Meg turned to her sister.

'What did you think of Morley's wife?' she asked more forcefully.

'She is very beautiful and young,' Meg said slowly. 'And yet it was as though Morley looked at her for direction before he spoke. Why would he need to be wary around family?'

'Would they cause trouble? Could they cause trouble, do you think?'

'No,' Meg said, smiling at her sister, but then she stood quickly. 'Why would they? We have always been friends, there has been no animosity between the families and there is a clear expectation that the crown would be inherited by one of Father's daughters.'

She swung around to find Kellin grinning.

'You do not agree?'

'I think there was a different daughter expected to take the crown,' Kellin said softly, patting the seat beside her, and Meg slowly sat back down.

'It will go to Elalia. I don't begrudge her for it. Do you think they bring the soothsayer to prove it should be one of them?'

'There has never been such an event,' Kellin said. 'They may fuss all they like, but the gods choose.'

'That choice could change,' Meg murmured. 'Long ago, in the early days of Rocfeld, one son was granted the raven hair on his father's death, but in the days following his hair faded to grey and the younger brother's hair became the raven black. The gods changed their choice.'

Kellin pulled a loop of hair around her finger and studied it for a long moment before turning to Meg and running her fingers gently over her tightly woven braids. She smiled sadly before leaning forward and kissing Meg's cheek. 'You would make an excellent queen. But no choice has yet been made. Do you suppose they mean to influence the gods?'

'That seems an even more impossible feat. How could they do such a thing?'

'They could prove that Elalia is not the queen we need her to be.'

Meg nodded slowly.

'Yet Elalia lived with the Silent Sisters,' Kellin continued. 'There is no greater devotion to the gods. And what could they gain if the crown went to you or me?'

Meg shrugged. She couldn't guess at what they may be thinking. She wondered, again, if the Silent Sisters were as everyone thought that they were. 'There could be no way to change the choice. Or would they mean to kill us all?' The look of utter fear on Kellin's face took Meg by surprise. 'It is only a thought,' she whispered, taking her hands and squeezing them tight. 'They are our cousins, our blood. I am certain that no such idea has crossed their minds.'

Kellin nodded mutely, pulling from Meg's hold. She turned away and left the room without her usual goodnight wishes. As the door clicked closed, Meg leant forward into her hands, her eyes squeezed closed. She was starting to get paranoid, uncertain of everyone at every turn. Perhaps Brother Erasmus was correct and she had simply misinterpreted some part of the conversation with the Silent Mother. She knelt before the fire, the heat against her face, and stared into the flames. She thought for an instant that she could see the image of her father's face, and then it was gone and the heat was too much and she sat back.

11

Brodwyn found it a strange relief to walk through the Temple doors, despite visiting every day since the funeral, and probably for longer than expected. Striding across the expansive floor toward the platform of the gods, he wondered, as he did at each visit, how the Temple could be so much more impressive than the one he had left in Tands. Not that it was an ornate space—in fact it was far simpler. But he thought the tall, exposed stone walls were far more beautiful than the painted ones he knew.

Brodwyn glanced around the people moving through the space, either toward the gods or on their way out. Several faces he recognised from earlier visits or the Hall, and he gave a polite nod as he moved toward the feet. But the face he searched for was never present when he entered the Temple, despite his having heard that she was devoted.

The gods and the followers smiled down on him and he smiled back as he rubbed his hands over their feet, each and every one. As he moved among the people before the gods to find a space to kneel, Brodwyn smiled on Brother Adroth's motionless form.

He knelt silently, clasped his hands before him and closed his eyes. But as he tried to focus his mind on the gods, the smiling face of the princess that he had caught through the crowd in the hall last evening kept swimming into view. Brother Adroth coughed beside him and whispered, 'Are you here to pray?'

Brodwyn nodded rather than spoke. How the old man did it he would never know, but he wasn't going to open his eyes and ask the question in fear of losing the image of the beautiful woman before him.

'Please,' he found himself asking the gods. For weren't they the ones conspiring against him? The reason that he had not managed the opportunity to speak with her yet? And she was curious of Tands. Someone had mentioned the other night that she wanted to know if it snowed, but he couldn't get away, or she was occupied or simply gone from the Hall when he tried to get an introduction. It was almost as though someone—again he thought of the gods— would not allow them to meet.

The brief introduction at her father's funeral had not helped his cause, for she had been too distressed. She had nodded politely as they were named. But her eyes had been on her father. She had appeared so broken, for a moment he wasn't sure if he regretted interrupting such a moment by travelling to Rocfeld, or whether he wanted to take her in his arms and let her cry against his chest.

He sighed; no one at Rocfeld knew who he was. The royal commander had been quick to recognise him, but he hadn't told his secret. He was just another advisor. Maybe it was simply that he wasn't seen as important enough in this role to meet such a princess. Or maybe it was because until the new queen was marked and crowned they couldn't finalise the agreement and so the betrothal was not set.

He stepped forward to brush his hands over the feet of the gods. He took his time, taking in the smooth, cool texture of the stone, refocusing his mind and calming his frustrations. As he stepped back, he noticed the royal commander kneeling amongst the people; he was straight and tall even kneeling before the gods. His eyes were also closed to the surroundings, as those around him.

The royal commander appeared to be a good man, and Brodwyn wondered why he kept quiet. Did the old man trust him? He sighed with the relief such an idea brought with it. He wondered if Commander Rainger would be so accommodating, but he had only seen him in the yard in Tands, and it may be that the soldier didn't fully appreciate his position.

Brother Adroth stood beside him silently, his eyebrows raised.

'What?'

'We are to meet with Brother Erasmus,' he said. 'Have you forgotten? We are not just here to watch the people.'

Brodwyn nodded and the weight of what was required of them settled on his shoulders. For negotiations around the sovereignty of Rocfeld with a new queen, his father should have come. Not an old Brother, two elderly advisors and a sneaky prince who should have stayed at home. And there was still no queen to negotiate with.

He sighed again before he could prevent it. His father had good reason for not coming himself. If only he knew what that reason was. Despite talking his father into allowing Alva to have his way, Brodwyn knew his father had his own reasons for allowing such a journey. As he followed Brother Adroth toward the back of the Temple, a younger Brother stepped forward and opened a door for them.

Entering a small room on the other side, Lords Caris and Alva were waiting. They both looked pointedly at Brodwyn before following the Brother through the next door. He just had to remember why they were there, and why he was there. Embarrassing his father or his kingdom would not do at this point, or the whole betrothal would be off. He was an advisor, he reminded himself as they walked quickly along the narrow passageways of the Brotherhood. The occasional candle was enough to indicate where the passage went, but he wouldn't like to find his way in or out of here on his own.

He just had to think before he spoke. Remember where he was and who he was supposed to be, rather than a prince who could speak as he thought.

The room they entered was a wonder and Brodwyn tried to keep up with the others, rather than stop and stare as they moved through dimly lit shelves toward a long table. Brother Erasmus stood as they approached, and thankfully there were more candles on the table than Brodwyn had seen throughout the Brotherhood.

'Thank you for coming,' Brother Erasmus said, indicating the group sit at the table littered with papers. A young Sister appeared from the dark with goblets, strangely out of place in the simple Brotherhood with their ornate patterns. Another Sister followed with a large pitcher of wine, which she poured slowly into each goblet. At the impatient wave of Brother Erasmus's hand, she placed it on the end of the table and disappeared back into the dark.

Brodwyn had an uneasy moment where he wondered just who else might be hiding amongst the dark shelves.

'Thank you,' Lord Alva said, lifting his goblet slowly to his mouth.

'It will not be long before a Raven Queen is marked, and then you may discuss with her all you came to discuss,' Brother Erasmus said. 'Yet she is still young, and as her advisor, I ask to review the main matters now so that I can prepare a response for our new queen, once she is selected.'

Lord Alva nodded again and Lord Caris glanced briefly at Brodwyn before taking a large gulp from his goblet. They appeared far too nervous for a simple summing up of matters. Surely his father had given them much to discuss with the new queen.

After a moment's silence that made Brodwyn more nervous than it should have, Brother Erasmus sat forward, resting his elbows on the table.

'What exactly do you wish to discuss with the new queen?' he asked.

'A few matters,' Lord Alva said.

Brother Erasmus didn't move.

'Trade between towns at the border,' Lord Alva said quickly.

Brother Erasmus raised his eyebrows.

'Marriage,' Brodwyn whispered.

'I am assuming, Sire, that you do not want the Rocfeld Court to know who you are,' Erasmus said, looking directly into his soul, and then glaring at Brother Adroth.

The other two advisors looked somewhat nervous, and then a grin stretched across the Brother's face.

'How did you know?' Brodwyn asked with a sigh.

'You have your father's eyes,' he said.

Brodwyn watched the man across the table and Adroth coughed.

'I will not share your secret,' he said. 'I am sure that you father sent you for a reason?'

'He doesn't know,' Brodwyn admitted, and Adroth sighed. 'But I'm sure he has worked it out by now.'

'A month away, I would say so. What was your reason?' Erasmus asked Brother Adroth.

'The boy begged,' he said with a shrug. 'He wants to be sure that he still gets his princess.'

Brodwyn's face grew hot. 'I am sure there is more than that.'

Erasmus raised an eyebrow. 'What does your father think of the match?'

Brodwyn looked down at the table.

'I did hear that he was keen enough when King Oren visited with him,' Erasmus said.

'I think he is unsure as to what a new queen might do.'

'Or he is hoping for a particular queen,' Erasmus offered quietly.

'Elalia is the eldest, is she not?' Brodwyn asked. 'We would not like to speculate as to whom the gods would choose.'

'Yet Meggie is the favourite, hence your father's agreement to the match.'

'Have there not been marriages between the kingdoms before?' Brodwyn asked.

'You forget your lessons,' Adroth admonished.

'Distant relatives of the crown, but never this close, never close enough to be a queen herself perhaps.'

'She will be Queen of Tands.'

'What would the world be if she were Queen of both?' Erasmus asked.

Brodwyn opened his mouth and then closed it again, looking at the advisors. One chewed a lip and the other sighed.

'We are here to negotiate on behalf of our king,' Lord Alva said. 'I cannot guess at what he thought might happen. As it stands, he is not confident in any previous arrangements made and would like to reconsider.'

Erasmus nodded and eyed Brodwyn, who turned his head and closed his eyes.

'Highness?' Erasmus asked.

'I do not know what it is that I wish for,' he answered.

'I am sure that you do, now that you have seen her.'

'But I have not been introduced,' he said, hoping his voice didn't sound like that of a whinging child.

'Nor can you be,' Lord Caris snapped. 'Not when you were not announced, not when you have masqueraded as Advisor Danel.'

'You may have done more to put the girl off,' Lord Alva said.

'You might be surprised,' Brother Erasmus said quietly. 'The girl is bright; she may understand your reasons for the lie better than her sisters will.'

Brodwyn sighed and focused on the swirling pattern of his goblet. 'I understand.'

'Take heart,' Brother Erasmus continued. 'It may be that the betrothal goes ahead. And that very little will change.'

'I do hope you are correct,' he said. 'That our negotiations are more ritual than politics.'

The Brother spread his hands open. 'But politics is the reason we are here.'

'A meeting, a proper introduction? Surely a little time with the princess could not harm the talks.'

'Possibly not, but it could influence how a new queen is willing to work with you once she is crowned, if it is one of the sisters that is marked.'

'Yet if she supports the match?'

'Support or not, if the princess has the opportunity to talk with you before a new queen, you may undo all your dreams before they have started.'

He looked down at his hands and nodded slowly. 'Will she want the match, do you think?'

'Meggie?'

He nodded.

'She is a good girl; she will do what is required of her.'

'Duty bound?' he asked, feeling somewhat disappointed.

Erasmus nodded. 'But she is a sweet girl. She would do her best to ensure the match worked for you both.'

Brodwyn nodded slowly. He understood, but now that he had seen her across the Temple that first time, he simply wanted her to love him for the man he was and not the king he was to be.

CR&SO

Morley looked at Tyne across the table as he laughed and then thumped his goblet on the table in the lavish rooms they had managed to secure. The manservant stepped forward, carefully raised the pitcher on the table and filled the cup. As he slowed the flow Tyne coughed and, meeting the man's eyes, raised his eyebrows. The servant tipped the jug again to fill the goblet to the brim. Tyne tipped his head to the man and then proceeded to spill most of the contents as he raised it shakily to his lips.

'The wine is good,' he said.

'How would you know? You can hardly taste it,' Morley said.

'If you notice that, then you need to drink some more yourself. Fill it,' he said to the servant, indicating Morley's cup with a tip of his head that moved his whole body and spilled more wine. 'Mine too,' he said, looking with puzzlement into his nearly dry cup.

'Enough,' Morley said, holding out his hand. 'That will be all tonight,' he said to the servant, who nodded politely and disappeared.

'We are not here to appreciate my cousin's wine,' he said.

'I know,' Tyne slurred. 'We are here for the crown.'

'Shh, the walls have ears.'

Tyne looked about him in surprise.

'We may have our own servants, but the gods only know who may be lurking behind tapestries,' Morley said, imagining men standing pressed between the hard, grey stone and the tapestries, their legs lining the walls

Tyne narrowed his eyes and leaned across the table. 'The husband is strange,' he said in a loud whisper.

Morley nodded. 'I puzzle at him myself. Born of a high family, but not what I would have expected my uncle to choose for a son or future king.'

'Perhaps he did not think Elalia would inherit,' he said with surprising clarity, and Morley looked more closely at the man before him.

'Perhaps,' he said slowly. 'Who might he have thought would succeed him?'

'Meggie is lovely,' Tyne mused.

'She is the youngest,' Morley said.

'But the brightest and loveliest...' He drifted for a moment and then refocused on Morley. 'It was your mother's brother's wife that was the Raven Queen, was it not?'

Morley nodded. 'Yet my uncle was chosen by the gods when she died. My cousins were very young at the time, and it has happened that way before.' He paused for a moment, stroking his pointed beard. 'King Ba had very young sons, still in the cradle, when he died, and his wife was chosen to rule. Much to his younger brother's frustrations. But the brother was unable to change the choice of the gods.'

'And yet here we are,' Tyne said, 'attempting to influence the gods.'

'I would not use the word "influence" as such. It is important to remember that what occurs in Rocfeld will have a direct effect on us. Tands may not stop at our borders.'

Tyne sipped at the dregs in his cup. 'So how can we influence them?' he asked, looking into the cup rather than at his cousin.

'I had hoped that I could organise a strategic marriage, but it seems my uncle had those plans already.'

'For Kellin?' Tyne asked, screwing up his face. 'They look so alike and yet so different,' he said.

'Megora.' Morley paused to sip his own wine. 'You are correct, cousin; she is by far the best of all the sisters, and if something were to happen to Elalia I'm sure she would be chosen. Yet it seems my uncle had some forethought, for he had promised her to Tands.'

'That is unfortunate,' Tyne agreed. 'He secured much there.'

'And what if Megora had been chosen by the gods? Tands would get their hands on Rocfeld and we would be lost to them as well.'

'With your cousin as their queen, it may not be such a terrible idea.'

Morley shrugged. 'And that leaves Kellin.'

Tyne leaned into his hand and tapped at his cheek with his index finger, and then he sat forward and shook his head. 'I would rather have the younger.'

'Perhaps if you spoilt the younger, Tands would not want her and...'

'This is your cousin you discuss,' Creena said, joining them at the table, a blanket wrapped tight around her shoulders, her fine, blond hair loose around her shoulders. 'Spoiling the girl may only bring more trouble.'

'You should be sleeping,' Morley said.

'How can I when you plot so loudly? I am surprised your young wife is able to sleep at all.'

'She would sleep through a war,' Morley muttered. 'And we do not plot.'

'Of course you do. We know Elalia to be unsuitable for this

position. Has the old woman said anything yet?' she asked, indicating a door with a subtle nod.

Morley shook his head. 'Not yet. I wonder if Father was right to send her.'

'If she could give some indication as to where the crown will go before it is marked, we may have a chance to be a part of this.' She stood and peered into the pitcher on the table, took the goblet from Tyne and splashed wine into it. 'I have some news,' she said with a smile.

Both men watched her closely as she slowly sipped her wine.

'It could be an advantage or two. Firstly, our cousin Kellin is quite taken with Tyne.' He rolled his eyes. 'She could hardly take her eyes from you and may have used the word "handsome".'

'Not surprising,' Tyne muttered.

'It appears that Elalia's husband spends far too much time with other young ladies.'

'Explain,' Morley prompted.

'He seems to be out on the hunt, so to speak, quite a lot. To the point he was out when the king died.'

'In the snow?' Tyne asked. 'What could he hunt in the snow?'

'His companion's sister, by the whispers around the castle, and it may be that she carries his child. And...' She paused again to sip her wine, and both men studied her closely. 'It is said that although this is their second winter married, there is no sign of a child for Elalia. It is whispered that he visits her rooms rarely, and then he often leaves before he would have time to bed her.'

'Perhaps he is easily satisfied,' Tyne said, grinning.

'Perhaps he is satisfied elsewhere,' Morley said with a quick laugh. 'But this is much per chancing. We need to be sure before we can use this. Are we sure the woman is pregnant?' he asked.

'Reasonably,' Creena said.

'And Elalia not?'

'I think it would be announced to all if she were.'

'Could there be other women or other children?'

Creena shrugged. 'He spends much time with Lord Robert; and the sister was ever present, until lately. For a man to rarely visit with his wife, it would be noticed if he was visiting someone else nightly.'

'Perhaps you should provide some test,' Tyne suggested.

'Not directly,' Morley pointedly added.

'It is well enough for you to offer your cousin's virtue,' she smiled.

'Morley,' a soft voice called from the doorway. 'Come to bed.'

He nodded without turning and stood from the table. 'Go to bed,' he said to Creena. 'And Tyne,' he said as his cousin lifted his eyes to him, 'consider the young sisters. For the old woman may give us something we can act on.'

Without waiting for a response, he slipped through the door left open for him by his young wife. The firelight threw strange shadow creatures around the room, consuming his wife's naked body as she climbed into the bed. He paused to undress before the flames, taking in the heat and the silence to think over his recent conversation, both with his cousin, who appeared to see more than he let on, and Creena, who had gleaned some interesting gossip from her young cousins.

Warm, soft hands were a shock as they worked up beneath his shirt, her firm body pressed against his. 'Has he made a decision about Kellin?' she asked.

He shook his head as her gentle touch reached his chest and her fingers curled in the thick hair they found there.

'Why not?'

'He prefers the youngest sister.'

'She is already promised to Tands,' she sighed. 'And everyone knows it. He will leave her alone and attempt to sway a sister we can get to.'

'But the youngest is the favourite.' He winced as she pulled sharply at the hair on his chest and as she withdrew her hands, he turned to her.

'She is no longer an option. Risking war with Tands by tainting their betrothal will not assist us. Kellin is to be the object of Tyne's interest. Grandmother will soon know the truth of it.'

Morley nodded slowly and pulled his shirt over his head before he climbed into the bed. Annar climbed in beside him, sliding down between the sheets and then turning her back to him.

'You know what I say makes sense,' she uttered quietly but forcefully. 'Megora is the youngest and certainly the brightest, but untouchable at this point.'

Morley nodded mutely.

'And she is closest to Kellin, so that if the middle sister is won, the younger may be influenced. We will find a way,' she said, rolling into him and pulling herself close against him. 'But first we get closer. First we become family.'

12

Elalia was tired of waiting to be marked. The Silent Mother appeared so confident, and yet she remained unchanged. The sooner it was clear that she was to be Queen, the better. Malin was also slipping in his duties as though he doubted she would be Queen, but there was a small part of him she still needed.

She sat before a foggy, silver-framed glass, studying her own reflection. She was still a beautiful woman, and when she was able to get him to her bed, he appeared to want to be there. But he still visited Lady Sera. It was clear to all that she was with child, and it chewed at her heart that he had so easily given her what she struggled to have.

She stared at her blurred image, trying to visualise her long hair turned to raven black flowing around her shoulders. It remained brown, and she needed Terra to work it into the intricate braids. Closing her eyes, she took in a slow, deep breath and imagined herself in the comfortable silence of the Sanctuary.

When her mother had died, Elalia had longed for the comfort of the Silent Sisters her mother had told her of. They all knew the stories and her mother had briefly spent time as a girl at the Sanctuary; it had seemed the only place for Elalia to go. Her father had been too busy in his new role as King to spend time with her; her younger sisters had been too young to be of any comfort, shutting themselves away with a nurse.

The Silent Sisters had welcomed her into the Sanctuary and she had been allowed the peace she was so desperate for, and the love she craved and missed with the passing of her mother.

She missed the Silence.

'Terra,' she called and the girl appeared at the doorway. 'Hair,' she said with a wave of her hand.

The girl nodded and went to work, quickly brushing through her long hair before starting the process of working it into tight braids.

Elalia's reflection seemed to swim and change before her, her dark curls becoming silvery as she stared at herself in the foggy glass. She blinked and rubbed at her eyes and the strange reflection returned to what it should have been. 'Have my cousins settled?' she asked, distracting herself with the idea of the strange man that reminded her so much of Rance. She preferred them when they were far away, particularly since her uncle had sent a soothsayer. And the young Annar was far too beautiful a girl to be married to Morley, so short and broad and hairy; yet she hung on his every word, and his arm. She was too tall, Elalia decided, much taller than Meggie and Kellin.

She sighed at the idea of Meggie and how she was well liked and faithful. Was it really so difficult a choice that the gods would take so long to decide? The old woman who had stepped from her uncle's carriage may have been an unwelcome sight but perhaps she could be of use. She wondered if her cousins would allow her some time with her. Elalia looked up and caught sight of Terra standing silently behind her. 'Cousins?' she asked again.

'Well settled, Your Highness. Their manservant comes directly to me with their wishes.'

'Does he?' she asked slowly, turning on the small chair to look at the girl directly.

Terra nodded. 'I send him to the kitchens, Your Highness, but he says that I have eldest sister's ear.'

'Does he want a word in it?' she asked, running her fingers over her hair.

'I do not know,' Terra stammered, reaching out to capture locks of hair before Elalia undid the work she had done.

'Has he mentioned anything particular of the cousins, or their discussions?' Elalia asked, turning back to the mirror.

'Only that they are somewhat demanding about the amount of wine and types of food to be provided.'

'He is right to come to you. Direct him as you see fit,' she said, and then waved the girl away.

'I haven't finished,' she blurted.

'Just go,' Elalia said, pulling at the little work the girl had done.

Terra appeared quite relieved to be released and backed out of the room. A capable girl, she was on hand at all times. But doubt seeped through Elalia as to whether she could be trusted. If anyone could be trusted. Everyone had their own agenda, herself included.

She turned back to the glass to check her hair and paused. The face looking back at her was not her own. She raised a hand slowly and ran it over her hair, again appearing silver in the glass. Her reflection worked in time, but she leaned forward to study the unfamiliar face that smiled at her and mouthed one word, "Sythia," before it changed before her eyes and she was staring at her own face. Elalia touched her face and then the glass, cool beneath her fingers.

⊂⊃⊄⊃

Meg looked about the room as she stood alone by the fire at one end of the Hall. The noise of so many conversations was overwhelming. More and more people were arriving every day and despite her best efforts, Meg found the increasing number more worrying. She knew they came to watch over them and to guess at who might be Queen or why the choice was taking so long to be declared. Yet she wondered, as she looked around the groups before her, how many of them thought that they might be able to influence that decision.

The cost alone to feed the visitors was worrying. Although Elalia, again too comfortable in making decisions as the eldest, had directed for more taxes to be collected, the longer this continued the harder it would be on everyone.

She was becoming paranoid, even of those that smiled at her, for she feared what they might do on her behalf. Meg smoothed her dress and took a steadying breath. Brother Erasmus had assured her that the gods watched over her and yet it didn't give her the same comfort as it once had.

She knew these people, she told herself as she watched her cousins through the crowd. But then she wondered how many of these faces she would see again once the queen was marked. And she probably knew a son or the like if she asked who these people were; but it was not her place to do so. She had to wait until she was introduced.

And then Brother Erasmus was standing before her with a strange man, tall and slender with tanned, brown skin. His hair, pulled back from his face, fell in a long plait down his back, and he wore a long, coarse moustache and a pointed beard in a style not worn in Rocfeld. His cloak was the most beautiful thing Meg had ever seen. The detailed embroidery over red silk was so beautiful she felt a stab of jealousy for the material and wondered if she could find the like for a dress. She resisted the urge to reach out and run her fingers over it by pulling them into a fist behind her back.

'Emperor Baghi of Luana,' Brother Erasmus said, and Meg instantly dipped into a low curtsy. 'The youngest sister, Princess Megora.'

'The most beautiful of them all,' he said and a strange unease prickled at the back of Meg's neck.

'Sire, please forgive my staring.'

'You have a fine eye for silks, it appears. Do not fear. Stand, girl, and let me look you over properly.'

Meg stood straight and raised her eyes to his to find them inspecting her own attire.

'I expected a girl,' he said. 'But you are clearly a woman. And you wear your own silks so well. An interesting style,' he added quietly.

'Your Eminence,' she said with a tip of her head.

'I shall send you more. Luana is home to the best silks and the best embroiderers. I shall send a selection so that you can have your favourites made into the finest dresses.' He looked her over again.

'You are too kind,' Meg said, unsure as to why he would send such a gift to her.

'I have daughters too, you know. I would have you appreciate the Luanian silk.'

Meg had not noticed his accent until his words did not quite flow as well as they had. 'How many daughters do you have?' Meg asked, glancing at Erasmus. She had learnt of the many sons of Luana, but had not heard of daughters.

'I may spoil them, but they are not worth counting,' he said with a wave of his hand. 'Their mothers are important in ensuring that one day they will be important to other men.'

Meg nodded politely and gave him a small smile. She wondered if she would ever be important or useful in her own right one day. She certainly wished to be, hoped to be more than just a wife.

'How many sons do you have?' Brother Erasmus asked.

'Nine,' he said.

'Nine?' Meg asked.

'Many children ensure strength,' he said with a slight bow. 'The strongest will be emperor after I am gone. His brothers will lead the armies and the vessels, and become important leaders within our empire.'

Meg gave him a nod. 'Such a large family,' she said. 'So many armies and ships.'

'You have your cousins here, do you not?'

Meg glanced again at her cousins across the room, standing in a small group, and wondered again why her uncle had not come.

'The defence of an empire so beautiful is essential,' the emperor said, returning to his earlier point. 'You would enjoy Luana. So different to Rocfeld, but you would enjoy it, I think,' he added softly.

Meg gave him a small smile.

'So many sons and brothers that would enjoy such a wife,' he continued.

'I am not sure the princess would appreciate your marital system, Your Eminence.' Lord Alva winked at Meg. 'Nor would her faith.'

Meg took in the old man who had just joined them and spoken so openly to the emperor. His eyes were now only on the man before him.

'Sir Alva,' the emperor said with a not-so-friendly tone. 'Do you wish to insult our way of life?'

The older man shook his head and gave an easy laugh. 'Never, Sire. I simply point out the differences may be too much for the young lass.'

The emperor gave Meg a low bow. 'It was a pleasure, Princess.'

Meg watched as Brother Erasmus indicated through the crowd toward Elalia and they weaved forward quickly. She was left for a moment with Sir Alva, unknown to her, and she was frustrated that he had not been introduced.

'Allow me to introduce myself, Princess Megora. I am Lord Alva. I am a representative of the king of Tands.' He bowed low before Meg. Softly, he said, 'We were introduced in the Temple.'

Meg nodded slowly, remembering the lines of people who had spoken to her that day, but she couldn't remember any of them. Meg found her face becoming hot.

'Do not be embarrassed. It was a difficult time. I am pleased to see that you are able to converse with a range of people and hold your own.'

She looked at him seriously and then across at the emperor; his last statement had been quite strange. She smiled, glad that he had arrived when he did.

'We are watching you to ensure that your father's words were true regarding the promise of marriage and that the right choice is made.'

Was everyone watching her? she wondered. She nodded politely, wanting suddenly to be back in her rooms. 'Does that mean that my father's wishes still stand?' she asked.

He gave a shrug then and looked past her.

Meg bit her lip.

'Why did your king not come?' she asked and then instantly regretted it, groaning inwardly.

'He was unable to make the journey.'

'And no one of the family came?' She watched as his face reddened. 'Rocfeld may take it as an offence.'

'That I cannot help,' he said. 'I can only do as I am directed.'

'As must we all,' she sighed. She noticed that through the crowd, the Silent Mother seemed to stare in her direction. 'Forgive me, sir, but I think it is time I retired.'

'Your Highness,' the royal commander said, bowing low before her as he joined them. 'I see you have met Lord Alva.'

'I have, yes. You must excuse me; it has been a long day.'

'Of course,' he said, bowing again. 'I'm sure you have asked Lord Alva many questions of Tands.'

'I'm afraid the princess has not had the chance,' Lord Alva said. 'What is it you would like to know?'

Meg paused. She so wanted to ask after their prince. 'Does it snow in the winter?'

He laughed and she smiled easily at the warm sound.

'Yes,' he said softly. 'Our weather is very much like yours.'

'Is it not hotter in the summer?'

'I have not experienced a summer in Rocfeld to compare.'

She looked at the royal commander and then toward the door.

'Your Highness,' the royal commander said, taking her arm and pulling her attention back to Lord Alva, 'what is it you want to ask?'

She shook her head. 'It does no good to dwell on things that may not come to pass,' she said and turned for the door, the Silent Mother still watching from across the room. 'Will you please excuse me, Lord Alva.'

She had made it a statement, not a question, but he politely answered, 'Of course, Princess.' His eyes held concern for her now.

She strode ahead, urgently needing to be on her own. The people seemed to be pressing her from all around. Her breathing increased and her heart raced.

'What of your guard?' the royal commander called after her as Raf stepped into the doorway and Meg headed straight toward him. Why should she worry about how good a man may be, if she never gets to meet the man?

She gave Raf a nod as she approached him, but another hand took her arm and she was dragged into a conversation with Lady Scott. She glanced toward Raf as he hovered beside her. She was tired of the prying and appraising eyes constantly on her. She wondered if her cousins would allow her some time with the soothsayer; she may be able to answer some more direct questions and allow her some peace. She refocused on Lady Scott and nodded politely.

Brodwyn watched the princess move swiftly toward the doorway, disappointed that he hadn't been quicker to extricate himself from the conversation that had kept him from meeting her. From the soft smile on Alva's face he seemed impressed, so there may be a chance yet to talk with her.

'That was her,' he said, coming to stand beside him.

Alva nodded.

'I would have liked an introduction.'

The royal commander coughed beside him and Brodwyn felt the world stop around him.

'Sir,' he said, bowing just a little. 'How nice to see you again.'

'Hmm,' the royal commander said.

'I do have good reason for appearing as I do,' he said quickly.

'We meant no offence,' Lord Alva said.

The royal commander waved the idea away. 'Your visit is only to discover who will be Queen, I am sure,' he said. 'It is only luck that no one else has recognised you.'

'I'm staying away from those that might.'

The royal commander nodded.

'I was hoping to meet with the princess.'

'I think you would be better keeping your distance,' Alva said.

Brodwyn was sure that his face betrayed his disappointment, for Lord Alva maintained his serious look.

'I agree,' the royal commander added and followed the princess's path toward the door.

'Where is Lord Caris?'

'Meeting Princess Elalia's husband.' Brodwyn indicated across the room with a general wave of his hand.

'And what did you make of him?' Lord Alva asked in a low whisper.

'I am not sure. He appears to be all charm and friendliness. It is hard to get the man to talk of anything of substance and so I do not know how clever he may be. Yet that may be the cleverness, to hide his intelligence away?'

'I think he does as his wife directs him.'

Brodwyn watched Princess Elalia through the people, talking and smiling with the emperor of Luana. She certainly appeared to be in control. He would have to keep out of the way of the emperor. They had met when he was a small child and he could still remember the man scalding his father for his lack of insight in only having one son. One child. He was sure that he would recognise some familiarity in him, and may give the disguise away and threaten them all.

He had remembered his mother, if only just, being asked by his father to consider another child, but she had shaken her head sadly. She had not lived much longer. No matter how he tried, he could not remember the birth of his sister, or her death only a short time later. It upset him that he couldn't remember any of her short life between, but then he had only been a child at the time. His mother had died from the sadness of it, leaving him alone with a father more determined to build a nation to leave him with than spending time with him as he grew. And so he ran amongst the other children of the castle with a number of nurses that he could never grow close to; when he grew to a boy too difficult for them to watch, he was left to play with the soldiers.

He learnt a lot and with the run of the castle, he met and spoke with a variety of people who were only too happy to assist him. His one true constant in all those years had been Seren. He had more respect for him than any other man he knew, including his father. If only he had come with them, this would have been a lot easier. Yet if the soldier had joined them, he was sure that his father would have realised what he was up to.

'You are very alike,' Alva said and Brodwyn snapped back to his serious face.

'Excuse me?' he said, thinking of his father still.

'You and the princess. I can see some similarities there.'

'Really?'

'She seems somewhat apprehensive, but I am sure that is the uncertainty of the situation. That of the match and who will be Queen. There is too much speculation in this room. You may make a good pair,' he added softly.

Brodwyn raised his eyebrows and the other man held up his hands. 'Not that I am promising the match occurs.'

Brodwyn nodded. He would love the chance to talk to her himself. She was certainly beautiful and he could watch her walk the room all day. She appeared to talk with ease to those around her but so far she had not spoken to him. 'You could have introduced me,' he said again.

'The lady was retiring,' he said.

'She does not appear to be leaving the room.'

'She tries. Watch her; she is polite and friendly but she stands in the doorway.'

'Would she not want to remain and talk some more? There could be dancing.'

'You will not dance with her,' Alva said sternly and Brodwyn turned from the woman talking by the door. 'It is not right that you should meet at all until this is decided. I do not want you getting excited and then it does not come off,' the man added in a more friendly tone.

Brodwyn nodded, but when he looked back she was gone and despite himself, he sighed. When would anything go as he hoped it would?

13

Elalia felt so tired. Would ruling really be this hard when she was Queen? So many people to talk with, so many hours standing in the Hall smiling. The Silent Sisters knew what they were doing and she had her place and tasks to do. All would be well, the Silent Mother had assured her, but she wasn't as sure that she was right. She gulped at the wine before her and regretted it instantly as a wave of nausea washed over her. She pushed the goblet away. 'Terra,' she called. She heard her gentle footsteps on the rushes but she squeezed her eyes closed and rested her head on her arm. 'Fetch a nurse.'

Without a word, the footsteps faded away. She sat up slowly, feeling more unwell with every movement, and peered into the goblet. Perhaps it was poisoned. She knocked it over as she pushed herself shakily to her feet.

She had only made it as far as the doorway when a plump nurse appeared before her. 'They want to kill me,' she muttered.

The nurse easily took her weight and directed her to the bed where she lowered her carefully and slowly. She lifted her legs up and pressed the back of her hand to Elalia's forehead.

'Have you vomited?' she asked.

Elalia shook her head and then put her hands out as her head swam and the room seemed to shift before her.

The nurse gently raised her arms and prodded under them, and then with a pressing movement she felt down her side and across her breasts. Elalia wanted to call out, but she kept as still as she could. The nurse lowered her arms and then, moving down the bed, slipped Elalia's shoes off and looked at her feet. She looked at Elalia seriously. 'How much have you eaten today?'

Elalia looked down at her hands; it had been so busy and she had spent so long standing in the Hall. 'I don't know,' she said.

The nurse gave her a disapproving look and then gently ran her hand over Elalia's stomach. 'It is early, but you must look after yourself and the child.'

Elalia ran a hand over her stomach and then grabbed the arm of the woman standing beside her. 'Are you sure?'

'Yes, Your Highness, you are with child.' She curtsied.

'Don't tell anyone,' Elalia blurted.

The nurse sat carefully on the edge of the bed. 'It is early, but you are young and healthy. There is no reason to think this child will not grow.'

'Thank you,' Elalia said softly. 'I worry for the child's safety. Please tell no one, not even Erasmus, until it has grown a little and a queen is chosen. Someone may wish me harm.'

'You must eat,' the nurse said, standing slowly.

Elalia nodded carefully. She wondered if the nurse would keep her silence or whether the Brotherhood was told everything, whether she wanted it known or not. When she looked up, Malin stood in the doorway.

'Are you unwell?' he asked. She couldn't be sure if he cared for the answer or simply asked, and she was reminded of how little she knew this man.

'I haven't had the chance to eat today, and I felt a little faint. It is nothing and I am sure that with a little sustenance I shall be back on my feet.' The nurse nodded and, giving Elalia a long nod, left the room.

'The girl is laying out food on the table now—not your usual dried fruit, but meat. I thought you might be entertaining another.'

She smiled as she slowly swung her legs around and he was quick with a hand to pull her to her feet. He offered his arm and she took it gratefully. She had never seen as much food on her table as what covered it now, but she was hungry, she realised, more hungry than she had ever been. She smiled again as Malin piled venison onto a plate for her and sat beside her at the table. Would he care, she wondered, if she entertained another? Would he stop visiting if he knew that he had completed the duty she set him?

CRSO

Elalia watched the Silent Mother kneeling before the altar and knew that she should have come to her as soon as she had seen Sythia in the glass. But she was required to show her worth to the people and visitors of Rocfeld, and had neglected the Silent Mother and her duties with her. Elalia reined in her excitement that she was finally with child; the Silent Mother would not share that joy. She would see the child as a distraction from what they were to do. What she was to do.

'She thinks you are ready,' the Silent Mother whispered, her voice carrying around the stone walls of the chapel.

Elalia stepped forward and bowed her head to the candles burning on the altar. No shadows moved across the walls. She was tempted to ask how the Silent Mother knew such a thing, but she was sure that the Silent Mother had more ways of learning the ways of Sythia than just the shadows that whispered.

'What must I do?' she asked.

'Must?' the Silent Mother asked in return, her face questioning, and Elalia only just stopped herself from stepping backward. 'You need to want for Sythia and her ways.'

Elalia nodded and dropped to her knees. 'With everything that I have and everything that I am,' she whispered. 'For I am Sythia's vessel. What would you have me do in Sythia's name?'

The Silent Mother knelt before her and took her hands. 'You are the key,' she said, her smile warm and friendly. 'Come to my room, for I have an elixir to make you stronger, to prepare you to assist Sythia in what she needs.'

Elalia nodded and followed the woman back to the room, and it was only as she closed the door and turned back that she realised just how different this room was. A moment of panic covered her body at what Brother Erasmus would do with such a find.

Even with the fire burning brightly, the room was gloomy. Elalia searched the shadows for the Mother's white tunic, but it was lost to her. Her hands found a table covered in cups and clay pots, and she could smell the bitterness of the herbs and something musky. She paused. There was an animal somewhere in the room, and she willed her eyes to adjust to the dark but they wouldn't.

'Shhh.' The sound filled the room and a single candle in the middle of the table flickered to life. 'You are the vessel,' the Silent Mother whispered suddenly, appearing on the other side of the table. 'I must make you stronger so that Sythia can grow stronger. Do you understand?'

Elalia nodded, looking over the various pots and cups on the table, and tried not to gag at the smells that seemed to invade her very being. She glanced around but could see nothing beyond the table. She was sure she could hear something scratching, but she refocused on the woman standing across the table.

'You must do as directed.'

Elalia nodded. 'Anything.'

'Drink,' she said, holding out a cup.

Elalia only paused once she had it in her hand. The contents reflected the candlelight and moved like water within the cup and yet the smells confused her, again the animal scent and earth and the smell of a cold, wet cellar. It was the smell of the underground, and she glanced at the Silent Mother, her face growing hard before Elalia downed the contents as quickly as she could.

'Are you losing faith?' she asked, her voice harsh and low.

Elalia shook her head quickly.

'There is something different,' she said, stepping closer and sniffing at Elalia. 'Something that should not be.'

'No,' she said quickly. 'I am as I should be.'

'Do you fear the marking and the burden of the crown?'

Elalia blinked back her surprise. 'No, I know that is what I am meant to do. That I am to be the Raven Queen. Once the choice is clear, I shall be secure. We shall be secure. Sythia shall be secure.'

The Silent Mother nodded once. 'Go and rest. Allow Sythia to guide you.'

Elalia slowly released the breath she had been holding and headed along the hallway to her own rooms. She wondered how the Silent Mother had managed to secure all of her ingredients. She could still taste the liquid and she wondered if Sythia had lived with such a smell for so long. What else could be in the Silence? Could the liquid have any effect on her child?

She opened the door to find Meggie sitting before the fire, her white hair tightly braided against her scalp and her hands held just as tightly before her.

'Are you well?' Elalia asked and the young woman nodded, then looked down at her hands. Elalia groaned inwardly. 'We should discuss this later,' she said.

'We may not be able to discuss this later,' Meggie said, surprising Elalia with her force. 'I fear what may be done.'

'That you may not be chosen as Queen,' Elalia said quickly. 'You know how to do your duty. You have done so all your life. Can you not trust in the gods now?' she asked with surprising softness.

Meggie looked at her seriously. 'There is too much talk,' she said. 'Soothsayers and potions. I overheard someone in the Hall mention that Kellin was being too friendly, that she had bewitched the people. What if someone else believes them, or hurts her?'

'You fear the same for yourself then? That someone may harm you to ensure you are not marked.'

Meggie nodded once.

Elalia sighed and sat beside her. 'The right choice will be made as it always is,' she said softly, more certain now that the Silent Mother was correct and it would be her. 'It takes too long. That is why they talk and guess, but the people trust in the gods and so they will wait.'

'I'm not sure that they will,' Meggie whispered.

Elalia wondered if she knew more than she had already said, but she didn't want to talk anymore; she wanted to sleep. She stood slowly and opened the door, but Meggie remained where she was. Elalia indicated the door and the girl stood slowly. 'I am tired of talking,' Elalia said. 'We cannot answer what we do not know.'

Meggie nodded slowly, moving to stand before her at the open door. Elalia could feel the energy slipping and struggled to keep her eyes open. Just what had the Silent Mother given her?

'Cousin.' Tyne grinned in the doorway and both sisters looked at him.

'What lovely timing,' Elalia said. 'Perhaps you could be of assistance and escort Meggie back to her rooms.'

'Cousin,' he said, bowing again. 'I would be honoured.' He held out his arm for Meggie.

Elalia simply nodded once and closed the door on them. She

had only just made it to the bed when the door opened again and there was Malin.

'I did not expect to see you,' she said quietly.

He grabbed her arm suddenly; his grip too tight, and a nervousness she hadn't felt in some time took her breath away. 'I loved you once,' he whispered, throwing her completely off guard and pulling her close, kissed her softly.

'I am with child,' she said.

'Truly?' he asked, stepping back.

She nodded.

'You do want the child?' he asked seriously.

'Yes, yes. But I worry, it is still early. I fear someone might try to harm us. I don't want to tell anyone.'

He nodded and then took her in his arms and held her tight. She felt comfortable for the first time in as long as she could remember. But she didn't need him now; she only needed the show of a good husband, and she hoped he could hold onto such an idea for a little longer.

'I'm tired,' she muttered.

'Of course,' he said. He helped her out of her dress and into the bed and before she could tell him that she didn't need him to stay, he turned too quickly for the door.

Meg tried not to think of her cousin Rance as she walked away from her sister's door on Tyne's arm. The similarity was so striking. Could cousins look more alike than brothers? She looked up at him and he smiled down at her. He was so like Rance, so like her uncle.

'Cousin,' she said slowly. 'Tell me, is your father or your mother sibling to my uncle?'

'Do you not remember me?' he asked, his eyes sparkling as he spoke, so like Rance she found herself looking away again. 'My father is the relation,' he said.

Meg found herself nodding but she could not remember the history, nor a younger Tyne playing with them when they were children.

'I am named for him,' he said.

She looked up at him for a moment, 'Your father?'

'My uncle,' he said with a smile. 'Ustyn.'

113

'You are Ustyn too?'

'That would be strange,' he said as the slow walk continued. 'Tyne is all I am.'

Meg was nodding again. They were almost at her rooms. She wondered how they had reached it and how he knew where they were going.

'Thank you, Tyne,' she said, releasing his arm.

'I have not spent much time with you, Megora,' he said. 'Meggie, I feel I don't know you. Share a cup of wine and some stories with me,' he said, leaning in close, and Meg suddenly saw a difference to her beloved cousin Rance. He leaned a little too close and as she stepped back, her loyal guard stepped forward almost between them. 'Who was your mother?' she blurted.

Tyne straightened up and beamed a large smile. 'She died when I was young,' he said, bowed and disappeared.

Meg realised they were outside her rooms and the door opened to reveal Kellin. 'He still looks like Rance,' she said, stepping back and holding the door open. 'Those eyes, so blue.'

'He is not that much like Rance, now I have had a chance to look at him.' Although possibly more closely related to him than we would like discussed at court, she thought.

'Thank you, Raf,' she said and he gave her a nod as he took up his post outside the door and she closed it against him.

'Where have you been?' Kellin asked.

'I was with Elalia,' she said, pouring herself a cup of wine and sitting before the fire.

'What happened?' Kellin asked.

Meg shook her head. 'Just talking.'

Kellin watched her a little too closely.

'Tyne smiled before telling me his mother died.'

'Not so like Rance then,' Kellin said, still studying her.

'I think I need to sleep,' Meg said. 'Tomorrow is going to be another long day.'

14

'Lord Alva,' Meg said, standing beside him at the feet of the gods in the Temple, and he jumped as though she had prodded him with a stick. 'I am sorry, sir. I did not mean to startle you.'

'It is my fault entirely, Your Highness,' he said, bowing low before her. 'I was thinking only of the gods.'

She dipped her head in return. 'I have interrupted your prayer.'

'Not at all. I was offering my thanks and then I thought I would explore the garden. Is it too cold to ask you to join me after such a snowfall last evening?'

'I would like that very much,' she said, taking his offered arm and walking with him out into the crisp air. 'The exercise will keep us warm,' she said as they entered the garden and the white world before them.

'Do you propose we run?' he asked, pulling her to a stop.

'Not at all,' she said, laughing. 'How could we talk?'

Lord Alva laughed comfortably, patted her hand and pointed to a path on the left lined with tall, neatly clipped hedges. 'This is such a treasure to have hidden away in the castle.'

'And despite the cold and wet that winter brings,' she added, releasing his arm and holding her skirts up just enough that they didn't drag through the slush that covered the path, 'it is one of my favourite places to visit.'

'I feared, Princess Megora, that you would be a quiet lass, spending your time indoors with a needle.'

'Is that what the ladies of Tands do?' she asked, stepping before him on the path so that he had to stop. The guard behind Lord Alva looked for a moment and then turned to look back the way they had come.

'They do not have a garden such as this to enjoy,' he said. 'I understand that you work with the poor of the kingdom, the orphans and the like.'

She nodded once and sighed before continuing along the path until it led into a small, open area, the fountain still and frozen. Lord Alva and the solider appeared not long after. 'Why is it that no one will tell me anything of significance about Tands?' she asked, sounding as disappointed as she felt. But Lord Alva looked across the garden rather than at her, and his face had lost its soft friendliness.

She turned slowly to follow his gaze to find a dark-haired man standing in the shadows. 'What is it the princess would like to know?' the man asked.

Meg couldn't find the words she wanted to ask. Her heart caught in her throat as he stepped from the shadow into the grey light of the day. He was handsome beyond anything Meg had seen before. She had barely glimpsed the man before, because she thought she would have remembered him for the rest of her life. His strong, square face blocked out the world around him as he smiled, a smile reflected in his dark-brown eyes. Due to her loss of voice, Meg could only smile in return.

'Danel, what are you doing?' Lord Alva asked, his voice surprisingly harsh.

'I was walking and discovered this wonderful place. If only we had a garden like this in Tands.'

'Mmm,' Lord Alva said. Meg looked at him closely; he appeared angry that Danel was here. The conversation and the walk stalled, she waited.

'The princess is curious of our land it seems, Lord Alva, and yet you do not answer her. Why would that be?' Lord Danel asked. Despite his station, he still smiled and appeared quite at ease, although Lord Alva remained firm and clearly angry.

Lord Alva mumbled. 'Princess Megora, have you had the chance to meet with Lord Danel, our third and youngest delegate from Tands?'

He bowed low and Meg tipped her head. He may have been

another advisor, but there was something very different about him. She couldn't find her voice and her face felt hot.

'Do you enjoy the garden often?' Lord Danel asked.

She nodded mutely and the two men waited.

'Could you show us your favourite winter spot?' he asked and as he stepped forward, Meg found herself stepping back, and his friendly smile slipped.

She nodded again and, taking Lord Alva's arm, directed them along a small path that led from the garden they were in. The roses lining the path were naked and Meg suddenly longed for their vibrant colours. Lord Danel followed behind and she was acutely aware of his steps crunching through the ice on the path behind them, wondering if he watched the garden beds they passed or her back. She gulped down the sudden panic. There were still too many uncertainties in her life and she was promised to a prince; yet as they walked she wondered if it would be as overwhelming to walk on Lord Danel's arm as she imagined.

Meg shook her head again and tried to calm her breathing. She had only just met the man, and she knew better than to trust a man by appearance alone.

She glanced back along the path to find the advisor chewing on his lip; his earlier confidence appeared to have disappeared. The soldier beside him was shaking his head and she stopped again, seeing a similarity between the two men she had not seen before. 'Lord Alva,' she said, surprised in the strength of her voice. 'Would you and Lord Danel like to explore a little further without me? I need a word with my guard and I shall catch you up.'

Lord Alva nodded and Lord Danel tipped his head to her before they moved along the path and out of sight.

'What do you think you are doing?' Lord Alva snapped and Meg wondered if he should have waited a little longer before he chastised the younger man. 'Do you want to destroy these negotiations before there is a queen to negotiate with? You will have more than your father to answer to if that is the case.'

Meg turned slowly to the guard behind her, who suddenly dropped to one knee and bowed his head. She had only seen this stance before her father when very bad news was delivered.

'He is not what he seems,' she said.

'I fear not, Your Highness.'

'What is it that you see?'

The guard paused and turned his concerned face up from the ground.

'What?' she whispered.

'He is a soldier, Your Highness.'

Meg nodded. When the two had been standing beside each other it was as though they were brothers. The broad shoulders, the musculature defined even beneath his heavy cloak. The way he stood, the way he walked, he expressed a confidence that she was drawn to. He was what she imagined Commander Brent would appear as, if he were dressed as a man of the court.

'He is a spy,' the soldier whispered loudly, interrupting her thoughts.

Meg shook her head slowly. He might not be what he was reported to be, but he wasn't a spy.

'I want you to wait here,' she said.

'No, Your Highness,' he said, quickly climbing back to his feet.

'It is not a request,' she said. 'I have an idea who this man might be, but he won't tell me the truth if you are there. I am safe. And if not, I'll scream loudly,' she added.

He opened his mouth to protest, but she held up her hand and then headed along the path to find the advisor and his young charge.

Both men turned as she neared them on the path. As the young man's dark eyes focused on her, she felt the need to smooth over her dress and check her hair. She kept herself still, although was disappointed to find that she had allowed her skirts to drag in the snow-covered path and she was not only wet but dirty.

She smiled sweetly. 'I wish to know about your prince,' she said quickly. 'No one will tell me anything of significance of Tands, but surely you can tell me of him.'

The men exchanged a brief look, but it was enough for Meg.

'Lord Danel, why don't you share your ideas of the prince?' she asked.

'He is a good man,' he said.

'Is that all?' she asked, as Lord Danel chewed his lip again. 'He is simply a good man. He sounds quite dull.'

'Not at all,' he said quickly. 'I think he has what is important in mind at all times. He does what he can for Tands.'

Meg nodded slowly. 'Duty bound.' she said. 'But that doesn't tell me of his nature. Is he kind, funny, impulsive, brave?'

'I wonder if he is as bright as his father would like him to be,' Lord Alva muttered.

'Hey,' Lord Danel responded.

Meg dropped into a low curtsy.

'There is no need for that,' the young man stammered, stepping forward.

'I would apologise, Your Highness, for not greeting you appropriately sooner, but you appear to have misled the people of Rocfeld.'

'Stand up,' he snapped, stepping forward, taking her by the hands and lifting her out of the curtsy.

The warmth of his skin tingled through her, and yet the strong, calloused hands reinforced her knowledge that he was a soldier.

'What is it that you hope to learn?' she asked. 'Or influence,' she added slowly, 'before a choice is marked.' She pulled her hands from his as she stepped back, glancing quickly over her shoulder. Had she put herself in harm's way? she wondered, fearful suddenly that they worked for their own agenda, and cursed herself for leaving the guard behind.

'I wanted to see you,' the prince said. 'Meet you.'

'As someone else? And when Rocfeld and the new queen finds out that you met with me before her, it will end badly for us all.'

'The new queen has not been marked yet; it may be you,' he said, stepping forward.

'It may not,' Meg threw back. She took a moment to calm herself or the guard would be running in, and she didn't think anyone else should know the truth. 'Who else knows?' she asked.

The prince shook his head.

'Who else?' she asked slowly.

'Brother Erasmus and the royal commander.'

Meg stared off into the garden. It looked dead and bare. She had the urge to run from it and back to her rooms when a small wren flitted onto a branch and then away. The royal commander would have known the prince from his visit to Tands, and yet he had said nothing.

She looked back over the two men, but she had no idea at all as to what she should do. Or what it would mean for them. 'Did you not expect the match to go ahead?' she asked.

'What?'

'Did you think that the match would not occur and so it would not matter if you were seen here as someone else?'

He shook his head slowly. 'I just wanted to see you. To be sure that your father was right about you. That you weren't some silly girl.'

'I am certainly feeling silly now,' she said. 'And you have only given my sister reason to end this betrothal when she is Queen. And maybe she is right; maybe it is for the best.' Meg curtsied again and headed back toward her guard.

'You do not like me?' he asked, grabbing her arm.

Meg wanted to be angry at him for such impropriety and for putting her in such a position, and angry at herself for wanting this only because it was what her father wanted for her. But he looked so disappointed that she may not like him that she had to smile, just to bring a little light back into his eyes. 'I do not know you,' she said.

'Please give me a chance to make amends,' he said, releasing his hold on her and taking a single step back.

Meg rubbed over her arm where he had held her so tight. 'Why have you come here as you have? Why not declare yourself?'

He clenched his fist. 'Princess Meggie, my father would not have allowed me to come.'

'I prefer Meg, and your father might have been correct. If you are discovered, you may risk more than yourself and increase tensions between our kingdoms.'

Lord Alva sighed and the prince nodded slowly.

'If my sister Elalia is marked as Queen, and she suspects that you have deceived her deliberately, then you will not receive anything you have come to negotiate for.'

'You talk as though you are property to be bargained for at the market.'

Meg laughed. 'That is exactly what I am,' she said, resting her hand on his arm as his face darkened. 'I was a negotiation piece for a king, and soon for a new queen. The first thought of me; the second only thinks of how the trade will benefit her.'

The prince shook his head and Meg stepped back, giving him another curtsy. Before she could turn and run back toward her guard, for she should have done so long before this, he stepped up close to her, took her hand and gently pressed it to his lips.

'Brodwyn,' she whispered, pulling her hand from his. 'Do not let her discover your deception. And do not try to meet with me again.'

He opened his mouth to speak and she turned quickly and walked away. It would only take someone to overhear them and she would be accused of plotting and trying to influence the gods, as someone had whispered not quietly enough in the Temple that very morning. And she didn't know if the prince might be someone else's device in influencing the choice.

She was angry that he had hidden himself and tried to deceive her, but there was something likeable about him, and she hoped he hadn't been disappointed by her. She nodded to the guard still waiting on the path as she veered along another, continuing at her fast pace, the guard moving quickly behind her. She wanted to stop and watch Brodwyn leave the gardens but she didn't want to risk him seeing her again.

'What are you doing?' Kellin said, far too close behind her, and Meg squealed. Kellin's face was scrunched in confusion when she turned. 'You wouldn't be doing something you shouldn't?'

Meg shook her head quickly.

'You look guilty,' Kellin continued. 'Why are you walking alone?'

'I'm not,' Meg answered quickly, nodding her head toward the guard.

'I thought you were in the Temple.'

'I was, and then I met Lord Alva and I walked with him and...'

Kellin crossed her arms.

'Why are you in the garden alone, and in the snow?' Meg asked.

'I just needed the air,' she muttered. 'Will you walk with me?'

Meg nodded and linked her sister's arm. 'You won't tell Elalia that I was talking to the Tandian delegates, will you?'

'When would I see her?' she snapped and then nodded slowly. 'Did they say anything of the prince?'

Meg pressed her lips together, involving her sister in the secret exposed her to Elalia's possible anger. 'Little,' she said. 'It is all dependent of Elalia now; she may wish to end the agreement and sell me off to someone else.'

Kellin pulled her to a stop. 'Do you see marriage in such a way?'

'I am a negotiation piece. Maybe not in Father's eyes when he promised me, but I am certain that Elalia would see me as little else.'

As Kellin opened her mouth to respond, they both turned at the sound of shouting and a number of boots running toward them. Meg's guard moved quickly between her and the approaching ruckus but Kellin's guard was a step too late. The man rushing forward, wildly slashing back and forth caught Kellin's arm with the sword and she screamed before the large soldier behind him tackled him to the ground.

'You are killing us!' he shouted. 'Killing us,' he repeated a little more quietly as the soldier pushed his face down into the snow.

Kellin started to cry. Meg looked from the torn cloak and the small amount of blood growing around its edges to the man pinned beneath the soldier. 'Commander Rainger?' she asked and he looked up but took a moment to focus on her before he smiled and bowed his head politely, his body still pinning the man to the ground.

'Your Highness,' he said. 'Are you well?'

'Princess Kellin is hurt,' another soldier said and Commander Rainger was on his feet dragging the man to standing with him.

'Why did you say that?' Meg asked the man.

'Trade has stopped at the border and we are starving. You are letting your people die.'

Meg shook her head and he spat on her before she had the chance to react. Commander Rainger swung the man around and handed him directly into the arms of two waiting soldiers.

'Your Highness, I didn't think...' her guard started, but she held up her hand as she wiped the wet slime from her face with the other, doing her best to imagine it as something else so that she didn't gag.

'Let us have a look at this,' Commander Rainger said to Kellin. He quickly but carefully pulled her cloak back and pulled at the torn material around the wound. 'I've seen worse,' he whispered with a smile, but Kellin's lip trembled. 'I think we should get you back inside and a nurse to look you over more carefully.' He gently pulled her cloak back around her shoulders and offered her his arm.

'Thank you,' she whispered, dabbing at her face, and allowed him to lead her back through the garden.

Meg followed but soon realised that the remaining guard seemed to be surrounding them. There was one walking before the commander and one to each side of her, as well as her own guard behind. She glanced back at the soldier behind her, but he was looking out into the garden they moved through. There would be little place to hide, she thought, looking at the bare garden beds, but then as they moved into the pathways surrounded by tall hedges she began to wonder who might be hiding in them, and she shivered.

15

'How fares your lady?' Bessie, the cook, asked Terra as she dashed past her and into the store for wine.

'As well as could be expected,' she called back from the dark room.

The cook raised her eyebrows as Lora raced into the kitchens, her face red.

'What is it, lass?' Bessie asked, wiping her floury hands across her bosom and resting a hand on the young woman's shoulder.

'The princess has been attacked,' she puffed.

The entire kitchen dropped into silence.

'Which princess?' Terra asked in a hoarse whisper.

'The two younger princesses were together in the garden when a man ran at them with a sword?'

'What man?' Bessie asked.

Lora shook her head. 'I don't know.'

The room was heavy with anticipation and the silence stretched on, Lora's laboured breathing and the crackle of the fires the only sounds. A little voice across the kitchen called out, 'Which princess?'

'Princess Kellin was cut.'

The room dissolved into murmurs. Bessie motioned for the little parlour girl to fetch a stool for Lora, and Terra poured a cup of wine from the pitcher she held.

'Why would someone do such a thing?' Lora asked.

'Someone who wants Elalia to be Queen,' someone whispered

across the kitchen, but the sound travelled and Terra straightened up and frowned across the room.

'She wouldn't do that,' she snapped.

'I didn't say 'twas her,' the voice replied. 'Just someone wanting her to be Queen.'

Bessie flushed, feeling guilty for immediately thinking the kitchen maid meant Elalia.

'Why haven't the gods made a choice yet?' someone else asked.

Bessie shook her head slowly. She had never heard of such a delay and she couldn't understand it either. Any of the princesses would make a lovely queen. She hoped for Meggie if she could pick one, but she didn't wish harm to any of them. 'Did they catch the man?' she asked.

Lora nodded vigorously. 'Commander Rainger raced in and tackled him to the ground before he could do any more harm.'

'I saw Lord Tarrant in the garden this morning,' Mary, another cook muttered.

'I saw one of the Tandian lords walking with Princess Meggie,' someone else offered.

'When did the attack happen?' Bessie asked.

Lora shook her head. 'I'm not sure. Maybe late this morning.'

The murmuring started again and the conversation got louder. The young maid looked like a frightened rabbit. 'It isn't your fault dear,' Bessie whispered, pulling Lora's small frame against her soft body.

'What if something happens to the princess?' she sniffed.

'Nothing will happen to her,' she whispered, looking over the girl's head at the whispers and conversation in the kitchen. 'Get back to work,' she yelled.

Movement was slow as people turned back to their work, but the conversation continued in whispers. It was a conversation that seemed to be constantly had about the castle, but given the amount of time since the death of the king and no queen marked still, people could talk of nothing else. Soon they'd be looking outside the castle walls for someone's hair to change.

CR∞

Elalia tried to remain calm as Meggie paced back and forth

before the fire.

'We must do something,' Meggie said again, her feet still moving and her eyes focused on the floor.

'Must we?' she asked slowly. 'Stop that,' she snapped and Meggie froze mid-step. 'I will not have you telling me what I must do.'

'He cut Kellin. With a sword. Why do you not see how serious this is?' she asked loudly.

'It was one man,' Elalia scoffed, 'Besides, it's been a problem for some time.'

'Really?' Meg asked. 'Why would we not have heard something about it?'

'You have only been focused on the crown,' Elalia said sadly, shaking her head, 'There is more to the world than who will be Queen.'

'But if trade has ceased and the people are hungry, is it not best to do something about it before they are all marching on the castle swinging swords?' Meg asked.

'I was well aware of the situation. Without a marked queen there is only so much I can do, and I have things well in hand. Tands does what it will.' Elalia pitied her sister for her narrow view of the world. Now that they had been personally assaulted, they were confronted with the true nature of ruling. 'Being Queen isn't just smiling, balls and gowns.'

Meggie threw her a dark look. 'There is a delegation from the king of Tands here. Surely they are here to negotiate on his behalf.'

'Who do they negotiate with? You?'

'They could talk to all of us. If there isn't a choice, we could make the decisions together,' Meggie suggested, sitting at the table.

Elalia tried not to show just how annoyed she was at the suggestion, for it was a good idea, but it didn't fit at all with what she wanted. 'You would like to show how good a queen you would make?'

'By the gods,' she snapped, taking Elalia by surprise. 'I want to help the people of Rocfeld first and foremost.'

Elalia nodded once, but she wasn't ready to give her sister the chance to show that she might be a better option for the crown. 'You may not be Queen of Tands. It may be that whichever of us is marked as Queen must remain here, or that you would serve Rocfeld better from another kingdom or empire,' she added, struggling to hide the grin at her sister's discomfort.

'Why don't we ask Brother Erasmus to sit with us?' Meggie asked, focusing on the goblet on the table before her.

Elalia waved her hand and stood up from the table.

'But he has met with the Tandians, I'm sure, and we could negotiate as a kingdom for the kingdom.'

'And why would the Brother be negotiating on our behalf?' Elalia asked, leaning over the table, wondering how Meggie had become so shrewd politically.

'I'm sure he helped Father with negotiations,' Meggie said quietly. 'We can't continue as we are. Until the decision is made, we need to work together. Or there may not be a kingdom to rule over once the decision is made.'

Elalia nodded once and turned to the fire. She would rather have the Silent Mother's advice first, but there could be a way for her to show how well she could be queen. 'Terra,' she called and the girl appeared in the doorway. 'Send for Brother Erasmus.'

'To come here, Your Highness?' she asked nervously.

Elalia nodded and waved her off.

Meg stood slowly from the table. 'I will tell Kellin,' she said. She stopped at the door. 'Thank you,' she said softly.

'Oh, Meggie.'

'Yes?'

'You will follow my lead on this,' Elalia directed and almost smiled at Meggie's expression. Meggie may have some political knowledge, but Elalia knew how to wield it.

Meg hesitated and then nodded before pulling the door closed behind her.

Elalia turned to the fire. No matter how she handled this, it couldn't look as though Meggie had the forethought to meet with them in this manner.

⁊⁊

'I am well,' Kellin said softly, taking Meg's hand and giving it a squeeze. 'Do not fret. The nurse has treated the wound and I am no longer in any real pain.'

Meg nodded slowly, but watched her sister closely.

'But I am still scared,' she whispered and Meg nodded.

Both girls jumped at the loud knock at the door. They looked for a moment, before there was a second. 'Where is Cate?'

'I don't know. The kitchen perhaps.'

Meg walked swiftly to the door and opened it to the guard. Brodwyn stood behind him with a Brother.

'The delegate from Tands wishes to enquire after the welfare of the princess,' the guard said.

Meg turned to Kellin, who stood somewhat uncertainly before the fire.

'Lord Danel,' Meg said turning back to the door. 'This is possibly not the best...' She lost her voice as he smiled at her.

'Who is it?' Kellin asked.

'Lord Danel and Brother Adroth from the Tandian delegation,' the guard reported. 'They said they were concerned after the attack, Your Highness.'

Kellin nodded slowly and the two men entered the room, Brodwyn glancing sideways at Meg as he passed. The guard remained in the doorway.

'The man responsible has been arrested, I hope,' Brodwyn asked the guard, and he nodded slowly.

'It appears to have been one man working alone,' Kellin said with a slight shudder, and Meg realised that she was more deeply affected than she had admitted.

'Do not fear, Your Highness,' Brother Adroth said softly, pushing past Brodwyn, taking Kellin's hand and guiding her into a chair at the table. 'Your guards will keep you safe from attack.'

He hadn't been quite quick enough in the garden, Meg thought. But she nodded at the man in the doorway and he pulled the door closed.

'There is some dispute at the border,' Meg said. 'Tands, it appears, has ceased trade with our towns. The people have become somewhat desperate.'

'You must be mistaken, Meg,' Brodwyn said quickly.

'Not at all, and if it continues this may only be the first retaliation by our own people.'

'You blame us for this attack on your sister?' he asked too loudly.

'It could have been either of us,' she snapped. 'We were together in the garden; it could have easily been me that caught the brunt of the man's anger.' Her voice caught as it finally settled on her just how close she had come to being in Kellin's position, and she realised just how scared she should be.

Brodwyn took a step toward her with his hand outstretched, but stopped and indicated the chair beside her sister. She stood behind it and took a deep breath.

'Why are you really here?' she asked. 'What are you negotiating for?'

Brodwyn turned to Brother Adroth instead of answering.

'The issues at the border need to be discussed,' she said more calmly.

'A time has been set,' he murmured.

Meg groaned with frustration and then scowled as he smiled at her, small creases appearing at the corners of his eyes.

'Meg stop it,' Kellin said, standing slowly. 'The old one, Lord...' she waved her hand as she searched for the memory of his name.

'Alva,' Brodwyn said.

'Yes, Lord Alva will be doing all the negotiating. He is the important part of this. What does it matter what they discuss?'

'Of course it is important,' Meg said, forgetting the company completely. 'A man attacked us; he hurt you. Trade and the border must be discussed and...' Meg's frustrations died out. Tands was here for its own reasons and she realised that the discussion she hoped for would only be superficial. And even if the three sisters worked together, it may not garner the results she hoped for.

'And what?' Kellin asked. 'Your betrothal to the prince,' she whispered.

Meg's whole body grew hot and she could tell from the sparkle that had appeared with the cheeky grin on the prince's face that her own face was as red hot as it felt. 'That is for the queen to discuss, once she is marked,' she said. 'The prince might not be very interested in the match, and I don't think this is the time to be discussing it,' she added, trying to indicate the others in the room with her eyes.

'I'm sure the prince is agreeable to the match. His father did agree to it, did he not? And I'm sure the young man will do as he is told,' Brother Adroth said.

'I'm sure he does what he pleases, no matter the propriety or the consequence,' Meg returned and then took a deep breath. 'I am sorry,' she said more calmly. 'You are right, I am sure. He would do his duty as required by his kingdom, as we all would.' Brodwyn's face had grown serious. 'We have had a scare with the attack. I think it best that we discuss this no further until the meeting.'

'Negotiations,' Brodwyn said quietly.

'Maybe if you met the prince, you might think differently,' Kellin said. 'This isn't like you,' she added, taking Meg's hands in hers. 'Father thought it best and so it must be. You would not be so very far away that we would not see each other again. And as Lord Danel said, surely it is a misunderstanding at the border. It will all be well.'

Meg pulled Kellin into her arms.

'Just wait until you meet him,' Kellin said again.

Meg opened her mouth to speak but Brodwyn slowly shook his head. 'I think that you and the prince could do much for Tands and Rocfeld,' he said. 'Your sister is wise and offers good advice.'

'Thank you, sir,' Kellin said with a smile as Meg released her. 'Please sit,' she said, indicating the table.

Meg served wine as they sat in silence around the table, trying not to look at Brodwyn, who didn't appear to look anywhere but at her.

'Did you call her Meg?' Kellin suddenly asked, breaking the silence, and Meg tried not to smile as Brodwyn's face reddened. She looked at Meg seriously and suddenly stood from the table. 'What have you done?'

'Nothing,' Meg said quickly. 'It is all well.'

'All well! You have talked with these men before. Elalia will be furious if you have met with them before her. She already thinks you do too much, that you are trying to influence the decision. And now you share looks with a man who is supposed to be negotiating your marriage to another. And calls you Meg.'

'Kellin, please calm down. It is not like that at all. They have only come today to ensure you are well.'

'Do you want to endanger the match? Do you not want to marry Tands?'

'I may not have a choice,' Meg said.

'Why?' Brodwyn asked.

'Elalia has already hinted that it may be beneficial for me to go another path.'

'What path?' he asked forcefully and Kellin stared between the two of them.

'Luana.'

'That cannot be an option,' he said standing from the table and almost knocking the chair backwards.

Meg stood at the same time. 'I don't get a choice. Why can you not see that? I must do as directed, first by my father and soon by my sister.'

'And you would let them make that choice for you, if she is to be queen?'

'I must,' she said.

'Your Highness,' Brother Adroth said loudly.

'What?' they both asked in unison turning on him.

'By the gods,' Kellin whispered.

Meg sat slowly at the table and Brodwyn moved over to stoke the fire.

'This is not like you,' Kellin whispered.

'He frustrates me,' she said.

'What can we do?' Kellin asked.

'Stay away from him in public places,' Meg murmured.

'You would rather go to Luana,' he said.

Meg tried to contain the shiver that covered her body and her skin prickled. 'I want to stay here and help.'

'You can't help from Tands?' he asked, turning his back on the fire.

'It does us no good talking about what may not happen. Talk with us all tomorrow and when the new queen is marked, negotiate what it was you came here for.'

'I came for you,' he said.

Meg looked down into her lap.

'You will talk about the border?' Kellin asked. 'When we are all together tomorrow?'

Brodwyn nodded slowly.

Brother Adroth pushed his old body up from the table and motioned the prince toward the door. 'I am glad you are well,' he said to Kellin, taking her hand and giving it a little squeeze. He nodded to Meg as she opened the door. Brodwyn bowed low to Kellin and then stood before Meg. She shook her head before he could say anything and with a single nod he followed the Brother out into the hall. She closed the door quickly before he had a chance to look back.

Kellin glared at her. 'The prince.'

'Is a liar and may not be what he appears to be, although I'm not sure of what that is.'

'Whatever he may be, you cannot say a word.'

'Who would I tell? Who would believe me?' Meg asked. 'And I already knew; it is you that I should be asking to keep the secret.'

'Elalia would end it immediately.'

'She may end it yet. Too many know him for what he is.'

'Well at least you are not attached to him,' Kellin said, a grin spreading across her face.

'He lied to me,' Meg said softly. She kissed Kellin's cheek and was out the door before Kellin could say anything further. She moved quickly along the hallway, wondering at the peacefulness of the castle so early in the evening. She only stopped briefly as she opened her door to ensure the guard was behind her; she hadn't even heard his leather squeak as it usually did beneath his armour. She gave him a quick nod as she closed the door, disappointed to find the candles all alight and the room empty. She stood just inside the door wondering what lay in the Silence, and why Brodwyn's lying to her mattered.

16

Elalia stood at the Silent Mother's door and focused her thoughts only on what she could do for Sythia.

'You look weary,' the Silent Mother said, without turning from her workbench.

Elalia pulled her hand into a fist to prevent it running over her stomach. How quickly it had become a need to ensure the child was growing every time she thought of him. 'There are many demands on my time, and I must talk with so many.'

'Megora is the problem,' she said.

'She is concerned for the kingdom,' Elalia said, walking into the dimly lit room and peering into the cup the Silent Mother held.

'She does not think you worthy,' the Silent Mother said slowly.

Elalia shook her head.

'She doubts your ability to be queen.'

'It does not matter what she thinks or what she wants. The decision will soon be made and the crown will sit on my head, amidst my raven hair. She cannot influence that, no matter what she thinks she can do.'

'Unless you are dead.'

'There is speculation, but I do not fear for myself.' she said quickly. If something were to happen to her, the line was secure; there was another option for Sythia. The child growing inside her would carry their hope. Unless the child was a boy.

'And yet there is the threat of the youngest.'

'Meggie may question my decisions, but she wouldn't try to kill me.'

The Silent Mother shrugged. 'She will be gone soon enough. She will have her own crown and will no longer try to influence you. That is if you wish to allow her to go to Tands.'

'It may be that another place would be better for her, but it would be away from Rocfeld no matter the choice,' Elalia said softly. 'I will be queen, with Sythia watching over me.'

'Sythia will watch over us all.'

'How can I help her?' she asked, and the Silent Mother held out the cup.

The liquid appeared clear like water and yet Elalia could not see through it—clear and yet dark—and she doubted for a single moment that the Silent Sisters' plan was the best way. The Silent Mother smiled and she nodded once before gulping it down, surprised by the lack of taste, as though it were simply water after all. And then a honey-like sweetness coated her lips and down her throat, and she felt warm in the embrace of it before the feeling was lost in an instant.

'You are the way for Sythia,' the Silent Mother said. 'You shall be marked as such before long.'

Elalia nodded and moved quickly back to her own room. She felt calmer than when she had entered the Silent Mother's room. And yet she felt an uncertainty in her ability to truly do as she had been asked to do.

She was at the door when she realised that she should be in the Hall, ready to meet the delegation, and if she was early enough then she might have the chance to talk with them before her sisters arrived.

Elalia arrived in the Hall to find it strangely quiet in its near-empty state. She was so used to the bustle and noise of it full of people that for a moment she thought she had entered the wrong doorway. The room was empty except for a single table, and Brother Erasmus already sitting at it. Terra raced past her with a tray of goblets, and another girl was not far behind with a pitcher of wine.

'Is this meeting about Kellin or Meggie?' Brother Erasmus asked as she walked toward the table.

As Elalia opened her mouth to respond, Meggie's clear voice

answered before she had the chance. 'We are to talk about trade.'

'And what would you trade?' Elalia asked with a grin, turning to watch her sister walk through the door, only for the grin to slip as she grabbed at the back of a chair.

Meggie entered the Hall on the arm of Lord Alva, Kellin only a step behind on the arm of the youngest advisor. The Brother and third advisor silently entered behind them. 'Have you started the discussion without me?' she asked, trying to keep her voice level, but when she glanced at Brother Erasmus he shook his head very slightly.

She indicated the table and took a seat before her sisters had reached her. Terra poured wine into a cup and handed it to her, but her hand shook and she set it down quickly, hoping that no one had noticed.

'The Tandian delegation,' Brother Erasmus said softly as they took their seats at the table, Lord Alva pausing to pull out the chair for Meggie. Elalia tried to focus on the Brother. 'The Tandian delegation,' he began again, 'has a list of issues it wishes to discuss with the Rocfeld Crown.'

'Which has not been marked yet,' Lord Caris said swiftly.

'Issues have arisen that need to be addressed now, and I thought that we could all talk together,' Meggie said.

'Your list of discussion points is very small,' Elalia said, taking the parchment from Brother Erasmus and studying it closely. 'I have several points of my own to discuss, but please let us begin with trade.'

Lord Alva nodded solemnly. 'There appears to be some dispute around the border,' he said slowly, and she noted that the youngest of the men nodded slowly.

'And to what type of dispute are you referring? For I am sure you are not talking about the trade between the villages on either side of the border,' Elalia said.

Now the young man's face turned serious and she gulped quickly at the wine, hoping her hands had stopped shaking.

'There have been some price disputes between the towns which has slowed the trade,' Elalia continued.

'That isn't what we were told,' Kellin said.

'And who have you been talking to?' Elalia asked quickly and then regretted her tone when the whole table turned to her and

Kellin's hand moved quickly to her arm. 'He may have been more angry than accurate,' she said softly, but Kellin shook her head vigorously.

'How can we fix this?' Meggie asked the young advisor and Elalia took another gulp of her wine.

Her skin felt hot. 'Tands is the answer to this, as they are the cause of the problem.'

'Trade?' Lord Alva asked.

'The incident in the garden,' she said.

Meggie and the young man shared another look across the table and she did her best not to thump her fist down. She felt uncomfortable, hot and sticky. She was certain that Meggie had been trying to find out more about her prince, that she thought she had the right to negotiate before a queen was marked.

'The only relation of the attack to our discussion here is that the man came from a border town,' Meggie said.

'Tands is responsible for the attack on the princess.'

The young man pushed up quickly from the table and two guards stepped forward quickly from the doorway.

'This is not Tands' doing,' he implored. 'We would never hurt them.'

She waved him off and stood from the table. She waved the parchment, still tight in her hand. 'You wish to take Rocfeld back for yourself. You wish to take it before a queen can be chosen. You were seen in the garden not long before the attack. If you were not a part of it, explain your presence there.'

'We were exploring,' Lord Alva said quickly. 'It is a beautiful spot.'

'It is winter; hardly anything grows.'

'I was curious of the design,' the young one said.

Lord Alva stood from the table, shaking his head. 'The matter has already been investigated. The man responsible has been arrested. He is not Tandian, he was not working for Tands, nor was Tands responsible in any way for such an attack.'

'I do not believe you,' she said, raising the cup to her lips. 'If you could not take Rocfeld easily, then you would take it by marriage or force.' She was disappointed to find her cup nearly empty, but she sat it down carefully. 'If Meggie is not marked as queen, I think you would not feel as strongly about her marriage to your prince.'

'It doesn't matter if she is queen or not,' the young one stammered.

'You have until the sun rises to leave Rocfeld and return to Tands. You can then report to your king that you were not able to secure the kingdom as you thought. You will give up your hope of the princess and will leave us in peace.'

'Elalia,' Meggie started, 'you can't make this decision; you aren't queen yet.'

'Are you so attached to a man you have not yet met? One who would covet your crown and kingdom, one who orchestrates attacks on you and your sister?'

'The prince is not responsible,' Meggie cried. 'Tands is not responsible for this attack. The people of Rocfeld turn against us in their desperation. We need these talks, we need this trade to help our people.'

'You are too young to understand,' Elalia said, waving the soldiers forward. 'Please return the delegation to their rooms.'

The Brother and Lord Caris stood beside the others as the guards indicated the doorway and despite their dark looks, they followed them. The Brother glanced back at Brother Erasmus, but the young man again looked back at Meggie; although this time she looked down at the table.

'I like this idea of yours, Meggie,' Elalia said as the doors were closed behind them. 'I think we should meet with the emperor next.'

'Elalia, enough,' Brother Erasmus snapped, standing slowly. 'You will start a war with power that is not yet yours.'

She shrugged her shoulders and sat back at the table. The strange heat still covered her body, but she felt more secure in the feeling now, and poured herself another cup of wine.

CRISO

'Again, Your Highness, I can only apologise for calling on you so late,' Lord Alva said.

'Maybe she heard something,' Meg said, pulling the shawl tighter around her shoulders.

'Would Kellin have said something?' Brodwyn asked.

'No,' Meg said, thinking of her sister's childish grin when she had learnt the truth. 'She told me I had to remain quiet.'

'What can I do?' he asked.

Meg studied him for just a moment. 'Leave,' she said. 'It is not worth your heads to remain here. Particularly as she claims the attack was your doing. Your father might try to take Rocfeld by force.'

'This won't help,' Lord Alva muttered.

'Does she want a war?' Lord Caris asked, surprising Meg with his shrill voice.

'I cannot guess at the reasons for my sister's actions.'

'Where will you go?' Brodwyn asked.

'I'm not going anywhere,' she said slowly as the two advisors stood and bowed, and then left the room. She looked after them and shook her head. 'But you must.'

'She does not know who I am,' he said, taking her hand, but she pulled from his grasp and stepped back.

'That would make it all the worse. Your father would be sure that she knowingly took his son and sent him back in pieces. He would not hesitate.'

'He might not act quite so quickly to defend me,' he said, chewing his lip again.

'The notion of you then.'

'What is your notion of me?'

Meg sighed and shifted beneath the shawl. 'It matters not what I think,' she said. 'But I do not want to see you dead.'

'Will I see you again?' he asked, stepping forward again.

'My husband may bring me to Tands one day.'

He shook his head.

'This match was organised between our fathers when our only task was to do what they saw best for our kingdoms. My sister has named Tands a risk and threat to the kingdom of Rocfeld, even if she is not yet Raven Queen. The match is dissolved.'

'She does this for herself,' he muttered.

'Yes,' Meg agreed. 'The world is not what it was, but I cannot change it.'

'Are you certain she will be queen?' he asked.

She nodded slowly and turned to the fire; she could see no way to change what was said.

Gentle hands rested on her shoulders and a soft, warm breath made her scalp tingle before he kissed the top of her head. She turned to watch him walk toward the door. He paused momentarily, looking back at her with sad eyes before he pulled the door closed.

Meg wondered if Elalia would have noticed if she had run away to Tands with Brodwyn, or whether it would have given Elalia the opportunity to take the control she wanted.

17

Meg sighed inwardly as Elalia, smiling far too much, walked quickly toward her across the Hall.

'You look tired, Meggie,' Elalia crooned as she joined her by the fire. 'Have you been sitting up late with your sister?'

Meg shook her head.

'I must tell you that the right decision was made about Tands,' she said, looking across the room. 'This match is not ideal for you. I fear the king only wishes to use you to gain control of Rocfeld,' she said, turning back to Meg, her fingers laced before her.

Meg nodded slowly.

'I thought you might be a little more disappointed,' Elalia said as Kellin and their cousins joined them.

'I had not formed any sort of attachment, for I have not met the man,' Meg said, fearing her voice betrayed her lack of strength. 'I fear your sharp words might have offended them and risked some form of retaliation.'

'They were a threat and they have been called on it; I'm sure they slink home to Tands to tell the king they were too easily discovered.'

Tyne pushed his way past Creena to the front of the group. But Meg looked past him to Kellin's sad face; she looked heartbroken.

'I am sorry, cousin,' Tyne said. 'But perhaps you may find a match somewhat closer to home.'

Elalia sighed loudly. 'I do not hope you think yourself an option, cousin. I am afraid Meggie must marry to strengthen our kingdom.'

'I am sure that my history and family would add strength,' he said quickly.

'They may, but not enough,' she said with a flick of her hand to dismiss him. But he narrowed his eyes and stood his ground and again, Meg saw the difference between this man and her beloved cousin Rance.

Kellin opened her mouth, no doubt to ask a question, so Meg held up her hand quickly and gave her a subtle shake of the head. 'It will be as it must. Where is the Silent Mother today?'

'At prayer,' Elalia said, looking her over closely.

'She prays a lot,' Creena muttered.

'The Silent Mother's work is never done,' Elalia snapped, then coughed politely and smoothed out her dress. 'I pray with her as often as I can.'

'And what do you pray for?' Meg asked.

'Excuse me?'

'Do you pray for peace and prosperity for the kingdom of Rocfeld and those within her borders, or for all mankind? Do you pray that the Silence maintains its hold over the goddess?'

'Meg,' Kellin whispered loudly, shaking her head.

Silence descended on the group and Meg's gaze shifted from her sister's red face to the people moving around the Hall beyond them; Meg wondered how long until they were discussing her and the severed ties to Tands. She wondered if their king would find it as difficult to take as Brodwyn had seemed to. She blinked away the image of his face as he had left her rooms the night before.

Malin and his guard appeared and the group came back to life.

'My love,' he said, taking Elalia's hand. 'You look well.'

She smiled but pulled her hand from his.

'Commander Rainger wished to check on you after the attack,' he said, turning to Kellin. 'Are you well?'

Kellin nodded quickly and gave the large soldier a smile. 'Thank you,' she said timidly.

'I believe Tands had more to do with that than they would admit,' Elalia said quickly. 'And so I said to the delegation.'

'I think...' Meg started.

'It was one of the main reasons for ending the agreement for Meggie.'

Meg gulped down her frustrations. Elalia didn't have to explain their discussion to this group.

'The man in question will not be able to harm you again,' Commander Rainger reassured Kellin.

She nodded slowly.

'You have ended the agreement with Tands?' Malin asked. 'Why?'

'It was the right thing to do. Meg is not heartbroken; you should not be. And they are gone.'

Malin looked Meg over critically.

'I am well,' she said. 'I would much rather be here than far away in Tands.'

'We will find somewhere for you to go,' Elalia said.

Meg bit back the question on her lips.

Elalia grinned. 'I may have had a word with Emperor Baghi.'

'When?' Malin asked too loudly.

'After Father's funeral,' she said, the smile not reaching her eyes.

'You always planned to end the betrothal that Father arranged, then?' Kellin asked.

Elalia's hard gaze shifted from her husband's face to Kellin's and Meg cringed on her behalf. 'He asked after her at the time. I said nothing was sealed. There is always room for negotiation and not all of Father's plans may have been for the best.'

'If only he had thought to make plans for me.' Kellin huffed despite Meg's vigorous shaking of her head. And as the silence settled on the group, Kellin turned fully to her sister. 'Did Father have plans for me?'

'Of course he did.' Elalia grinned, and this time the mischief twinkled in her green eyes. 'You, dear sister, are destined for the Sisters of the Brotherhood.'

Kellin took a step back and would have tripped had she not stepped into Commander Rainger, who was quick to take her arm and hold her upright.

Kellin's jaw had dropped open. 'The Brotherhood,' she whispered and a tear escaped before she could stop it. 'A life alone, hidden away in a rough, grey tunic,' she said, gulping down more tears. 'I couldn't.'

Elalia shrugged and Meg stepped forward in an attempt to calm her, but she put up her hands.

'Princess, let me escort you back to your rooms,' the commander said, offering her an arm as Malin rolled his eyes.

'I can take her,' Meg said.

'Oh, let him do it; it makes him look important. Following me around all day must get tiresome.'

'It is for your protection, Sire,' he said formally. 'I shall send a replacement.'

'Do not bother,' Malin said sharply. He looked at Elalia and then around the room 'I am sure these soldiers will not allow me to die before you get back.'

He bowed and gently moved Kellin toward the door.

'That was unnecessary,' Meg snapped.

'When will you two learn that you may not always get what you want?'

'We don't ask for much, just the chance to be of use to our kingdom. And you have not yet been marked as Queen.'

Elalia tipped her head a little to the side and smirked.

'Prince Malin, how is the Lady Sera?' Creena asked suddenly in the following silence.

'Excuse me?' he asked. He seemed genuinely confused by the question.

'I thought her brother a friend of yours, and I heard she was unwell. She seemed a sweet thing when I met her.'

Malin nodded. 'I don't know,' he said, looking at Elalia rather than Creena, and the smile Elalia had worn slipped away.

'Perhaps when you see her next you could offer her my wishes for her health.'

Malin bowed politely to the group and marched away. Tyne, not far behind him, moved off to find Morley, who was talking with his young wife and Lady Scott.

Meg tried to focus on those around her as Creena and Elalia talked, but she was too tired to maintain the required effort. Elalia would do as she wanted and there was no chance for her to change her mind and consider Tands. Now that they had been asked to leave, with the implication that they were behind the attack, they would not be favourably received even if they were to return.

'I am so silly,' Meg said. 'I would forget myself, I am sure. Remind me Creena, how is Tyne our cousin?'

Creena smiled indulgently. 'His father is a relative of ours,' Creena said.

'Oh,' Meg said. 'A close relative? For I cannot seem to place him on our tree.'

Elalia watched her too closely, but she didn't interrupt.

'Not too distant,' Creena said. 'For he has our father's handsome features.'

'True,' Meg said as she watched him with Morley. He could have been their Uncle Ustyn many years younger. And then he ran his fingers through his hair, the movement making Meg gasp. Elalia turned to look where she was, but had missed the gesture.

'Kellin always has news,' Creena said. 'Now that she is gone I feel lost. 'If she goes to the Brotherhood, we will never hear anything of interest.'

Meg shook her head slowly. She doubted there was little that Creena and her cousins didn't already know. 'I'm tired; I think it time I retired.'

'Do not worry, Meggie, I will find you a husband.'

Meg headed for the door without acknowledging either of them. She knew it was her duty to do as she was directed, but knowing that marriage to Brodwyn was no longer an option was much harder to deal with than she expected. She was sure she simply needed a reminder as to what was important, how she could still help her kingdom in her own way.

Instead of heading back to her room, Meg made her way along the hallways toward the family's private chapel. She needed a quiet moment with the gods and she wasn't up to facing anyone in the Temple.

Strange lights moved across the stone walls. Standing in the doorway, the shadows flickered in the pale light across the floor and ceiling, and it took Meg a moment to realise that the Silent Mother was standing in the middle of it all, her white tunic lost amongst the shadows.

Meg pressed herself into the doorframe as the random shadows formed into shapes and an uneasiness pulled at the hairs on her arms and neck. The small altar still only contained the two candles and she missed the gods in the space, as though they had been stolen away. She pushed herself harder into the door. Her fingers gripped the wood in an attempt to ground her as her legs felt weak.

And then the shape came into focus and a tall, slender woman stood against the wall. The image was so clear and lifelike, Meg was certain she was actually standing in the room with them.

When the Silent Mother turned to the shadow and held out her hand, the shadow stepped from the wall, and it took all of Meg's strength not to cry out. The older woman dropped to her knees and lay her forehead on the stone floor, and the shadow stepped forward and put a hand on the back of her head.

The Silent Mother looked up and nodded once. The silence felt thick and oppressive and for a moment Meg wondered if what she saw was the Silence. A woman working with the Silent Sisters to keep the goddess at bay. But then the Silent Mother sat up, leaned back on her heels and her lips moved; although it appeared that the two were conversing, no sound emanated.

Meg was desperate to move closer but feared what would happen if she was seen by either. Although she wanted to believe as much as Brother Erasmus that this woman worked for the good of all men, she was certain that nothing was as it seemed.

The shadow woman pointed to the wall and more shadows passed over it, like clouds across a blue sky. And then they pulled together and a raven flew across the wall. Meg was sure she could hear its cry. The raven turned into the raven crest of the Raven Crown and Meg's heart stopped beating.

The raven became the shadow of another woman and a crown glowed above her head; it was clearly Elalia. The shadow Elalia moved across the wall and a flash of light pushed away all shadows but for the one standing in the room. Elalia's shadow returned, with many people bowing down before her. Meg shivered.

The Silent Mother bowed down again before the shadow and it dissipated into a dark mist and then disappeared. As the random shadows from the flickering candles covered the walls again, the Silent Mother whispered, 'Sythia.' The word echoed in the bare room. Meg stepped backward as slowly as she could. Once she was out of sight of the doorway she turned and bolted toward her room, hoping this time the Silent Mother wasn't waiting for her, because she wasn't sure how she could convince anyone else that she was working with Sythia, not against her.

18

Meg found Brother Erasmus leaning over a bowl of soup in his study. He looked up at her before dropping the spoon and standing. 'What is it, child?' he asked.

She wasn't sure how to explain what she had seen, and her concerns returned around his reaction to the arrival of the Silent Mother. And then he did not believe what had occurred in her rooms, with the strange fire and the Silent Mother preventing her from leaving.

'I want to talk to you about the legend of Sythia and the Silence.'

'Why?' he asked, sitting slowly and looking into his bowl.

'I believe,' she said very softly, her voice sounding strange amongst the books and dust, 'that you have not told us the whole truth of Sythia.'

'Really?' he asked, slowly stirring the soup. 'Why do you think that?'

'There is something strange in the Silent Mother, something secretive that I would not expect.'

'They live with the Silence; it is hard to leave such peace to visit a loud castle such as Rocfeld.'

Meg looked down at her hands in her lap. She couldn't say exactly what she had seen in the chapel, for he wouldn't believe her and she may have been mistaken as to who the shadow figure was. 'How did Sythia kill the Raven Queen?'

'Why?' he asked softly, reaching out and taking her hand.

'In the stories we were told as children, we only learn that Sythia killed the queen to take her power and that was why she was banished to the Silence. There is more to the story, and I would like to hear it,' she said, giving his hand a gentle squeeze.

'I'm not sure,' he said.

'Brother, please. A god could do so much—why kill the queen? Why do such a thing?'

The Brother sighed and stood from the table. He disappeared into the shadows of the book shelves and although she knew he was still in the room, it was unnerving that she couldn't see him.

'The goddess whispered to the queen that she would be stronger working with her,' his disembodied voice said from the shelves and despite knowing him so well, a shiver moved down her spine. 'She whispered for years.'

Again Meg shivered. Wondering if the voice sounded like someone the Queen had trusted. 'She didn't listen,' Meg stated, already knowing the answer.

'No, she didn't,' he said, appearing in the candlelight with a narrow book. 'She wanted to rule for the good of the people rather than to the whim of a goddess. But Sythia was determined; she may even have tried'to influence those of the Raven Crown before the Raven Queen of the story.'

Meg waited, her hands clenched in her lap as he tapped the book beneath his fingers.

'Sythia thought to take the body of the queen for herself and rule in her place. But such a transformation takes a lot of magic. The queen had been gifted magic by the gods and was very powerful in her own right. After she died, the gift of magic was never again offered to the Raven Crown, and the gods' only influence was from a distance in marking the rightful heir.'

'So a queen without magic would be safe?' Meg asked.

'There are other ways to rule,' he said. 'In trying to influence the queen, a strange illness entered the castle, killing two of the queen's three sons.'

Meg wondered why she had never heard of the children before. 'Did the gods help? Did Kira and Kion help the people?'

'There was little they could do, for the people started to fear the gods rather than love them, and the gods feared panic and unrest rather than assistance if they stepped in to help.'

'And so they let her kill the queen?'

'It is not clear how the queen was killed, but either way it was too late for Sythia, she was bent on ruling over the people and the only way left to her was to replace the queen. Despite her best efforts and magic of her own, she could not turn her silver hair to the raven black that marked a queen.'

Meg's hand moved over her own white hair and Brother Erasmus gave her a friendly smile. 'Do not worry, child.'

'So with no other option, Sythia attempted to take over the queen and take over her crown that way. But when it didn't work, she killed her?'

'Desperation does strange things to the mind,' Brother Erasmus said. 'The gods were concerned that she would continue to try to take the crown by force, and so they banished her to the Silence where she could do no harm. The Silent Sisters work with the Silence to ensure it maintains its strength and that Sythia remains locked away.'

'What does the Silence look like?' Meg asked quickly.

'I don't know that it has a particular appearance. It is not a being as we would understand it. I imagine it as a void.'

'A place,' Meg murmured. 'Not a being.'

The Brother nodded.

'How was she trapped there?' she asked.

Brother Erasmus shook his head. 'That is a question for the gods, for there is no detail within any story as to how that was achieved.'

'What if she were to escape?' Meg asked, leaning forward and squeezing his hand.

His soft smile went a little way to calm her. 'There is no escape for Sythia,' he said.

Meg nodded slowly, but she wasn't as sure as the Brother. It wasn't the Silence she had seen with the Silent Mother, and she wondered if she could have been corrupted by the whispers of the goddess. She opened her mouth to ask the question when he shook his head. 'There is nothing to fear now from Sythia,' he said, pushing the book across the table. 'It is brief and will offer you no more than I have, but the story may put your mind at ease.'

Meg stood slowly from the table with the small book in hand, and worked her way along the narrow hallways of the Brotherhood to the Temple. She sighed as she entered the space, the gods smiling down on the people, and she wondered if anyone would be able to answer her questions.

On her way back through the castle, she paused at the door of the Hall and watched her cousins deep in conversation, the small group looking only inward, and she wondered why they had come to Rocfeld at all. Had they been sent by their father to learn more of the new queen, and would they support the sister that was marked? She had heard that they had arrived with a soothsayer and she wondered what the old woman would be able to tell them, or what she might have told them already.

Meg moved quietly along the passage and then more quickly up the stairs. She stopped for a moment at the sound of running behind her and turned to find the guard following her. She nodded once, turned and ran on. She only paused at the door to her cousin's rooms to hand the book the Brother had given her to the guard and as she opened the door, the guard turned his back to stand watch.

The room was dimly lit and she wasn't quite sure where to start, but she was sure the old woman might be her only chance at the truth of what she had seen.

'Come,' the old voice called from near the fireplace, and Meg stepped forward carefully. 'I have been expecting you,' she said, reaching out an old hand, and Meg was surprised by the strength of it as it closed around her hand.

'Were you?' she asked, kneeling before the woman as she turned her hand over and studied her palm.

'You have seen what cannot be explained,' she said.

Meg nodded slowly. 'Shadows,' she whispered.

'Dark and dangerous,' the old woman said, pulling Meg's hand closer to her softly wrinkled face, the breath hot and damp on her palm.

'Can you tell me what I saw?'

The old woman's dark eyes searched Meg's skin and then the soothsayer licked her palm, and it took all of her strength not to pull from her grip. She gulped down her repulsion and waited.

'Death,' the crone whispered, lifting sad eyes from her palm to look deep into Meg's soul. 'There is much death coming. Darkness and shadows shall lead the way, and you will experience more darkness than any other.'

Meg tugged at her hand then, unsure she wanted to hear any more, but the woman held her tight.

'There is much pain and loss to come your way, little queen. You have been marked for power, but it is a difficult road to reach your throne.'

Meg gulped down the fear building in her chest. 'Elalia is to be Queen,' she whispered.

'She will be a queen,' the old woman said, nodding slowly. 'Her pain will be easier to bear.'

The old woman released her hand quickly and Meg slipped backward, sitting hard on the floor. 'Can you tell me of the Silent Mother, of the Silence?'

'You have seen for yourself what it is.'

Meg shook her head. 'I thought...'

'Do not speak of it again, for your words are meaningless to those around you.'

'But is what I have seen meaningless?'

'Of course not,' the old woman said, leaning back in the chair and crossing her arms. 'But you will know what to do.'

'I don't,' she said quickly.

'But you will,' the soothsayer said, closing her eyes to the world, and shivered a little. 'So much pain for one so young,' she murmured. 'The men love you. Stay close, for they will keep you where you need to be.'

'What men?' Meg asked, exasperated with the riddles.

'Your men,' she said. 'Now go away, child. Your cousins would not appreciate your visit.'

'Thank you,' Meg said, climbing to her feet. The old woman waved her toward the door. The guard stood to attention as she opened the door, and she looked him over critically before she pulled the door closed and headed back toward her own rooms.

She wasn't sure if the old woman had meant Brodwyn or the Brothers when she referred to "her men" or where they might keep her. She shivered, thinking of her dark eyes, so piercing as she focused on her that she could almost see the shadows of the chapel in them, and she wondered what darkness was to come.

19

Malin chastised himself for not realising the connection sooner. Tyne was clearly more than a cousin to Rance, with whom he shared his looks, but he had inherited his father's mannerisms and they couldn't be hidden. How had Elalia's uncle hidden a bastard son in his own home? Or had he? Perhaps the point being that the child was his was all the reason he needed to keep him close.

If her aunt could do such a thing, then perhaps Elalia could raise another's child in her home. She knew of the existence of the child after all, he mused, heading from the Hall to find her. And now that she was secure with a child of her own, she might be more forgiving.

Moving quickly, Malin almost ran into Robert as he appeared in the doorway. He looked tired and stressed. But Malin was sure that with the right words, he could talk Elalia into accepting the child in the castle. Malin slapped him on the back and turned him about so that they walked together. He ran over in his mind what he would tell Elalia and how he could change her mind while Robert muttered away at his side.

They were almost to Elalia's rooms when the urgency of Robert's words sank in. 'It will all be well, my friend; I have just found the answer to our problem.'

'There no longer is a problem,' Robert said, holding out his arm and then grabbing Malin's sleeve to stop his progress.

'Not now that I have found the answer,' Malin said smugly.

'Listen to me,' Robert yelled, taking him by the shoulders. 'The child has died.'

Malin was sure his heart actually stopped beating as his whole body became cool and shivery. He shook his head but his friend's slow nodding confirmed it. He allowed Robert to turn him about and they walked with far less urgency toward Robert's rooms.

The scent of bitter copper met him at the door as he shooed the approaching nurse away and pushed past a maid that gathered bedding from the floor. The room was stifling hot.

Sera's pale face was focused on some distant point as she rolled her back to him. 'Go away, Malin,' she said, her voice sad and broken.

Malin sat on the bed despite her words, taking in the destruction around her. The maid came in quietly and swept the rushes away from around the bed, taking them in an armful through the door.

'I had found a way to keep the child,' he whispered.

She rolled away from him again, her sobs filling the room and shaking her small frame. He leaned across and put a hand on her shoulder, then lay along her back, his arm around her. His hand found her stomach, strangely soft, and she pushed his hand violently away.

'Sera,' he said quietly.

She hit him, smacked his face and chest, forcing him out of the bed. Then she was up on her knees pushing him, punching him as best she could, an angry energy giving strength to every strike he did not know she had. And then he grabbed her wrists, scared of what she might do to him or herself, her fresh sheets splattered with blood. 'Sera,' he said, struggling with her, 'calm yourself.'

And then the nurse was back, taking her into her arms, directing the maid to change the sheets and glaring at him.

'Get out,' Sera said, all fight gone.

He staggered from the room to find Robert waiting, his face drawn. 'It has been a long night,' he muttered.

'We should hunt,' Malin said, pulling his shoulders back.

'You have broken her,' Robert said, looking down into the fire rather than his face. 'And no other man shall want her.'

'When she is healed, we will set things right,' Malin said, but Robert's face was darker than Malin thought he would ever see. And then Malin, Prince of Rocfeld, found himself walked backwards from his friend's rooms, and the door shut in his face.

He stood in the dimly lit passageway, the large, thick wooden door between them, and all he could hear was Sera's sobs.

He walked away from the door, unsure where to go or what to do, and then he was standing at the private chapel, two candles flickering strange shadows around the walls, Elalia on her knees on the hard flagstones before a simple wooden altar, a stark contrast in her black cloak to the white tunic of the sister beside her. It was strange that there were no gods in this chapel. No images to remind them of what they worshiped. She remained unmoving as he stood silently behind her. Not knowing if she knew he was there or not. In the strange light, the dark cloak made it appear as though she was the raven itself, her wings at the ready to fly away.

He had a moment of desperate wanting, to fly with Elalia to achieve some kind of peace. But he knew she would never let him. He would have to be content to watch her from the ground. He closed his eyes and he could see the blood-stained sheets and Sera's angry fists. He moved as slowly and silently as he could from the chapel and ran across the courtyard towards the stables.

Focused only on flying away on horseback, he didn't see the manservant step from the shadows until he blocked his path.

'I need a moment, Your Highness.'

Malin stopped dead, suddenly feeling exposed. He rested his hand on the sword in his belt, but the man's quiet demeanour didn't falter.

'Why would you need a word with me?'

'It is your cousins that require the word; I am only sent to deliver a request for you to attend them.'

'When?'

'Now.'

Malin waited for pleasantries to follow, but they didn't. 'They would demand my audience?'

'They simply ask if you would visit with them.'

He sighed and looked back toward the stable. More men were milling around and he could hear the soldiers in the barracks. He nodded once and followed the servant silently. Perhaps he could ask Tyne about his life at Lekland, he thought as he focused on the man's back. And then he should visit with Elalia; it was time that they announced the child. He gulped down his regret for Sera.

Morley and Tyne sat at the table, the ladies not present—or at least not visible—when the servant led Malin into the room. He could have done with a closer look at the strange, young wife of Morley, he'd had very little opportunity in the Hall to make conversation and when he had, she had stared at him with little expression.

The two men stood as he stepped closer, giving a short bow, and he indicated that they sit down again.

'We thank you for your visit, Highness,' Morley said.

'I was surprised by your request for a private audience,' Malin said. 'I am sure that you could have come to me.'

A large goblet was placed before him and the manservant filled it before he refilled the one before Tyne. Morley waved him off.

'We wish to talk in private, Highness, and we do not want our secrets shared.'

Malin looked at Tyne. 'Some of your secrets are not so well hidden,' he said.

Tyne, still grinning, tipped his head. 'Neither are yours.'

'What do you wish to talk about?' Malin asked, sipping at the wine, he wasn't going to explain himself to these people.

'Your wife, mostly, and the state of the kingdom.'

Malin raised his eyebrows.

'Do not mistake me, Sire,' Morley said. 'We love our cousin, yet we wonder if she is the best choice for the kingdom.'

'Did your soothsayer tell you that?' Malin asked, leaning back in his chair. 'Can she be sure which sister the gods will choose?'

He shook his head. 'Will Elalia protect us if she is marked the Raven Queen?' he asked.

'From what?'

Morley sighed. 'You are aware of the history and threat with Tands?'

Malin nodded. 'You believe she is not?'

'I wonder at her rejecting their prince for Meggie, and sending them away under blame for an act undertaken by a Rocfeld villager.'

'She believes they were a threat,' Malin said. 'Would you want your cousin married into a family that may try to kill her?'

Morley shook his head slowly. 'Are we sure that Tands is the threat?'

'I wonder with the attention you are paying to the running of our kingdom that you did not meet with them. Do you wish to negotiate above my wife or her sisters, cousin?' he asked drawing out the last word for full effect.

'She was always a silly child,' he said, appearing to let his guard down completely. 'Perhaps once she has children of her own they may focus her. For women are different creatures when it comes to children.'

Malin nodded slowly, deciding to allow this farce of a meeting to play out. He should chastise Morley but he wanted to see where this went. Was Elalia in danger and thereby affecting his own ambitions?

'Is there a problem producing a child?' Tyne asked suddenly.

Malin stared at him and the man grinned again. He found himself squaring his shoulders. 'My wife is still young,' he snapped. 'She has many years to produce children, we have many years,' he added. 'And the young princesses are not yet wed.'

'Forgive my cousin,' Morley said, glaring at the still grinning Tyne. 'He forgets himself.'

Malin thought, Tyne wasn't the only one to "forget himself".

Tyne shrugged and stood a little shakily from the table. He was taller than Morley and despite the grinning Malin thought there was possibly something darker in him. They could be friends if he were on the same side. Malin was struggling to work out who was on which side with this table.

'Now that the connection with Tands is dissolved I wonder if our young cousins will ever marry. They are certainly past an age where they could be offered out,' Morley added, looking more into his wine than at Malin.

Malin shook his head. 'Do you think the crown would pass to your side of the family?' he asked. He tried to focus on Morley but with the younger man walking slowly behind him he felt the uneasiness he had felt in the stables return.

Morley shrugged. 'Who can guess at the Gods,' he said. 'We only want to ensure the security of the kingdom, for our own children.'

'Why am I here?' Malin asked. 'What do you want?'

'We want the opportunity to talk with Elalia, to help ensure she has the right ideas in running the kingdom,' Tyne said, far too close behind him, and Malin heard the real man beneath the mask.

'We want our cousin in the crown with the *right* ideas.'

'You mean your ideas,' Malin said, but he looked at Morley as he said it.

'We wish to help her,' he said. 'But we cannot do that when she will not listen, nor even allow us the time to talk. You could help us.' He was glad now he allowed them to freely speak. It provided him with more opportunities now.

Malin looked at him seriously as he sipped from the large goblet in front of him and Tyne walked slowly toward the window, looking out into the dark night. 'I'm not certain she will listen to me,' he said.

'You are her husband; surely you are her first choice for counsel. We simply want an opportunity to talk, at length.'

He stood slowly from the table, unsure Morley was asking for what he really wanted of Elalia. Malin watched Tyne's profile as he stared into the black of the night beyond the thick panes of glass. 'Why me?' he asked. 'Why not approach Elalia directly?'

'She will not see us,' Tyne said, 'and you are the only one that could persuade her.'

Malin nodded once and the manservant opened the door for him.

'Thank you, Your Highness,' Morley said without looking up from his wine, 'that you took the time to visit with us.'

Now it was Malin's turn to grin, thinking of them without their heads, should he so choose. He had them all now. Tyne faltered in his own stupid grin.

The guard at the door had been replaced by Commander Rainger, shadowing his steps back toward his rooms. He was desperate to see Sera. *Let him follow*, he thought. *The man is mine. We will find him what he wants and perhaps he will keep my secrets.*

Malin knocked on the door, but the maid that opened it was not one he knew. She bobbed a quick curtsy but shook her head. His mouth went dry and he pushed his way past her. Sera sat by the fire, her face pale and still wet with tears. Robert stood at her side. Malin sighed and Robert moved toward him quickly, his hands on his chest pushing him back to the door.

He looked at Sera as he stumbled backwards, wondering now where the commander was.

'Out,' she croaked and stared back at the fire.

The door was closed and he found himself in the hall, the door shut in his face. Again.

Damn Robert, Malin thought, he was right. He had broken the girl and she was the only one he had truly cared for. That was, he drifted into sleep every night with the image of her perfect breasts in his mind. And they helped him do his duty with Elalia as well.

CRED

Meg arrived in Elalia's room to find a bigger mess than she had seen before. Papers and food littered the tables and clothes covered the floors. Meg was almost hesitant to enter, but at the sound of vomiting she rushed forward.

Elalia lay in her bed, many of the covers pulled back or pushed onto the floor, and a nurse knelt in front of her with a large bowl. Elalia heaved into it and lay back. As the nurse went to sit it down, she started to heave again. The smell in the room was bitter and overpowering.

'You are ill,' Meg said, unable to state anything but the obvious. The nurse looked up in desperation.

She stepped around her and opened the small window, then travelled back the way she had come and opened the doors. Elalia continued to heave, the nurse unable to leave her station.

Meg stepped in and took the bowl from her. 'Go,' Meg said. 'Send another nurse as soon as you can, and another bowl.' She winced. And as the woman's grey tunic disappeared through the doorway, she called, 'And find Terra.'

'I am here, Your Highness,' she said, appearing in the doorway. 'What has happened?'

Meg sighed and then took a cloth from another bowl by the bed and wiped over Elalia's face and neck between heaves. Meg shrugged and held the bowl higher for Elalia. 'I think we need a Brother,' she muttered and Terra headed for the door.

'No,' Elalia groaned. 'I want none of them here.'

'But you are ill,' Meg said.

'I am with child,' she said.

'That does not explain this mess,' Meg said.

'You question me,' she said, and then vomited again into the bowl.

'Should this not be a time of joy?' Meg asked, thinking of how this could raise the morale of their people. It could also act as a distraction and stop many from worrying about the crown. 'Terra can clear the tables and the floor.'

The girl nodded and nervously looked over the table before her.

'I am not moving from this bed,' Elalia said.

'Fine,' Meg answered, and she sat the bowl on the floor and moved over to help Terra.

'Please, Meg,' she called.

'You go to her,' she told the girl, who looked like she might also vomit. 'The nurse will return soon.'

She nodded and moved over to the bed, carefully picking up the bowl and holding it closer to Elalia. Meg moved back to the main room, and piled up the plates and tipped goblets. She dusted off the parchments covered in crumbs and piled them on the only clean part of the table she could find.

'Do not touch anything,' Elalia called out and then vomited.

'I am surprised that continues,' Meg said sharply. 'I do not read your papers, just move them.' She continued to pull the pile together.

'Why are you here?' Elalia called out.

Meg opened her mouth and then closed it. She'd had a clear idea in her mind as she had walked toward her sister's rooms that she could convince her that she had been mistaken about Tand's hand in the attack in the garden. But as she listened to her sister in the next room, she realised that no words would help; in fact, they would probably only act to push her in another direction, and that direction was looking more and more like Luana.

As the nurse entered the room, she slowed to look at the mess before her. Meg indicated the bedchamber and followed her in. The nurse felt her patient's forehead before sitting in the space Terra had just vacated. 'Take that out,' she said to the girl. 'And bring fresh water.'

She nodded and took off quickly. Meg could send her on another errand with the countless plates when she returned. As the nurse took over with Elalia's care, Meg moved around the room picking up clothing and material from the floor. Beautiful gowns lay crumpled on the rushes and when she picked them up, there were shoes and various things beneath them.

One dress she picked up was torn so badly it would never be repaired. She held it up for Elalia to see, but she waved her off. Terra reappeared with water and the look of someone wanting to run.

'She would not let me in,' the girl said, standing in the doorway. Meg nodded.

'Gossip and lies,' Elalia said.

'It is not, Your Highness,' the girl implored.

'What is?' Meg asked, dropping the dress over a chair and relieving the girl of the pitcher. She poured a little into the bowl beside the bed and then sat it on the newly cleared table. 'What is gossip and lies?' she repeated, turning back to the girl.

'I fear the princess is in danger,' she said.

Meg looked from Elalia back to Terra. 'What danger?'

'Her husband plots with her cousins,' she said, her eyes never leaving Elalia.

'Elalia, you should have this checked.'

'Malin would not,' she wheezed. 'I am carrying his child.'

She heaved again into the dish and lay back against the soiled sheets.

'How do you know this?' Meg asked the girl.

She paused, still looking at Elalia, who now sat back with her eyes shut. 'I met a man in the kitchen,' she said quietly. The sister muttered something under her breath and Meg urged the maid to go on.

'A nice man. He is the manservant of your cousins. Princess Elalia said I am to give him whatever he needs.'

Meg raised her eyebrows and the girl blushed. 'I was in the kitchen store and I heard him telling someone that your cousins are strange. And the girl he was talking with said all royalty was strange in some way, begging your pardon.'

Meg smiled.

'He said,' she went on, 'that the older brother is very serious but spends all his time with his lady wife, in their bed chamber, and she wears no clothes and...'

'How is that a threat?' Meg prompted.

She took a deep breath. 'They have talked of removing the princess before, he said. And then the prince visited with them and they enlisted his help.'

'Lies,' Elalia called weakly. She swallowed and the nurse wiped her face with the cloth. She nodded and Meg waited.

'There is more,' the maid whispered.

Meg nodded for her to go on.

'The Lady Sera is unwell.'

'Unwell?' Meg asked.

The girl chewed her lip and looked at the floor. Elalia reached out to grab her arm but she stepped out of her reach. She looked like a frightened bird. 'Lady Sera,' she began shakily, 'is sick because her baby died.'

'Oh my,' breathed Meg.

'Thank the... gods,' Elalia muttered, pushing the bowl and nurse away from her. 'Bring me water,' she muttered as the woman headed out of the room. 'Tell me all.'

'It came too early. There was too much blood.'

'Who was there?' Elalia asked.

'Her maid and a nurse from the Brotherhood.'

'Is that all?' Elalia pressed.

'Her brother,' Terra answered. 'They are quite close.'

'Was it his child?' Elalia asked.

'Seriously?' Meg bit down hard on her lip and took a step back, her sister's green eyes dangerously bright. 'Your husband visited his friend after the child was removed.'

Elalia stared her down.

'They say in the kitchens that she would not let him in and he forced his way, and that she hit him and it made her worse.'

'She has spurned him, it seems. Let us be sure,' she said. 'Send for the Lady Sera. I would like to check her illness for myself.'

'I think you would be best to focus on your own health for the moment.'

Elalia glared at her again.

'Where is the Silent Mother?' Meg asked suddenly, thinking it strange that Elalia would have excluded her friend at such a time. 'And when are you to announce the news?'

'Not your concern,' Elalia muttered, sipping slowly from the cup the nurse held.

Meg looked back at the girl. 'You can order the rest,' she said. Everyone knew what Malin was up to, including Elalia. If it was for the nurse's sake that she continued the denial, it was wasted breath, for the Sisters of the Brotherhood knew better than to share secrets. Although she was sure some secrets had been told already.

'Should I send for the Silent Mother?'

'No,' Elalia said quickly, waving the nurse away.

Meg watched her for a moment, unsure why she would not want the woman close. The image of the shadows in the chapel made her shiver and she wondered if her sister had any idea of what the Silent Mother really did.

Meg watched the girl collecting dresses from the floor. 'Are you sure about Malin?' she asked her.

'He was, Your Highness, and that was enough for me.'

Meg nodded, unless it was an idea planted to unsettle Elalia. She glanced at her sister. 'Well at least you are not dying,' Meg said. 'I suggest the bedding next,' she said to Terra.

'Where are you going?' Elalia asked.

'Someone from this family must make an appearance in the Hall or more questions will be asked than we could think to answer.' She rushed out into the crisp air and sucked in a deep breath. What would Malin hope to achieve by siding with her cousins? How much could Meg believe of Terra's story? Terra had no reason to lie, but Meg suddenly saw shadows everywhere and not just in the rooms.

'Cousin,' Creena called, as Meg walked into the Hall. 'I have not seen Elalia today.'

'I am afraid she is unwell,' Meg said.

'Oh dear, perhaps I should visit,' Creena suggested.

'I would not recommend it,' she said with a shiver. 'Some stomach illness.' She screwed up her face. 'And the nurses are with her, for she has been vomiting all day.'

'Oh,' Creena said, looking a little green. She took a step back. 'And Kellin? I hope she has not caught this illness as well.'

Meg looked about the Hall for a moment. It wasn't like Kellin to miss an evening of talk and gossip with others. 'I haven't seen her,' she murmured.

'Nor the Lady Sera. I hear she too is unwell.'

Meg did her best to keep her attention on the room in fear she may ask for the truth from her cousin. She was surprised to see

Brother Erasmus enter the Hall.

She walked quickly toward him, aware that he would only be there if it was essential. 'Brother Erasmus, I would like to talk with you.'

'And I you,' he said. 'I...'

Malin swept into the room clapping his hands loudly, and the conversations around the room died. 'I have some news,' he shouted at the room.

Meg found herself stepping closer to the Brother. 'This is not a good idea,' she muttered.

'What isn't?' Brother Erasmus asked, but Meg was focused on the passive face of the Silent Mother across the room and she wondered why she was here, or at least what she was here for, rather than at her prayer or with Elalia. The woman's eyes were focused on Malin and Meg realised that Elalia didn't want the woman to know she was with child. But she couldn't determine why that would be.

'Princess Elalia and I are delighted to announce that we expect our first child in the summer.' He grinned broadly to the room.

'He already knew,' Meg whispered, wondering how long they had kept the secret and whether Elalia knew of the other child.

A cheer went up in the room and clapping started, he bowed politely and then turned on his heel. Meg hoped it was to visit with his wife rather than the Lady Sera, but then she might be forgotten now that there was another child on the way.

'Well,' Brother Eramus said. 'I had not expected that news.'

'I would have thought they would have waited, and announced the news together. She is quite unwell.'

Brother Erasmus nodded, but she was watching across the room. The passive face of the Silent Sister cracked a little, her cheeks reddened, and she turned her back on the room to look into the fire. As Meg left the Hall, she realised that she and Brother Erasmus had not continued their conversation.

20

Meg was surprised to see Malin sitting on the edge of the bed wiping over Elalia's brow with the soft cloth when she entered the room. Elalia laid back with her eyes closed and murmured thanks while he sat over her.

'How does she feel today?' she asked.

'Better,' Elalia murmured, 'now that my nurse is more handsome.'

'It will pass, so I believe,' Meg murmured so that they didn't hear her. Loudly she said, 'Is there anything I can do to be of assistance while you are confined to your bed?'

Elalia shook her head slowly.

'Brother Erasmus said he was happy for me to...'

'Brother Erasmus,' she croaked, interrupting, 'is not Queen.'

'Nor is anyone else yet,' Meg whispered.

'I am still the eldest sister and well enough, I am sure, to do what is required.' She pushed his hand away from her brow. 'I know my duty to the kingdom.'

Malin stood suddenly. 'Duty,' he said. 'I did mine; you are pregnant and I deserve some recognition. Yet you can only complain that I would make the announcement without you.'

Meg took a step back and nearly knocked over a frozen Terra in the process. Both women took another slow step backward.

'Duty,' Elalia said again, 'Duty. That is all you saw it as.' She started to cry, large tears rolling down her cheeks, and Meg wanted to rush forward but she stayed where she was. 'They say you plot against me, that you bed any woman with breath in her body.'

'I prefer a good bosom,' he said.

Elalia launched the bowl beside her at him with surprising force and it shattered on the ground at his feet, water spilling across the rushes.

Terra made to move forward but Meg caught her arm. Meg realised the two had completely forgotten that she and Terra were in the room, so engrossed they were in their... Meg swallowed hard, not even knowing what to call it.

Elalia suddenly pulled her night shirt open and held her own breasts up to him. 'I have a good bosom,' she said.

'And they will grow,' he muttered, moving closer. 'As the child grows and swells in your belly...' he reached forward but Elalia smacked his hand away, pulling her shirt around her again.

The scene unravelling before Meg revolted her. Terra was frozen in place, horror reflected in her brown eyes. Her skin was pale. Meg was sure her own was drained of blood as well.

'I am still your husband,' Malin was saying, practically leering.

'Now that I have what I wanted, I may not need you. And you were hardly keen to be my husband and all that such a position entailed before.'

Meg could feel Terra shaking. Her hand still tight on the girl's slender arm, she quietly backed the two of them out of the room. 'You will not speak a word of this to anyone,' she said, turning on the girl, and she nodded. 'Not one.'

Terra nodded more vigorously. 'Yes, Highness,' she mumbled.

Meg let go and stood straight, giving the girl a small nod, and she fled. Meg, stunned by the display, stood for a moment longer and heard no further conversation from the bed chamber. She slowly followed Terra's path once the noise had died down and she was certain they wouldn't hurt one another.

She passed the Silent Mother in the Hallway, and she nodded slowly to the woman but received no acknowledgement in return. Meg walked quicker and then stopped at the top of the stairs to see the woman enter Elalia's rooms without knocking. She wondered if this was the woman's first visit since learning of Elalia's condition.

As she crossed the courtyard, Meg saw Kellin and waved. She was dressed for the cold weather with a thick cape. 'Where are you going?' Meg asked.

'I thought Elalia might like some fresh air and we could go for a walk.'

'A walk?' Meg asked. 'She has hardly left her bed all week.'

'And so she needs the exercise. She loves the snow and it is nearly gone.' The two looked at each other for a moment. 'I thought I could talk to her about Tands,' she said softly and Meg smiled, taking her hand.

'She won't listen,' Meg said, trying hard to come up with another reason. 'She has made up her mind and there is little that could change it.'

'I am hoping she is in a good mood now that she is with child, and despite my reservations, the prince is a good man. I think you would make an excellent pair.'

Meg opened her mouth and then closed it.

'I won't tell,' Kellin said. 'Did you think I would tell?'

Meg shook her head, wondering if she should just tell Kellin not to go. 'But it isn't worth dwelling on; she won't change her mind,' Meg said again. 'You only risk angering her further and she isn't exactly receptive to new ideas today.'

Kellin shook her head with a grin. 'I am only walking with my sister to talk about her child and if something else comes up, we can discuss that too.' She kissed Meg's cheek and walked swiftly across the courtyard. In relief, she spotted Malin going in the opposite direction. At least he wasn't in Elalia's room now.

CRULKO

Kellin had hoped to walk in the garden, but Elalia was having none of it. The Silent Mother had been standing at the foot of the bed, looking even more serious than she usually did, when Kellin had entered the room. At the suggestion of a walk, Elalia was only too keen but she baulked at the idea of the garden. Kellin worried that if she didn't walk there again soon, she would never enter the gates again.

'The garden holds too many risks,' Elalia said as they stood in the courtyard. The last of the snow blew around them and Elalia pulled up the hood of her cape. 'I would have thought that you wouldn't want to visit there again.'

'I fear that might be my problem,' Kellin said, looking across at the gates that led to the garden. 'There are guards with us, and the commander assured me that there was no risk.'

'I think there is always a risk,' Elalia said, looking about the courtyard. 'There are very few about today.'

'It is cold,' Kellin said. 'Which way shall we walk?'

Elalia shrugged but walked toward the market. More people moved around between the stalls despite the cold and Kellin wondered how long it had been since she'd had the chance to walk amongst them herself. The guards, following a few paces behind, coughed and when Kellin turned, one moved around to stand beside her. 'It is too crowded, Your Highness,' he said. Kellin sighed and Elalia nodded.

'We could walk the halls,' Kellin moaned, looking beyond the market to the barracks and wondering if the commander was close by.

'I want to walk in the air,' Elalia said. 'I suppose we could try the garden.'

Kellin smiled but her guard frowned. 'The commander said there was no further risk,' she said.

He nodded once. 'Are you sure?' he asked.

'I don't think we need take questions from you,' Elalia snapped.

'He is only trying to keep us safe,' Kellin said. 'He may be right.'

Elalia waved her hand and walked quickly toward the garden gate, Kellin skipping to keep up with her, and the two guards fell into place behind them.

As they entered the tall, hedge-lined path, Kellin stopped and Elalia motioned to her to keep going. 'This might have been a bad idea,' she whispered.

Elalia continued and, taking a deep breath, Kellin followed. Elalia marched along the path and Kellin realised that there was no way her sister would be open to any discussion about Tands and Meg. She cursed herself for thinking she could sway her so easily. The prince appeared to be a good man, and he so clearly cared for Meg. Too late, Kellin thought the garden walk would probably now only reinforce Elalia's feelings about Tands.

After a little while, Kellin was lost in her thoughts, dreaming of Meg and Brodwyn together, sitting side by side before the people of Rocfeld and Tands when she stopped. There wasn't a sound in the garden but she had the strangest feeling someone was watching them.

Kellin screamed as the shadows beneath the trees on the other side of the garden moved. The guards rushed forward but something shiny raced at them and she threw herself at Elalia, knocking her to the ground.

Elalia cried out and pushed at Kellin but she stayed as she was, fear causing her to freeze. The guards ran off through the garden, chasing down the shadow, and Kellin focused on Elalia's hard stare. 'I'm sorry,' she said, sitting back in the cold, wet mud of the garden bed. She tried to lighten the mood. 'I think I killed a flower. Are you hurt?' she asked.

Elalia's sharp slap across her cheek was a surprise.

'There was someone there,' she said, her hand to her cheek.

The guards returned at the same moment, one nodding agreement.

'You did this,' Elalia screamed, holding out her hand for the guard to help her to her feet.

Kellin shook her head vigorously. 'I was trying to push you out of the way.'

'Of an attack you orchestrated,' she said, brushing at the mud on her cape and dress.

'No.'

'Yes,' she said, her voice strangely calm as she indicated to the guards. 'My sister has tried to have me killed. You will arrest her.'

'Elalia,' Kellin pleaded as each guard took her beneath the arm and lifted her to her feet.

'I am sorry,' one of them murmured.

'Don't you dare apologise to her. She is a threat to the kingdom. Or I shall have you locked up for conspiring with her.'

Neither spoke again as they maintained their hold on her and directed her toward the castle, too stunned to do anything but let them direct her. It was only as they headed toward the stairs that led to her rooms that Elalia spoke again.

'I don't think locking the princess in her room is appropriate,' she snapped. 'Take her down to the cells.'

The guards froze, Kellin still held tight between them, only now she writhed about, trying to pull from their tight hold, her feet barely touching the ground.

'I am the eldest,' Elalia said loudly. 'You will do as I direct until such time as a queen is marked.'

'Yes, Your Highness,' the one on Kellin's right said, turning her about.

'Elalia, please,' she begged, still trying to break free of the iron grip they maintained on her arms. 'I love you. I would never hurt you.'

Her sister waved a hand and disappeared. As she left them, the tight grip on each arm loosened a little, but they still directed her to a part of the castle she hadn't been before. The stairs were dark and narrow and she nearly slipped several times, but they maintained their hold.

The smell of rotting straw was overpowering as she entered the underground space, and she blinked to adjust to the dim light but couldn't see. She could hear murmurs and the movement of others but she couldn't make out who was there. A door squeaked open and she was led into a small room. A small, barred window let in very little light and the door was not solid, but made of bars.

'I shall organise some more straw to make you comfortable,' one guard said and disappeared.

The other simply bowed his head and pushed the bars closed, turning a large key. Kellin struggled to swallow as the lock clicked loudly. She dropped to the floor and pulled her wet cape tight around her. The straw was damp and smelt of urine. As the walls came into focus she could make out scratch marks, and what could have been blood splattered across one wall. She closed her eyes; she didn't want to think about who had been here before her or how long she might remain here. She sniffed to prevent the tears, but instantly regretted it as the smell of urine and mould made her gag.

Hot tears ran down her face. This morning she had been nervous about discussing Tands with her sister. Now she thought it would have been much easier to deal with than this. She pushed herself up and stood against the door, the bars icy cold in her hands and against her face. The light was dim in the room beyond and she couldn't hear anything.

'Hello?' she called out.

'No one comes til evening, miss,' a rough voice called out.

Kellin stepped back from the bars and shivered. She pulled her wet cape around her again, but it wasn't going to help her. She ran her hand over one of the grooves carved into the wall to find the stone as cold as the bars. She was going to freeze to death before she had the chance to defend herself against Elalia's accusations. As she stood shivering in the middle of the cell, she wondered who had been under the tree. Someone was trying to hurt Elalia. Or was it Elalia trying to hurt her?

CRED

Elalia pulled the blanket tighter around her shoulders as she huddled before the fire. She couldn't stop shivering. Her clothes had long since dried but the idea that someone was actively working against her scared her more than she thought it would.

There was muffled discussion at the door and she hoped that the guards wouldn't allow anyone else to enter. Malin had appeared only briefly to confirm that she had survived and then disappeared again. She needed the image of the perfect family, but she didn't need him pestering her day and night.

She watched the door closely but breathed a sigh of relief when the Silent Mother entered.

'Tell me they weren't trying to keep you out?' Elalia asked at the dark look on her face.

She shook her head. 'I was curious as to what they did to find the culprit and how such a thing happened in the first place.'

Elalia looked back at the fire. 'I know my sisters are jealous of me, but I did not realise just how strongly Kellin felt about who should be Queen.'

'Are you sure your sister was involved?'

Elalia nodded, her eyes still fixed on the dance of the flames before her.

'Sure that she would kill you?'

'Maybe she only wanted to scare me,' she said, looking up to the woman standing beside her. 'She did push me out of the way— or it might have been into the way. I don't know,' she said, standing quickly. 'Perhaps she wasn't involved and she saw something and was trying to warn me.'

'What did you see?' the Sister asked, taking her hands.

'Shadows,' Elalia muttered, pulling away from her. She pulled at the blanket around her shoulders and sat at the table. She reached forward, poured wine into a goblet and took a large gulp before looking back at the Silent Mother, still standing by the fire. 'What do you know?' she asked, putting the goblet down slowly. There was something stiff about her. She was always self-assured, but she seemed far more distant and it made Elalia more nervous. 'Do you think Sythia is in danger? That someone attempts to prevent our help?'

The woman's face softened a little and sat at the table. 'No one would know of our work unless they were told directly.'

Elalia stared for a moment and then shook her head. 'No,' she whispered.

'I did not think you would tell,' she said softly. 'But I would hope that you would tell me everything, for the only way to assist Sythia is together.'

Elalia nodded and felt her face heat. She took another gulp of the wine.

'The news of your child was shared with all Rocfeld by your husband, and yet you have not said a word.'

Elalia studied the movement of the wine in the cup. 'I know it was not part of the plan.'

'Not everything goes to plan,' she replied. 'But we will find a way to bring you back onto the path.'

Elalia looked up sharply to be met with the same serious stillness in the Silent Mother, and she wondered if she should not have waited. 'We have been married long enough that people talked that we did not yet have a child. There are certain expectations,' she said softly.

'Perhaps,' the Silent Mother said, slowly nodding. 'And yet you know Sythia's expectations are more important than those of the people of Rocfeld.'

'But without the people of Rocfeld, I will never be queen,' she said, trying to stress the importance of what she had done without sounding like she was whining about it.

The Silent Mother raised her eyebrows and Elalia realised that she hadn't succeeded. 'There is time,' she stated firmly. 'You must refocus. We will pray and then I have another drink for you.'

Elalia felt the same reservation she had when she had taken the last cup from the Silent Mother, and she struggled to respond.

'Is this child more important than Sythia?' The Silent Mother, leaning forward just a little, asked it kindly but her eyes were hard.

Elalia felt a fear she had never experienced with this woman. She shook her head slowly.

'If you are worthy, Sythia herself may visit with you in prayer.'

'Will she be angry with me?' she whispered, her mouth drying and her heart beating so fast Elalia was sure that it would leave her chest.

'You are the way for Sythia,' the Silent Mother said slowly. 'We cannot help her return without you. You,' she said firmly, reaching forward and taking Elalia by the chin, her strong fingers biting into the skin, 'are the only way.'

Elalia nodded and she released her hold.

'Now warm yourself and put your sisters out of your mind. Tomorrow morning I shall come for you before the sun rises.'

Elalia nodded again and sat still, watching the woman leave the room. Once the door closed, she drained what wine was left in her cup and then refilled it and drained it again. The warmth of the wine filtered out to her fingers and her fear dulled a little. She refilled the cup once more and then pushed up from the table. Taking the cup back to the fire, she dropped down before it and focused on the flames. If Kellin hadn't been trying to kill her, who could it have been?

21

Kellin sat up at the sound of the bars rattling and was surprised that she had managed to fall asleep. She was still wet through, and was sure she smelt as bad as the cell around her. Her face was as cold as the stone she had slept against.

'Get up,' a voice screamed as the door squeaked open.

'By the gods.'

The deep voice startled her and she looked up at the bulk of a man coming through the door. She shuffled back out of his reach.

'It is me,' he said softly, squatting down before her, 'Commander Rainger.'

Large tears welled and slid down her face before she could stop them, unsure if his presence indicated things were better or worse than she imagined.

'The prisoner attempted to kill Princess Elalia,' another guard snapped, stepping into the light.

'The prisoner is Princess Kellin,' Commander Rainger said. 'I wonder how you would explain her illness and death from cold to the people of Rocfeld?'

'She was ordered locked up,' the other man said, not quite as confidently.

'Perhaps her sister only wanted her removed from sight. What is the evidence?' Commander Rainger asked, standing slowly.

The man shrugged and Kellin wiped the back of her hand across her face.

'Fetch a Sister, hot water and dry clothes,' the commander said with a strange calmness, and the man saluted and disappeared.

'Can I come out now?' Kellin asked.

The commander shook his head slowly. 'I'm afraid not. An allegation has been made that you were involved in an attack on a royal person; a witness saw you push the princess into the path of danger and so you must remain here.'

Kellin sniffed in a sob before it could escape. 'I wouldn't hurt Elalia.'

'There is a lot of speculation as to who should be queen and maybe someone is trying to influence that,' he said. 'Your sister announced that you would go to the Brotherhood; perhaps you wanted that changed.'

'That was Father's wish,' she whispered. 'I don't want to be Queen.'

The man sighed and then looked around the space. 'Did they bring fresh straw?'

She shook her head.

There was some grumbling from outside the cell and Kellin longed to look out and see who was there.

'Fresh straw,' the commander said. 'And where is the Sister?'

More mumbling and then quiet.

'Come,' he said, holding out his hand.

Kellin carefully put her hand in his and allowed him to pull her to her feet. Unsteady on her feet, he was quick to put his hand under her elbow and direct her out of the narrow doorway to a table that sat in the small space outside the cells. The fireplace was dark and cold and a single candle burned on the table.

The commander directed her into a chair, and there was bread and a cup of wine before her. Without waiting, she picked up the bread and tore into it with her teeth. She had never been so hungry in her life and she chewed quickly and swallowed, tearing off another chunk. She tried to eat as quickly as possible, but it stuck in her throat. She clung tight to the bread in one hand and reached for the wine, gulping it down, hoping it would unstick the bread, but all she did was cough.

'Slow down,' the commander said softly, gently patting her back until the coughing subsided.

She nodded slowly and took another bite of the bread.

The other man arrived with a steaming bucket, which he sat

heavily on the table, some of the water sloshing over the sides, a Sister just behind him holding what she hoped was dry clothes. Kellin dropped the bread and stood quickly, using the table to balance, and took the Sister's outstretched hands in hers.

'Let us get you cleaned and dry,' the Sister said, pointing toward the steaming bucket.

Kellin pushed her hands into the water, her sleeves along with them. It was such a relief and yet she wondered how long until she was left in the cold again. She shivered and the Sister pushed a small cloth into the hot water.

'Fetch two blankets,' the commander ordered the other man, and Kellin listened to his steps disappeared along the corridor. 'We shall try to make you as comfortable as possible,' he said softly and disappeared inside the cell.

The Sister allowed her to keep her hands in the water as she gently washed her face, and then she took it in her hands. 'You need to change out of the wet and into the dry,' she said, glancing over her shoulder toward the cell. 'Commander,' she called. 'I need you to stay where you are.'

A young boy arrived with a shovel just as she said it and he stopped, looking between the two women and the cell. 'In here, boy,' the commander called.

The sound of scraping metal across the stones echoed through the space and Kellin shivered. The Sister quickly unlaced her dress and helped her out of it and her damp under dress. Kellin shivered and prayed no one else would be arriving to see her in this state.

The clean under dress was soft and dry and she was thankful to be covered at least. The dress itself had a grey, rough weave and was coarse against her skin as the Sister pulled it over her head. She ran her hands over it, trying not to be disappointed. Even her maid wore better. But she was warmer.

Looking down at her muddy shoes, she realised the dress was shorter than it should have been, and the Sister held up a shoe. Nodding, Kellin sat back in the chair and picked up the bread, pulling smaller pieces from it, but as hungry as she was she couldn't swallow it.

'How long is this to continue?' she asked, lifting the cup and finding that her hand still shook. The Commander reappeared at the cell door.

'As long as it must,' he said, leaning on the back of the other chair. 'I'm afraid it will depend on your sister.'

'Does Meg know?' she asked.

He shook his head. 'I can't take a message from a prisoner, Your Highness.'

She nodded slowly but glanced at the Sister who gave her a little smile. She gave a nod to the commander, scooped up Kellin's wet clothes and, taking the bucket, she moved quickly toward the steps. Kellin couldn't take her eyes from the grey tunic as she carefully navigated her way into the light.

The scraping of metal on stone started again as the boy pushed the putrid straw out into the small area by the table. Kellin covered her face and then he too was running after the Sister, up the steps and away.

Kellin focused on the little flame sitting strong and tall on the candle. Not a hint of a breeze, and she gulped down the fear of suffocation. She only looked away from the flame at the sound of movement, and Commander Rainger had come to stand beside her.

'It is time,' he said softly and nodded toward the cell.

She stood slowly and walked unassisted into her new home. Fresh straw had been piled in one corner and it smelt so sweet. Before she had the chance to ask anything else, the guard returned with two blankets, which he tossed onto the straw and then he glared at the Commander.

Commander Rainger closed the cell door behind her and she discovered that the new straw went only a little way to improving the overpowering smell of the cell.

'Take a blanket and spread it out,' the Commander said, 'then wrap yourself in the other. It will go a long way to keeping you warmer.'

She glanced from the blankets to him and picked one up, trying to untangle it from its folds. The guard tittered in the darkness beyond the bars.

'Enough,' the Commander chastised.

In the new silence, she shook the blanket to unravel it and she dropped it over the straw—in more of a pile than she had aimed for, but it would work. She shook out the other and pulled it around her shoulders like a cape. It wasn't nearly as warm as her other would have been if it were dry, but it would have to do. She sat down slowly, pulling her legs in underneath herself, her new bed somewhat sharper than it was before.

The commander nodded and gave her a small smile. 'I have work to do,' he said softly. 'I will return.'

She nodded once and listened to his regular steps move away into the darkness. The unsettling, toothy smile of the guard appeared at the bars and then disappeared, but he didn't seem to travel far and she wondered if he remained just out of the light, watching her.

22

'I said no visitors,' the young woman by the fire said quietly as Elalia was shown into the room.

How long since she had seen her? The plump, rosy girl had disappeared and was replaced with a pale, broken woman. Elalia fought back her pity for the girl and stepped forward.

'I heard you were unwell,' she said. 'I came to see if there is anything I can do?'

'To see what your husband has done,' Sera responded without looking away from the flames.

Elalia tried to keep the smile in place as she sat in the chair beside the girl, the sheen of the material reflecting the light as she smoothed out her dress. 'How can I help?' she asked.

'You cannot,' Sera said. 'There is nothing to help. There is no help. My child is gone,' she croaked and looked up with red eyes.

'You will have more.' Elalia forced the words from her lips. 'When you marry...'

'I cannot marry,' she said, wiping at the tears that fell. 'I am spoilt and no man shall have me.'

She was right, and Elalia had come to press that very point; she had come to make threats and tell of rumours that did not exist of her and her brother. But she felt a kinship to this woman that she did not want to feel.

'I will arrange something,' she said, softly. 'We will find a way.'

Sera looked at her with curiosity. 'What will Malin say to that?'

she asked quietly.

'Malin will do as he is told,' Elalia snapped. Taking a deep breath, she smiled for the woman beside her.

'He will not leave me alone,' she said, her shoulders slumping. 'He calls and yet I cannot make him understand that I do not wish to see him.' She looked Elalia square in the eye. 'For I do not, Your Highness, wish to ever see him again.'

Elalia nodded. 'I could organise a marriage far away,' she said.

The woman leaned forward in her chair. 'How far?'

'My cousins visit from Lekland. My young cousin, and a favourite of my uncle, is searching for a wife. It could be a way to keep you safe.'

'And far away,' she said. 'I am not the only one, Highness.' She reached forward and clutched Elalia's hand.

'I am with child myself.' Elalia pulled her hand out of the girl's hold, ignoring her words.

'Why are you here?' she asked.

Elalia followed the girl's gaze into the fireplace and wondered if she found it as calming as Elalia did herself. She wanted the little distraction gone. 'I was attacked in the garden,' she said quickly. 'I wanted to ensure you were not involved.'

'Why would I attack you?' the girl asked, more confused than taken back, and Elalia wondered what Malin saw in her.

'So that you can have my husband,' Elalia said, locking eyes with Sera. She was pretty, she had to give her that.

She shook her head vigorously. 'I told you,' she said. 'I don't want him here.'

'Maybe you want one of my sisters to be queen,' Elalia said with care.

Sera pushed up slowly from the chair and Elalia winced at the obvious pain it took her to do so. 'Why are you here?' she asked. 'You think I plot against you and yet you offer your cousin in marriage. You sound as though you care and yet you doubt my every move.'

Elalia sighed. 'I want you away from my husband. The cousin is a good compromise, and the only offer you will get.' She stood and smoothed over her dress. 'My family must come first.'

Sera nodded slowly. 'That I do understand.'

'Try to make yourself presentable and I shall organise the

introduction.'

Sera sat down slowly and refocused on the flames. 'You will do as you please.'

'Yes,' Elalia said, watching the girl for a moment, and then left, unsure if she had succeeded in what she had come for. The Silent Mother would call it another distraction, but she had to remove the distractions before they influenced whether or not she would be queen.

As she entered the private chapel, Elalia was almost sure that the shadows in the room withdrew. Without looking up from her position of prayer, the Silent Mother motioned her closer. 'All I do, I do for Sythia,' she murmured as she knelt beside the Silent Mother. She might doubt me, she thought, but Sythia will see it for what it is when she comes again.

'Were you lost?' the Silent Mother asked after a moment.

'I had something to take care of,' she said. 'Have the shadows spoken?'

'I am sure they have much to say to you,' she said quietly, 'And yet here is silence.'

Elalia opened her mouth and then closed it again. Silence assisted them. In the Silence they heard Sythia. 'Do you doubt me?' she asked, sitting back on the cold flagstones and studying the woman beside her. 'Do you think it a mistake that Sythia has chosen me as her vessel?'

The Silent Mother didn't turn away from the small altar, but shook her head. 'I doubt your commitment to Sythia.'

Elalia was taken by surprise. 'All I do, I do for Sythia!'

'The child is not part of Sythia's plan. Your husband was not part of Sythia's plan,' she said quickly, and Elalia wondered how long the Silent Mother had been hiding such thoughts.

'Sythia's plan involves me being Queen. If I am not Queen, it doesn't matter how much we have tried to prepare. There is too much speculation as to why a queen was not chosen at my father's death. And why the gods wait, still, to mark one. I must do all I can to show that I am what this kingdom needs, for the gods and the people to want me as Queen. A stable marriage and children is part of that image. You know that I do all I can for Her. And I will continue to do all I can in Her name.'

The Silent Mother nodded once. 'Do you feel well?' she asked.

The question surprised Elalia and she didn't respond.

'Do you feel the heat?'

Elalia remembered the sticky heat she had felt after the last cup she had taken from the Silent Mother and she shook her head slowly.

'It will return; we will do all we can together.'

Elalia stood and followed the woman out of the chapel. As she entered the dark room, the same uneasiness settled on her. 'This will not harm the child?' she asked.

'If Sythia wills it, no harm shall come to your child.'

Elalia nodded slowly, but the Silent Mother's words gave her little comfort. 'Could we not find a way to encourage the mark?' Elalia asked.

'The gods would see it for what it was and all would be lost.'

'Yet they cannot see what we do for Sythia.'

'The Silence we work within shrouds us from the gods. We protect them from the evils of what lies within as well as protect mankind. They cannot see us. Elalia, precious one,' she added in a whisper, taking Elalia's hands, her own soft yet strong. 'Sythia named you at your birth as her chosen one. Have faith that she chose for good reason.'

'Rocfeld is a distraction,' she muttered.

'True, but you are strong enough to fight it. Focus as you did at the Sanctuary.'

'What if I can't?'

'Do you doubt now?' the Silent Mother asked, her voice harsh. She reached out an old hand toward Elalia's stomach and she stepped back. 'This child is a distraction.'

Elalia shook her head quickly. 'It is the risk to us from my sisters, or others trying to implicate my sisters.' She paused, looking seriously at the woman in the dim light. 'What would they gain from such action?' she asked.

The Silent Mother turned her back and moved small clay bowls around on the far bench. A raven cried out. 'Perhaps there are some that think the crown will be marked outside the family,' she said.

'What do we do?' Elalia pleaded.

It was the soft and gentle face that she knew that turned back to her with a cup held firmly in her outstretched hand. 'You have faith that Sythia does what is best.'

Elalia took the cup and hoped that Sythia wasn't as disappointed in her behaviour as the Silent Mother was, and decide that the crown would sit best on someone else's head.

'Faith,' the Silent Mother whispered as the raven called softly from its cage in the dark.

'Sythia,' Elalia mouthed silently and gulped down the contents of the cup. She tried not to screw up her face at the bitterness of the thick liquid, and she was thankful for the dark. But as soon as she handed the cup back to the waiting woman, her whole body felt light and not as solid as it was before. As though it didn't belong to her anymore, and she couldn't stop her arms from floating away. She ran a hand over her arm and the sensation on her skin was vague, as though her fingers didn't quite exist. She wondered for a moment if she was turning into a shadow herself, and then with surprising force the weight returned and she felt heavy and full and tired.

'The feeling may come and go,' the Silent Mother said. 'Go.'

Elalia bowed her head and turned slowly, surprised at the effort required to turn her body. Once outside the room she leaned heavily into the wall. She shook her head slowly and pushed up to walk toward her own door, where a guard stepped forward.

'Elalia,' Meggie called, racing toward her.

She tried to wave her off, but her arm was too heavy.

The guard surprised her by lifting her into his arms as the world seemed to spin before her, and he followed Meggie into the room. She raced ahead, pulling the covers back on the bed, but Elalia shook her head. The room stopped spinning, but Meggie remained where she was and the guard placed Elalia down and stood with his back to the door.

Meggie pulled her shoes quickly from her feet, plumped pillows and guided her back before pulling up the covers. 'Do you want for anything?'

'You to stand back,' she muttered.

'I heard there was an attack in the garden. I worry that it isn't safe.'

Elalia shook her head.

'Were you hurt?' Meggie asked, sitting carefully on the side of the bed and reaching out for her hand.

She wanted to pull it away but she had never felt so heavy.

'I can't find Kellin,' she whispered. 'I'm so worried.'

As Elalia took a deep breath, lightness filled her again. Her hands seemed uncontrollable and when she studied them she was sure she could see right through them. She wondered if she would turn into a shadow after all.

'Elalia,' Meggie said loudly and she looked up at her concerned face, wondering what Meggie would do if she faded before her. 'Have you seen Kellin?'

'No,' she whispered.

'When was the attack in the garden?' Meggie asked forcefully, and then looked at the guard.

'Yesterday,' he said.

'Yesterday?' she repeated loudly, and Elalia squeezed her eyes closed against her. 'Why didn't you say? What if something has happened to Kellin?' she said.

'Kellin is fine,' Elalia murmured and then opened her eyes just as the guard opened his mouth, but she glared at him and he closed it quickly.

'How do you know?' Meggie asked, but Elalia closed her eyes again as the heaviness washed over her. 'Do you want me to fetch someone for you? Malin or the Silent Mother?'

'No,' Elalia said. 'I want to sleep.'

'A nurse?'

'Go away,' she said, pulling the blankets up around her shoulders and squeezing her eyes closed even tighter, hoping they would simply leave her alone.

In the silence that followed, Elalia slipped into sleep but she dreamt of the chapel, the door closed against the world and the candles burning down too quickly. She tried the latch but her hand faded in and out of focus and she couldn't get hold of anything. And then the door swung open and Sythia stood tall and strong in the doorway, preventing her from leaving, and as she smiled, Elalia faded away to nothing.

She woke with a start, her heart beating fast, her skin clammy, and she had thrown the blankets back. She held her hands up before her and they appeared as solid as they ever had.

23

Meg searched the room as the usual people started arriving. Kellin still hadn't appeared and she was concerned. Malin entered, flagged by two guards who he directed to stand by the door, his usual commander nowhere in sight.

'Where is your charming sister?' Tyne asked, catching her by surprise, and she looked up into his grinning face, any similarity he had to her kind cousin now vague and distant. And she tried not to shiver as he stepped forward to take her hand.

'I am trying to find her myself,' she said politely. 'And our cousins? Do they join you today?'

He nodded once. 'Creena comes now,' he said and pointed toward her as she worked her way through the people.

'Cousin,' she said sweetly. 'Kellin not with you today?'

'I cannot seem to find her,' Meg repeated. Uneasiness grew as a lump in her chest, making it harder to breathe. 'Where is Annar?' she asked quickly.

'She is feeling unwell, I fear, and Morley would not leave her side.'

'I hope it is nothing serious,' Meg said. 'I shall send for the nurse.' She turned but Creena grabbed her arm.

'Do not bother yourself, cousin. It will pass, I am sure.'

Meg smiled and nodded and wondered what ailment could possibly afflict Morley's perfect wife, and was frustrated at her chance to find her sister.

'The three of us.' Tyne smiled, drawing Meg's attention back to him. 'Have you any news from Tands?' he asked.

Meg shook her head.

'Such a shame that Elalia thought them involved in the attack. She must be busy preparing for her child,' he said. 'I have not seen her of late.'

'You may see her now,' Meg said, indicating the doorway where her sister floated through, all smiles and confidence.

'Where could Kellin be?' Creena asked again. 'She so likes to talk of court news, and we have spent so much time away from Rocfeld.'

'Your cousins say they do not know you. That they should like to know the two of you better,' Tyne whispered, standing too close to her.

Meg focused on his strange words. 'What is to know,' she asked, 'that you do not already?'

'Come, cousin.' Tyne added, 'You are too modest. I am sure your sister and yourself have many talents and interests that I am not aware of. You talk so long of a day to Creena and Annar, and yet you have nothing to share with me.'

'I fear,' she said, 'that we would have little to discuss of interest for a man such as yourself. Gossip and gowns and hair styles. Surely men of your position and education would not want to discuss such things.'

'Surely your education, as princess, would be of more than fine clothing and needlework,' Tyne said. 'Elalia was educated with the Silent Sisters, I understand.'

'She spent many years with them, but I fear Brother Erasmus would take far more credit with her education than they could.'

He raised his eyebrows and Meg smiled sweetly. What were they digging for? And why the interest in Kellin? He could hardly look at her when they arrived.

'Are you betrothed?' she found herself asking out loud and the smile slipped momentarily from Tyne's grinning face.

'At present, no, dear cousin. Do you have someone in mind?'

As she shook her head, her sister's voice said, 'I do.'

'Truly?' he said, turning his smile on her and dipping into a shallow bow. 'How lucky am I?' he asked.

'Very.' Elalia beamed. 'She is a dear, sweet creature. Although still young, you would find her good company.'

'And have I met the lady in question?' he asked, the charm appearing forced for the first time.

'Not yet,' she said. 'I am afraid she has been unwell, but she has a strong constitution and I hope to introduce you before you leave.'

'Leave?' Creena asked, her voice squeaky.

'Surely you travel homeward at some point,' she said.

Creena frowned. 'We are here to see the crowning,' she said. 'And Annar, my sister by marriage, is unwell and Morley worries for her health.'

'She seems so healthy,' Elalia mused. 'Meggie should fetch the nurse to her.'

'There is no need for such a bother,' Creena said quickly.

'It is no bother,' she said, still smiling, more than Meg had seen previously. 'Meggie would be honoured,' she added, waving Meg away.

'Have you seen Kellin?' she asked quickly.

Elalia shook her head and waved her off again.

Meg rushed from the room, almost running over a young Brother in the hallway. 'Can you direct me to a nurse?' she said.

'Are you ill, Your Highness?'

She shook her head. 'It is for my cousin, Annar.'

'I shall send a Sister to her rooms, do not fear.' He hurried off.

'Meggie,' Elalia said, appearing silently beside her as she entered the Hall. 'Did you find a nurse?'

She nodded and glanced toward Creena and Tyne speaking in hushed angry tones. 'She will go directly to Annar,' she said.

'Are you looking for someone?' Elalia asked.

'Kellin,' Meg said. And then blurted, 'Shouldn't Uncle find a wife for his... relative?' she could feel her face burning at her near blunder.

Elalia raised her eyebrows. 'Perhaps. But they are here and I have a dear friend I thought would suit him well.'

'A dear friend?'

'I do have friends,' she whispered and Meg bit her lip, wondering if her disbelief had shown on her face. Elalia didn't spend time with anyone. She didn't even have the time for her own sisters. She only had time for the Silent Mother. The idea made Meg shiver.

Meg looked about the room, unsure what else they could

discuss. Tands had gone, along with any chance at a connection. The emperor of Luana still filled the port with his boats and occasionally the Hall with his many men, most of them Meg was sure were his sons. But then none of them looked alike and yet they all looked the same in their long silk robes, long black hair and pointy beards.

She was tired of the people. She was tired of the noise. Not just the constant chatter and movement around the castle, but the whispers and stares and innuendo. She no longer cared who was marked as the Raven Queen; she only wanted the chance to get back to her life. Or a semblance of what it had been before her father's death.

Meg reached out and gently took Elalia's arm. 'Are you sure you haven't seen Kellin?' she asked slowly as she lifted her hand away. 'You are so hot,' she uttered with concern. 'Are you unwell?'

Elalia's face set into a blank canvas and Meg took a step back. 'It is the child,' she said softly. 'The body changes to accommodate the growing child.'

Meg nodded once but tried again, asking, 'Kellin?'

She had met many women with child over the years and none of them had changed in such a way. Why was Elalia so changeable and evasive? Meg tried again and raised her voice slightly, compelling Elalia to answer. 'Kellin? Have you seen her or know where she is?'

'I don't know,' she said, more forcefully than Meg was expecting, and she swung around and marched off across the room. Meg knew Elalia was lying. It had something to do with the attack, and no one was talking.

Meg took a deep breath. Her fingers still tingled from the heat she had felt through Elalia's sleeve. She shook her head and headed for the door. She kept going until she was standing in the quiet of the courtyard, the cool air blowing around her, snow still settling on the stones.

Looking across to the Temple she thought of the stories of Sythia, how she had tried to take over the Raven Queen and how the gods trapped her in the Silence. The cods had removed magic from the Raven Crown line, but could it be possible for magic to reappear?

'Your Highness,' a guard said, stepping from the shadows.

Meg jumped, pulled from her thoughts.

'I am sorry, Your Highness. I worry at you being in the cold.'

She nodded but remained where she was. 'Have you seen Kellin?' she asked.

The man nodded once.

She waited.

'She has been arrested.'

'Arrested?' she asked. 'For what crime?'

'An attack on Princess Elalia.'

Meg sighed before she could stop herself. 'And where is she?'

'In the dungeon.'

Dungeon? Meg clutched her hands in front of her before she could do or say anything silly. The world was not as it was, or was it that she was finally seeing the truth of it? Whatever the way of it, it would never be the same again. 'Take me to her, now,' she said authoritatively. The man turned on his heel immediately and led the way.

The castle appeared like a foreign land as she moved through doorways previously unknown and hallways that led to a part of the world she didn't want to understand. How could Kellin be pulled to such a place, and how much could Elalia do before she was clearly marked by the gods?

The overpowering smell of men and urine made her stop in the doorway.

'It is this way, Your Highness,' the guard called from ahead. She sucked in a breath and then started to cough. Covering her face with her sleeve, she nodded once and continued down the rough, worn steps.

How could Elalia have her own dear sister locked up in this horrid place? Meg reached the bottom and saw Commander Rainger standing from the small table as she entered the dimly lit space. Knowing he was here made her angry. Why hadn't he come and told her?

'Meg,' Kellin called from the gated doorway to the side. Meg looked between the two of them and then stepped up to the bars and took Kellin's hands.

'What has happened?' she asked. 'How long have you been here?'

'This is my second night,' she whispered, her teeth chattering and her fingers like ice. 'Elalia was attacked in the garden. We were attacked in the garden. But I saw something or someone and I pushed her out of the way, and she thinks that I was trying to kill her, that I had dragged her into the garden to meet her death.' She took a deep breath as her words had run quickly over each other. But the breath only rattled in her chest.

'Surely she doesn't need to be down here,' Meg said, turning to the commander.

'I have tried, Your Highness, but your sister is insistent.'

Meg shook her head. 'She'll die down here.'

'No,' Kellin whispered, pulling the rough blanket tighter around her shoulders. 'I'm sure Elalia will work out how to have me executed before then.'

Shocked to the core at Kellin's words and even believing her, she asked, suddenly distracted, 'What are you wearing?'

'I hardly think that is the most important point at the moment.'

'But it is always important to you,' Meg said as a tear tracked through the dirt on Kellin's cheek. 'You are always the most beautiful in the room.'

'Still am,' she whispered, a small smile pulling at her lips. 'You know I couldn't be outdone, not even here.'

Meg laughed despite the sharp pain in her chest and she pulled her sister close, the cold bars between them as she clung tight, and Kellin started to cry.

'She can't do this,' Meg whispered, wiping ineffectually at the tears running down Kellin's cheeks. She gave her sister's hands around the bars one last squeeze and she was up and out the stairs as quickly as she was able. She dragged in a deep breath of the fresh, icy air, trying to rid herself of the smell of the dungeons, but it clung to her skin. She turned to find the guard hard on her heels. 'Where is the royal commander?'

'At the barracks,' he said.

She nodded once and headed in the direction, the guard walking quickly beside her. 'He may not be able to assist you.'

She continued on without acknowledging his words. Someone had to have a way out of this. Once she reached the barracks she stopped, taking in the movement of men and horses around the space, and the guard pointed to a small, wooden building attached to the walls of the castle itself.

Meg didn't knock but pushed straight into the room, finding the royal commander and Commander Brent sitting together in the small space at the table. 'She'll die,' she announced to the room as they hastily stood.

The royal commander shook his head and indicated a chair, then poured wine into a cup and sat it in front of her. 'She won't die,' he said firmly, resuming his seat, as Commander Brent did the same. 'Rainger watches over her. She may be cold, but she is safe where she is.'

'Safe?' Meg clenched and unclenched her hands and then gripped the cup tightly and drank deeply.

'Someone wants to harm Elalia or Kellin or both,' he said calmly. 'Princess Elalia thinks Princess Kellin is the threat.' He held up his hand as Meg opened her mouth. 'We know that cannot be true, but we do not know who may wish them harm, and so it is best that Princess Elalia thinks that her wishes are being met and that we can keep a close eye on Princess Kellin.'

'To keep her safe,' Meg said slowly, comprehension dawning on her.

He nodded and gave her a soft, encouraging smile. Meg took another gulp of wine, considering the implications. The commander sat silently at the table between them.

'No one knows she is there,' she said, thankful that these men watched over them.

'Not really. Several people know of the arrest, but they would assume she was kept elsewhere, and for those that know the true whereabouts it must look as though she is arrested.'

'Hence the dress, and the cold and the smell.' Meg shuddered.

He nodded again, the smile lost from his dark-brown eyes.

She gulped down the rest of the cup and focused on the room around her; a narrow bed ran along one wall, the table taking up the rest of the small space. 'Why don't you have rooms in the castle?' she asked.

'My place is here with the men. I don't need anything fancy.'

Meg nodded slowly and somewhat dismayed, she said, 'I didn't know.'

'What didn't you know?'

'That you lived here, that Kellin had been arrested, that we had that place beneath our feet.' She glanced sideways and caught Commander Brent staring at her. Then he pushed his chair back, bowed slightly and left the room.

'Your Highness,' the royal commander said, moving to sit in the chair Brent had vacated and reaching out to take her hand. 'Much has happened over the last weeks and months. I have no doubt that you pay attention to all that occurs around you. There are many that would hide from you, or wish to hide from you, what is really happening in Rocfeld, but it will all be well.'

'How can you be so sure?'

'I have faith,' he said softly, squeezing his hand around hers. 'I know you have faith, and the gods will mark a new queen soon.'

Meg thought he was still treating her like a girl. She squeezed his hand, stood and stepped back, placing the cup on the table. She straightened her back, tried to mask the doubt she was sure was obvious on her face and clasped her hands in front of her.

'What if they mark Kellin while she is locked up?' she asked. 'She must be released.'

'I cannot undo what your sister has done,' he said, leaning back in his chair. 'I can only do my best to ensure she comes to no further harm.'

'Which one?'

'Both of them.'

Meg nodded slowly. 'Thank you,' she said.

As she made for the door the old man grabbed her forearm, stopping her in her tracks. 'Don't visit with her. If people see you coming and going from such an area, they will grow suspicious.'

'People are already suspicious,' she said, thinking she had already made a blunder. Determined to learn fast, she replied, 'I will take care.'

'Please, Princess, not everyone is what you think.'

'I am well aware of that already. I recently met a prince.'

The royal commander sighed and released his hold on her arm.

'You didn't say anything.'

He shook his head. 'I did not think him a threat.'

'He wasn't. He isn't,' she said, shaking her head, the same disappointment she had felt when she discovered the connection dissolved, washing over her again, and she gulped down the rising lump in her throat.

The royal commander pushed back his chair with a scraping noise across the floor and opened the door, standing back for her. 'Once a queen is marked, life will be different.'

She shook her head as she headed out into the dark night. 'I'm sure it will continue on as it has my whole life,' she muttered.

'Escort Princess Meg back, Brent,' the old man boomed before closing the door.

Commander Brent appeared at her side as she looked out into the dark night. She took his offered arm and two guards stepped up behind her. 'Are you ready, Your Highness?' the commander asked, indicating forward with his other hand.

She nodded once and they walked back through the yard toward the castle. It was eerily quiet, and in the sporadic torchlight only shadows seemed to move around. She stepped in closer to the commander, moving a little quicker.

'You need not fear,' he said.

There doesn't seem to be a moment in the day when I'm not scared of something, she thought. To the Commander she said, 'Father said fear hones the senses.'

'He did indeed, Your Highness,' Commander Brent said, pulling her to a stop, but she shook her head.

'I just want to be back in my rooms.'

He nodded and without another word, he walked her back through the castle and to her rooms. She stopped at the door, another fear taking hold.

'Raf,' Commander Brent said, opening the door and moving Meg back from the opening. He stood against her, the wall at her back.

The big soldier moved around them and into the room. She could hear him moving slowly through the rooms; it took an age before he returned to the doorway with a nod. The commander walked her in and she sat before the fire, every limb shaking, her body sore from holding herself up. Would the tension ever end? she wondered, realising just how cold she was.

'Do you need anything else?' he asked.

She shook her head without looking away from the flames. 'Thank you for the escort.'

'Raf will stay by the door. Call out if you are worried.'

'I'm worried all the time,' she said, standing quickly. She

focused on his serious face. 'I'll be fine,' she said quickly, trying to smile. 'Thank you again.' She walked quickly toward the door and held it open for him.

He opened his mouth as though to speak, but he bowed instead. 'Good night, Your Highness.'

She simply nodded and then closed the door behind him. She couldn't sit back and do nothing now that she knew what was going on, and as much as she respected the royal commander, she didn't agree with him.

She would try to free Kellin before Elalia allowed her to die in that cell.

24

The opportunity came the following day.

'What are you doing?' Elalia asked, interrupting Meg's conversation with Lord Tarrant.

'I was just...' Meg started, but Elalia held up her hand.

'Please excuse us,' she said pointedly to the man, who looked at Meg before bowing to the princesses and walking away.

'That was rude,' Meg said, disappointed that they had been interrupted before she had the chance to discover more.

'You seem to be asking a lot of questions?'

'So far it is only you that have asked a question, and you are yet to make any sense.'

Elalia's face darkened and a strange chill covered her skin. 'What have I done?' she asked, wondering if Elalia would tell her the truth.

'You are to leave Kellin alone. Asking everyone you come across what can be done to free her—I won't have it.'

'Kellin is of no threat to you,' she said, trying to sound decisive. 'It isn't fair to keep her where she is. How does it look to the many visitors we have at Rocfeld at the moment? Wondering which sister will be queen, and one locks another away.'

Elalia worked her jaw and Meg gulped down her regret. Her argument had sounded better in the darkness in her room, under the covers, as she had worked over her plan the night before.

'Are you going to lock me away as well?'

'Only if you try to kill me.'

Meg managed to scoff. 'Kellin tried no such thing, and you know it. It isn't right to keep her there.'

'Stay away,' Elalia hissed, leaning closer. Meg nodded. 'Find some other cause to keep you occupied.' She stalked off across the room.

Meg watched her for a little while, talking with a group of ladies. Elalia turned only once to glance at Meg over her shoulder, something dark in her look, and Meg shivered.

'Are you cold, Your Highness?' Commander Brent asked, and she jumped just a little. 'I am sorry,' he muttered, bowing and backing up.

'Wait,' she said and he stopped and straightened up. 'Do you think the royal commander is correct?' she asked softly.

'He often is,' he said. 'But I assume you mean about your sister?'

She nodded and glanced back at Elalia, now standing beside Malin, her arm through his.

'She is safer with Commander Rainger watching over her.'

'But surely he can't watch her every moment of the day.'

'It appears that he is trying to,' he said, shifting a little uncomfortably.

'You agree that I should stay away,' she said.

'It is not the place for a princess,' he said and as she opened her mouth, he held up his hand. 'Please try to understand that we do as we do to keep you safe.' He looked around the room, taking his time to study everyone standing in the Hall.

She certainly felt safer with them; even in the Temple there was always someone watching over her. But knowing that Kellin was where she was, so cold and dirty, she worried. 'What if Elalia does have her killed?' she whispered, more to herself than the commander, and he turned from the room back to her with a seriousness even more severe than his usual expression.

'No one but a Raven Queen could order such a thing.'

She nodded slowly. Although her mother had never ordered an execution that she could remember, her father certainly had. Meg had watched from a window overlooking the yards, half hidden in a curtain so that the Sister didn't catch her, for her father had ordered her away. But there had been so much talk of the punishment and the cruel nature of the crime, although Meg had not understood what that meant, and now she couldn't remember what the crime was. But she clearly remembered the head of the man attached to his body and then so easily, with the swing of the giant axe, it was cleaved and rolled away across the dirt. She squeezed her eyes closed, but she could just as easily imagine Kellin in such a place, her red-blonde hair catching the sunlight as it rolled across the dirt.

'Excuse me,' she mumbled to the commander and headed out the door, running along the corridor and out into the cool air.

She stopped, hearing the sound of boots behind her, and although he didn't speak she knew one of the guards had followed her out. Some people moved through the courtyard, most leaving the Temple, and headed towards the Hall or their rooms. She shivered—she had left her cloak behind again—and headed for the Temple.

The expanse of the Temple was cool, and yet she was comforted as she walked quickly toward the gods with the subtle squeak of the guard's leather behind her. She had so many questions, and for the first time she couldn't bring herself to touch even the feet of the gods, holding her hand above Kira's toes. She clenched her fists together and knelt directly in front of the platform. Instead of closing her eyes, she looked up into their faces, trying to guess at the emotions they wore.

What she wouldn't give to talk with them, hear their voices and comforting words. 'Why?' she whispered. Why would they allow this to happen to Kellin? Why would they not mark a queen?

'What is it, child, that you would ask of the gods?' Brother Erasmus whispered in her ear, and she turned quickly to him kneeling beside her.

She choked out a sob instead of the words she wanted to and he pulled her into his arms, holding her damp face to the rough cloth of his tunic.

'Come,' he whispered into her hair, pulling her to her feet and through the Temple. She allowed him to lead her, not taking in her surroundings other than the silence that seemed to surround them and the squeak of a soldier's leather beneath his armour. Then she was sitting at the long table in the Brother's study and a cup of wine was sat in front of her.

'Talk to me,' he said softly, sitting on the bench beside her.

'I don't understand what is happening.' She hoped her voice didn't sound as cracked as it felt.

'In what way?'

'Kellin,' she whispered.

'The royal commander did think it best that she stay where she was,' Commander Brent said, and she wiped at her face as she looked up at him standing beside the table.

Brother Erasmus nodded and waved him into a seat.

'Why have the gods not chosen a new queen?' she asked, swivelling to face the Brother. 'What if they have chosen someone from outside Rocfeld and we must wait for them to arrive?'

'I am sure that a queen will be chosen from amongst King Oren's daughters,' the commander said. 'And soon,' he added in a murmur as Brother Erasmus scowled at him.

'But it has been so long, and I worry what might happen while we wait,' Meg said as the image of Kellin's head rolling onto the dirt came back to her.

'Kellin will be well,' the Brother said. 'The commander watches over her. Elalia won't harm her; she just wants her out of the way.'

'I'm not sure what Elalia wants,' she said, taking the cup of wine and draining it.

'You cannot worry about what may not be.'

'The castle grows more full every day. I didn't think that could happen, and yet the longer we wait the more come to see what might happen, or what could have happened. Our cousins only wait for the crown might go to one of them.'

'Megora, it is in the hands of the gods.'

'It has been far too long,' she said.

'And so you ask the gods for a resolution?'

She shook her head vigorously. 'I only asked why they have not made a choice yet. Why they don't talk to me,' she added in a barely audible whisper.

'They cannot,' the Brother said quickly. 'You know that they could only talk to you if you possessed magic, and they took magic from the line long ago.'

'But am I descended from that line?'

'Why do you ask this?' he asked softly, shooing the commander from the room.

She took a deep breath and waited for the door to close behind him.

'What if we are not meant to be Raven Queens?'

'Both of your parents wore the crown,' he said softly, taking her hands in his. 'Why do you doubt yourself?'

She shrugged.

'Nothing feels as it should. Nothing appears as I thought it was before Father's death. The whole world I thought I knew is not what I find myself living in.'

'If this is about Kellin, it is unfortunate but it will be righted.'

'Not just Kellin,' she said, thinking particularly about the Silent Mother and the strangeness that surrounded her. 'I always loved your telling of the downfall of Sythia,' she said, running her hand over the edge of the table. 'I could picture it so clearly. The queen, the gods, all seemed tangible to me when you described it.'

'I am sure the Silent Mother knows what she does by being here,' he said quietly. 'That there is no danger of Sythia escaping. Do you fear her?'

'I think we should always fear an angry god, no matter what prison she is locked in.' Meg stood slowly and wiped over her face. 'I am not doing as well as I thought I would,' she said, 'and I fear that Father would be very disappointed in me.'

'Never,' the old man said forcefully. 'He knew your true worth, as do we all. It was hard to see him go, and then the loss of Tands and the lack of a queen. Trust that the gods know what they do and that they do it for good reason.'

She nodded once and opened the door, surprised to find the commander waiting on the other side.

'I fear the castle is not as safe as we would like to think,' he said softly.

She nodded and turned to Brother Erasmus standing beside the long table. He smiled and waved her on.

'Do you want to stop in the Temple?' he asked as they worked their way along the shadowy hallways of the Brotherhood.

'No, thank you,' she muttered, but as they entered into the back of the Temple and the gods all smiled at her from their platform, she rushed forward to kiss the feet of the gods she loved, her lips lingering on the cold, salty stone.

'I'm ready.' She stood straight and calm and the commander

nodded before leading the way to the door. She shivered as the cool night air wrapped around her, and hugged her arms to herself, for she was still without her cloak. The wind seemed to whisper and she stopped, straining to listen to what it might be saying.

'I don't think you should visit with your sister,' the commander offered.

She looked at him blankly for a moment and then shook her head. 'I want to return to my room,' she said.

He nodded and they moved quickly out of the wind and into the chill of the castle.

A soldier waited at her door, but again she asked for him to check the room before she would enter it. As he left her standing by the fire, she asked the commander, 'Can I send another blanket for Kellin?'

'Of course,' he said. 'I'll take it myself.'

She nodded slowly and indicated for the maid to fetch one. 'It is cold tonight,' she said as the maid handed it over.

'The royal commander worries that you talk to too many about your sister's predicament,' he said.

She shook her head and turned back to the fire. She was ready for this line of argument. 'I'm only asking general questions, not letting anyone know what has really happened.'

'And yet your sister is still not at court. They will guess at the meaning behind your questions.'

She sighed and nodded, giving up. 'I'll trust the royal commander to do what is best,' she said. 'He has always looked out for me.'

'He watches over all of you.'

'True,' she murmured. 'Thank you, Commander Brent, for your assistance.'

'Your Highness,' he said with a low bow and left her. She could hear muffled conversation through the door and was thankful that the guard remained outside the door. What else, she wondered, was not as she thought it was?

CSEO

Kellin watched the large man through the doorway as he stoked the fire, pushing as much wood into the small hearth as he could, and then sat at the table so that he wasn't between her and the flames. The metal bars were cold against her face and her body ached. She looked back into the small cell. She didn't even have the energy to walk around it, although she thought she should, for the exercise would warm her. She slumped back against the bars and sighed.

'Does the fire help?' he asked gruffly but kindly.

She shook her head, and then nodded. 'Maybe a little.'

'When the meal arrives, you can sit here at the table. It is closer to the fire and will lift you out of the straw for a time.'

'You are too kind,' she said with a catch in her throat.

When he didn't respond, she looked around to find him staring into the fire. 'I meant it,' she said. 'You are much kinder to me than you should be under such circumstances.'

'I understand it is difficult for you,' he said. 'And there is little I can do to make the experience easier.'

'Commander,' she said, pulling herself to her feet, groaning a little with the effort and pulling the blanket around her shoulders closer. 'You have done far more than you should for me. I am a prisoner, after all. A woman arrested for an attack on a princess.'

'That you were not responsible for.'

'Have you managed to find who was?' she asked, wondering if there was someone still wandering the garden waiting for another chance to kill Elalia, or Meg. 'Is Meg safe?'

He nodded. 'She is closely watched, Your Highness. But we have not found the person responsible.'

'I'm not comfortable with that title down here,' she said with a smile. 'But I'm glad she is watched over. Is there any sign of the mark of the Raven Crown?'

He shook his head and turned back to the fire.

'What would you call me if I were just a regular woman locked up down here?'

'Lots of names that shouldn't be said before a princess,' he said, turning back to her and she grinned. 'Miss,' he said after a time. 'I might call you Miss.'

'You could call me Kellin,' she offered.

'I don't think that would be appropriate, Your... Miss.'

She laughed at his struggle, feeling the joy and release of the sound. 'What do you call me when you talk with the royal commander about my situation?'

'Princess Kellin,' he said solemnly.

She strained to see who was coming at the sound of footsteps on the stairs. A young soldier appeared with a tray, but she couldn't see what was on it and with only a cursory glance at the princess in the cell, he disappeared.

'Stew and bread,' he said, placing the key in the lock of the door, and she stepped back a little, waiting for him to motion her toward the table.

As hungry as she was, she needed to maintain some semblance of control. She walked slowly to the table, sitting closer to the fire and breathing in the warmth of it. She dragged the tray across the table toward her and smiled. The bowl was much larger than what she had been offered before, and the lump of bread beside it was still warm from the oven. She held it in her hands, taking in the warmth of it, and then held it to her nose. Bread had never smelt so sweet.

'Thank the gods,' she said before picking up the rough spoon and diving into the bowl.

'Slow down,' the commander directed from across the room, 'or it will only come back up.'

She nodded, trying to savour the next spoonful, but she was too hungry to taste anything other than the heat of it.

The young soldier returned with another tray and stopped. 'But sir,' he started, as the commander held up a hand.

'Just put it on the table,' he said.

He nodded and slid the tray onto the table, and Kellin lowered her spoon. The young man looked between the two of them and then hurried away.

The commander sat down slowly and moved the spoon through the small bowl before him. Kellin's eyes misted before she could do anything to stop them.

'Eat,' he coaxed before putting the spoon into his mouth.

'But you gave me yours.' Kellin felt terrible.

'You need it more than I, and it will be the only meal you get today.'

She nodded slowly, moving the spoon more slowly to her mouth and finding her hand shook a little more than she would have liked. 'Thank you.'

He shrugged and continued to eat.

'Would you like some bread?' she asked, holding the small loaf out to him.

'You've had your hands on it,' he said.

Despite his grin, the tear rolled away down Kellin's cheek as she sat the loaf down slowly beside her bowl. He leaned across the table, took her bread, tore a piece off it and then dunked it into his bowl. 'Now eat,' he said before poking the bread into his mouth and raising his eyebrows at her.

She wanted to smile at him, his handsome face and oddly pale brown eyes that made her look twice; but the weight of her situation pressed down on her again and closed her throat and as hungry as she was, she didn't think she could get another spoonful down.

'I'm sorry.' He sighed, looking down into his own bowl. 'I thought...'

'When will Meg come again?' she asked, to stop him from making an already awkward situation worse. She wanted to cry, but clenched her fist under the table to stop herself.

'The royal commander didn't think it was safe for her to visit,' he said, still looking into his bowl.

'Because I might hurt her?' she asked, dropping the spoon onto the table.

'No,' he said quickly. 'Because not many people know you are here. It is to protect you both.'

She nodded slowly, closing her hand around the spoon, but she didn't lift it from the table. 'Could I be locked away here forever?' she asked quietly.

'Not forever,' he said, his honey-brown eyes studying her too closely.

'Does that mean I might go free, or Elalia will have her way and I'll be executed?'

'She hasn't asked for such a thing,' he said, studying the bowl instead of her. 'And unless she became the Raven Queen, she could not order such a thing.'

'Just a matter of time.' Despair hit her hard.

She watched him for a time and slowly dipped the spoon back into the stew, now losing some of its heat but it still warmed her. 'Who do you think will wear the crown?' she asked after a time, before biting into the bread.

He shrugged.

'There must be speculation, ideas, gossip,' she said, leaning forward, realising how much she had missed such conversations.

'I'm sure everyone has an opinion.'

'But I'm asking for yours.'

'I don't think it appropriate to give,' he said, scraping his spoon across the bottom of the bowl.

'We all know it can't be me,' she said softly, looking again at the stew. 'Meg would be a good choice.'

'Why can't it be you?' he asked.

The strange cackle escaped her lips before she realised it was building, and she slapped a hand over her mouth. 'It was never going to be me,' she said once the strange noise stopped threatening to escape, and an odd calmness came over her.

'But you are a princess, daughter of King Oren and Queen Melia.'

'And surly and gossipy and shallow and not concerned enough with the welfare of the kingdom as I am with my own dresses.'

'I don't think that is true,' he said. 'Not at all. You are concerned with your sisters' welfare. And I am sure you want the right person in the crown.'

'Do you not think Elalia is that person?'

'I did not say that,' he said, pushing up from the table and lifting a small log from the pile and dropping it onto the others already burning brightly in the fireplace.

'Please commander, everyone has an idea of who should wear the crown and that is partly why this castle is as full as it is, so that they are all here when the choice is made and they can congratulate themselves on guessing correctly.'

'I am sure some are here to support you and your sisters during this difficult time.'

'Or help the gods with their choice by limiting the options. I wonder at you, Commander, have you not lived in Rocfeld long?'

'All my life,' he said. 'I know there is nothing but love for your family.'

'That may change.' She looked down at her dress and ran her hands over the coarse material. Dejectedly she said, 'It may have already changed.'

'You cannot consider yourself here because we want it.'

'And yet here I am.' *Why would he not commit to an answer?*

'If you are marked as Queen,' he said, tapping the side of her bowl, 'you could have yourself released.'

'Then I am here for the rest of my life.' The certainty in her voice didn't match her body as she shakily stood.

His eyes reflected his frustration and sadness. 'You haven't finished.'

'I can't get it down,' she replied dismally, moving back toward her cell door.

'You could sit by the fire some more, Your Highness.'

She shook her head and without turning back to him, she opened the door herself, pulled the bars closed behind her and sat with her back to the wall, just out of sight of the commander, and the fire.

25

Meg stopped in the doorway to her sister's room. Surprised, she saw several men at the table, the Luanian emperor amongst them, and took in the quiet conversation. Elalia looked across at her and motioned her into the room.

'You wanted to see me?' she asked, staying where she was.

'I thought you might like to visit Luana,' the emperor said, rising slowly from the chair in a fluid, snakelike movement.

'I thank you for the offer,' she said. 'I am sure there is enough to keep me busy in Rocfeld that I may not get the chance to travel for some time.'

'There is so much I would like to show you,' he said.

Meg looked at Elalia, who despite her fake smile, motioned more vigorously for her to move into the room. 'Did you need me to do something for you?' Meg asked softly, taking a single step forward.

'I called you to visit with our neighbours,' Elalia said, standing herself now, and the other men in the room followed the motion.

'We are saddened by the behaviour of our northern neighbours,' Lord Libry said, indicating his seat for Meg. 'We come to offer alternatives.'

She looked around the room, saw Elalia nodding about the tragedy of Tands, and despite the uncomfortable feeling growing in her stomach, Meg took the seat.

'There is no evidence that Tands misbehaved on their visit here,' she said directly to Lord Libry, who squinted across the table at her and then looked to Elalia, as though asking how to respond. 'I assure you, sir, that I am not heartbroken at the loss of Tands; although I had heard good things of their prince. I am happy to be of use to Rocfeld. I am not in any hurry to run away,' she said, looking at the emperor as she spoke.

'And yet for a woman of your age, you should consider an arrangement sooner rather than later.'

'Surely it would be for the new queen, once she is marked, to make such a decision. Or...' She glanced around the room, her heart beating fast in her chest, 'Are you suggesting that the choice is mine?'

'Of course you would have a say in who you were to wed.' Elalia's voice was strained. 'As long as it was prudent for the kingdom and any issue the marriage may produce.' She gently rubbed her hand over her stomach and several of the lords looked between each other.

'I would rather wait,' she said.

'For you may be marked as Queen,' the emperor said and the room dropped into a strange silence, although Meg was sure she could hear Elalia's teeth grinding together.

'I would never presume such a thing, Your Eminence. I trust the gods to choose well.'

'What if the gods are wrong?' Elalia asked, almost snapping out the words.

'They never have been before,' she said and the lords exchanged glances again. 'They may mark Kellin as Queen.'

'And the world will be a very different place,' Lord Libry said and then appeared to remember where he was, his round face reddening in blotchy patches.

'What if my gods chose you to come to Luana?'

'I know very little of your gods and why they may be interested in me,' Meg said softly, and Elalia actually rolled her eyes.

'They may not be seen as your gods are, and they allow us to determine our own heirs and successors.'

Meg nodded slowly, but she wasn't sure what Libry's words meant.

'If you are determined to stay in Rocfeld,' he said, 'perhaps you would consider one from among the noble sons.'

Meg looked over the old men and tried her best not to shudder.

'I would rather dedicate myself to the people, rather than just one man.'

'Do you suggest the Brotherhood?' Elalia asked, with a smirk on her lips. 'You and Kellin together, perhaps?'

'I do not think that the best option,' Lord Libry said quickly. 'I think no clear decisions are made until the queen is marked.'

Elalia's eyes narrowed. 'Perhaps.'

'Can I go now?' Meg asked.

'Do you not wish to take the opportunity to talk and learn more of Luana?' the emperor asked.

'I thank you, Emperor Baghi, for the consideration, but I'm afraid I had promised to help the Sisters with an errand and I must be going.'

'What could be so important?' Elalia asked, no longer hiding her fake disappointment.

'I am sure it is not nearly as important as the work of the Silent Sisters, but it is for the people after all.'

Elalia nodded and waved her hand at her sister, dismissing her. Meg leapt up from her seat, paused to curtsy to the emperor of Luana and turned for the door. 'Good day, gentlemen.' She moved so quickly through the door that she nearly ran into the guard on the other side.

'Could I visit with—' she said, when the door opened behind her.

'Meggie, I do hope that you are not plotting something,' Elalia said, pulling the door closed behind her.

'Not at all.'

'Why are you talking to the soldier?' she asked, her suspicion clear on her face.

'The royal commander has imposed some limitations on our travel around the castle, it seems. I'm sure he only wants to ensure our safety, but it is most frustrating. I have found that I have to ask if I can walk somewhere before I even start.'

The soldier looked at the wall.

'Really? Such as where?'

'The gardens seem to be a trouble spot, and as the snow is melting I would so love the chance to walk amongst the hedges.'

The guard shook his head slowly.

'And so you see?' Meg said, raising her hands to indicate the man. 'So frustrating.'

'I think the threat from the garden is gone,' Elalia said slowly.

'Is it?' Meg asked. 'Did you see who was beneath the trees?'

Elalia glared.

'Did you?' the whispering voice of the Silent Mother asked behind her, and she turned with a smile but shook her head. 'Was your sister involved?'

'I thought she stood beside you,' Meg said, looking more at the guard than Elalia. She sighed loudly. 'Either way, I cannot go there. But I'm sure the Temple is safe enough in the eyes of the royal commander.' The guard nodded once. 'And so I shall spend my time there.'

'So diligent in your prayer,' the Silent Mother said. 'What do you pray for?'

'I pray for all of Rocfeld.'

'You do not ask for anything in particular?'

'It is not for me to ask anything of the gods,' Meg said, her hand on her chest. 'Only that they provide what they think best for us.'

The Silent Mother bowed her head slowly, hiding what Meg thought was a patronizing expression, the same one Elalia wore openly.

Meg swung around and marched along the hallway. She paused at the top of the stairs, the guard behind her. She could hear Elalia and the Sister whispering, but not what they said.

'I want to see Kellin,' she said, marching on ahead of the guard.

When she entered the cells, her sleeve over her mouth and nose, she found the two commanders standing by the small fire in conversation and her sister possibly sleeping on the straw piled in the corner of her cell.

They both turned around and Commander Brent stepped forward. 'The royal commander told you to stay away,' he said sternly.

'I'm not very good at taking direction,' she said.

He raised an eyebrow and she blushed despite herself and turned her attention to her sister's still form.

'Elalia is trying to exert her power.' Persistently she continued, saying, 'I wanted to be sure she is safe.'

'Your sister hasn't been marked yet. It is not until a queen is marked that any decision could be made.'

'And yet she has dissolved the agreement with Tands and tries now to marry me off to Luana or worse, one of Lord Libry's sons.'

Commander Rainger swayed on his feet and she looked around at him. 'Are you well?'

He nodded, but Commander Brent's face clouded. 'You have to rest,' he said. He swung on the guard trying to hang back behind Meg and pointed a sharp finger at him. 'Make sure he gets back to the barracks and sleeps and then send someone to return the princess to her rooms.'

'Oh thank you,' Meg said, sighing with relief and stepping toward Kellin's cell door.

'Not Kellin. You,' he snapped.

'But,' she started, but focused on his angry face she stopped, nodded and moved over to sit at the small table. 'You know you can't speak to me like this.'

'It is my job to keep you safe, and if I need to move you to safer quarters with force, then I can speak to you however I choose.'

'I wonder if we will ever be truly safe again.'

'You do not realise just how unsafe your world was before this point.'

She stared at him across the small table and he sighed as he shifted from foot to foot. 'Things are not as we would wish them to be,' he said more quietly.

'She's not safe even here,' Meg whispered, looking across at her sister beneath the blankets. Not from the cold or the scandal or from anyone who may wish to advance one of her sisters. She stood quickly and headed for the door.

'You need to wait for a guard,' he called after her, but she shook her head and ran, lifting her skirts high to make it up the rough steps, almost tripping and then out into the cold night air. She continued to run until she found herself standing before the gods in the Temple.

In the silent space, the candles flickered. Not even a brother hovered in the space. 'Why?' she asked, looking up into their serene faces. 'Is this some strange test? Why won't you make a choice?'

Doubt and fear took hold that her world would never be the same. That Elalia would just assume control and without being marked appropriately there would be fighting, too many trying to influence her, others trying to take control or take over.

Meg wondered about the emperor, still so long away from his own land. Living on the boats in the harbour, rarely visiting. Did Elalia really think that she would agree to marry one of his sons? And that if she did, he would go away? She shook her head. He would use the connection for his own benefit. Everyone worked for themselves; no one was thinking of the people or the kingdom in any of this, only the power and control.

'I don't want it,' Meg whispered to the gods. 'I only want to ensure my parents' legacy is continued, that the people of Rocfeld grow and prosper and are safe.' She was sure that Water smiled a little more than she had before.

Without following the rituals of the Temple, as she hadn't when she arrived, Meg left. Her footsteps echoed across the empty space and she shivered as the cold night air wrapped around her. The silence of the courtyard was unexpected and the gooseflesh that formed was due to more than the cold. The shadows grew misshapen before her, and she stood frozen to the spot, unable to run, unable to catch her breath.

Each dark corner appeared to be a man, and just as she thought she could see the glint of a sword, she heard shouting and then Commander Brent and two other men appeared in the courtyard, and the shadows lessened and the sword Meg thought she saw disappeared.

'I told you to wait,' the commander snapped as the other soldiers moved around her, staring into the dark.

She nodded as she wrapped her arms around herself, shivering uncontrollably, and one of the guards wrapped his large cloak around her. Commander Brent grabbed her elbow and directed her back inside as the other two soldiers walked quickly beside her.

She was pushed inside her room as Commander Brent slammed the door shut behind him. 'I couldn't follow you,' he said, the anger clear in his voice and his hard face. 'That would have left your sister at risk.'

She nodded mutely again, unsure if the lump in her throat would ever dissolve.

'Do you want to put yourself in danger?' he asked harshly, taking a step toward her.

Meg backed up, shaking her head quickly, pulling the black cape tighter around her shoulders; it smelt of oil and metal and the man who had worn it.

'Well?' he crossed his arms.

'There was someone in the courtyard,' she whispered.

He stared her down.

'Something in the shadows, or the shadows were something,' she added, almost under her breath. 'I saw a sword.'

'I promised your father,' he said loudly, the anger still rolling off him, and then he swung around and stomped toward the door.

'What did you promise?' she asked, taking a step after him, surprised her voice worked.

He sighed then and the anger dropped from his shoulders before he turned away from the door. 'When he went to Tands, he asked me to take particular care that you were well. That you remained safe.'

'You look after all of us very well,' she said.

'You,' he said, sounding defeated. 'King Oren told me to watch over you, Princess Megora, and I am not doing a very good job.' He was through the door and pulling it closed with a bang before she could articulate any of the questions running through her head.

She sucked in a sob as she sat heavily on the floor.

26

Elalia stared at the nurse, her face serious as her hands moved gently but firmly over Elalia's body. 'The child grows well,' she said after too long. 'What is your concern?'

Elalia shook her head, unsure what she could say about her worries. She motioned Terra forward to help her back into her gown.

'It is a happy time,' the nurse continued as she stood back and waited for Elalia. 'Your cousin's wife is not faring as well.'

Elalia stopped. 'What do you mean?'

'She is very sick with her child.'

'Annar is with child?' she asked, swatting Terra away.

'I thought you knew,' the nurse said. 'You had asked for a nurse to be sent to her.'

'I thought she was sick, not that a child was the reason. Is there a risk to the child?'

'I am not certain; it is early.'

'Hurry up,' she snapped at the girl. 'I think I should visit with my cousins. I do have someone I would introduce to them.'

The nurse simply nodded and left the room.

'Send for the Lady Sera,' Elalia said at the girl and she hurried off.

'What would you want with her?' the Silent Mother asked, appearing in the room.

'Just removing a distraction.'

'Another?' the woman asked, standing by the fire.

Elalia felt a nervousness that was new to her, although as it shivered over her skin she felt as though she had the feeling more and more often.

'How is the child?' the sister asked.

'He grows well,' she said, finding the smile spread easily across her face.

'A boy?' she asked seriously, turning from the fire.

Elalia shrugged and the smile dropped. 'I do not know. Just a feeling.'

'Would you prefer a male child?'

'No,' she said quickly, trying and failing to read the Silent Mother's face.

'I have things I need of you,' the Silent Mother said. 'How long will your distraction with the girl take?'

'Not long,' she muttered. 'Do you have another drink for me?'

The Silent Mother nodded once and Elalia grimaced. 'I want to test you.'

'I will come to you once I have dealt with my cousins.'

'Why are they worth your time?'

'My new cousin thinks himself worthy to marry one of my sisters. I mean to put an end to that and end my husband's distraction at the same time.'

'They are not important.'

'Perhaps, but left unchecked they may become another threat to the crown. They may be working against me already. I only seek to smooth the way.'

'Sythia will ensure the way is smooth.'

Elalia nodded once and the Silent Mother smiled, taking her by surprise.

'Deal with your distractions then, and I will be waiting for you in the chapel.'

As the door opened, Terra showed in the small and frail and frightened-looking Sera, and without any acknowledgement, the Silent Mother walked past them and into the hall.

Sera wrung her hands together.

'There is someone I would like you to meet,' she said.

'I'm not ready to see people,' she said, her voice quiet.

'Nonsense, it is a small group and they are family, soon to be yours too.'

The girl didn't look any happier.

'They will need your assistance, and I think it a way for you to show my cousin what a wife you will make.'

'What if he will not have me?'

'I'm not offering a choice here, but showing the benefits.'

'I'm not really of any benefit to anyone; I'm spoilt.'

Elalia sighed. 'Come along,' she snapped and, taking the girl by the arm so that she couldn't change her mind, she headed toward her cousins' rooms.

The introduction hadn't quite gone as smoothly as Elalia had anticipated it. Annar didn't seem particularly grateful that she had suggested assistance, despite her pale face and obvious discomfort. Tyne stared out the window rather than try to interact with Sera, who spent the entire visit looking down into her lap, threatening tears. Morley was the only one that appeared interested in Elalia's visit, but he talked over the top of her, asked too many questions as to what was occurring throughout the kingdom, and she glared at him rather than answer any of his questions.

She had stayed far too long before dragging Sera out of the room and promising to return her the following day. It was exhausting. As she leant against the wall, peering out through the arrow slots at the clear sky, she wondered if she had benefited from the event at all. The Silent Mother was right, she was distracted, and even her attempts to remove the distractions were not helping.

But nothing was secure until she was Queen. And she would need to continue her current efforts to ensure that happened. Touches of green hinted at the end of winter and she sighed before continuing up the steps toward the Silent Mother's room and, she was sure, the Silent Mother's continued disappointment.

'I thought you were to come directly,' the Silent Mother's voice accused from the dark shadows of the room.

'I have been working on removing trouble.' Elalia tried to sound as confident as she had felt earlier.

'Removing it or moving it?'

Elalia sat slowly on the stool before the fire. 'I do all that you ask,' she said, slowly looking into the flames rather than trying to find the Silent Mother in the room. 'And I have explained that if I am to become Queen I need to ensure that I do as a queen would, and there are some things that need to be done to ensure it happens.'

'Such as the child,' the Silent Mother said.

Elalia nodded and rubbed her hand over her stomach. She wanted to feel him so much and yet there was nothing other than her own occasional sickness that confirmed his presence.

The Silent Mother sighed.

'These are necessary steps,' Elalia said softly. 'They do not distract me from the path to Sythia.' She looked up at the woman now standing beside her, a small cup in her outstretched hand.

Elalia took it without pausing to look or, she hoped, taste the drink, but it was thick and stuck to her tongue. There was an overwhelming taste of honey, which surprised Elalia, and she looked up at the woman beside her. 'When are we to test it?' she asked. 'You did say that you wanted to test me.'

'It will work,' she said, turning back to the bench. 'I don't know that you are ready yet.'

'That is why we must test it.'

The Silent Mother shook her head.

'You don't think I'm committed,' she whispered, disappointment washing over her. 'I have dedicated my life to being the queen Sythia needs me to be.'

The Silent Mother nodded once, but waved her hand toward the door without turning around. Elalia gulped down the threatening tears and left. As she reached her door she stopped, then raced down the steps to the private chapel and knelt on the floor before the candles. She sighed, trying hard to clear her mind of all her fears, but she couldn't.

She stood and walked slowly to the little altar. Focused only on Sythia, she closed her eyes and moved her hands over the candles. The warmth of the flame was startling and she stood back and then smiled as the candlelight flickered the dance of shadows across the walls.

Elalia moved back from the altar and knelt again on the cold stone floor. She bowed down, her head on her hands, and she felt the cold stone seep into her skin. When she sat back up, her hands moved again to her stomach, certain that Sythia would only allow this if it fit with her plans.

'Thank you,' she whispered.

'It is not for you that I do this,' a quiet voice whispered around the walls.

Elalia looked, but she was still alone in the small chapel. Images within the shadows moved in and out of focus. Elalia closed her hands around her stomach.

'I will not take the child,' the voice whispered.

'I said I would give you anything,' Elalia said.

'And you will give me all that I need.'

'What is that?'

'You will know when it is time. You will do as I instruct.'

She nodded. 'Anything.'

'The Silent Sisters assist us. You will help with the Silent Mother's magic and do exactly as she directs.'

Elalia nodded again. 'Will I be Raven Queen?'

A raven's strong shadow wings beat against the light and pushed it around the room, gliding effortlessly across the stone walls. She watched it for some time and then the raven turned into a woman, tall and slender, and a ring of light, like a crown, descended onto her head from above. A man, tall and broad, walked past her and disappeared into the light but she looked after him. Strange, dark flames rose from her skin and she burned before a flash of light was followed by the darkness. When the shadows began to move again, the woman sat upon a throne and many figures knelt before her.

'You will become the strongest queen this world has seen. But there will be sacrifice.'

'Yes, Sythia,' she whispered, lowering her head to the floor again. 'I give you my all.'

'I ask for nothing less.'

She would be the queen they needed her to be and her son would follow. Yet as she imagined the child in her arms, she was filled with the bitter taste of panic. The Silent Sisters believed they could do as Sythia required without men; how would they react to the son, the future king, that she was sure Sythia had given them?

27

'Why are you here?' Morley asked the young woman sitting before the fire, needlework clenched in her hand.

'The princess thought I would be of use to your wife,' Sera whispered, looking at the mess in her lap rather than at him.

He glanced at the closed door behind which his wife slept and then back to the girl. 'You don't appear to be useful.'

She shook her head and a tear slid down her cheek.

'Leave her alone,' Creena said from the window seat where she played a game with Tyne. 'She was sent; she had little choice.'

'And what does Elalia hope to gain by placing the girl here? Does she want news of our activities?' he asked, looking between his sister and the girl, still crying, her eyes focused on some distant point. He sighed.

'She hasn't been well,' Tyne muttered and he glared at him with raised eyebrows.

'Is she defective?'

'I am in the room.' Her voice low and despondent, she stood slowly. 'Not that I matter. I shall leave you.' She gave Morley a little curtsy and with her needlework still scrunched tightly in her hand, she made for the door.

Before she reached it, Tyne was standing beside her, his arm around her waist, guiding her toward the window seat. 'Ignore him,' he whispered theatrically. 'Sit with us; let us learn more of you. For I think my cousin intends for you to become a more permanent part of our family.'

'She cannot force such a thing until she is queen,' Morley said, sitting beside his sister. 'If she becomes queen.'

'Do you not think she will?' the girl asked.

Morley looked at her seriously but didn't know where to start with her. 'What do you know of politics?'

She shrugged. 'Only what I heard my brother and his friends discuss. I do know that nothing is ever as it seems, that promises made are rarely kept.' She glanced at Tyne and then back to Morley. 'I know the chances of this match occurring are small.'

'And yet here you are.'

'She told me to come and this is my only chance.'

'You are such a pretty thing,' Creena offered, pushing Morley out of the small seat beside her. 'Why would this be your only chance?'

She looked nervous then, as though she had thought the secret shared only to find she was the only one that knew, and telling would change everything. She shook her head quickly.

'My cousin,' Tyne said, leaning in toward her, 'has put you in a difficult situation. It appears she wants you out of the way.' A tear rolled down the girl's face and she wiped at it as she nodded slowly. 'Why?'

'She feels I am a distraction for her husband.'

'He might enjoy the distraction,' Tyne quipped, but she turned an angry glare on him.

'I will not see the man,' she said firmly. 'He is not a man I trust.'

'He has used you ill,' Tyne said more softly, taking her hand in his. 'What did he do?'

She shook her head then and pulled out of his grip. 'I should go,' she said softly. 'I was sent to watch over your wife,' she said to Morley, 'but she will sleep more and more and will not want for my company.'

Tyne stood with her. 'Elalia said that you were unwell. Was that Malin's doing?'

'Good evening.' She curtsied to the room and turned again for the door.

'I will agree to the match,' Tyne blurted as her hand reached the latch.

'You will not,' Morley said, stepping between them. 'This is something that Father should be involved in. It is not for our cousin to design your future.'

'I have just as little choice as the girl. Your father will only match me with some woman for his benefit, not mine. And this match could benefit all of us.'

'How so?'

'Elalia will think us compliant to her wishes...'

'Which we are.'

'And that would give us the advantage if she were to be marked as the Raven Queen,' Tyne continued. 'The girl has no link to Elalia, no loyalty there. She knows full well that Elalia just wants her out of the way of her husband. He may express some doubts, but how loudly could he complain?'

'I am happy to be out of the way of Malin,' she said softly, still standing by the door watching them.

'But why would no other man be interested?' Morley asked.

'I am spoilt,' she uttered quietly, looking down at the ground.

'Her child died.' Creena's voice was sympathetic in his ear and Tyne stepped forward and took Sera in his arms, pulling her tight against his chest.

'I do not think this a good idea,' Morley said.

'She holds no love for the prince and I guess no loyalty to the princess. Perhaps Tyne is right. Elalia would think us simply following her instructions,' Creena said.

'It will put Malin offside.'

'Was he ever on side? He may help us if he thinks he will gain an advantage; we just have to sell the right advantage.'

'He is only interested in power,' Sera said from Tyne's chest. 'He wants to be King.'

'I doubt the gods would share his ideals,' Morley said. He studied Tyne, and knew by the way he continued to hold the woman to his chest that his mind was made up and he would bear the consequences when they returned to Lekland. Unless they could use the situation to manipulate another.

Morley shook his head.

'I will walk you back to your rooms,' Tyne murmured soothingly, pulling away from the woman, who at least appeared calmer. Once the door was closed behind them, Morley marched to the table and poured wine into a goblet.

'What is it?' his sister asked as he handed it to her. 'What are you thinking?'

He poured another and lifted it slowly to his lips. 'There is no advantage to this. We may show Elalia that we will do as we are told. But nothing more.' He pulled out a chair and sat at the table. 'We were to influence the decision, be an influence over the new queen, whoever she may be. But with Tyne married to another, how can that be done?'

'It may show his caring side to our younger cousins.'

'We rarely see them. Where has Kellin got to? She was rumoured to have been involved in an attack or the like in the garden, but then we haven't seen her. Was she injured? Killed?'

'Someone would have mentioned it if she were killed,' Creena said, draining her goblet and helping herself to more wine. 'Perhaps she is being kept safe somewhere.'

'There are too many unknowns, and it looks more like Elalia will become the next queen.'

'There is still Meggie.'

'But Elalia puts herself forward, talks with the nobles; she is making directions, dissolving the agreement with Tands, talking with the emperor. Spending her time with the Silent Mother, showing the gods how perfect she is.'

'It is the gods that make the choice,' Creena stated quietly, but Morley heard the sarcastic undertones.

'Do you really think that Father would be happy with that reasoning alone?'

She shook her head and sat slowly beside him at the table. 'What do we do?' she asked.

'We remove Elalia from view and work on the younger sisters.'

'Kellin is very self-assured and Meggie is very clever; what could we offer them that would influence them in any way at all?'

He shook his head. 'One step at a time.'

❑80

The knock was gentle on Meg's door but it still made her jump. She turned slowly as Lora opened it. 'Lady Sera?' she asked, stepping forward. 'I...' She stopped as she took in her cousin,

Tyne, standing behind her in the doorway.

'Please forgive our intrusion,' the young woman said, curtsying. 'But there is something we would ask of you.'

Meg indicated the table and they sat side by side as Lora put goblets on the table and a pitcher of wine. 'Thank you,' Meg said as the girl disappeared. She looked between the two; they appeared quite happy and yet she sensed a nervousness.

'How are you?' Meg asked Sera. 'Are you quite recovered?'

She looked more solemn, but nodded slowly. 'I know that many rumours have circulated the castle,' she said shyly.

'It does not matter,' Meg said. 'What is it you want to ask?'

Sera looked to Tyne, who took a deep breath. Where had his confidence gone? Meg wondered.

'We are to wed,' he said, cocking his head slightly.

'Excuse me?' she asked quickly.

'Your sister suggested the match,' he said, looking a little hurt. 'But it is you we would like to witness us before the gods.'

'I had no idea that you had met,' Meg continued, wondering why Elalia would pair them together.

'I fear she wanted me out of the way,' Sera muttered and Meg sighed. Elalia seemed to be taking on a lot of late. 'And she worried for Tyne's interest in Princess Kellin.'

'What interest?' she asked without thinking and then stood quickly. She noticed the glance that passed between them as she turned back to the table. With her hands on the back of the chair, Meg asked, 'When is this to occur?'

'Today, Brother Erasmus is to meet us in an hour.'

Meg sat back down slowly.

'When did you decide upon this?'

'Yesterday,' Tyne answered. 'But do not let that influence you. We have talked and we know our current positions would not be beneficial for any other match, and we have found a connection we did not expect to find.'

'Positions?' Meg asked.

The pair glanced at each other again, but she nodded. 'I understand,' she said. 'But I do not understand why you ask me.'

'You have always been kind,' Sera said.

'But it was Elalia that brought you together.'

'For her own means,' Tyne said.

'And you do not invite me for yours?'

Tyne grinned. 'It would be of benefit for our union to be supported by a royal cousin, it would help dispel any rumours or possible threats.'

'What threat?' Meg asked slowly, looking toward the door.

'I fear Prince Malin may cause a disruption,' Sera whispered, looking down at her hands. Tyne looked concerned for her, which had Meg nodding and standing again.

'I will be your witness,' she said.

'Thank you,' Sera squealed, jumping up from the table and throwing her arms around Meg before she realised what was happening.

The door swung open with a bang and the girl stepped back as the large guard filled the doorway. Meg nodded in his direction and then, taking Sera's hands, gently kissed her cheek. 'I shall see you in the Temple.'

Tyne bowed low before her. 'Thank you, cousin,' he said.

The guard stepped back and they left, the wine still untouched on the table.

When Meg arrived in the Temple, the small group led by her cousins stood at the feet of the gods with Brother Peras. She looked around the Temple and found Brother Erasmus at the back of the Temple, almost lost to the shadows of the space as the candles had only been lit around the feet of the gods this evening. He shook his head and then stepped back to be lost completely.

Was it that he thought this a bad idea, she wondered as she took a deep breath and moved toward the group.

Sera looked very beautiful and surprisingly calm, her hand on Tyne's arm, and even he smiled more naturally than Meg had ever seen. Had Elalia actually made a happy connection here? Annar, on the other hand, wore an ugly scowl; she smiled at Meg as she arrived, but it didn't travel to her eyes.

'All will be well.' Morley was trying to sooth Annar.

'Good evening,' Meg said softly as she joined the group and found only her cousins and the young Brother amongst them. 'Is Elalia to come?'

'Too busy,' Annar muttered.

'How do you feel, cousin?' Meg asked sweetly. 'We have not

seen you in the Hall.'

She nodded once but didn't answer, looking to the Brother, who looked at Meg. She gave a short nod and he cleared his throat.

'Lady Sera, is your brother to come?' Meg interrupted quickly.

'He is busy at present,' Tyne said. 'He will join us in our rooms for the feast.'

He was possibly occupying Malin, but she wondered how he could be around the man, considering what he had done. But then, he may have known full well. She refocused on Brother Peras watching her and she gave another little nod.

'We stand before the gods to bind this couple as one. To join their hands in the love of Kira and Kion.' Tyne held his hand out palm up, and Sera put hers in it. 'Do you promise this before the gods?'

'In the name of the gods, I am bound,' Sera said.

'In the name of the gods, I am bound,' Tyne repeated.

Brother Peras nodded. 'You are bound together in the light and love of the gods.'

Still holding hands, the new couple turned for the door, the group moving with them. Meg looked up at the gods watching over them, their faces unreadable. 'Thank you,' Meg said to the young Brother, and he moved away. Meg stepped forward and kissed the feet of the gods before following the group toward the door. Lord Robert should be hosting for his little sister and her new family this evening, but he didn't even have that privilege of tradition. Was he simply happy to do as requested by her new family because it was the only option the girl had?

She glanced quickly over her shoulder as she headed out of the Temple, but Brother Erasmus could not be seen and Brother Peras had disappeared as well. She shook her head quickly and raced to catch the small group walking through the cool evening.

The room Meg entered did not look any different to how it had before. There were no decorations at all. Not even a centrepiece on the table. She stopped inside the door, watching the room for a moment. A manservant offered to take her cloak and she nodded as she let it drop from her shoulders. Annar sat down in a seat at the centre of the table, and her husband next to her. Despite having his back to her, Meg could feel the look of anger on Tyne's face as he pulled out a chair opposite them for his new wife. Creena leaned to the side and motioned for more wine although Meg worried that she might have had far more before the ceremony than she should have had.

Meg was directed by the manservant to the end of the table, and she felt isolated from the group. The conversation was non-existent. And although there was movement when there was a knock at the door, nothing changed.

Platters were carried in by a train of servants, although once they were on the table and the servants had left, it was as though nothing had changed. Meg thought that Sera seemed to smile a little less naturally as she looked over the food before her. There appeared to be quite a lot of it for the small party that they were, but there was nothing special or outstanding amongst it. A large roast leg that Meg thought might have been pork, but wasn't sure. Vegetables, gravy, a small roasted bird, but certainly not swan or even goose, worthy of such an occasion.

'Eat,' Annar said without ceremony, and Sera's lip began to tremble. Tyne's hand closed around hers tight, but nothing was said.

'We must wait,' Sera started when the door opened and she turned to see her brother. She was up from the table and threw her arms around his waist, but he pulled her back, looked into her face and then gently kissed her forehead.

The manservant stepped forward and indicated his place at the opposite end to Meg.

'Please,' she said as he moved toward the table. 'Sit by me.' She indicated the chair and he nodded and sat beside her, still somewhat removed from the rest of the group.

'How are you, Your Highness?' he asked politely, looking over the table, his eyebrows drawing together a little. 'It was nice of you to attend for my sister.'

'She asked and I was only too happy,' Meg said. 'I am glad you could join us, although sadly not your parents.'

He nodded once, but his attention was still on the table.

'Is something wrong?' she asked quietly.

'I should have done this for her,' he said, looking over the food. 'I would have given her what she deserved. Is that a chicken?'

'It appears so,' Meg whispered.

'They wouldn't let me,' he whispered back. 'I think they were worried about Malin, or so they said, but I worry that they have not truly accepted her for what she is.'

'I think we are well aware of what she is,' Annar said loudly, and the quiet whispering between the newly joined couple stopped. 'A whore of the prince the princess wanted out of the way.'

Sera's hand covered her mouth and large tears spilled down her cheeks.

'Now is not the time for your objections,' Tyne said loudly, putting his arm around Sera's shoulders and pulling her to his chest.

'When will be?' she asked. 'You have not listened to my advice so far. What do you think will happen when we return to Lekland?'

Tyne glared but didn't say another word.

'Perhaps it is best if she remains with me, or returns to our mother,' Robert said, pushing his chair back from the table.

Sera hung her head as the tears flowed even more. This time Tyne shook his head. 'We are joined and we shall remain so.'

A small smile lit up her face as she looked up at him.

'I am sure Uncle will be accepting of Tyne's new bride once he sees them together,' Meg said, motioning for Lord Robert to sit back down at the table. 'Let us focus on the future rather than the past.'

'Thank you,' Sera whispered.

Meg gave her a nod and lifted her cup. 'To Sera and Tyne.'

The group mumbled the same words and they drank to the new couple.

Meg ate as little as possible and when she pushed back her chair and stood, the room stood with her. 'I'm sorry to leave the festivities so early,' she said. She took Tyne's hand and then kissed Sera on the cheek. 'I wish you good fortune in your life together.'

'Thank you again, Your Highness,' Sera said.

Meg nodded. 'Good night,' she said to the table and took the cloak from the manservant rather than waiting for him to help her into it. She moved quickly down the hallway, pulling the cloak around her. It was another example of Elalia making sure her will was adhered to. Making decisions not hers to make. Although, she had to admit that the couple were happy with each other, if no one else.

The sooner the Raven Queen was marked, the better for everyone.

28

Malin paced in his rooms and then stopped and poked at the fire. He was still saddened at the news of Sera's marriage and although it was only duty, he was strangely drawn to Elalia in her current state. He stabbed again at the fire. He had expected life to become somewhat easier when she got her way, and yet it hadn't.

When he had seen them in the Hall, Sera's hand had been so tight around Tyne's arm, as though it would protect her from him in some way. He couldn't touch her again, and it hurt him far more than he realised.

He stabbed again at a log but didn't know where he could get the answers he needed, and he wasn't sure he had the questions formed clearly enough in his head. Maybe he had been mistaken with Sera. Maybe she didn't want to leave with Tyne and he still had a chance.

He pushed his way into the rooms his wife's cousins shared to find them all seated around the table. They all turned and the manservant stepped forward with a pitcher of wine.

Malin waved him off and glared at the smiling faces, except for Sera, who did not look as happy to see him as he had hoped she would.

She drained the goblet in her hand and stood from the table, 'Excuse me,' she said and moved to an adjoining room. He watched her walk away, her slender figure and subtle curves accentuated by the elegant dress. Tyne glared at him as he stood from the table and silently followed, closing the door behind them.

Malin took Tyne's seat at the table and the manservant filled his goblet. 'Your cousin's wife appears well,' he said, taking a long drink.

'Why are you here?' Annar asked.

Malin gulped down another mouthful of wine and shrugged.

'Your wife is difficult to find,' Morley said, sitting beside him.

Malin focused on the closed door.

'I would appreciate some time with her,' Morley continued.

'You could go hunting,' Annar said.

'Hunting? Elalia? She would rather bed your manservant.'

'I could call him back for you.' Annar grinned.

Malin narrowed his eyes. 'Why hunting?'

'It is a diversion you enjoy, is it not?' Morley said. 'We could join you; Creena and I love a good hunt. Time away from the castle would give us opportunity to talk uninterrupted.'

Malin looked at Annar. 'I am unwell, My Lord,' she said, rubbing her slender stomach. 'I could not possibly travel so far.'

He raised his eyebrows.

'I can assure you I am with child. One of your nurses has reported the certainty of the fact, I am sure,' she said with surprising venom, and Malin wondered where the quiet, usually dull girl had gone.

'How did you make her do that?' he asked, still focused on her body.

'I filled her with my seed and started a child growing,' Morley said, pulling Malin's attention from her. 'They would have known if it were a lie,' he said. 'The nurses are clever that way, despite never knowing a man.'

Malin sat back and held out his cup for the manservant, but he didn't come. Annar pushed the pitcher across the table.

'You hunt so often, you would surely know the most exciting spots; and you and our cousin would be excellent hunting partners,' Morley said.

Malin nodded. 'What do you want to discuss with her?' he asked.

'Organise the hunt,' Annar said stiffly. 'Somewhere with a good chance of a kill; Creena loves to run down a decent buck and I am sure you would be able to find her one.'

Malin grinned across the table at Creena. 'Would you like a

companion at the hunt, cousin?'

'I think we could do without the chance of scandal,' Annar snapped. 'But guards, of course, would be essential. Given recent events, it would not be safe for the princess to travel without them. The tall, broad one,' she said, clicking her fingers.

'Commander Rainger,' Creena said.

'That is him; he seems sensible.'

Creena nodded across the table.

'I haven't seen him of late. The royal commander may have him on a task of some kind.'

'You are the Prince,' Annar said more sweetly. 'You could have him reassigned to the hunt.'

'A hunt with Elalia?' he said, trying to picture her on horseback with a bow in her hands.

'Why yes, cousin,' Annar drawled, 'we would love to accompany you on such a venture.' She stood and curtsied low before him. 'We are most grateful for the invitation,' she said, motioning to the door. 'Please tell your wife I am not yet able to travel, but my husband and his sister are keen for such adventure.'

Malin stood slowly, noting the manservant had reappeared.

'Are you sure Tyne and his new wife would not care to join us?' he asked.

'My cousin's young wife is my dearest companion; I would insist she keep me company whilst my husband is away. Her new husband is still much in love,' Annar said, 'and would rather remain with her. I am sure you remember when you were newlywed, Your Highness?'

'I will inform you of the details once they are settled,' he said and stalked through the door, held open by the manservant.

Elalia stared at Malin in disbelief and then back out the window that looked over the courtyard.

'It could be exciting,' he offered. 'And it is quiet at the lodge.'

'The Silent Mother will be here shortly,' she said, still staring out. 'I can't leave her.'

'How long since you have been on a horse?' he asked.

'Too long,' she said.

'Remember the freedom?' he asked, a small smile on his lips.

She sighed. She did remember that feeling, of the horse strong beneath her and the wind in her hair. 'When?' she found herself asking, and he beamed at her. Then she looked toward the Temple and sighed. 'I do not know,' she muttered.

'I shall arrange it all,' he said, standing beside her. 'I will send for supplies, and word to your cousins, and once it is set we shall leave immediately.'

She smiled at his enthusiasm and took his hand as his eyes ran over her body. Doubt flickered across his face before the smile settled and he reached out for her. She remained unmoving for a moment. 'What prompted this idea?' she asked.

'What idea?' the Silent Mother asked from the doorway.

'Malin wishes us to go hunting with our cousins,' she said.

'Why is that? Do you hope your cousin's new wife will travel with you?' she asked, her hard eyes on Malin.

Malin shook his head as Elalia took a step back.

'You went to see her,' she muttered.

'I talked with Morley,' he said. 'He doesn't get the chance to talk with you when so many others do, and I thought it would be a chance to have some time away from Rocfeld; it is so busy, so many vying for your attention.'

She looked at him seriously for a moment, wondering at the true motive for this trip.

'There has been so much pressure of late,' he continued. 'I thought it would be a chance for you to spend some time with your family.'

'I think it is a good idea,' the Silent Mother said and they both turned to her in surprise. 'Some fresh air and peace will help refocus you.'

Elalia nodded slowly.

'I will talk with the commander and organise it all,' he said, racing from the room.

The Silent Mother smiled. 'It might do you good,' she said slowly, and she followed Malin from the room.

CREED

Elalia breathed in the rich scents of the forest as she stepped down from the carriage. She wondered why she had not come before, but she realised with a pang she had never been given the opportunity. With her hand still in Malin's, she stepped forward to take in the splendour of the hunting lodge. For unknown reasons, she had pictured it as a small house amongst the woods, yet the building stretched away from her.

Her grandfather had it built when her mother was a child, yet as far as she could remember her mother had never travelled here either. She smiled as the manservant opened the door for her with a nod.

The expanse of the room beyond the foyer was a surprise and despite the large fires burning at each end of the room, it was cool and dark. Candles burned along the length of the table that could have seated the entire court if required, and yet the dark panelling of the room seemed to absorb the light rather than reflect it. Deer heads and antlers covered the walls. It was a masculine space, created for men with no idea of women at all. And yet despite the unfamiliarity of it, Elalia felt calmed by the shadows.

A young woman bobbed a curtsy in a distant doorway and disappeared quickly.

'How lovely,' Creena said, standing beside her. 'Have you not been here before?' she asked.

Elalia shook her head.

Terra appeared before her and curtsied. 'I have unpacked your rooms, Your Highness. Shall I show you the way?'

Elalia nodded and made to follow the girl when Creena took her arm. Elalia wondered at the gesture when Creena let her go, clutching her hands before her. 'Cousin,' she said, a little less confidently than Elalia expected. 'I am keen to see the woods around the house. When you return, will you explore with me?'

'I would like that.'

Elalia followed Terra and found her room not far from the main hall. Large and spacious, it was almost the size of her bedchamber at the castle. 'Is there a chapel?' she asked and as Terra shook her head, Elalia rubbed her side. The girl looked concerned, and Elalia smiled to reassure them both. 'I am uncomfortable; it has been a long journey,' she said and the girl nodded but looked just as worried.

'Perhaps you should not hunt, Highness.'

Elalia sighed. 'My husband wishes it,' she said. 'And I am eager to learn.'

The girl looked pointedly at her barely swollen stomach and Elalia glared at her until she bobbed again and disappeared.

Elalia took her time to look through doors as she moved toward the main hall where Creena was waiting with Morley and Commander Rainger.

'We are only going to walk around the lodge,' she was saying sweetly.

He nodded politely. 'Then you will not mind two men walking behind you.'

Creena sighed and smiled at Elalia. 'You look so well. I am so keen to see the place, yet the commander is somewhat nervous and so I have bowed to his better judgement.'

Elalia nodded and allowed Creena to take her hand and lead her out of the house. She paused to breathe in the fresh air, sweet with the scent of the trees, before they followed the path around the lodge. The only hint of the soldiers was the crunch of their boots on the gravel behind them.

'He knows best,' Creena said, indicating over her shoulder.

Elalia nodded and looked into the dense trees around the lodge. She wondered how it had been built in such close proximity to the forest. As they rounded the corner they saw the stables; Malin and Morley looked over horses with cups in hand.

'When do we go out?' she asked as they joined them.

'So eager to hunt,' Creena said. 'Let us recuperate from our journey before we chase deer through the woods.'

Elalia nodded. 'It will be a difficult chase,' she said, looking again into the dense forest.

'There are some paths,' Malin said. 'And once we are out from the lodge, there are more clearings.'

'Come,' Creena said. 'We have not explored this side.'

They slowly walked back around the lodge. 'What beautiful stone work,' Elalia said, wondering why such effort would be taken with a building so lost in the forest. A hidden gem. She vowed to return again.

'Too pretty for men,' Creena said, and Elalia patted a hand on her arm.

She took in the sweet smells that surrounded her. It reminded her of playing as a child in the hidden garden at her uncle's house. She hadn't allowed herself time for distractions and although she enjoyed the house, she felt a stab of guilt that she had left important work behind.

The guards followed them along to the front door and when they reached it Creena asked, 'Would you like to see every room?'

She nodded and followed Creena through the door. 'You may wait here,' she told the guards, and they took their place either side of the door.

They moved through rooms that did not seem as big as the women had expected from the outside, and they were almost disappointed when they discovered a staircase behind a door at the far end of the house.

'Interesting,' Creena said.

Elalia looked up, but could not see or hear anything. She carefully put a hand on the wall to steady herself and started to climb the stairs.

Creena took her hand. 'I do not think this is a good idea,' she whispered. 'We do not know what is there.'

'Which is why we go to look,' Elalia said, taking another step. The Silent Mother had been right, she thought as she took another step; she was too concerned with what others would think of her and not what promises she had made to Sythia. She marched up the steps quickly and found herself in an open, dusty attic space.

Creena, behind her, pulled at her arm.

'There is nothing here,' Elalia said, pushing past her and back down the stairs. She had only come hunting because she needed the time to focus on what was important. Without the distractions of Rocfeld, that should be easy enough.

The air was still and the forest made little noise as the small group on horseback travelled between the giant trees that crowded the path. A bird called somewhere in the distance and when Elalia turned to look for it, she saw Rainger looking deep into the trees. Malin flinched in the saddle when she reached for him, and she watched him for a moment before he gave her a nervous smile.

'Has Morley spoken with you?' he asked. She shook her head. 'I thought that the reason he wanted time with you, to talk, but he hasn't?'

She shook her head again. 'How far away are the deer?' she asked. 'I am getting sore from sitting so long.'

'Not far,' he mumbled and looked into the trees ahead.

'You have hunted before?' she asked Creena, trotting up beside her, surprised at the size of the bow she held in her hand.

'With my father,' she said. 'There is great power in taking the life of an animal.'

Elalia smiled but gulped down the revulsion she felt. The idea of blood made her queasy, and she wondered if this was a good idea. She placed a hand over her stomach as a strange shiver covered her body.

'Are you well, Your Highness?' Commander Rainger asked behind her, and as she nodded a thud slammed into her and she fell, the world moving slowly around her before it went dark. She struggled to open her eyes and Creena's strange smile came into focus, and then the world went dark again.

Her stomach twisted and burned; blinding light hit her eyes and she raised an arm to shield them but it wouldn't work. She was shaking, being shaken and jostled around, and Creena and Morley sat opposite her, jiggling and shaking too. It was too hard to keep her eyes open, and she closed them against the burning pain.

CR80

Meg pushed her way through the silent group that surrounded her sister's bed. 'Where is Terra?' she asked.

'At the lodge,' Creena offered. 'We left in such a hurry.'

'The nurse?'

There was no response. Silence continued as they stared at the broken woman in the bed. Meg glared between them. 'Commander,' she hissed, and Commander Rainger snapped to attention. 'Fetch a Sister-nurse and a Brother.'

She focused on her sister. It was hard to tell what the damage was with her so covered in blood; the room reeked with the bitter scent of it. Her face was scratched and already bruised, her arm swollen and disfigured.

'Why did you move her?' she asked quietly.

'We could not get help,' Malin whined.

Meg's frustration grew at the lack of action around her. 'Out,' she screamed, turning on them. 'All of you, out!'

Creena and Morley turned quickly and fled. Malin took a step back but remained where he was. She glared at him, and he nearly ran into the returning commander in his haste to disappear.

'By the gods,' the nurse murmured as she leant over Elalia's broken body.

Meg turned on the commander and, taking his arm, led him from the bed just as the Brother entered the room. He took one look at Elalia and fled. She hoped it was for more help.

'What happened?' she asked the soldier, keeping his focus away from Elalia.

He shook his head. 'So fast,' he said. 'An arrow, a large arrow.' His eyes narrowed. 'A Tandian arrow.'

Meg took a deep breath.

'It missed her, but I know not how. It killed her horse in an instant and she fell badly, the horse across her body.'

Meg winced.

'I carried her back to the lodge,' he said, looking down, and Meg realised then that he was covered in her sister's blood. 'But the carriage was there and Lady Creena said it would take too long to get help, that it would be faster to return to the castle. That it would be better for her to return to the castle.'

Another nurse raced into the room and Brother Peras not far behind. He paused and squeezed Meg's arm on the way past. She drew a ragged breath.

'It was too far,' Commander Rainger said seriously. 'I should have insisted, but Lady Creena was so sure, and the prince took her from my arms and climbed into the carriage.'

Meg shook her head. 'It was too far. It would have been much better if she had remained where she was and you sent for help.' Meg sighed. 'Too far or not, she is here now and the nurses will do all they can.'

Elalia screamed behind them and the second nurse shook her head at Brother Peras. He glanced at Meg and the commander, and with a small wave of his hand they left the room.

'I have failed,' he said, his shoulders rounding.

Meg shook her head. 'You have seen far worse, I am sure.'

He nodded, his eyes on the door. 'But not to a princess.'

'Go and rest, wash or whatever you need to do,' she said. 'You have done all you can for her today.'

He stood to attention and left the room, and then she raced through the door after him. 'Commander Rainger,' she called across the hall. 'Send for Kellin. Not you, someone else; but have her sent here, now.'

He nodded and ran on.

Meg stood at the doorway of her sister's bed chamber and watched the nurses. The Brother nodded toward the door, but she shook her head. Someone who loved her needed to be near.

Elalia was terribly pale. Her arm was tightly strapped and her body was battered and bruised, and she seemed so frail in her nakedness.

The nurse looked at the Brother and gave a small nod. He stood and moved toward the door, taking Meg with him into the other room and closing the door.

'She will live,' he said and Meg let out a sob of relief. 'The child...'

'I understand,' she said.

A nurse came through the door, a bundle of bloody sheets and cloth in her arms. And then Kellin pushed through the door, looking just as she had the last time Meg saw her, covered in straw, her hair a mess, her face and hands a similar grey colour as the dress she wore. She looked at the bloody nurse and back to Meg.

'She is alive,' Meg said, taking her in her arms. 'She will be well.'

'I was so angry with her,' Kellin sobbed. 'But I would not wish her dead. By the gods, may she live.'

Meg directed her to the table and the Brother poured wine. Kellin took a shaky sip.

'What happens now?' Meg asked him.

He shrugged.

'We cannot say it was a Tandian attack,' she said calmly. 'It will create panic, and the Tandians are already ill at ease with us; they will be knocking on our gates or trying to push them down.'

'You do not think that Tands is behind this?'

She shook her head.

Kellin grabbed her arm. 'Why would Tands want to kill Elalia?'

Meg and the Brother looked at her. 'Many reasons spring to mind,' Brother Peras said.

'But they would not be so obvious,' Meg said. 'They would not risk a lone man in a forest. They would be cleverer, or they would come in force. It makes no sense,' she said, getting up from the table.

She noticed the Brother watching her closely. 'I am sorry, Brother, it is not my place to guess at what Tands may do. I hardly know what they might do. Tell me,' she said, sitting again at the table. 'Do you think Tands is behind this?'

'You are correct, Princess Megora,' he said slowly.

'Then who?' Kellin blurted. 'Who tried to kill her?'

Meg looked up to see Malin in the doorway, his hands covered in blood, and a hot anger grew in her chest.

'It is lucky for you that she lives,' Meg said.

'She lives?' he asked, his voice shaky. 'Thank the gods.'

'How could you have put her in such danger?' she asked, her hand forming into a tight fist to prevent the rage she felt pushing through to the surface. As he shook his head slowly, she stood. 'You took her into a forest with very little protection when you knew someone had tried to kill her. What did you want to prove?'

He looked at Kellin; confusion flickered across his face and then he shook his head.

'What if she had died?' Meg pushed. 'She could have died with her child.'

'Her child?' he whispered, and made to push past her into the room.

'Let her rest,' Meg said, her voice strong.

He backed up, glanced at Brother Peras and back to Meg. 'I shall be in my rooms,' he said. 'You will notify me when she wakes.' He stalked from the room.

Meg blew out a slow breath and her shoulders sagged. She looked back at the Brother, who nodded encouragement. 'I think I see Brother Erasmus's meaning,' he said, and took a sip from his cup.

'Excuse me?' she asked softly, and Kellin took her hand and gave it a squeeze.

'You will do well in Tands,' he said softly.

Kellin raised the goblet back to her lips with shaky hands, and Meg sighed; she was never going to reach Tands. She glanced through the doorway into the other room and then back to the table as a gentle hand rested on her shoulder.

The royal commander pulled her into a quick embrace and just as she thought she would start to cry, he released her, patted her shoulder again and joined the Brother at the table. 'You had best start at the beginning,' he said.

Meg nodded, poured more wine into her goblet and sat slowly at the table.

29

Creena barrelled through the door. 'You fool,' she screamed. 'You missed her,' she said more slowly, and then stopped.

The soothsayer slowly rocked back and forth, her old head shaking. Annar sat at her feet, pale and clearly frightened.

Morley looked between the woman and his wife. 'Where is Tyne?' he asked.

Annar started to shake her head in the same manner as her Grandmother, and Morley had a startling image of the future.

'Has he not come back?' he asked. Where could he be? Some damage had been done, but he hadn't managed to kill Elalia as he had hoped. If he was still out in the forest there was a chance that he might be found, and then they would all be lost.

'Darkness comes,' the old woman whispered.

'Annar, where is Tyne?'

'Packing,' she said softly, never taking her eyes from the old woman, and she reached out slowly and took her hand.

'Can someone please explain what is going on?' Morley said.

'She was in the forest,' Tyne said, appearing in the doorway to his room, still covered in dirt and leaves, his clothing torn where it appeared he had caught on a tree or the like and his hair dishevelled.

'Who was in the forest?' Morley asked. 'Someone saw you?'

He nodded quickly, running a hand along the other arm as he trembled.

'Oh, by the gods,' he said. 'What happened?'

'Sythia,' the soothsayer said, lifting her eyes to him, and he blinked back the idea that he could see something in them.

'We must leave,' Annar said.

He shook his head. 'We have not done what we came to do,' he said clearly. 'How could Sythia be in the forest?'

'There was a woman. I raised the bow, released the arrow, but it did not go where I directed it.'

'You missed and you are trying to blame someone else,' Morley said, his arms crossed over his chest. 'This won't help you once you stand before Father. And you only loosed one arrow. I thought the plan to at least injure Malin as well.'

'The arrow turned toward Malin. My aim was true,' he said desperately as he stepped forward and then glanced at the old woman still rocking in her chair. 'It would have hit her in the chest, but it swayed and dipped and struck the horse.'

Morley sighed.

'There was someone in those trees,' he said, taking Morley's shoulders in his hands, his grip tight, his face anxious. 'A woman in white. I couldn't see her clearly, but she was there.'

'Sythia works within these walls,' the old woman murmured. 'There is much darkness and more to come.'

'We have seen no signs of such things; Tyne might have been distracted.'

Shaking his head, Tyne returned to his room where Morley could see Sera hurriedly pushing clothes into the trunk.

Annar slowly got to her feet. 'We have to leave.'

Morley shook his head as Creena, still standing silent before him, started to nod.

'Death,' the old woman said. 'We will be dead by morning.'

Creena ran for her room as Annar took his hand. 'We must go,' she said. 'Grandmother knows.'

Morley followed Annar into their bedchamber to find the trunks already filled and locked. She glanced around the room and then moved quickly back out to her grandmother. The manservant pushed past him, dragging the trunk toward the doorway, Tyne not far behind with his own.

'She knows,' Annar said again as she helped the old woman to her feet.

239

Meg smiled across the table at Brother Peras. 'I think that is a good idea,' she said.

'When there is no reasonable theory as to who is behind this, then it was our only option,' he said. 'You were correct in your thinking, and the royal commander and Brother Erasmus agree.'

Commander Rainger pushed through the door. 'I do not like this,' he said, his voice booming off the walls and his arms crossed. Kellin appeared in the bedchamber doorway and he glanced at her. She smoothed quickly over the grey dress, and tucked her hair behind an ear. 'It was a Tandian arrow that struck the princess's horse. These rumours of a hunting accident are a mistake,' he said to Meg.

'We are not going to seek revenge for an act that may not have happened,' Meg said clearly.

Kellin stepped from the doorway. 'Rainger saw the arrow,' she said.

Meg shook her head.

'The Brotherhood has ensured that Rocfeld knows it was a hunting accident,' Brother Peras said.

Meg nodded.

'Meggie,' Elalia's shaky voice called from the other room and she rose from the table and rushed in after Kellin.

'Elalia,' she said, sitting on the bed. 'How do you feel?'

'Bruised,' she said, lifting her broken arm carefully. Her other hand moved immediately to her stomach and the fat tears splashed down her pale cheeks as she squeezed her eyes shut. 'No,' she murmured.

The Brother pulled Commander Rainger back from the door and slowly closed it. Meg took her sister in her arms.

'I am so sorry,' Kellin said. 'It was such a terrible fall and the horse...' she trailed off.

'I don't remember,' Elalia whispered.

'That may be best,' Meg offered, laying her back down. 'Fetch the nurse, Kel,' she said over her shoulder.

Elalia shook her head, and Kellin stayed where she was.

'What were you discussing?' she asked Meg, taking her hand, her grip surprisingly tight. Meg shook her head.

'Tands,' Kellin said, and Meg glared at her. 'Rainger thinks it was a Tandian arrow that hit you.'

'No,' Elalia whispered.

'You do not have to remember,' Meg said. 'We have said it was a hunting accident.'

'Accident?' Elalia repeated.

'Yes.' Meg nodded slowly. 'You fell from your horse.'

'She smiled,' she said. 'I remember her smiling, and the shaking.'

'That would have been the carriage,' Meg said. 'They rushed you home.'

'It hurt,' she said, another large tear escaping. 'She smiled and smiled. They were happy,' she said, looking at Meg.

'Who was happy?' Kellin asked.

'Creena was happy,' Elalia said. 'She smiled.'

Meg and Kellin exchanged a glance. Kellin nodded and moved to the door, but Meg stood quickly and grabbed her hand. 'It is not safe,' she whispered.

'I will take the commander with me.'

'We do not know for sure that they meant to kill her,' she continued in the same hushed tones, 'but they were happy to let her die.'

Kellin nodded and left the room. Elalia groaned and Meg moved back to her side. She pulled the blanket around her and sat back on the edge of the bed.

Brother Peras appeared in the doorway and Meg stood slowly to meet him.

'She needs sleep,' Meg said.

'It will take time.'

'The child was the hardest,' she said.

Malin pushed past them to stand at the end of the bed. He looked a little lost. 'How could this happen?' he asked.

'Where is the Silent Mother?' Elalia asked.

'I haven't seen her,' Meg answered. 'Would you like me to send someone to find her?'

She shook her head and then squeezed her eyes closed as a large tear worked its way down her face. 'She will come when she wants to see me.' She sucked in a ragged breath. 'She is disappointed in me,' she whispered.

'Who is responsible for this?' Malin asked and Meg refocused on his tired stature.

'Go and rest,' she said. 'There is nothing you can do here.'

'I could...'

'Leave,' Meg said, moving quickly toward him. 'You took her out there. You put her in harm's way. Did you know that this might happen?'

He shook his head vigorously. 'Morley wanted to talk to her,' he murmured, backing up.

'About what?' she asked, slowing her pace. Perhaps Elalia's strange recollections from the day were accurate; Meg's heart skipped at beat knowing Kellin had gone marching in there to see what they knew.

'Let her sleep,' Brother Peras said, pushing them from the room. Malin sat slowly in a chair by the fire and Meg stood beside him, staring at the flickering flames.

'There will be more speculation,' Meg said. 'Suggestions as to who else might benefit from her death.'

'Such as yourself,' Malin whispered.

She glared at him and Kellin threw the door back, the bulk of Commander Rainger behind her. She shook her head as she walked quickly toward Meg and took her hands. 'Our cousins are gone,' she said.

'Gone?' Malin asked, looking at her.

'All of them, nothing left.'

'Does that mean they were involved?' Malin asked. 'Would they lie to me to get Elalia in a position where they could kill her?'

'But she isn't dead,' Meg said softly. 'And leaving like this would only make them look responsible. Why would they leave?'

Kellin shook her head. 'Maybe they saw who was responsible and feared what might come next.'

'Then why not tell us?'

'Perhaps they saw something that could not be explained,' a quiet voice said from the doorway.

Meg stared at the Silent Mother as the hairs on the back of her neck stood slowly to attention. The Silent Mother had come at Elalia's request; would she try to kill her? She seemed to be the only one that knew what the Silent Sisters really did.

'She lives?' she asked, and Meg nodded. The Silent Mother looked toward the door but didn't move. 'The child?' she asked. Malin shook his head slowly, and Meg was sure there was a small smile on her lips as she turned back through the door.

'You don't want to sit with her?' Meg asked quickly.

'It is time for my prayer,' she said without turning back. 'We will talk when she is better.'

Meg shivered and Kellin put her arms around her and pulled her close. 'It will be well,' she whispered.

But Meg wondered just what the Silent Mother and her shadows were doing in Rocfeld, and if Elalia was in on all their secrets.

'Do we send someone after our cousins?' Kellin asked.

Meg nodded and Commander Rainger bowed low before he left the room.

'You should change,' Meg offered, stepping out of her sister's embrace and trying to smooth down her hair.

'I would rather stay with you.'

Meg nodded slowly and Malin stood from the chair and indicated Kellin sit down. Meg sat beside Brother Peras, wondering if he would believe what she had seen in the chapel. She stared into the flames as they sat in silence and Meg shivered again as the soothsayer's words of darkness and death replayed over and over in her mind. How much more darkness would they see? Elalia had survived; who was it that would die?

30

Elalia stumbled along the dark passageway, bouncing off the wall, cringing and yelping when her arm touched against the rough stones. She should have picked up a candle, but she was desperate for the Silent Mother and had taken the first chance to find her way to her room. She had ordered the guard to wait back at her door, and despite not wanting him to follow, she regretted that he wasn't there to assist her. She realised with overwhelming sadness that she could not find her own way and she sank to the floor, catching her dress on the rough, stone walls as she slipped.

It felt like an age that she sat against the cold stone, and then warm hands were guiding her to her feet. As the gentle light of the room spilled into the hallway, the Silent Mother appeared before her. She threw her arms around her and sobbed against the rough material of her tunic.

She was helped to a stool beside the fire and handed a cup of water. She gulped it down thirstily and rubbed at her face with the back of her hand.

'What have you done?' the Silent Mother asked softly, taking her broken arm in hand.

Elalia flinched at her touch. Her arm was still sore and swollen and now ached from the fall in the hallway, and she realised both arms were scratched and bleeding.

She looked up into her friend's face. 'The baby died,' she whispered.

'Yes it did,' the Silent Mother said sternly, letting the arm drop, and Elalia yelped and pulled it to her. 'What did you do?' she asked, her voice harsh and cruel.

'There was an accident, in the woods, when I was hunting.'

The older woman raised her eyebrows and crossed her arms.

'Malin wanted me to,' she said. 'He wanted me with him,' she whispered, more unsure now, concerned he may have been part of the plot with her cousins. She looked up, pleading with her to understand.

'You have lost your focus,' she said, 'for a man.'

'He is my husband,' she breathed. 'He wanted the child—he wanted me when I was with child.'

'He wanted what he always did: power. Power over you, power over people.'

'I have the power,' Elalia said, her voice small. 'He was mine.'

'He was never yours,' she said. 'Never.'

'Help me,' she pleaded.

'You have squandered my help,' she said. 'Worse, you have squandered your goddess's assistance. You do not listen to her. You do not do as she bids.'

'No,' Elalia said, reaching out and grabbing hold of her friend, even though pain shot up her arm. She held her tightly. 'Please help me. I shall do as you direct. I promise. I shall do as Sythia asks, for she is everything.'

The Silent Mother nodded once and took Elalia's broken arm gently in her hands. She closed her eyes and rubbed over the skin, mouthing her silent words. When she took her hands away, the pain had left her, and Elalia stretched out her fingers and breathed with relief.

'Thank you,' she said.

The Silent Mother turned her back and started mixing ingredients at the work bench, the silence between them eating away at Elalia. She gulped down tears. 'Sythia had said I could keep him,' she said.

The Silent Mother turned on her with a dark look. 'You would follow your own way,' she said loudly, her voice harsh in the small room. 'You do not listen to Sythia or her needs.'

'She told me...'

'I know what Sythia needs more than you. You are the vessel. You must remain safe; you must be the queen that Sythia needs you to be. You put yourself in danger.'

'What do I do?' Elalia asked. 'Tell me what to do.'

'I may not be able to save you again,' she said more quietly, turning back to the bench.

Elalia watched her bend over her work. Strange smells filled the room, making Elalia's head spin. 'You were there,' she whispered.

'Drink,' she said, turning from the bench with a cup in her hand, its contents a concentration of the bitter scent, and Elalia's eyes watered.

She gulped it down. The familiar warmth filled her body and the pain of her accident slowly ebbed away. She rolled her shoulders and flexed her fingers. 'That was different,' she said, licking her lips, savouring the bitterness.

'You need the focus,' the Silent Mother whispered. 'Do you feel more focused?'

Elalia nodded. 'I long to test it,' she said, her voice reflecting the new calm that filled her.

The Silent Mother held out her hand, indicating the room.

Elalia found herself grinning as she walked around the cluttered space. On the wall hung fresh herbs, and the strong, sweet scent of the mint drew her in. She stood for a moment and then gently ran her hand over the leaves. She chewed on her lip with excitement as the leaves curled and dried.

The Silent Mother gave a little shrug and Elalia felt the sting. She set her jaw and ran her hand over the dried herb, willing it back to life. The desiccated leaves uncurled as she touched them, and their bright-green colour came back. As she stepped back, the bunch began to flower, and wispy roots grew from the ends of the stalks.

'You might have done a little much there,' the Silent Mother said, stepping forward as the bunch grew and thickened, 'but it works.'

Elalia nodded silently, watching with wonder what she had done. She looked closely at her hands.

'You are not ready to do too much,' the Silent Mother warned, taking her hands between her own. 'It is not time.'

Elalia nodded slowly. 'I need to be Queen first.'

'Yes,' the Silent Mother said, kissing her cheek. 'You need to be Queen, and then you can be who Sythia needs you to be.'

She smiled then, relaxed and comfortable. 'The child?' she asked.

'Forget the child,' the Silent Mother said sharply. 'There may be others, when the time is right.'

Elalia nodded slowly.

'Go. Pray and sleep.'

Elalia turned back at the door. 'You won't leave me, will you?'

'I do what I must for Sythia,' she said. 'As do you.'

Elalia was able to make it back to her rooms without falling down, despite her overwhelming tiredness. She sat on the bed, her gown pulled and damaged from where she had rubbed against the walls. She knew Terra would say something to Meg, but she shook the idea off and lay down.

She would focus as she had been told to, and Sythia would assist her with Meg in return, for she had spent too much time giving directions since the accident.

Elalia dreamt, vivid and dark, of the accident in the woods. The world around her strangely focused. People moved slowly. Morley and Creena looked into the forest around them, but she was sure it wasn't for deer. Malin stared unseeing on his horse, and Elalia wondered if he had really wanted to hunt, or bring her with him.

The Silent Mother was clear amongst the trees, her white tunic a beacon in the shadows. She pointed at Elalia, her whole arm raised and directed at her. And then she was falling; the ground, hard and unforgiving, had knocked the air from her lungs. The weight of the horse across her body made her cry out. But she was numb. She looked up at the grey sky through the tree tops, her cousins muttering, Malin screaming. The commander—she had forgotten him—was calm and she felt strangely light as the horse was lifted from her body.

But she was empty; she knew in that instant that the child was gone, despite not really knowing he was there, and her face was pressed into the cold metal of the commander's breastplate. The raven etched upon it flapped its wings. 'Do as you promised,' it screamed.

Elalia woke with a start. The Silent Mother had been in the woods. But was she responsible for saving her life or taking her child's? Either way it was Sythia's doing, Her design, and she stood slowly, looking over the tatters of her dress. The child could no longer be her focus. The Silent Mother had been correct; it was a distraction and she had more important matters to focus on.

Unsure how long she had stood beside the bed, she was surprised by Terra helping her into a fresh dress. 'Focus,' she whispered to herself, noting the lack of pain as Terra laced her in.

'I am sorry, Your Highness, did I hurt you?' the girl asked in a fragile voice.

She shook her head and walked out into the sunshine. Pushing through the clouds, touches of green tried to grow into the world. Elalia stopped and looked toward the garden. How long had she been hiding away? Tinges of bright green seemed to cover the garden, and she stepped slowly toward the gate and then stopped.

She turned instead for the Temple, taking her time to study the door, the weight of it, the weathered grey of the wood, the grain and the pattern carved upon it.

The guard behind her cleared his throat and she entered. She hadn't been inside the Temple since her father's funeral, and she walked slowly but deliberately toward the gods. They seemed to watch her with interest and she smiled up at them, her heart beating too fast in her chest.

As she reached Kira's feet, she took a deep breath as her hands lingered on the cool, smooth stone. 'I'm sorry,' she whispered, as she did the same to Kion. She took her time to greet all of the gods, studying their faces, and then she took her place amongst the people and knelt before the gods.

I have neglected you. I have not worshiped you as I should have. I only want to be the ruler my people need me to be. I have spent so much of my life protecting us from what lies within the Silence. Now it is time for me to protect the people in another way. But if you do not think me worthy, I shall return to the Sanctuary of the Silent Sisters and continue your work there.

When she slowly opened her eyes, the gods appeared to be smiling down on her. Elalia took her time to repeat the rituals of the Temple, showing her respect to each god. She nodded and smiled at the people she passed on the way out, but she didn't stop to talk.

She was sure that Brother Erasmus would have been there

somewhere, watching her, but she didn't look for him. That hadn't been her reason for entering the Temple.

She walked more confidently and the guard behind her moved quickly. 'Are you sure?' he asked. She stopped then and realised she was at the gate to the gardens. She nodded once and walked in.

Standing in the spot where Kellin had pushed her out of the way, Elalia closed her eyes and could clearly see the image of the Silent Mother beneath the branches. She nodded once and gulped down the feeling in her chest. Despite the hurt it caused, she knew why the Silent Mother had acted as she did. For she only did as Sythia needed her to do.

When she opened her eyes, the shadows moved differently beneath the trees and Elalia took a step forward. A woman, tall and slender, moved amongst the shadows of the dappled light beneath the trees. She glanced quickly at the guard, but he looked the other way. Elalia stepped forward again and the shadow appeared to nod, and then it disappeared.

Focus, it seemed, was exactly what she needed.

31

Meg wondered at Elalia as she watched her kneel down before the gods. She had only looked up from her own prayer because the noise of the Temple had dropped to nothing. If she had seen Meg amidst the crowd, she didn't acknowledge her. Meg shook her head and squeezed her eyes closed, then opened them again in the next breath so that she could be sure that it was in fact her sister kneeling there.

Meg glanced up at the gods, smiling down on them and then back to Elalia's bent form.

Again she closed her eyes and tried not to sigh. What could she be trying to prove? Elalia had been focused on the Silent Sisters' way of life since she returned, and she only appeared in the Temple when she really needed to. Meg hadn't seen her there since her father's funeral.

She sighed again and then stood up, moving slowly through the people to pay her respects to the gods before she left. When she turned from their feet, Elalia remained bent in prayer, her body still, her eyes closed, her face serious. Meg caught Brother Erasmus's eye at the back of the Temple, and she moved as quickly as she could without running or stepping into people, so that she could catch him before he disappeared. It seemed so long since she'd had the chance to sit and talk with him.

He smiled softly and took her hand as she approached, and then looked concerned as he focused on her face. 'What is it, child, that the gods couldn't calm for you?'

She shook her head softly, but found herself turning to watch her sister again.

'It is nice to see her here, for a second time in as many days,' he said. 'How does Kellin fare?'

'She keeps to herself,' Meg murmured, still watching her sister, and then turned to him slowly. 'It was harder than she is willing to admit,' she said.

'Has she forgiven your sister for locking her away?'

'She hasn't mentioned her. Do you think she was justified in locking Kellin up like that?'

'It was more fear than forethought,' he said.

'Do you think she has changed?'

'Kellin?'

'Elalia, since the accident in the woods, and the loss of the child? She seems so calm,' she said slowly, not giving him the chance to answer her question.

'What would you want her to do?'

Meg shrugged.

'But you are surprised that she would turn to the gods for comfort.'

'I expected her to lock herself away with the Silent Mother, praying to the Silence. It seems to be where she is comfortable.'

'She looks comfortable here,' he said, looking out over the people. 'Just another worshipper.'

Meg shook her head again, fearing something else, and she wasn't sure where the feeling came from or even why it had originated. She had sat for so long beside her sister's bed, holding her hand, being of comfort; and then she was pain free, and calm, and she didn't need her any more.

'I don't appear to be of any use,' she whispered, turning back to the Brother as the truth of her words stabbed at her chest. 'Father wanted more for me, and I fear I will sit here and grow old without ever being of any real use to my own people.'

He smiled and slowly shook his head. 'You are always of use, always a comfort to your people, such great work you have done for the less fortunate. Do you miss Tands?'

She nodded before she could stop herself, a little tear escaping.

'The agreement might have been dissolved, but it does not mean it may not still happen.'

She shook her head. 'I should go.'

'It has been so long,' he said, pulling her focus to him as he spoke quietly. 'The prince is a good man; he may find a way back to you.'

'I can't rely on that,' she whispered.

He nodded. 'Go and find your sister; spend some time as you once did.'

Meg nodded, but she couldn't find the strength to leave the Temple. The strange, sick feeling that something was wrong sat with her, as it had when her father had stumbled that day in the Hall. She was staring unseeing when Brother Erasmus squeezed her hand so tight she yelped. He had the same vacant look that she was sure she had worn only moments before.

She turned to look where he was, the noise slowly building in the Temple, and she saw the slow movement of colour through her sister's hair. Starting at the roots, it was turning the dark, midnight black of the raven's feathers.

The movement in the Temple stopped and the people turned toward her sister and knelt. 'We kiss the crown,' they said as one, and Meg mouthed the words with them.

Disappointment washed over her, followed quickly by fear, of what Elalia might do and what she certainly wouldn't allow to happen. And then, smiling, she stepped forward and threw her arms around her sister as she stood, then curtsied low before her, trying to stem the tears that seemed to prickle the backs of her eyes.

The excitement moved through the whole Temple. Meg could feel the buzz against her skin and she glanced quickly toward the gods smiling down on them.

'They have made their choice,' she said softly.

'Yes they have,' Elalia said, taking her arm. 'The whispers and speculation will stop now, and I have the chance to get on with ruling the land.'

Meg gave her a small smile and made to move away.

'You are disappointed?' Elalia asked, holding her close.

Meg paused. 'I always knew you would be marked, Elalia.'

She smiled, a real smile that Meg couldn't remember seeing before. 'It is as it should be,' she said. 'How soon can we place the crown upon my head?' she asked Brother Erasmus, whose calm smile grew tight for a moment.

'Tomorrow,' he said.

'I need to see the Silent Mother,' she said, moving toward the doorway, dragging Meg with her, and the people still bowed down before her.

'You don't need me for that,' Meg whispered.

'I'm not sure what I can do with you,' she whispered back.

Meg chewed on her lip, wondering if she should mention Tands, or if she wanted to. Even if her sister changed her mind, the damage was done to the relationship with their neighbours to the North, and the chances of them wanting to continue the arrangement were gone.

'You did help,' Elalia said softly, pulling them to a stop. 'After...' she looked down.

Meg nodded once.

'But then,' Elalia went on, dragging her along again, ignoring the people that stopped in the courtyard to stare and bow down before their new Queen, 'you would do your duty to Rocfeld, no matter what I think that might be.'

Meg tried to pull from her grip, but her hand tightened around her arm. 'I think I know what you need to do to prove your duty for the kingdom and be of assistance to your new Queen.'

'So marrying me off to some old man will help you?'

'Now Meggie, it may be that marrying you to some old man's son would be better, and no different to what Father had in mind.'

Meg knew she was right. Despite his words and concerns for her happiness, the connection with Tands was for Rocfeld first. 'Not Luana,' Meg begged, her voice catching.

Elalia shrugged but continued walking. Her pace had increased, and Meg was almost skipping to keep up to prevent her being pulled over. 'Where are we going?'

Elalia stopped and released her tight hold of Meg's arm. 'Go and tell Kellin the happy news,' she said. 'I have a coronation to prepare for.'

Meg watched her walk away, still moving quickly, the guards marching along behind her, and she found herself alone. It was a strange sensation and she walked slowly toward Kellin's rooms. The guard on the door bowed as he stepped back to allow her to the door, and then looked at her quizzically. She simply shook her head and opened the door.

Kellin stood by the window, staring out across the garden, not even turning as Meg entered the room. 'Something feels different,' she said. 'Can you feel it?' she asked, turning.

'Elalia has been marked,' she said.

'Oh.' Kellin sat in the window seat. 'We expected that,' she said softly as Meg took the seat opposite. 'But it doesn't feel right.'

Meg nodded slowly. 'I had the same feeling in the Temple.'

'Did you see her?'

'She changed before my eyes and a Temple full of people.'

'Elalia was in the Temple?'

Meg nodded again. 'And not her first visit, it appears. The gods smiled down on her and the raven hair followed.'

'Why did we have to wait so long?'

'I don't know,' Meg said, standing now and looking over the garden. 'But the decision is made and tomorrow she will be crowned, and then perhaps she can focus on Rocfeld and the people, and things can be put right.'

'What can be put right?'

'There is still trouble at the border towns...'

'You would have been a good queen,' Kellin said, throwing her arms around her and pulling her close. 'Do you think she might talk to Tands about Brodwyn?'

Meg shook her head against her sister's neck. 'I think it more likely she sends me off to Luana.'

'I think the prince might have something to say about that.'

Meg pushed out of her sister's hold. 'He has no say,' Meg said softly. 'I need to sleep; tomorrow is going to be a long day.'

32

Elalia smoothed her hands over the front of the black dress and paused with her hands over her flat stomach. She sucked in a large breath and turned to admire the feathered cloak again in the long glass within her rooms. Those crowned before her had worn a cloak with a ring of raven feathers around the neck. Elalia's cloak was all feathers, tight and smooth, and she smiled at the wings folded around her. She was not only the Raven Queen; she was the raven.

Behind her reflection, Malin stood tall and still. Was there a look of wonder there? He appeared as the man she had thought he was when she met him before the gods to make her promise to him. As if sensing her thoughts, he stepped forward.

She ran her hands across his chest, brushing her fingers over the silver raven feather pin. His hands found her hips and he gently pushed her back a step to take her in. The warmth of his hands reminded her of something she had longed for once, but she shook the memory away.

'You look well,' he said, kissing her forehead. 'You didn't answer my question last night.'

'Which question was that?' she asked, turning back to the mirror. He had asked so many, most about himself.

'Whether you would like to try for another child.'

Elalia focused on her tight braids, ensuring no wisps of hair had escaped. 'Now is not the time,' she said.

'We can wait until after the ceremony,' he said, grinning over her shoulder in the glass.

'I am Queen,' she said, straightening up and smoothing over her dress one more time. 'My focus is elsewhere.'

His grin dropped and he looked at her far too closely. 'All you wanted was children.'

'And now I don't,' she said, giving the Brother at the door a nod. She took Malin's arm and directed him after the Brother. 'I'm sure you can find some young thing to play with if you need to.'

He pulled against her, stopping her movement, and the Brother continued on ahead. 'Why did you send Sera away?' he asked in a low whisper.

'Who?' she asked.

A growl escaped, and the Brother ahead of them stopped and turned back. 'You married her to your bastard cousin.'

'I didn't know you were so attached,' she said, giving his arm a gentle tug, and was relieved that he started walking again. 'You can do as you like,' she said. 'I only ask that you attempt to act as the husband of a queen when I need you to.'

'What would the husband of a queen be?' he asked, disappointed. Or was it anger in his voice? She tried not to sigh.

'Lord Rocfeld, I think.'

He stopped then, and she had no choice but to stop with him, his eyes focused on a distant point.

'Does that suit?' she asked, and a large grin covered his face.

The Temple was silent behind the closed doors, and she wanted to release Malin's arm and walk in on her own. She stood tall and calm, and she nodded once and the doors opened with the slightest of squeaks before her.

The Temple was full. All of these people were here for her, to see her, to kneel down before her as their new queen. Despite the number of people, there was a clear path across the Temple toward the platform of the gods. As they slowly walked toward Kira and Kion, a gentle whisper moved through the silence, and she could sense the power she would soon hold. She looked up only briefly into the faces of the gods as they smiled down on her.

Brother Erasmus stood at their feet, motioning her toward him. Elalia released her hold on Malin and stepped forward. As she made to kneel before him, he gave a slight sideways movement with his head. Her heart stopped as she realised her mistake, and she hoped that no one else had noticed it.

She stepped straight to the feet of Kira, as though she had only paused to greet Erasmus, but as she ran her hands over the cool stone she was sure the whispers echoed her error. Elalia took her time, offering thanks to Kira for her position. Then she moved to Kion and did the same. Then she bent and kissed his feet and, returning to Kira, did the same. More briefly she moved over the followers, sliding her hand over the pale stone and then kissing them before moving back to stand before Brother Erasmus.

He gave her a slow nod, but she could feel his disappointment. Not that it would matter; she was soon to be Queen, and there was nothing he could do then. She focused on the uneven weave of his grey tunic as he started to speak. All murmuring stopped.

'You are all welcome here this day, to stand before the gods and bear witness to the crowning of their choice.'

With her back to the people, she was grateful they had braided her hair to show off the full splendour of the raven cloak. So heavy with feathers, she wondered for a moment if she could turn into the raven itself and fly away.

'Are you ready to hold the burden of the Raven Crown?'

'I am,' she said clearly, her voice loud in the silence of the Temple.

As the ceremony continued, her last concerns of being what she needed to be lifted from her shoulders. She was Queen now and could be just what Sythia and the Silent Sisters needed her to be.

The royal commander appeared at her side, but she remained kneeling. A Brother and Sister stepped forward with the crown. Such a simple crown, she realised, looking at the ring of silver. She was sure it had looked far more impressive upon her mother.

Erasmus stepped forward and placed it on her head. She feared for a moment that it would be lost amongst the braids and knots, and then the disappointment that there was not more ritual to the actual crowning settled on her. It was only a day. One day. She would show what she was tomorrow, when she could make the decisions for herself.

As the crown touched her head, Elalia expected some response from the people, but there was nothing but silence. Taking the royal commander's offered hand she stood slowly, looked up into the serious faces of the gods and then turned to her people to look on them for the first time as their queen.

She curtsied low, as she remembered her father doing something similar after her mother's death, and the applause began. It was polite, quiet clapping, but it moved through the space and up to the ears of the gods. Even Kellin and Meggie were clapping, although neither of them appeared very happy about the gods' choice.

Erasmus named Malin as Lord Rocfeld as he stepped forward, and she took the chance to smile up at him. A small smile, one the people would expect, one he would expect; but she couldn't quite catch his eye. He looked out across the people, far more serious than she had expected him to be. Perhaps her words had more impact than she had expected.

The Silent Mother stood at the very back of the temple, her white tunic standing out in the sea of people filling the space. She nodded once and Elalia breathed out slowly. She turned back to Erasmus as he gently touched the pin on Malin's chest. There was no other ceremony to mark him. Brother Peras, standing behind Erasmus, nodded and Elalia used Malin's hand to steady herself as she stepped forward to kiss the feet of the gods again.

How much lighter she felt now that the crown sat snugly upon her head and she was officially Queen. She allowed Malin to lead her out of the Temple and into the sunshine. They would greet everyone as they entered the Hall, and everyone would want the time to talk with her.

'My Queen, how beautifully raven like you are today,' Emperor Baghi said behind her.

'Your Eminence,' she said, giving him a slight curtsy although it hurt her to do so. 'I am glad you stayed.'

'I would not have missed such an event.' He smiled sweetly, although it didn't carry to his eyes as he leaned forward to take her hand and raised it slowly to his lips, his long moustache scratchy across her skin. 'Let me escort you to the feast, for I would talk with you about your new kingdom. I must leave for Luana tomorrow.'

She carefully slid her hand from his grasp and wrapped it around Malin's waiting arm. 'I would enjoy the conversation,' she said. 'But it must wait until we are seated, for today is about traditions, and it is for my husband to escort me.'

He bowed low and indicated with a flourish that they lead the way.

'What would he want to talk about?' Malin asked in a hoarse whisper.

She shook her head but said nothing. The man probably thought as a woman she would need help. How she would show them all. She looked around the group moving toward the Hall, but she couldn't see the Silent Mother. There would be certain expectations now that she was crowned, but she needed the Silent Mother closer than before.

33

'I do not understand why you are so unhappy,' Elalia said, making herself comfortable before the fire in Meg's room.

'I am not unhappy. The gods have made their choice, I only ask what choices you will make for us.'

'When they are made, you will know.'

Meg tried not to sigh. She had expected her sister's earlier frustrations to resurface, but she was still smiling and calm. Too calm.

'Is the Silent Mother to stay?' she asked and saw the first flicker of something else pass over Elalia's face. 'Surely she is needed at the Sanctuary.'

'She is needed here,' she said quickly, and stood up.

'I have not seen you in the Temple over the last few days,' Meg continued to push.

'I continue to pray in the private chapel, as I have since I returned from the Sanctuary. Are you trying to make things difficult?' Elalia asked, the same level calmness to her voice, but she swayed from foot to foot, her back to the fire, and Meg gulped down her uneasiness. 'Do you think you can still influence the gods? Do you think that if I were not here that you would be Queen?'

Meg shook her head quickly.

'Are you and Kellin still plotting?' She stopped her movement and leant forward.

'We were never plotting against you,' Meg said quickly,

standing to face her sister. 'I thought the paranoia stopped once you were Queen.'

'The danger didn't end when the crown was placed on my head.'

'That danger never came from us, and of course it did. There has never been a Raven Queen killed for her crown.'

'Are you sure? Are you certain of that, Megora? For our mother died young.'

Meg gulped back the bitter taste of bile at the back of her throat. 'Why would you say such a thing? She was ill.'

'You were a child; how can you be sure?'

'So were you.' Meg stopped and looked over the strange calmness of her sister. Even with the nature of the conversation and her apparent fear of danger, she was composed. 'Is that why you went to the Silent Sisters?'

'What do you want, Megora?' Elalia asked, picking up a goblet and taking a sip. She tilted her head a little to the side, looking Meg directly in the eye. 'Do you think that Tands will take you, that you will be Queen of another land?'

She wanted to shake her head again, but she stared her sister down.

'Did meeting your prince determine your path?'

Meg opened her mouth and then closed it. Did she really know that Brodwyn had been here?

'Did you know that they only wanted you out of the way?'

Meg shook her head then, remembering Brodwyn's sad face when he'd had to say goodbye.

'They wanted us all out of the way so that they could take Rocfeld back,' Elalia continued.

'That wasn't why he was here,' Meg said.

Elalia shook her head slowly. 'Poor Meggie, you have no idea of how the world works. And I have told the royal commander that I think it a strong possibility that Tands will try again.'

Meg chewed on her lip, unsure what she could say. Elalia clearly had a message and she would have to hear it. The royal commander was a sensible man and he knew Brodwyn; he understood that he wasn't a threat. 'We established that it wasn't a Tandian attack in the forest that caused you to fall from the horse,' Meg said, and then sat slowly in the chair as something dark and unknown passed across Elalia's face.

'How do you know that?'

'If it were them, they would have tried again. No one would attack only once.'

'You thought our cousins involved, and yet they didn't try again.' There was an edge to her voice now, the ever-present calm starting to crack.

'And we only guessed at their involvement, and yet they ran— and not to Lekland. Or at least they haven't been found between here and there.'

'There was the attack on you and Kellin in the garden,' Elalia said quickly.

'That was more our doing than Tands. It was a Rocfeld man, desperate for his family, for his village.'

Elalia shook her head.

'We have been surrounded by danger since Father died. Those wanting a hand in who was marked, those wanting the ear of who was marked, those wanting power over who was marked.'

Her anger slipped away and she was the calm queen again. 'I was marked,' she said. 'I am the Raven Queen. I shall stamp out these threats to the kingdom and the Raven Crown.' She turned and swept from the room.

⊂ℜℰ⊃

Meg wasn't surprised when Elalia called her to the solar; she was surprised it had taken so long since their last conversation. Elalia stood at the window and the Silent Mother sat at the table. Meg waited for one of them to speak first, and when Elalia continued to stare, Meg stepped forward and found her staring unseeing across the courtyard.

'Elalia?' she asked softly, her hand on her arm, which seemed unnaturally warm. 'Are you unwell?' she asked slowly, remembering another time when her sister had felt hot and had claimed it was the child.

She nodded slowly, focused on some distant place.

'You wanted to see me,' she said.

Elalia repeated the slow nod. Other than the two unmoving women, the room appeared unused. The rushes were fresh and undisturbed, the fire out, the table bare. A chill settled on Meg and she walked quickly toward the unlit fire.

'Leave it,' the Silent Mother said.

Meg looked from her to Elalia's vacant face. 'Why did I want you?' Elalia asked, turning from the window and sitting beside the Silent Mother at the table.

'I have no idea,' Meg said. 'You haven't spoken to me since our conversation in my rooms, where you told me I was to do as you directed.'

'You want to go to Tands,' she said, focusing for the first time on Meg's face.

'Why did you call me here?' Meg asked, finding her own frustrations growing. 'I don't want this same conversation.'

'But you do not see the threat.'

'From where? Tands?' Meg asked and Elalia nodded. 'Because it is not there.'

'You are so blind to him,' Elalia said.

Meg shook her head and turned for the door.

'You want to be Queen,' Elalia called after her, her voice strained for the first time, and Meg stopped.

'You are the Raven Queen,' Meg said, dipping into a deep curtsy, unsure at her sudden need to reassure her sister of her position. 'No one but the gods can change that.'

'I know what you are,' the Silent Mother said softly. 'I know what you see.'

'Do you?' Meg asked quickly. 'And what do you see?'

'I see a threat to the Raven Crown,' she said. A smile pulled at her lips and Meg took a step back, shaking her head.

'I am not a threat to the crown. Elalia is Queen; I knew she would be Queen.'

'You will try to stop her,' she said slowly, standing from the table, and Meg took another step back.

'Why would I try to stop her? What would she do?' Meg looked between the two strange faces before her—Elalia's vacant stare, the grinning Sister. 'Who would I try to stop?' she asked as her chest tightened and the hairs at the back of her neck stood up.

'You want to be Queen,' the Silent Mother said.

There was a single knock at the door and Meg turned as Commander Rainger entered the room. 'We are ready,' he said, glancing briefly at Meg before bowing before Elalia.

'They took my baby,' she whispered.

'There was an accident, Your Highness,' he reminded her gently, glancing quickly at Meg, who felt as concerned as he looked.

'It is not safe,' she continued in her quiet voice.

'You are to go away,' the Silent Mother said, her cold eyes focused on Meg.

'I can leave you and return later,' Meg said, giving another curtsy, trying to maintain her breathing. After the initial shock from the accident at the loss of her child, she hadn't seemed concerned by it, but Meg realised that she should not have so easily accepted Elalia's peace with the situation. For Elalia hadn't seemed concerned by anything.

The Silent Mother gently touched Elalia's arm and she stood slowly. 'There is a threat to the crown and thus the family,' Elalia said slowly, not quite focusing on Meg. 'It is no longer safe for you here.'

'Where am I to go?' Meg asked. 'What are you up to?' she asked the Silent Mother.

Elalia focused on her then, her green eyes hard and her voice clear. 'I am the queen,' she said. 'I know what is best, and you shall be moved to a safer place to be protected.'

The commander was standing beside her. 'Your Highness,' he said softly. 'Surely we can protect the princesses here.'

'You will not question me or my decisions,' she said loudly, the calm façade cracking. 'I know what I do and this plan is set with the royal commander.'

Commander Rainger bowed low before her.

'You can take them and protect them.' She was standing again, moving around the table toward them, her hand outstretched. Elalia took a deep breath and blinked at Meg, as though she had just discovered her in the room. 'You must prepare to leave,' she said softly. 'Help Kellin to prepare her things. You must leave now.'

Meg blinked back angry tears and backed out of the room. She pulled the door shut and stood for a moment in the hallway, wondering what might be happening in her sister's mind to think that this was any sort of option. What had the Silent Mother done or said to have them removed from Rocfeld? She shook her head and raced toward Kellin's room. They just had to sit it out; surely it would pass in time and given Elalia's strange moods, it might only be a matter of hours before she was rational again.

Meg froze in the doorway. 'What is this?' she asked.

Kellin raced into her arms, sobbing. 'We are being sent away.'

'She meant that we are leaving today,' she said.

The maid bobbed a curtsy and continued past Meg. 'Cate has been packing since daybreak,' Kellin said. 'I do not want to go.'

'Nor me, but I think we have little choice,' Meg said, looking over the state of the room and realising that this wasn't a temporary madness that would pass. 'Who goes with us?' she asked Cate as she came back into the room.

The girl bobbed again. 'Myself and your lady maid,' she said. 'And a cook and scullery maid.'

'A cook?' Meg asked. 'Where are we going?'

The girl shrugged.

'How long?' Kellin asked.

The girl shook her head again, her own lip quivering somewhat.

'I need to check my rooms,' Meg said as Kellin clung to her. 'I will be back.'

But when she reached her rooms, footmen were already carrying trunks through the doors. Lora curtsied but looked lost. Meg gave her a reassuring smile that she didn't really feel and the girl followed the men out of the doors. She handed Meg her cloak as she went, and she realised the girl was already dressed to travel. She took a moment to look out of her small window across the courtyard below and saw the wagons being loaded and the men gathering. What did Elalia think this would achieve?

'Meg?' Kellin's soft voice called through the room.

'I am coming.'

Arriving arm in arm in the courtyard, the maids were already seated in the front of the carriage and the cook with the luggage and supplies.

Meg felt sick, though she tried to smile for Kellin, whose sobs continued. Elalia appeared beside them and embraced each of them briefly.

'Please,' Kellin called as she was guided up into the carriage. 'Elalia, please don't send us away.'

'It is for your own protection,' she said, and walked back inside before any more could be said. The Silent Mother remained by the doorway, watching her.

Meg climbed in beside Kellin and wrapped an arm around her. One of the maids had started to cry as well. The horses picked up their pace and the castle disappeared behind them, and she was momentarily lost in the bustle of the streets and markets before they were surrounded by fields and the sound of the hooves on the hard road.

Where was Brother Erasmus, or the royal commander? Surely one of them would have come to say goodbye or reassure them. Meg gulped down the tears threatening to spill over as she stared out the window.

And then Kellin grabbed her arm as someone rode past the window of the carriage, and she noticed others doing the same. The soldiers that would accompany them. She wondered how many Elalia had sent and whether they would protect them or draw attention to them.

The broad figure of Commander Rainger came into view, and Kellin's grip tightened on her arm. He tipped his head and Meg tipped hers back. Then from the other window, she noticed Commander Brent and gave him a similar signal. 'It would be best, Your Highness, if you were to raise the shutters,' he said.

Meg nodded again and then stood to pull the shutter up and over the opening, blocking the light and the view. She reached across Kellin and did the same to the other side.

'He is seeing us off?' Kellin asked quietly, her voice nearly lost to the noise of the wheels and hooves.

Meg looked at her for a moment. 'Seeing us off?' she asked.

'The commander,' Kellin said.

'No,' Meg answered. 'They are coming with us.'

Kellin burst into fresh tears, followed closely by Cate. Meg leant back and closed her eyes, wondering how long they would be thrown around in the carriage and how far away their destination. Why the Silent Mother was so determined to have her removed from Rocfeld and to where, in the name of the gods, that may be, she didn't know. She hoped with everything she had that it wasn't the Empire of Luana.

ACKNOWLEDGMENTS

Darja at Deranged Doctor Designs (DDD) for absolutely brilliant cover design work and all the marketing extras. Kim for support and clear emails around what they needed from me to make the magic happen.

Melissa, my key reader and critic and ideas bouncing buddy, for without you this story wouldn't have become what it is today.

TWG members: Melissa, Matthew J Morrison, John Hargreaves, Sue Larsen, and newbie Nicholas Jansen for constant listening and support in all things writing related.

All the fantastic beta readers for their time and useful feedback: Matthew J Morrison, Yasmin van Tienen, Lisa Evola, Kierra Beeson, Brandy Prettyman, Paula Osheroff and Heather Ewings.

My proofreader Allison Wright, even though she's in the great big US of A, she is able to cope with my Ozzie-ness and save me from a lack of commas and a surprising number of typos.

My parents, Francine and Ken Smith. Amazing, supportive people that I don't thank nearly often enough. They keep me normal and for that I'm forever grateful. And they buy my books.

As always, Temwa for being the perfect daughter.

ABOUT THE AUTHOR

Georgina Makalani survives life as a servant of the public by hiding in cafes at lunch time with dragons, witches, a laptop and a little bit of magic.

For more about Georgina visit her website:
www.theflowofink.com

Other Stories:

The Mark of Oldra

The Legend of Iski Flare (Novella series):

The Legend Begins
Red Wolves
The Riddle of Daralis
The Last Child
The Tree Maiden

Short Stories:

Stuffed Frogs and Spinning Teacups
Searcher
The Silence (in Glimpses)

www.ingramcontent.com/pod-product-compliance
Lightning Source LLC
Chambersburg PA
CBHW031229120726
47905CB00002B/523